J. Daniels is the *New York Times* and *USA Today* bestselling author of the Sweet Addiction series, and the Alabama Summer series. She loves curling up with a good book, drinking a ridiculous amount of coffee, and writing stories her children will never read.

Daniels grew up in Baltimore and resides in Maryland with her family.

Visit J. Daniels online:

https://www.facebook.com/jdanielsauthor
Twitter: @JDanielsbooks
Instagram: authorjdaniels
www.authorjdaniels.com

D1392619

5 8882 82811 8822 2

FOUR
LETTER
WORD

A Dirty Deeds Novel

J. DANIELS

piatkus

PIATKUS

First published in the US in 2016 by Forever, an imprint of
Grand Central Publishing, a division of Hachette Book Group, Inc.
First published in Great Britain in 2016 by Piatkus

1 3 5 7 9 10 8 6 4 2

A CIP catalogue record for this book
is available from the British Library.

ISBN 978-0-349-41172-9

Printed and bound in Great Britain by
Clays Ltd, St Ives plc

Papers used by Piatkus are from well-managed forests
and other responsible sources.

MIX
Paper from
responsible sources
FSC® C104740

Piatkus
An imprint of
Little, Brown Book Group
Carmelite House
50 Victoria Embankment
London EC4Y 0DZ

An Hachette UK Company
www.hachette.co.uk

www.piatkus.co.uk

To Jeff. UU

ACKNOWLEDGMENTS

Thank you to my family for your unwavering love and support. For understanding when I was shut away writing and for not judging me when I would finally resurface hours later, still in my pajamas. I know how I looked, so again, thank you. Also, Mom, Dad, please skip over the sex scenes as usual. Let's keep Christmas as comfortable as possible.

To Beth Cranford, thank you for keeping me sane. For encouraging me and telling me I could do this, and for your help with all of the "little things" that aren't quite so little. Along with Beth, thank you to Kellie Richardson, Lisa Jayne, and Lana Kart for reading this book in its rough stages and, like always, giving me your honesty, enthusiasm, and voice messages. I was nervous, and you made me less nervous. To Lisa Wilson, Tiffany Ly, Yvette Trujillo, and Kellie, of course, thank you for your amazing teasers and the promoting you did for this baby. You girls are the BEST.

To my wonderful agent, Kimberly Brower. Thank you. Thank you. Thank you. How many times have you talked me off the ledge? I've lost count. Peanut butter cup sundaes on me.

To Megha and the Forever team, thank you for picking up this story and for supporting my vision in it. To the amazing book bloggers who have been on this journey with me from the beginning, I can't list you all here, but please know how grateful I am for each and every one of you. Special thanks to Give Me Books,

Kinky Girls Book Obsessions, Rock Stars of Romance, and The Literary Gossip.

To the author friends I've made along the way, you know who you are. And to my readers, for your love and warm hugs, thank you most of all.

FOUR LETTER WORD

Chapter One

SYDNEY

I had been sitting in the same spot for an hour.

Well, at least it felt like an hour. I honestly had no idea what time it was. I couldn't look at the clock to verify how long I'd been immobile. I couldn't look at anything besides the hand resting in my lap.

No, not resting. It shook violently, no matter how hard I pressed it flat against my jean-covered thigh.

My skin all over was clammy and frigid at the same time. Sweat tickled my palms, pooled at the base of my neck and in the hollow dip of my throat. It was quite possible I was running a fever.

I should feel sick. This *was* sickening.

The house felt eerily quiet, desolate, though I knew Marcus was in the other room. I hadn't heard the evidence of his departure—the front door closing or the low rumble of his truck starting up.

He hadn't left. And why would he? Why would *he* be the one leaving in this scenario?

You should be leaving, Sydney. Get up. Run. Grab your stuff and get the hell out of here.

I exhaled a trembling breath. I couldn't move. I couldn't stop shaking. I could barely remember how important oxygen intake was in the matter of staying alive. Long seconds stretched out before I would inhale in a panic, allow my lungs to taste the air in the room I shouldn't still be sitting in, then expel that breath all too quickly.

I needed to go. I needed to react somehow, because I hadn't thus far.

I felt numb. And this... this felt like a dream.

A paralyzing dream.

The kind you didn't wake up from.

My phone rang from my bag on the floor somewhere, but it sounded miles away. I couldn't lift my head to the noise. I couldn't even remember where I had tossed it after I endured the one-sided conversation with Marcus.

Endured. Not participated in.

Him, doing all the talking, all the explaining, and none of it sounding the least bit apologetic, his voice cold and distant, detached, final... having made the decision, *his* decision, while I stood there frozen.

Frozen.

Marcus turned on his heel and swiftly left the room. I collapsed into a pile of heavy limbs on the floor, where I'd remained, and where I had every intention of remaining.

That was my reaction. It was the only reaction I was capable of.

Until the phone rang... *again.*

Something felt off. It was a miracle I felt it, whatever it was, considering my deadened state.

Like a whispered warning against my ear.

My spine stiffened in an instant. I turned my head in the direction of my muffled ringtone, scanning with what felt like new eyes.

Fresh and alert.

I was up to count six of Taylor Swift singing about being young and reckless. I knew who was calling, and I contemplated ignoring my best friend again, slouching over and righting myself to my previous position, until I realized...

Shit.

Shit.

My already tight chest grew tighter.

Tori never called me that many times in a row. If I didn't answer her, I was usually in the middle of a shift at work, and she'd leave her standard "call me when you get a sec" message.

She never rang me up like this. Urgently.

Was something wrong?

I found my bag halfway under the bed and tugged it out by one of the straps. Palming my phone, I answered the call just before the last words of the verse sounded.

"H-hey, what's up?" I asked, voice strained and anxious, stumbling brokenly through my greeting.

My head hit the side of the mattress as I resumed my location on the floor with my knees pulled in close against my chest.

"Syd." Tori's voice cracked with a whimper. "Hon...hey, hey, are you busy right now? Do you have a minute to talk? I need to talk."

I blinked rapidly at her distressful tone.

I suddenly couldn't remember the last hour, or however long I had been in this room. I couldn't remember the bomb Marcus dropped in my lap before he dismissed me with a curt nod and went about his business doing God knows what.

My hands no longer shook. My breathing was even. Focused.

I had never heard my best friend cry. Never. Not once in the twelve years we'd known each other. And we'd been through some shit, let me tell you.

But she was crying now.

I was right. Something was off.

Worry consumed me. My blood ran warmer as I began to pace along the length of the bed, pressing the phone to my ear as I quickly collected myself.

"I have as much time as you need, sweetie. What's going on? Why are you upset?"

"Wes," she hiccupped.

Wes.

Tori's boyfriend of six months and serious enough he was obviously worth shedding tears over.

I hadn't had a chance to meet the guy yet, due to my busy work schedule and the three-hour drive time between Tori and myself. But I felt like I knew him. Ninety percent of Tori's and my conversations revolved around what amazingly sweet thing Wes did for her that week.

He seemed perfect.

My attention snapped back to the phone at my ear when I heard a crash, the sound of glass breaking, followed immediately by my best friend's livid but still distraught high-pitched voice.

"*Married.* He's fucking married, Syd! Can you believe that? That son of a bitch has a wife!"

I stopped pacing and stared openmouthed at the wall.

Married?

Oh, *God*...

Tori took in a shuddering breath and I started pacing again, needing to either move or hit someone. And I wasn't jumping at the chance to confront Marcus just yet, so option two was out.

Tori's voice shrank to a more vulnerable decibel when she finally continued.

"God, Sydney, how stupid am I? How did I not see this? His weeknight rule with being too busy to see me Monday through Friday, always sending my calls to voice mail only to return them minutes later, which I'm imagining now was enough time for him to make up some bullshit story to appease his wife so he could sneak out and call me back. *Asshole.* God...that stupid *fucking* asshole. How? How did that not set off alarms in my head? Was it that obvious? Was I that blind, Syd?"

I didn't know if it was from my frantic pacing, or from Tori's confession sinking in, but suddenly I needed to steady myself with a hand on the wall.

The room began to spin.

I blinked everything into focus before finding my own voice, which I kept quiet.

"Oh, my God, Tori. My *God*. How did you find out? What happened?"

"Saw him with her at the mall, pushing a damn stroller through the food court," she answered, sounding equal parts disgusted and destroyed. "They looked so fucking perfect together, I didn't know whether to throw up or scream."

She groaned, and I heard more things rattling in the background.

I pictured Tori testing the weight of different glass objects before she chose one to hurl against the closest wall.

"I walked right up to the son of a bitch. I saw her ring. I saw *his*. I was ready to confront him then and there. You know me. But you know what that bastard did?"

She sniffed loudly through the phone.

It broke my heart to hear her like this, but I didn't get to tell her that before she continued.

"He ... he threw his arm around her, smiled at me, and introduced us. He actually *introduced* his wife to me, Sydney. Told her I was an old friend from high school. Can you believe that? A *friend*."

She chuckled derisively at the word.

"I've done things with him I've never done with other men. I've talked with him ... you know? That kind of talking where you just share yourself with someone for hours and hours and you can't think of anything else you'd rather be doing. I don't know if I loved him, but I could've. I know I could've."

"What did you do?"

She breathed through a tight laugh.

"I know what I should've done. I should've called him out on it. Stomped his balls out. His wife deserved to know. *I* would want to know, but I couldn't do anything. I couldn't. I stood there like some *freak*, staring at him with my mouth hanging open. I probably looked psychotic. I couldn't believe what I was hearing. After God knows how long they walked away and I ... I just kept standing there until a security guard came up to me and asked if I was okay." She paused, then whispered, "I wasn't. I'm not."

I moved to the bed and sank onto the mattress, elbows on my knees, and rubbed my palm across my forehead.

I couldn't believe what I was hearing either. I couldn't believe people could be this malicious as to openly hurt someone this way, even though I was suffering from a pain similar to what Tori was experiencing. But at least she was acknowledging it. Admitting the effect it had on her and even going as far as confessing it to someone.

I couldn't do that yet. I wasn't feeling anything.

Until now.

The change was swift. I suddenly felt everything, as if someone had taken a book filled with the range of human emotions and chucked it at my head. I was overwhelmed. Alive with reaction. I wanted to cry. I wanted to scream. I was full of rage and bitterness, pain...God, the pain was undeniable now. It felt like a cancer eating away at my bones.

Tori let out a strangled yell. Something else shattered through the line.

I closed my eyes and imagined doing the same thing.

I knew her adoration for Wes ran deep and threatened to run deeper the more time she had spent with that man.

She saw him as her future.

He'd already planned one out with another woman.

Are all men complete pieces of shit?

My eyes flashed down at my left hand, lifeless on my leg. One particular finger felt foreign to me. Irritating. Like an itch I couldn't reach to scratch.

I couldn't remain still anymore.

My skin pricked at the base of my neck as I stood and pulled my suitcases from the walk-in closet, dragging them to the bed.

I knew my best friend better than anyone. I knew that sometimes she simply needed me to listen instead of offering my assurance or advice. Just knowing someone was there for you spoke louder than a lot of words.

So that's what I gave her. Silence.

She cried softly into my ear as I threw my entire life into two suitcases and one duffle bag. I ransacked the bathroom, not caring how I left it as I packed away my toiletries. I wiped away every memory of myself from that room.

Every photo. Anything tying me to Marcus. Everything personal.

I wanted them gone. But more important, *I* wanted to be gone.

I stripped the ring from my finger and held it tight in my fist, the blunt edge of the diamond threatening to break skin.

Tori dragged out an edgy breath, then told me quietly, "I'm sorry, hon. I just needed to get that off my chest. You're probably busy, right? Are you at work? It's cool, I'll let you go."

Work. That was another thing I had to deal with. Immediately. Sooner the better.

"Yeah, I'm kind of in the middle of something," I replied, which wasn't entirely a lie. I knew she would assume that meant I was at the hospital, when in reality I was in the middle of letting go of the life I thought I was meant to have.

The one I wrote vows for.

I had to get off the phone. The sooner I finished this, the better.

"All right. I gotta go anyway. There's glass everywhere. I should probably clean it up before I step on it. Call me tomorrow if you have a chance."

The call disconnected.

I chuckled, which seemed so strange given the reality of the situation.

My current, completely fucked-up situation.

Tori never waited on the line to hear anyone's good-bye. I knew that about her. I'd overheard many conversations she held growing up, but every time we spoke, I still readied myself with a response.

It was habitual, and the normal thing to do.

I envied her ability to cut the world off like that. To dominate life.

It wasn't too late for me to become a wrecking force. I had absolutely nothing to lose anymore.

I had nothing at all.

Securing the duffle strap over my shoulder, I lifted the suitcases and marched down the hallway.

Noise from the television grew louder as I descended the stairs. Marcus was continuing on with his night as if nothing had been revealed. As if we were still an "us," and he hadn't taken all of that away from me.

I briefly glanced in his direction when I moved past the living room.

He was sitting in his favorite chair and nursing a beer, his feet crossed at the ankles and propped up on our coffee table. His eyes glued to the game.

Typical.

He was a creature of habit, and he had already come to terms with a world we were no longer facing together. He chose it willingly.

Why should my departure affect him? He'd already let go of me.

Marcus didn't speak. I knew he wouldn't, but what surprised me was my silence. I had so much to say, to scream, in his face or from this distance, it didn't matter, but more than anything I wanted to get on the road before darkness blanketed the sky. I hated driving at night.

And most important, I wanted to get to my friend.

I didn't need to free up a hand to open the door. Our storm door never latched properly, and with a swift kick at the base, it would swing free and open, creaking at the hinges.

For the first time since we'd moved into that house, I was grateful for the minor imperfection.

I didn't need to free up my hand, but I did need to open it slightly. Two fingers letting go of the weight burning against my flesh.

The last noise I heard before I stepped outside and welcomed the damp air on my skin was the ping of gold striking the wood beneath my feet.

* * *

I rode with the windows down the entire drive to Dogwood Beach. I reveled in the clean scent of grass and earth, the sweet warmth of a May evening. Everyday things, beautiful things that would normally calm my restless mind, but not tonight. I kept the music off and just let myself *think*, piling on sign after obvious sign I had been too stupid or too disconnected to notice over the past three months.

It was all so clear now. Every color of our corrosion.

The naive veil had finally been lifted, and the longer I drove, the more I hated myself for becoming one of those women who allowed deceit to slip past them. Who stayed too detached and okay with little changes that should've been red-hot alarms, blaring with an incessant warning.

Our growing silence with each other, leaving our only conversations to be ones we needed to have, not ones we wanted to have. The indifferent way he began to look at me, or the late nights when he'd claim he was too tired to drag himself to bed and instead chose to camp out on the couch.

A couch I knew from experience wasn't the best for sleeping on.

I regretted every whispered word I uttered into the dark late at night when I wrapped myself around a cold pillow and reached with a seeking hand for a body I knew wasn't next to me.

What was I reaching for?

And why? Why didn't I see it? Where had I been?

Tori's questions from earlier became a mantra.

Was I that blind? How stupid was I?

With each passing minute, my hands formed tighter to the wheel until a crack of pain shot up my forearms. I adjusted and readjusted, flexing until my shoulders began to shake. I was a bottle of pent-up aggression, a warrior in a cage, watching as a threatening figure inched closer...closer until I saw the intimidation radiating off them in heated waves. Until I felt it on my skin. The warm bite of hunger scratched the back of my throat. I wanted to bare my teeth and sink them into flesh. Draw blood. I couldn't remember ever feeling this alive before, but I was ready.

Ready to release my anger onto someone who truly deserved it.

It was after nine when I finally arrived, parked my car behind Tori's Volvo, and grabbed my duffle, leaving my other bags in the backseat.

The smell of salt water soaked into my lungs as I climbed the stairs to the porch, and for a brief moment I thought about how peaceful my new life was about to become.

Living at the beach was a fairy tale to me. A pipe dream that was about to become a reality...at least I was hoping it would.

I was showing up at my friend's house, unannounced, seeking refuge.

Bag in hand, I held my breath and knocked three times.

Seconds passed before the door swung open.

Tori stood before me in her pajamas, a pair of pale blue linen shorts and an oversized T-shirt that hung off her shoulder.

Her jaw hit the floor as she looked me over with wide, startled eyes.

"Syd! What are you..." She paused, gaze lowering to the duffle in my hand. "What's going on? Where's Marcus? Is he with you?"

She glanced behind me in the direction of the driveway.

Explanations were in order. This was the boldest move I had ever made in all of my twenty-four years, aside from getting married straight out of high school.

I never visited Tori without planning out my trip, and she always knew about it well in advance.

This wasn't simply a visit, though. This was a permanent relocation.

But explanations could wait. I had to deal with something, or someone, to be specific, before I revealed anything.

I pushed past her and entered the house.

"No, he's not. And he won't be joining me either. I hope that offer you made me last year still stands. I know you were just joking about us ditching our men and starting a lesbian life together, but as long as we keep it purely platonic, I could swing it."

I tossed my bag on the couch in the large sitting room and spun to face a very, very confused-looking Tori.

Rightfully so.

She tilted her head, motioning around the room as if the house, and not the woman standing in front of her, had just magically appeared.

"What's going on here? What are you doing?"

"I need that asshole's number. Let me handle this first, and then I'll explain everything. I promise." I tugged my phone out of my back pocket. My hand shook ever so slightly. "What is it?"

She slowly inched closer.

"Who? Wes? Why? You're not going to call him, are you?"

"Tori," I growled. "Give. Me. His. Number."

My words, and the tone behind them, acted like a fire lit to blaze under her ass. She gasped, then moved with purpose through the tiny but lavish beach house.

Tori came from money. Her family came from money. You didn't live this close to the water and in digs like this without either having connections or a stacked bank account.

"Okayyy." She spoke with uncertainty, her tongue clinging to the word as she walked back into the room. "Okay, um, seriously, I have no clue what's going on right now, but I'm almost afraid you might choke me if I don't do what you say. You're a bit scary right now, Syd."

If I'd had it in me, I would've smiled at that.

But I didn't have it in me to smile.

Tori dug the heel of her hand into her eye while her other scrolled through the contacts on her phone.

Her long blond hair was haphazardly pulled back into a loose pony, with several pieces falling onto her shoulders and curling there.

She looked unkempt and exhausted, but still unbelievably gorgeous, because she always looked unbelievably gorgeous no matter how unkempt or exhausted she was.

Tori was a natural stunner and the definition of small-town beauty queen. She grew up in the pageant circuit, won every competition she ever entered without even caring enough about them to try, it was all her mother's doing, putting her in those pageants and exploiting her daughter's beauty, and Tori went through the motions to make her mother happy, but that didn't mean Tori didn't know when to put her foot down and that occurred when she was approached by some agency to do shampoo commercials when she was fourteen.

My best friend wasn't interested in the kind of attention appearing in a shampoo commercial would bring a fourteen-year-old who had developed a lot earlier than the rest of her peers.

So that offer was the end of Tori's pageant days and, subsequently, the beginning of her mother's descent into the world of plastic surgery.

If her daughter wasn't going to bring her attention, Mrs. Rivera would find her own way to grab it.

I watched another strand of hair fall out of Tori's messy yet still utterly perfect pony.

I imagined after she destroyed God knows how many breakables in the house, she probably tossed about in her bed, praying for sleep and dreams involving Wes's unfortunate but highly deserved demise.

Bastard.

Keeping her eyes on her phone, Tori shook her head then finally spoke.

"He probably won't answer you. That's his thing. But whatever. Ready? It's 919-555-6871."

I opened up the keypad on my phone and moved my thumb furiously over the numbers.

He would answer. I'd hit Redial until my fingers bled if needed.

I placed the phone to my ear and waited.

I felt anxious and slightly dizzy. My pulse was racing. I knew I probably needed to sit down, take a breath, but the second that motherfucker's deep voice seeped into my ear with a tired yet undeniably sexy "yeah," which pissed me off to no end seeing as I hated this man with every fiber of my being and had no business thinking his "yeahs" were sexy, I was on high alert and once again found myself pacing the room like a strung-out junkie.

"You," I growled, voice vibrating low and sore in my throat. "Stupid, worthless piece of dog shit."

Tori gasped behind me.

"*Excuse me?*" Wes sounded put off. "What the fuck—"

"Who the hell do you think you are, huh? And in what universe is a douche bag tool like you able to bag a wife? Is she *also* a fucking idiot?"

I heard his heavy breathing on the other line, but nothing else. His silence boiled my blood.

"Hello! Remove the dildo from your mouth and fucking speak!"

I spun around, shocked at my own coarse words, and looked up at Tori, curious to see her reaction.

She stood frozen between the couch and the wall, her eyes swollen and red from her earlier tears, doubled in size now that I'd let my mouth loose on this dipshit.

A light, amused chuckle hissed in my ear.

I pulled in a breath through my nose.

"Jesus Christ," he mumbled. "Think you might have the wrong number, Wild. I don't normally suck on dildos after six o'clock on Tuesdays."

I blinked at the floor.

Wild?

Was he making fun of me?

He was. He was making a joke, out of me, out of this, out of my best friend's pain.

I flattened a hand to my chest, feigning regret.

"Oh, I am so, so sorry. I forgot. You're into ass play. Hard and deep, right? Tori told me all about it. My mistake. Is that something your wife enjoys? Do you take turns fucking each other?"

"Fuck," he groaned. "You serious?"

"You hurt her," I bit out through clenched teeth. "You hurt my best friend. And you better pray to the God of assholes like you that I don't ever see your ugly, motherfucking face. Jail doesn't scare me, loser. I will cut your dick off and make you eat it in front of your mother."

He laughed again, only this time it was bold and straight from his belly. One of those laughs I knew had his head thrown back and tears brimming his eyes.

My feet stuck to the carpet. The hand at my side curled into a tight fist with nails threatening to break skin.

"You're...*wow*," he said, his voice floating with another soft laugh. "Damn. Just slow down a minute, all right? Quit yelling for a second." He cleared his throat. I heard the creak of the mattress. "Look, I'm not going to deny that I partake in a little ass play on occasion, but no joke, I'm the one delivering it. There is no other scenario. As for my dick? I really need him to stay attached. We're close. You get me?"

Did I *get* him?

"I hate you," I whispered, closing my eyes, my heart pounding.

Suddenly, I forgot who I had dialed and could only picture Marcus standing in the doorway of our bedroom.

Marcus, telling me it was over.

Marcus, digging his nails into my chest and clawing out my heart.

Marcus, my husband, who had stopped loving me and wanted out.

He didn't look remorseful in that moment. He looked...relieved.

There was no need to lie anymore. No need to pretend he was happy. He was free, and I was falling.

Down.

Down.

Into the unknown, where I had to find the person I was without him. I didn't even know where to begin looking for her.

Wes hesitated responding, finally giving me a quiet, "Don't even know me," followed by a heavy sigh. "Again, you got the wrong number. This guy who you *think* I am, he screwed over your friend? Right? Do me a favor and check the number you were supposed to dial. I'm betting you're only off by one."

"Fuck you," I spat.

I was sick of hearing his denial, but then strangely found myself pulling the phone back and studying the screen.

There was something in his voice when he dropped the enjoyment of my verbal lashing. A concealed sadness, and I didn't think the man who had shamelessly introduced his wife to his girlfriend had the ability to feel anything that deep.

You had to have a heart first. Wes clearly didn't.

I couldn't remember what number Tori had given me. It could easily have been the number lit up on my phone, but I wanted to be certain.

I lifted my head to look at her.

"What was that number again?"

Tori narrowed her eyes, her mouth dropping open. She then glanced down once more at the phone in her hand and slowly repeated, "Uh, 919-555-6871."

Shit.

Exactly one number off. I'd dialed 6872.

"What's going on?" Tori asked, stepping forward.

I knew the man on the other end of the line heard the confirmation he was betting on. By the time the phone touched my ear again, he was finishing the last subtle notes of a throaty chuckle.

"Sorry you're going to have to go through that epic speech again, Wild. You nailed it, though, if that helps."

Wild.

His voice was smooth and low, wickedly playful.

Sexy.

I was ready to dig a hole in the sand and bury myself in it.

God, I am such a shit.

I slapped a hand over my eyes, groaning.

"Oh, my God. I am so, *so* sorry. This...was clearly a call not meant for you. I'm sure you're not a douche bag tool."

"Who sucks on dildos and gets fucked by his wife?"

He chuckled again.

I could feel the heat burn across my cheeks and down my neck.

"Yeah," I said through a wince.

"Not really my thing."

Tori nudged my elbow, then held her hands out, silently questioning what was going on.

I shook my head. I needed to get off the phone with this guy. I'd abused him enough already.

I held up a finger to Tori and spun around, facing the large bay window at the front of the house.

"Right. Um, again, I'm very, *very* sorry I cussed you out and accused you of enjoying...those things. I don't normally go off like that. It's just been...one of those days. You know?" I blew out a quick breath. "Sorry again. Take care."

Quickly, before he had the chance to respond, I slid my thumb over the End Call button.

My body slumped into the nearby recliner and I curled into the leather, dropping my head back with a sigh.

That felt good. Even if I hadn't spewed that hatred at my intended victim, something in my chest felt lighter. It was bizarre. Maybe I didn't need to dial the correct number to chew out Wes, or face my new reality and lay into Marcus.

Speaking of douche bag tools.

Marcus had gotten off too easy. He pulled the pin on our relationship and walked away without any refusal from me. I'm not a wallflower. Far from it, actually. I would eventually face him and give him every word I was meant to say in that bedroom. He deserved to know how I felt, but more than that, he deserved to feel it.

"What...the *hell* was that?" Tori appeared in front of me, her hands stuck to her hips. "Did you seriously say all of that to a wrong number?"

I nodded.

"Holy shit, you badass. Way to commit." Her smile faded a second before her eyes went soft. "Are you going to try Wes again? Because really, Syd, you don't have to do that. I'm not asking you to fight my battles, and to be honest..." She trailed off, swallowing heavily as her eyes lowered. "I think I'm okay. I mean, I'm completely done with men for the time being, but I'm not chasing a bottle of pills with some hooch. I'll get over it. He was just another mistake."

After I was silent for a few seconds, she bent down and placed her hand gently on my knee.

"Hey," she whispered.

I rolled my head to the side until our eyes met, and before she spoke her next words, I knew from the look on her face what she was planning on asking me.

I decided to beat her to it.

"Marcus told me tonight he wants a divorce."

She sucked in a breath.

"What? Why? What happened?"

Before I could answer, she shot up abruptly, holding her hand out to keep me quiet.

"Wait. We need wine for this discussion, and all of the chocolate in this house. Give me a minute."

She turned to take a step, but halted, spinning back around and pointing at the floor.

"You will be living here."

My mouth lifted in the corner.

"Thank you."

She disappeared down the hallway in a blur of blond hair and long limbs as I tucked myself into a ball, staring off into the quiet house.

My new home.

Chapter Two

SYDNEY

"I just... I don't get it."

Tori slid down onto the floor next to me in front of the couch with another bottle of wine.

We had polished off the first one rather quickly while I revealed the details of my evening, which included everything involving Marcus, plus the ending of my employment in Raleigh I handled over a phone call on the drive here, and I was already starting to feel the effects of the alcohol. My cheeks were flushed and I was growing tired.

Wine always made me sleepy.

She popped the cork and poured herself another glass.

"How do you fall out of love with someone after seven years together?" she asked. "How does that even happen? And with no warning, that's the strangest part. It's like he just woke up and, boom, he wants out."

I took the bottle from her and brought it to my lips. The moscato warmed my throat.

"There were warnings," I confessed, staring straight ahead. I could instantly feel her eyes on me.

"Like?"

Tori sounded baffled, which was to be expected. I hadn't shared with her the details of the past few months with Marcus. Not because I wanted to keep her in the dark, but because at the time, I was lost in it myself. I didn't want to see what was happening to my marriage. I didn't want to feed any truth to it. So I made excuses for Marcus. I played down obvious cautions and ignored my suspicions. Anything to keep myself from acknowledging the reality.

"Syd."

Tori nudged my shoulder, snapping me out of my head.

"Sorry." I gave her a weak smile, then focused on the bottle in my hand. "You know how Marcus's job is. He's always worked crazy hours, but lately, it was nonstop. Twelve-to-fourteen-hour days. He'd pick up side jobs on the weekend for extra cash. We never saw each other anymore. If he was home, I was working and vice versa. It was like we were living separate lives in the same house."

"But you guys still talked to each other and stuff, right?"

I subtly shook my head.

"Not about anything other than stuff we had to discuss, like if a certain bill was paid or what I needed to pick up from the market. He became quiet, like really distant with me, but I figured it was just the job getting to him. I knew he had to be exhausted. He was never home."

"Mm." She brought her glass to her lips. "What about texting? Didn't you two talk on the phone at all?"

I gave Tori an odd look. She should've known the answer to that question.

"You know how Marcus is with technology. He hates cell phones. He rarely carries his with him. And texting is out of the question. He refuses to do it."

I took another swig of the wine, remembering the countless conversations we'd had about him never returning my messages.

"How am I supposed to respond to a smiley face? And I'm not typing on that small as shit keyboard. It's lame."

I took a deep breath before continuing on with my confession.

"We stopped having sex, too. That should've been the biggest red flag, but again...long hours. I just figured he was too tired."

I prayed he was too tired. The other possibility, my husband no longer finding me physically attractive, wasn't something I wanted to believe, and it wouldn't have been something I could've understood either.

I hadn't changed much since Marcus and I first met in high school. I still looked fairly the same. Yes, I was curvier and filled out my jeans a bit more, especially in the bottom, which seemed to be where I stored all the extra calories I consumed, but Marcus acted like he loved the freshman fifteen I held on to. Up until recently, he could barely keep his hands off me in public.

How could he go from wanting me insatiably to not at all? How does that even happen?

Tori leaned forward and exchanged her glass for the bag of chocolate-covered pretzels off the table.

"How long has it been?"

"Three months," I blurted out.

"*Three months?*" She whipped her head around and gaped at me. The bag crumpled in her grasp. "You haven't had sex in three months? Really? Jesus, that's..." She paused, blinking several times with her mouth hanging open, then leaning closer and whispering as if she didn't want her neighbors to know, "*Three months?* Did you at least try?"

I rolled my eyes.

"Of course I tried, but after the third rejection I gave up."

"I don't blame you."

She bit into a pretzel and offered me the bag.

I shook my head. Not even one of my favorite snacks appealed to me at the moment.

"And you just thought he was too tired for sex?" she asked.

"Yeah."

God, that observation sounded ridiculous now. It was so obvious, but denial can fool you. Hope can fool you, too. I knew what I wanted to believe, and that was the only thing I allowed myself to focus on.

For three months, I didn't just think my marriage was fine and my husband still wanted me, I knew that was the only possibility. I left no room in my head for doubt.

"Does he know you're here?" she asked.

"No. I just packed up and left. I didn't talk to him."

"Good. He doesn't deserve to know what you're doing. Fuck him."

A bubble of laughter caught in my throat. All I could think of was...

I tried.

"I'm going to say something, and I know this is a huge risk because there is a possibility you and Marcus could work out your shit and get back together, but I think he did you a huge favor tonight."

I slowly turned to look at Tori. I couldn't believe what I had just heard.

"What?"

"I know. I know. Just hear me out. Don't yell at me yet." She sat the bag of pretzels down and turned her body, angling herself toward me. She tucked a chunk of hair behind her ear. "I've always liked Marcus. You know that. But I think he kind of dulled you out a little, hon."

I narrowed my eyes at her.

"Dulled me out? What does that mean?"

She motioned at me. "You weren't *you* with him. I don't know. You two were always so serious together. It was like the guy couldn't take a joke."

I shrugged. "So what?"

"*So what?*" she repeated, sitting up on her knees. "I never saw you laugh with him, Syd. I mean, you two seemed happy, otherwise I would've said something to you, but...it was like you weren't friends at all. You were just married. He never played with you."

I slid my hand around my neck and squeezed while my eyes lost focus on the carpet.

I couldn't dispute what Tori was saying. Marcus wasn't really a playful guy, but I never needed him to be. He always, up until recent months, made me feel like I was the only woman he ever saw. He was affectionate, most of the time, and caring. He supported and encouraged me through college. I didn't need him to joke around or make me laugh. That wasn't important. I just needed him to love me. And he did.

He just didn't anymore.

Tori sighed. "I'm sorry. I'm not trying to upset you further, it's just...I've known you forever. I know the person you are when we're together. You're silly and a complete nut. Remember how we met?

Seventh grade? You told me your name was Tori, too, because you wanted us to be best friends and you thought it would happen faster if we had the same name?"

I smiled faintly.

"Had you calling me that for a week," I said.

"I know." Tori laughed. "I yelled at everyone who called you Sydney. Even teachers." She nudged my shoulder with hers. "I'm just saying, I missed that girl when Marcus was around. That's all."

She said those final two words on a shrug.

I slid down farther and rested my head on the cushion, staring up at the ceiling.

Tori joined me, putting herself into a similar pose.

After a minute or two of silence, I finally responded.

"Maybe you're right. Maybe Marcus and I weren't friends. Maybe we didn't play with each other and laugh all the time. But you know what? It doesn't matter anymore. Whatever we were, he no longer wants it. He's done. And I need to think about my life without him, starting with finding a job around here."

"Oh, I got you covered on that."

"You do?"

I stared at her profile. I had no idea what she was driving at.

She tilted her head to the side and smiled.

"Hell yeah I do. Come work with me at Whitecaps until you find an x-ray job."

"As a waitress?"

"Yep. Nate will work you into the schedule no problem. He's cool. And I'll make sure he puts us on the same shifts." She slapped my knee and stood, stretching her arms above her head with a yawn. "I'm beat. Do you need help bringing the rest of your stuff in?"

"Nah, I got it. When do you think I could talk to Nate about getting a job?"

I got on my feet to join her, both of us grabbing a bottle and the trash from the snacks we'd devoured during our conversation.

We carried our handfuls to the kitchen.

"Tomorrow," she answered, holding the lid of the trash can open for me. She then took the unfinished bottle of moscato and recorked it before sticking it into the refrigerator. "We'll take a drive down to Whitecaps and get you set up. I'm sure he'll want you to start immediately. We just had someone quit last week."

"It'll only be until I find an x-ray job. Are you sure he won't mind if it's temporary?"

I knew some managers frowned upon hiring someone who wasn't willing to stick around. I wouldn't blame Nate for being hesitant about bringing me on, and I would never keep my motives from him. I could very easily find a job in a couple weeks and leave them short staffed.

On the other hand, it could take me months to find an x-ray position here locally.

Tori placed her hands on my shoulders, gently squeezing. Her eyes got soft.

"You know you don't have to jump right into something. You could take a few weeks to relax—"

I cut her off.

"I need to work, Tori. I can't just sit around here. I'll go crazy."

Crazy thinking about how I was suddenly single for the first time in seven years, and how I'm going to be divorced—*divorced*—before my twenty-fifth birthday.

Crazy thinking about what I could've possibly done to cause this, or to prevent it.

Crazy.

This didn't feel like my life.

Tori stepped back, dropping her hands with a nod and a smile.

"Okay. You know what's best for you. And you'll like it there. Trust me." Mischief danced in her eyes.

I could only imagine what she meant by that.

"I'm heading to bed. Pick a room, any room. It's yours."

"Tori, wait."

She stopped almost to the stairs, gazing back over her shoulder.

"We've done nothing but talk about me all night. Are you okay, with Wes and everything?"

It took her a second, but a ghost of a smile tugged at her mouth.

"Getting there. I mean, it hurts, but you're here. That'll help.

I know I'll be okay." She winked at me before climbing the stairs. "Night, roomie," she called out.

I stood in the silence of the kitchen for a minute, maybe more, wondering when I could be okay, too.

* * *

I couldn't remember falling asleep last night.

I couldn't remember the slow drift of weightlessness that takes over your body when your mind is quiet.

I couldn't remember relaxing at all in the most comfortable bed I'd ever lain on.

I did, however, remember calling my mother and filling her in on my eventful evening after I carried my suitcases inside. I also unfortunately remembered her sweetly paired "I told you so's" and "God hates divorce" rantings in my ear.

She was never a huge fan of Marcus, for reasons she never expanded on, but more so, she thought my choice to leave him and move in with Tori, instead of staying and working things out with Marcus, was disappointing.

Disappointing. I disappointed her.

That hurt.

The conversation with my mother was kept brief. I made up an excuse and got off the phone while she was in the middle of yet another spiritual lecture, and I readied myself for bed.

I remembered hitting the soft, billowy mattress and wiping the tears from my eyes.

I remembered flipping my pillow over when I soaked the satin.

I remembered the peaceful hum of the fan spinning overhead, the clock on the wall ticking away the seconds of my misery, and the faint sounds of waves crashing outside my window, and how all of it, every calming noise, irritated me to no end.

But clearing my mind enough to welcome sleep? No. That I couldn't remember at all.

I woke in a tangle of sheets and blankets, my hair matted and soaked with sweat. My nightshirt twisted on my torso.

I sat up in a jerk, my eyes searching the room for someone. *Someone.* That was almost laughable.

I should be used to waking up alone at this point, but somehow this morning felt...different.

Permanent.

Irrefutable.

I used to be a morning person. A life person. Today, not so much.

* * *

"Hellooo?"

Tori waved her hand in my face as we drove down the long stretch of road that runs parallel with the shore.

I dragged my gaze off the dash.

"Huh? What's up?"

She chuckled softly, peering out the windshield.

"You were spacing out over there. We're almost at the restaurant. It's just up here on the right."

I flipped the visor down and checked my appearance in the mirror.

I fingered the ends of my long, bottle-dyed blond hair, then smeared on a quick application of lip gloss.

"You okay?"

"Fine," I replied through a rushed exhale. My stomach felt coiled into a rigid knot. I shifted in my seat, shrugging. "Just new job jitters, I guess. I hope he hires me."

Tori laughed again as I leaned back in the seat and tucked my lip gloss into the front pocket of my jeans.

"What?" I asked, turning to look at her as the car slowed down.

Her profile was devilish, lifted in amusement, matching her signature ruby lip she always wore no matter if she was going out or cleaning the house.

Tori always wore red lipstick. And she *rocked* it.

"Nate isn't an idiot. He knows what he's doing. You're in."

I thought about how strange that sounded, then decided to shift the attention off me and onto the one person I knew had to be hurting as badly as I was.

"How are you today?"

Tori didn't miss a beat. She also made me reevaluate my assumption that we were both in the same sinking boat.

"Getting better by the second," she replied, adjusting the volume on the stereo, wiggling her ass in her seat and smacking the steering wheel along to the beat of the Calvin Harris song pumping through the speakers.

She smiled at me before elaborating.

"My best girl is here, it's going to be a gorgeous day, by the looks of it, and I devoted all of my prayers last night to the hopes of Wes contracting a delightfully new STD and having that shit named after him. Hopefully soon, people will start getting diagnosed with 'the Wes.' Symptoms include swelling of the genitals, painful urination, and a wicked rash." She lifted her eyebrows, crystal blue eyes sparkling. "It's fatal."

I couldn't help laughing.

She pulled into a large lot surrounding a restaurant and parked along the side.

Whitecaps was a waterfront establishment, very beach chic, if there was such a thing. Colorful long boards were propped along the outer perimeter, with a few stuck into the sand on either side of the staircase. Boating oars framed the entrance of the restaurant, and the railing wrapping around the building was made up of a thick rope, the kind you would use to secure your boat to a pier.

I liked it instantly. It was such a contrast to the beige walls and dark environment of a radiology department.

"Let's get you a job."

I'd barely exited the car before Tori was grabbing my hand and dragging me up the stairs and through the doors.

My eyes blinked rapidly at my new surroundings.

The atmosphere inside was as energetic and refreshing as the exterior of the building.

Bold, vibrant color scheme, with lots of oranges, yellows, and bright blues. Surfboards and nautical knickknacks hanging on the walls.

I didn't like it.

I loved it.

Flo Rida poured softly through the overhead speakers as I was pulled through the restaurant toward the back of the room.

Tori waved to a few servers, then halted at a door with the word "Manager" written in white.

She knocked twice. A muted voice beckoned for her to enter.

"Nate, hey, are you busy?" Tori asked, swinging the door open and tugging me to follow.

The man behind the desk lifted his head.

He was a young guy, couldn't have been more than thirty, and really, *really* good-looking, with dark, short-styled hair and a muscular build, rough, sexy stubble marking his jaw, and eyes the color of a rich chocolate. His tie was loosened at the collar, and his thick shoulders pulled the material of his dress shirt taut across his body, highlighting his pecs.

He glanced briefly at me, then looked at Tori, pulled his dark-rimmed glasses off, and set them on top of a pile of papers.

"I'm always busy. What's up?"

"This"—Tori pulled me close beside her, still holding my hand—"is my best friend, Sydney. She just moved here and needs a job. Give her one."

I gasped at my best friend's bluntness.

Nate leaned back in his chair, eyes narrowing.

Shit.

"*Please* give her a job, is what you meant to say, right? Because I am your boss, not your friend, Tori. You seem to forget that every other time I see you."

"Didn't I say please?"

"No," he answered dryly.

I was suddenly panicked.

Good-bye, nice job with fantastic music and a chill environment.

Tori waved her free hand nonchalantly in the air.

"My bad. Please, can you give her a job? She's amazing, and you *know* she'll be very popular with the locals."

Nate trained his eyes on me, studied me briefly, then asked, "You have waitress experience?"

I nodded, reclaiming my hand and stepping forward.

"It's been a few years. I waitressed through high school and a little in college. But before you hire me, I have to tell you, this isn't permanent. I'll be actively looking for a radiology position while I . . . *if* I work here. I promise to give you two weeks' notice, but it could be soon that I'll end up leaving."

"Radiology?"

"Yes, sir. I'm certified in x-ray."

"Do you know how overly qualified you probably are for this?"

I smiled uncertainly, readying my knees to beg.

The carpet appeared soft. I might get away with little to no rug burn.

Nate cleared his throat, leaning farther back in his chair.

"So I could hire you today and you could quit on me this weekend if you found something else? That's what you're telling me, right?"

"Yes," I answered honestly.

"Do you have any idea how much hassle that'll be for me? The amount of paperwork and double coverage for training I'll set up, all for nothing? And when you do end up quitting, I'll have to scramble to get your shifts covered. That's not easy. Why should I even hire you?"

My breath caught in my throat as I stared at him, scrambling for a response.

Shit!

He was definitely leaning toward blowing me off. As he should. This was ridiculous. I could find a job tomorrow and not even get the opportunity to pick up a shift here.

I briefly glanced in Tori's direction, only to see how little invested she was in this discussion.

She was busy admiring the collection of sailboats lined along the bookshelf on the other side of the room, humming softly to herself.

Scowling, I turned back to Nate in time to catch the impatient tilt of his head.

I inhaled a deep, soothing breath before finally responding.

"Because I would really appreciate the opportunity to work here, probably more than half of your staff. Because I don't simply need this job, I want this job. Being over qualified isn't an issue. I didn't get a degree in waitressing. I have no idea how to work your computer system. But I am a fast learner. I'll work my ass off for you. Tori said she does doubles occasionally to help you out. I have no problem with that. I actually wouldn't mind the constant distraction. And again, I promise I'll give you notice if another job comes up. Even if I'm only here a few weeks, you won't regret hiring me."

Silence stretched between us. Nate seemed to mull over my request, running his hand along the back of his neck as he exhaled a thick breath.

I looked anywhere but his face.

The stripes in his shirt. The clutter of paperwork on his desk. The back of my best friend's head as she continued to forget I existed.

"I doubt half of my staff knows how to work the computer system. In fact, none of them use it," Nate admitted, drawing my attention back to his face. A subtle grin pulled at his mouth. "You'll fit right in."

My mouth stretched into my biggest smile in months. The tension pulled from my shoulders. I extended a hand to Nate as he stood up out of his chair.

"Thank you so, so much for this. I can start immediately. Today. Tonight."

He laughed, releasing my hand.

"How about Friday? I'll pair you up with Tori for training."

"Great."

"Awesome," Tori sang, skipping over to rejoin the conversation. She threw her arm over my shoulder. "Thanks, Nate. You're the best boss ever."

He jerked his chin, then reclaimed his seat, his eyes refocusing on the documents in front of him.

"Get Sydney set up with uniforms before you go."

Tori directed me out of the office, nodding at Nate's request.

"Thank you again," I said over my shoulder before the door to the office closed behind us.

I felt relieved, and a bit excited. I hadn't worked with Tori since we were sixteen and both living in Raleigh. We never got through a shift without cracking up at least a dozen times.

I needed this right now.

Tori pulled away from me when we reached the hostess desk.

"We're getting out of here 'cause I don't hang at work on my days off." She reached for the keys in her back pocket. "Wanna wait for me out in the car?"

I looked out the large window overlooking the dunes obscuring the ocean.

"I think I'm going to go check out the beach really quick. Text me when you're ready."

She gave me a double thumbs-up before spinning around and walking back in the direction we came.

I slipped out the door.

I crossed the pebble stone parking lot and ascended the staircase leading to the beach, wrapping my arms around myself even though I wasn't the least bit chilled.

The sun burned across a cloudless sky. I felt the intensity of it bake into the skin of my bare shoulders.

Waves crashed against the shore, some carrying surfers with them in the distance. A few feet ahead of me, a small child kicked a sand castle and giggled with his father.

I sat down on a step and slipped my sandals off.

The sand was warm underneath my feet as I dug my toes into it, staring out at the world in front of me. I rubbed a shell between my fingers as I watched a couple walk hand-in-hand toward the pier.

They looked happy. I tried to remember the last time Marcus held my hand, or even reached for it.

My chest burned when I couldn't conjure up an image in my mind.

I looked down at the faint line marking my left ring finger. The token I was left with now that I no longer wore my ring. It was subtle, thanks to my naturally pale skin, but to me it stood out like embers glowing in the dark.

I hated it. I didn't need a reminder of how I'd failed as a wife. Or how Marcus stopped seeing me as one.

Maybe I could coat my entire hand in sunblock except for that thin strip. Burn the memory away.

The idea seemed promising enough to consider.

From my back pocket, my cell beeped with an incoming message.

I wiped the tear from my cheek as I stood and palmed my phone, expecting to see Tori's name lit up on my screen.

I froze on the step, my free hand on the railing as I stared curiously at the message and the number it was sent from.

Wild Girl. Eaten any innocent men alive today yet?

My lip twitched, the hint of a smile.

I sat back down, reading the message a second time as I remembered my conversation with this stranger yesterday. My accidental verbal beat-down.

Jesus. I really let him have it.

I couldn't think of the last time I was that embarrassed.

I told the guy to remove a dildo from his mouth, for Christ sakes.

All in all, whoever this was seemed to be a good sport about it. He could've laid into me and cussed me out. Made me feel even more like a complete shit for dialing the wrong number and not confirming the identity of my intended victim before I tore into him like he owed me money.

He was more than decent about the whole thing. Easily forgiving.

And now he was messaging me out of nowhere and striking up conversation.

Wild.

He wanted to talk to me.

Huh.

I tapped my thumb on the edge of the phone case, then hovered over the letters of my keypad as I stared at the message.

Did I even want to talk to this guy anymore? Wasn't this weird? We didn't know each other. Our encounter was a mistake. A one-time mishap, never to be repeated.

Right?

Chapter Three

BRIAN

I passed out last night pissed off and ready to beat the shit out of my best friend/roommate, who didn't understand the premise of fucking quietly in the bedroom down the hall.

Moans and earsplitting screams echoed off the walls of our beach house, seeping underneath the crack of my door.

Filling my fucking head. Keeping me awake.

Nothing was unusual about that scenario. Jamie brought home lots of women, and I swore to Christ he tested out their vocal range before even considering their pussy as a temporary home for his dick. The louder the better seemed to be his philosophy.

I didn't give a fuck what he did, or who. I just didn't want to hear it.

Taking every pillow I owned, I submerged my head and muffled the sounds well enough to fall asleep.

Six hours, that was all I was asking for. Six hours and I could function enough to push through another mindlessly objectionable day in the life I was slowly living. Quickly hating. And unarguably deserved.

I barely settled into a dream when the shrill ring of my cell phone jerked me upright in bed.

It took a moment for my eyes to adjust to the darkness, for my hand to seek out the bastard device on my nightstand. I didn't recognize the number. I was fucking exhausted and could barely focus on the screen my thumb was hovering over.

I almost let the call go to voice mail. I almost said to hell with it and shattered the fucking thing by hurling it against the wall.

Thank fuck I didn't. I would've missed out on the most amusing conversation I've ever had and, quite possibly, the most perverse.

And the voice that gave it to me.

Unfuckingreal.

Didn't know what did it, the vulgar she was throwing at me, her fiery tone that paired with it, or the sweetness I heard underneath, but I was hooked. Every muscle in my body tightened as her voice seeped into my ear and awakened my mind.

Fuck sleep. I was no longer interested.

That feisty thing on the other end of the phone was filthy and unquestionably infuriated, ready to sink her claws into me and draw blood.

I would welcome an assault from her with arms outstretched and the biggest grin smeared across my face. I couldn't help it. She was fucking fantastic. Passionate in her defense. Silver-tongued and ballbusting.

My ears weren't the only parts of me enjoying that conversation.

I wanted to taste her voice. I thought about what her lips looked like as those words left her, if they were pink and wet and swollen and if she bit them while she was silent and waiting, hearing out my objections.

Strange how quickly an obsession can build.

One phone call had me reeling, and it was never even meant for me.

I hadn't laughed like that in months, and it felt good.

The kind of good I wanted to keep feeling, and I could've.

I could've kept her going. Lied. Revealed nothing and let her lay into me as much as she needed to. But she deserved to know I wasn't the person she was seeking out. And her response?

"Fuck you."

Yeah. Fuck me.

How long would I be consumed by this mystery woman?

Hours, at least. That was for certain. It was eleven o'clock and I was trying to busy myself at work on Wednesday, but nothing was taking my mind off that voice.

"Would you fuckin' relax?" I glared down at my lap, pressing my palm against the tent in my shorts.

I got hard every time I thought about her. It was becoming a major fucking problem.

My gaze lingered until the heat in my groin subsided, then I resumed the tedious task of staring at my phone on the counter. The very phone containing her number.

Fuck this. How pathetic was I going to allow myself to become today?

I pushed away from the counter with a grunt and went to the corkboard on the back wall displaying this week's lesson sign-ups.

I removed old advertisements and sales that no longer applied. I studied the list of names, noted the instructors posted next to them, then dropped my shoulders and glanced back at the phone.

If that piece of shit devil of a device had a mouth, it would've fucking smiled at me.

It was winning. No contest. I knew it. Apple knew it. It was only a matter of time before I caved and dialed her up, giving in and fully acknowledging my fucked-up obsession.

I raked a hand down my face as I remembered how abruptly she ended our conversation last night. How quick she was to apologize and get off the phone.

Red flag, right there, dick.

I didn't even get to utter a partial good-bye before she hung up and left me reeling. She wouldn't answer me. I'm the guy she didn't intend on calling.

I moved back to the counter, but instead of caving and grabbing my phone, I pulled the crossword puzzle off the shelf behind me and tossed it on the wood, grabbing a pen and leaning over the paper.

I read the clues. Filled in a few answers. Got pissed when I filled shit in wrong and had to write over it, all because my mind wasn't on that damn crossword or the answers I was filling in.

Not one bit.

I had officially run out of things to distract me.

My phone vibrated and shifted on the counter, snapping my attention off the spot on the paper I was spacing out on.

I reached for it and glanced down at the text from my sister. My hand readied to reply.

And then...it hit me.

A text...a text I might be able to coax her to respond to. It was, without a doubt, the less personal approach.

Decision made, I palmed my phone and pulled up my recent calls. My thumbs moved hurriedly over the keypad.

Wild Girl. Eaten any innocent men alive today yet?

I hit Send. I felt good.

Keeping it playful was most likely the best way to go about this. My other thought, confessing how hard I came last night after she hung up on me, might've backfired.

She'd respond, all right. With a restraining order.

The front door chimed, pulling my attention off the phone.

Jamie, the same motherfucker who I wanted to beat the piss out of last night, drifted into the shop with a small group of women floating in behind him. He jerked his chin in my direction, greeted me with a smug grin, then turned his head and watched as the three ladies moved to congregate by a table covered in T-shirts and board shorts.

Stopping on the other side of the counter I was standing behind, he ran a hand through his damp hair.

"What up? What are you doing?"

I placed the phone down.

"Nothing. Waiting on that shipment of boards to arrive."

Not a lie. I was waiting. The boards were set to arrive sometime today. I just couldn't seem to care one way or another about it.

I nodded toward the window facing the ocean. "How's it out there today?"

"Decent. A bit choppy." He lifted his brow. "You tryin' to get out? I can man the shop. I don't have any other lessons until later this afternoon. I think three o'clock is my next one."

I shook my head, stepped back, and leaned my weight against the table, crossing my arms tight across my chest.

Jamie and I co-owned Wax, a surf shop walking distance from the beach.

We opened the store a couple years back when both of us lived and breathed sand and salt water. Back when I did surf, it was purely for enjoyment. I craved the rush of adrenaline. The freedom and adventure it provided. Jamie was the same, but it was different for him. He was a local hero. A Dogwood Beach legend. He won three world championships back-to-back and was one of the most powerful free surfers I'd ever seen.

Kid was fucking talented. He split his days in the shop with me and out on the water.

"Where the fuck is Cole? Wasn't he supposed to be back with our lunch by now? I'm starving."

"He called. Screwed up the order and had to go back," I replied.

"Serious?"

"Yep."

"Idiot." Jamie laughed.

His gaze trained on the three women in the store as they checked out some long boards.

"How difficult is it to remember a Chinese take-out order for three? He needs to get his ass out of the sun. I think that hippy organic sunscreen he uses is killing off his brain cells. No joke."

"I don't know. I had some chick stop in here the other day and ask what brand he wears. Said he gave her a lesson and smelled good, or some shit. She ended up getting his number before she left."

Jamie straightened. He looked stunned.

It took everything in me not to crack up.

He narrowed his eyes.

"Shut the hell up. Cole got laid based on his love for the environment?"

I shrugged.

One of the three girls browsing around the shop came up to the counter. Her smile passed between myself and Jamie.

"Excuse me. Um..." She paused to bite at her bottom lip. "Can one of you help us reach those shirts up there?"

She pointed behind her at the wall of merchandise, allowing the tiny top she was wearing to ride up her body and reveal a pierced navel and a tribal tattoo surrounding it, making no attempt to cover herself after she lowered her hand.

My gaze barely lingered. I wasn't interested.

Jamie, on the other hand, smiled and threw his arm over her shoulder.

"Sure thing, baby," he said gently. "I can help you with that. I'll even lend a hand if you or either of your friends want to try one on. We're all about good service around here."

She giggled and hid her blush behind her hair, wrapping her arm around his waist.

"Might want to check IDs before you *assist* with anything," I suggested as the two of them stepped away.

That girl looked young as shit, and virgin pussy fucked with my best friend's better judgment. Made him a thoughtless moron completely controlled by a set of tits with legs. He had a thing for being a chick's first and rarely passed up that opportunity.

Jamie glanced back, acknowledging me with a jerk of his head, grinning like he was already sheathing up his cock and sinking himself balls deep into one of the girls while the others waited bent over and eager.

I shook my head.

Dumbass was going to get himself in trouble one of these days.

The phone on the counter vibrated, dragging my attention away from the foursome about to commence in the dressing room.

I snatched it up and glanced at the sender. My pulse jumped.

It's a little early. I usually wait until after dinner to randomly dial up men and cuss them out. Again, I'm SO sorry. I feel awful for saying that stuff to you.

My fingers moved vigorously.

Don't need to apologize. That was the most interesting conversation I've ever had.
Really?
Straight up. How did the intended guy take it? You make him cry?
I never called him.

Huh. That surprised me. She seemed dedicated to destroying that prick's ego last night. He sure as hell sounded like he deserved it.

You should've. I think you had a shot at causing some serious hurt.
I don't know.
Got some mouth on you.

I pinched my eyes shut as my cock reacted . . . a-fuckin'-gain.
Shit.
Did I seriously need to give myself another reminder of her mouth? Hadn't my brain been stripped of blood flow enough today?

Thanks? LOL. Not sure how to respond to that, so I'll just take it as a compliment.
It was a compliment. Trust me.
Okay.
You trust me?

Where the fuck was I going with that question?
Way to switch into full-on creeper mode, Brian.
Christ.
I needed to back up before she blocked me and prevented any future conversations.

Not sure why I asked that or what the fuck it meant. You don't know me. Can't trust people you don't know.
I don't NOT trust you. If that makes sense. People don't really earn trust with me. They lose it.

I stared at the screen, finding her response both interesting and cryptic, but not having time to dwell further on that as she hit me up again.

This is weird, right?
What?
This. Texting each other. I honestly wasn't expecting to talk to you again. Everything in my life is seriously messed up right now.

What's messed up about it?
EVERYTHING.
You gonna elaborate on that?
I'll bore you.
Try me.

I waited anxiously for her reply. I wasn't sure I was going to get one. This felt too personal, but fuck it, I wanted to know.

Honestly? I feel like I'm spinning out of control. You ever feel like that?
Can't say I have.
Like, I'm trying to focus on something steady to keep myself from falling, but I can't see it. I just keep picking up speed, spinning and spinning.

I was staring at her response when another message came through.

It's a really scary feeling.

Something pitted in my chest. I remembered a part of our conversation last night. The echo of pain shining through when she whispered she hated me, or the man she thought I was. There was more to her besides the anger coating her mouth, clinging to the hatred she was spewing.

And here it was again.

I forced my fingers to type the first thought that popped into my head, even though my brain was screaming, *screaming* at me to type anything else.

Focus right here.

Awesome. I was losing my mind. Or I had already lost it when I'd sent her that first message. There was no other explanation for my behavior.

She took a whole fucking minute to respond.

I'm Sydney, by the way. Hi.

I smiled. Relief warmed my blood.

Hey.

Hey...you. No name? That's not really fair. What am I supposed to program you in my phone as? Dildo sucker? Don't lie...you've considered it. ;)

I dropped my head with a laugh.

Damn, she was delightful.

And she wanted to program me into her phone. She wanted to know who I was.

That felt good.

Telling her my name wasn't a huge issue. Not my first name anyway.

Brian. And fuck no. Still not into anything involving dildos. You?

Desire bloomed with a warm ache in my groin.

Teetering on inappropriate? Yes. However, she opened the dildo discussion. I was simply continuing it.

Hi Brian.
Wild. Asked you a question.
SMH.

I didn't think she was going to give me an answer. Then a few seconds later she leveled me with one.

Dildos can be very useful when your husband stops wanting to have sex with you. I gotta run. My friend is waiting for me.

I stared, mouth hanging open, rereading the same sentence repeatedly until I was certain I wasn't imagining things.

Husband. The fuck? I had no fucking idea how to take that. I didn't believe she was married. The way she spoke last night, defending her friend with such conviction, there was no way she'd be going behind her husband's back to text me. Even if this was purely innocent, which I honestly wasn't sure if it was, what married woman would actively engage in a conversation about dildos with a man who wasn't her husband?

Maybe she *was* married? Isn't anymore? How fucking old is this chick?

The door chimed and Cole walked into the shop, carrying two bags of food. I quickly typed the only response I could think of without digging for answers.

Later.

I shoved my phone away and looked up as Cole dropped the bags on the counter. Jamie was right behind him.

"Dude, fucking finally. How did you screw up the order?" Jamie asked.

He began digging into one of the bags, pulling out containers and chopsticks and passing them out.

Cole slowly looked over at him and glowered.

"I didn't screw it up. I asked for chicken and broccoli, hold the broccoli, which by the way is the dumbest fuckin' thing I've ever heard. I could've just said chicken."

"Then I would've gotten plain chicken. I want it with the sauce, brother, and I don't like trees in my food." Jamie popped off the lid of his order. "What was the problem?"

"They put trees in your food. You're lucky I checked."

I watched the three girls exit the shop.

"Underage?" I asked as Jamie turned his head at the sound of the chime.

"Yep."

Cole laughed. "I'm surprised that stopped you."

"I like untapped pussy, not underage pussy, dick," Jamie said, shoving a piece of chicken into his mouth. "I have *some* fuckin' standards. Cut me some slack."

"For your *one* standard?" Cole asked.

My phone vibrated in my pocket.

I dropped my chopsticks, then my unopened container of noodles hit the counter so I could reach for the device, wondering if it was Sydney again.

"Jesus, Dash." Jamie laughed.

Jamie always called me Dash.

I ignored him and stared at the screen:

Be here in twenty. I have someone requesting you.

"Fuck," I whispered, shoving my phone away and digging out my keys.

I wasn't angry about the text. I *needed* that fucking text, and that's where my anger stemmed from. My dependence on it. I couldn't say no.

This was my life. My fucked-up life. And the only person I could hate for it was myself.

I glanced up. Jamie and Cole both gave me a look, *the* look, full of sympathy and a hint of sadness, because they knew what I was about to do and felt sorry for me, given the reason behind why I was doing it.

They were the only two people who knew about my other source of income.

No, not income. Income was something you acquired and kept. I've never banked a dime of this money and I never would.

I rounded the counter.

"I'll be back in a few hours. When that order arrives, make sure it's right before you let them leave. It was a pain in the ass last time getting them to ship out the correct shit 'cause of their own fuckup."

They both mumbled something. *Yeah*, or *you got it*. The chime overpowered whatever they said and I didn't care enough to turn back.

I slipped out the door and climbed into my Jeep, sending Mike a brief reply so he'd know I was coming before grabbing the bottle of pills in my glove compartment.

I popped the lid.

A laugh threatened in my throat as I held the tiny blue tablet in my hand.

How many times had I gotten hard today? I should've kept a tally.

I didn't have difficulty getting aroused at the thought of Sydney, at the memory of her voice, or the very idea of what she could possibly look like.

Dark hair and green eyes, I had decided. She was mysterious and a little shy.

I knew if I thought of her now, I could not only get an erection, but sustain one. I wouldn't need a drug to get through this. If I closed my eyes and pictured *her*, what I imagined she would feel like, sound like, the sweetness of her skin, I might even enjoy the next hour.

Shitty move, though. It felt wrong even contemplating that option.

Sex was nothing more than a mindless release to me these days. A necessary transaction.

I stopped looking at it as recreational three months ago. I no longer fucked because I wanted to. The women I slept with didn't care about me. None of them even got me hard without a fucking prescription.

What happened last night with Sydney...*that* was different.

Exhilarating.

Real.

I wouldn't associate that with this. I wouldn't use my body's reaction to her on someone else. They didn't fucking earn it. She did.

I placed the pill on my tongue and tipped my head back, swallowing it down with a bit of saliva.

Then I drove.

The studio was just off the highway, a mere fifteen minutes from the beach and in the seediest part of town. I parked along the back of the building. My usual location. I wasn't typically paranoid, but if I got messages to come out here in the daylight, I didn't want to risk anyone recognizing my Jeep.

I opened the side door and stepped inside the building.

I was told this place was originally an abandoned warehouse. Mike, the owner of Xstasy, acquired the space a year ago and stripped it, putting up makeshift walls to separate different areas, depending on the type of shoot.

It smelled like mildew and regrets. I hated everything about it.

"Dash."

Mike waved me over to the far corner where he stood next to one of the camera guys.

I passed a room where two chicks were moving their hands tentatively over each other. The start of a scene. A man stood behind them, stroking his cock as he watched the blonde dip her head between the legs of the other and eat her out.

The camera zoomed in.

I used to watch porn, and a scene like this would've had me vigorously working my dick in the past. There's not many guys who aren't into seeing two beautiful women together, but now when I see something like this or hear their sounds as I walk across the dark concrete, it does nothing for me.

Doesn't even warrant a twitch.

I reached Mike in quick strides, tipping my chin at the middle-aged creep.

"Hey."

He slapped my shoulder, smiling. I hid my disgust behind a smirk.

"Good. You made it in less than twenty. I got over three thousand active on the site right now and I need you ready. I want your best stuff."

"This is streaming live?" I asked.

I hadn't done that yet. Everything I shot was put up on the site later, usually the next day.

He gave me a hard look.

"That a problem?"

I shook my head.

It wasn't. I didn't see much of a difference if this shit went viral now or in two weeks. As long as I got cash out of it, I wasn't going to protest.

He tipped his head, then smiled as a young woman came to stand next to me.

She was tiny in all areas but one, which by the looks of it cost her a couple grand. Her dark hair was braided into two sections falling past her shoulders, making her look young and innocent, and if that didn't give away the theme of the shoot, her Catholic school uniform nailed it.

Mike brushed his finger along her cheek.

"Dash, meet Jayden. She's been anxiously awaiting your arrival. Isn't that right, sweetness?"

She stepped forward with hunger flaring in her eyes. Her small hands slid up my arms and around my neck. Her tits pressed hard against my ribs as she pulled me into a hug, pinning me against her.

I registered her warm breath and the hint of her perfume.

I barely reciprocated the affection. Just a light hand to her hip.

"Nice to meet you, Mr. Savage." She leaned back, batting her lashes. Her long nails raked down my chest. Then she brushed her hand against my cock, which was slowly hardening. The drugs were kicking in. "You ready to get started?"

I nodded, making sure Mike saw as he spoke to the camera crew.

"What's your name?" I asked her, bending to whisper so he couldn't hear.

"Jayden."

I shook my head.

"Your real name."

She studied me curiously.

"Sara," she murmured, as if she felt embarrassed revealing that secret about herself.

It was funny, her shyness. I was about to touch and taste every part of her. Give her pleasure until I couldn't stand another second of it and sought release myself.

But sharing her real name? That was apparently a little too personal for her.

The lights around us dimmed. Mike gave cues to the staff about angles and shots he wanted.

I took her hand and stepped into the darkness.

Chapter Four

SYDNEY

Merlot red.

I stared at myself in the hallway bathroom mirror at Tori's house, running my fingers through the ends of my freshly washed and dried hair.

The color wasn't spot on to my natural shade, but it was pretty damn close to it. As close as I was probably going to get doing a boxed hair dye kit at home.

It was vibrant. Bold and edgy.

I was slightly nervous I could even pull off this hair color anymore. It had been a long time.

In an attempt to find the person I was supposed to be now, my post-Marcus self, or pre-Marcus self, considering I was looking for the woman I had left behind and lost along the way, I decided a radical change was in order. Something I could make happen immediately. And while twirling a lock of my hair around my finger as I scrolled through online job postings earlier today, it hit me.

Red.

That was definitely something radical.

It had been nine years since I'd let my natural hair color shine.

Being a typical fifteen-year-old girl and wanting to copy everything my best friend was doing, at the time, I had started highlighting my hair right along with Tori. Then I highlighted it again. And again, repeating this ritual every four weeks until there wasn't much trace of natural shade left in my tresses, which turned out to be a good thing considering how vocal Marcus was on liking blondes when he transferred to my high school junior year and, more specifically, on liking my hair blond and no other color.

He expressed this opinion the day I showed him a picture of me as a kid, my red hair falling wild around me since I didn't like having it brushed much back then, mainly because my mother was rough about it and didn't bother spraying detangler on my hair before taking a comb to it.

I have thin hair, and a lot of it. Always have. It needs detangler.

Marcus took one look at that photo, shook his head, then handed it back to me, ordering, "Keep it blond, Syd. I'm not dating a ginger."

And that was that.

Well, not anymore.

I paused my online job searching, dashed to the nearest CVS, and scanned the boxes of L'Oréal hair dye, grabbing the one closest to my natural shade and also picking up a couple cute hair accessories while I was in there, purchasing them because along with disliking red hair, Marcus also turned his nose up at hair accessories, which kept me from wearing cute little clips with dainty fabric flowers and gorgeous turquoise head wraps.

Until now.

Now I was wondering if I'd gone a little too far.

But I was wondering this while smiling at myself in the mirror, thinking my reaction was a normal one for someone who had kept their true ginger self hidden for nine years.

I'd get used to it. It would just take a day or two.

And the color was truly beautiful. I couldn't deny that.

After cleaning up the mess in the bathroom and making sure I left it as immaculate as it was before I went all radical in there, I made myself some hot chocolate and returned to the bedroom I'd chosen out of the two available in Tori's house.

This one had a window facing the ocean. I'd never pass up a view like that.

I grabbed my laptop off the desk and carried it to the bed, careful of the steaming beverage in my hand as I maneuvered into a cross-legged position with my back against the pillows, placing the laptop in front of me and waking the screen. I blew the steam across the top of the mug and resumed scrolling for job opportunities in the area.

There wasn't a lot of scrolling. Pickings were slim.

I was sipping my hot chocolate and changing the header font on my résumé to something whimsical and completely unprofessional when I heard footsteps in the hallway, lifted my head, and saw Tori filling my doorway with her mouth agape.

"Oh, my God," she whispered.

I gripped my mug tighter and sat up straight.

"What?"

Her cherry-painted lips curled up, then she jumped into the room and clapped her hands repeatedly in front of her, shrieking, "*I love it! I love it! I love it!*"

"You love what?"

"Your hair, dummy," she clarified, stepping closer with her finger pointed at me. "I always loved you as a redhead. Rock on, sister! How long has it been? Freshman year?"

I smiled. It felt good having my best friend's much-appreciated approval, and it stripped away that tiny shred of doubt I was holding on to regarding my radical decision.

"Sophomore," I corrected her, sliding my laptop beside me and stretching my legs out. "I would've gone back sooner to the red, I think, if it weren't for Marcus's strong dislike for it. I was tired of the blond. Plus, it was really damaging to my hair, all that bleach. This," I said, tugging at a lock, "won't need to be maintained as much. And it's all silky now. Feel."

Tori took the three steps to reach me and moved her hand through the ends of my hair.

"Sweet," she murmured, plopping down beside my legs and smiling softly. "I'm going to be supportive and ask if you've found another job yet. Though, know this, I'm kinda hoping it takes you a few months and we get to kick ass at Whitecaps together for more than five seconds."

Tori was always flat-out honest with me, all the time. I appreciated it.

I laughed and slid my hand to the laptop, tapping it once.

"I only found one so far and it was posted eight months ago. Doesn't look good. You might get your wish."

"Shame," she said, a smile in her voice even though she kept her face indifferent. She bent her knee and rested her leg on the bed, asking, "You speak to him yet?"

Him being Marcus. There was no other him in my life, even though I had engaged in conversation yesterday with the man I'd accidentally ripped into two nights ago. It certainly didn't mean I had another "him" in my life. Though if I'm being honest, it was nice being texted back all the same.

But Tori didn't know anything about that, so she most certainly wasn't referring to Brian.

I shook my head, then dropped it back against the headboard.

"Still?" She appeared shocked.

"Not a word."

Her one hand curled into a fist.

"Bastard. What the hell? He doesn't care to know where you are?"

"Where would I be besides here?" I asked, shining a light on what was, in my mind, the obvious explanation for Marcus's silence.

Tori's mouth grew tight. She knew I couldn't go to my mom's place. She knew all about my mother and our nonexistent relationship.

Marcus knew, too. Still, he couldn't reach out and make sure I'd arrived safely?

"Right," she replied, studying her nails. "Well, you are always welcome here. You know that, hon."

It felt good hearing that, and Tori was right. I did know. But I didn't dwell on that good feeling because I was now grasping for an explanation as to why the man I'd married no longer gave a shit about me or my whereabouts.

It hurt. Marcus was the last person I wanted to talk to but, strangely enough, the one person I needed to hear from the most.

"Are you going to call *him*?"

At the sound of Tori's question, I refocused my attention on her, the hand in my hair starting to work that same lock again after going still during my pondering.

"I don't know," I answered honestly. "Do you think I should?"

She sat up a little taller. "Honestly? No, and I really don't care how immature this sounds, but I think he should be the one reaching out to *you*. He wanted out. He blindsided you and ended things, which was the entire reason you packed up and left. Not because you realized how much better off you are without him, or how living with me instead of Marcus would be *the shit*, because it clearly is. No, he should be calling you and begging for your forgiveness. And I. Mean. *Beg.*" She leaned closer, placing her hand on my knee and squeezing. "And when this happens, you shouldn't forgive him unless you *want* to forgive him."

I lowered my eyes until she gave my leg a squeeze again, prompting me to lift them and look into hers. She waited for this, then spoke with a softer tone.

"Promise me, Sydney, right now, that you will not go back to that man unless you want to stay married to him. Do what your heart tells you to do. It's the only voice that should matter."

I smiled a little, then felt the need to point out a fault in her theory.

"My heart told me to marry him six years ago. What if it was wrong then? What if I made a mistake?"

She pushed off from the bed, propped one hand on her hip, and said with some sass coating her tongue, "The heart is never wrong, honey. It's just stupidly hopeful like the rest of us. Can't blame her for the fault of man-kind. That's on them."

My mouth lifted in the corner.

I understood what Tori was saying. It was a nice thought, a simple one, too, putting all the blame on Marcus and taking this burden weighing heavily on my mind off me, allowing my heart to beat a little easier without all that guilt squeezing it tight.

Simple.

Right.

No matter how hard I tried to shift that blame, my head still throbbed and my heart still struggled to maintain a healthy, normal rhythm.

Tori interrupted the internal battle I was convinced I'd lose when she announced on her walk to the door, "I wish we both smoked. We could totally kick it on my roof and belt out some Alanis while working our way through a pack or two." She turned her head to add, "I got *Jagged Little Pill* on my playlist. Just sayin'."

I scrunched my nose. "Can we belt it out while *not* killing our lung tissue?"

"We probably won't look as cool doing it."

"No, but I won't have to use my inhaler. Nothing cool about whipping that thing out. Just sayin'."

I gave her a goofy grin, getting one in return.

She spun around, gripping the door frame. Her face went soft.

"You good, hon?"

I gave her the same soft look, then asked, "Are *you*?"

I didn't want her thinking I was forgetting about her pain and only focusing on my own.

She nodded. "Getting there," she said, slowly smiling to reveal brilliant white teeth. "Big day tomorrow. Your dream of becoming a waitress and living off tips is finally coming true."

I pulled my knees up and rested my chin there, laughing.

"I'm gonna go paint my nails," she announced, waved her fingers at me, then disappeared into the hallway before I had a chance to give her so much as a wave in return.

Typical.

I cut my eyes to the clock on the wall, noting how much time I had before I needed to start whipping up something for dinner, which I had decided early this morning I was handling as my first order of thank-you to Tori for letting me crash. Then I reached for my laptop to resume browsing for jobs when my phone beeped from across the room.

I knew, I *knew* it wasn't Marcus. He didn't text. He *never* texted.

But there I was, kicking out of bed and rushing over to the message I thought for sure was the first of many I was about to receive from my estranged husband, detailing all the hundreds of ways he was sorry for making the biggest mistake of his life and the regret for not following up sooner, shadowed immediately by the begging of forgiveness Tori insisted on.

I...was...*sure*.

But as I swiped my phone off the desk and studied the device in my hand, the grip around my heart grew tighter at the same time as something strange flipped and twisted in my belly.

It wasn't Marcus. That was the first thing I noticed and focused on, acknowledging the tightness in my chest a half second before feeling that strange flip and twist sensation, which distracted me momentarily from the tightness in my chest.

I stared at the name of the sender.

Was it weird he was messaging me again? Yes. Absolutely.

We didn't know each other. The only people I regularly texted were Tori or work associates when I needed a shift covered.

But even though I thought it was weird, I couldn't deny the way my body reacted to seeing Brian's name on my screen.

The flip and twist. No one can ignore the flip and twist. It only happens during certain occasions, and when it happens, you remember it.

I felt the flip and twist. I felt it more than I was feeling the tightness around my heart, and because of that, I swiped my thumb across the screen and opened up yet another text from a man I was never supposed to talk to in the first place, allowing myself to forget for a moment that Marcus didn't text me, and focusing on the one person who did.

I really wanted to smile again.

Wild. Help me out. Need a 4 letter word for something a runner might break.

While I was still reading the first message, he sent me another.

Starts with a T. Don't cheat. And it ain't toes.

I felt a wrinkle settle in my forehead as I read and reread his messages. They had to be the strangest set of messages I'd ever received from someone. And that nickname, Wild. That was strange, too.

It didn't fit me.

Yes, I had promised this man I'd make him eat his own penis

in front of his mother, screamed and acted like an out-of-my-mind crazy person, but that wasn't me.

Not the true me.

I was straight. Breezy. I was early Saturday nights and a Coldplay playlist. I was matching fingernails and toenails, a timid first kiss and lungs that couldn't tolerate cigarette smoke.

But this man called me Wild.

I liked it. I'd never had a nickname before.

I wanted to be Wild.

I *could* be Wild. Why not? What was stopping me?

While I was doing all this wondering, Brian grew impatient and sent me another message.

You busy?

I carried the phone to the bed while typing out my response and sat down on the edge.

No. Just thinking. You sure it isn't toes?

My mind automatically went to all 206 bones in the human body, specifically ones that began with the letter T.

None of them fit the four-letter requirement, except for toes. And runners could most certainly break toes.

It isn't.
Are you sure? That's the only thing that fits.
Positive.
How are you positive?
Doesn't fit with the next clue. Answer needs to end in an E.

I rolled my eyes and fell back on the bed, holding my phone above me.

Well THAT could've been helpful information. If you know two letters, why'd you only give me one?

Didn't want to make it too easy for you. Would've been impressed you got it with just the T.

I smiled. It felt good.
Really good.

Give me a sec. Putting my thinking cap on. Something a runner might break—starts with a T and ends in an E, right?
Yep.

I lowered my phone and blinked up at the ceiling.

My mind was stuck in the human anatomy, which wasn't surprising considering my profession and how many hours a week I typically spent viewing images of bones. But I knew if this was a crossword puzzle clue, and I was fairly certain it was, the answer wouldn't be obvious because they rarely ever were, and the clue would need to be looked at from a different angle, not taken literally like I was doing.

I looked at it from that different angle while filling Brian in.

Turning my thinking cap around. Things just got serious.
Whatever works. Mind if I ask you a question while you get serious?

I flipped onto my stomach, propped myself up on my elbows, and bent my knees, swinging my legs alternatively.

Shoot.
You married?

My legs stopped swinging.

Now, this was usually not a question I had difficulty answering. Up until two days ago I wouldn't have needed time to think before giving my automated response over the past six years, that being yes, but now I was having difficulty answering one of the simplest questions *to* answer, no matter who you were.

One was either married, or you weren't, right?

I didn't want to say I was married, because I didn't feel like I was anymore, but I didn't want to say I wasn't because that felt final. Conclusive.

So I gave the only answer I felt comfortable giving.

Separated. As of two days ago.
Shit.

I wasn't sure what he meant by that response, if he was disappointed or felt sorry for me, but I didn't have much time to think on it as his next message came rapidly through.

Sorry to hear that. How you doing with it? You hanging in?

Hanging in.
Was I? Is that what I was doing?

Well, I cussed out a stranger two days ago right after my husband told me he wanted out, and today I dyed my hair red.
Red?
It's my natural color. I was blond. I needed to do something radical.

Something Wild, I thought.

Red is definitely radical. Pictured you with dark hair.

He pictured me, what I looked like.
The flip and twist happened again.

It's a dark red.

I bit my lip and started swinging my legs again, thinking it was weird I felt inclined to inform Brian what he was picturing wasn't far off from what I actually looked like, then pushing that weirdness aside and focusing instead on the lingering sensation warming my belly.

It was a really nice feeling, and one I wanted to focus on.

Is it ok I'm talking to you like this?

I knew what he was asking. Our topics of discussion ranged from me wanting to chop off his penis to how either of us felt about dildos. Not exactly topics a woman recently separated, *very* recently separated, should be engaging in with a man who wasn't her estranged husband, especially if there was any hope for reconciliation and I honestly wasn't sure there was but I hadn't ruled that out, though estranged or not, I'm not sure I'd ever felt the desire to chop off Marcus's penis before and expressed that to him.

Actually, no, that was a lie. Two days ago I'm sure I could've expressed that to him.

Still, I didn't think this was wrong. It didn't feel wrong.

I was smiling. And that could never be a wrong thing. I was sure of it.

It's ok.
If I called, you'd answer?
Yes.
Good to know.
Can I ask why you want to talk to me?

This was something I had been curious about yesterday when Brian texted me after my interview with Nate.

I knew how I felt about it, but I had no idea why he wanted anything to do with me after everything I'd said to him. I *clearly* had baggage, plus my life was a bit of a mess. I didn't think I had anything to offer.

Brian made me smile when I really needed it. But what was I giving him?

Honest?
Absolutely.

My phone rang, startling me and sending my heart racing a mile a minute.

I pushed up onto my knees and answered it on a breathless, "Hello?"

"Started typing and realized I didn't feel like typing all that shit out, so I'm just gonna say it real quick then let you go, okay?"

His voice was low and husky, with a rough edge to it that made the hairs on my neck stand up.

Every. Single. One.

"Um...okay. Sure," I replied, reaching up and grabbing on to a lock of my hair and twisting it.

He then proceeded to give me all his shit, as he so put it.

"Not a lot in my life right now that's good. Hardly ever laugh like I did that night you told me to eat my own dick. Might've been the funniest shit I've ever heard. You were straight up defending your friend and I felt that shit. Felt what you told me yesterday, too. You seem cool and sweet. Definitely don't have sweet in my life and not sure I deserve it, but I'm not gonna think about that 'cause this feels better. Not thinking. If you end up at any point not wanting to continue speaking to me, I'm cool with that. If you end up being unseparated and *can't* continue speaking to me, I'm cool with that, too. You say the words and I'll disappear, but if you don't mind giving me more of what you've already shared, I'll take it, Syd. I like talking to you. I liked it enough to reach out yesterday and enough to do it again today."

"You texted me about a crossword puzzle," I pointed out, suddenly wondering if maybe he tricked me into more conversation, because I didn't know men who did crossword puzzles and who weren't also eating off the senior citizen's menu.

"You didn't need to do that," I elaborated. "You could've just sent me a 'Hey, what's up?'—you know? I would've answered."

"I could've if I wasn't currently stuck on a clue I thought maybe you could help me out with."

"You're *really* doing a crossword puzzle."

I still didn't believe him.

He sounded hot. Hot men didn't do crosswords. I was sure of it.

"Why would I lie?" he questioned back, then quickly followed that up as if he could read my mind with, "Didn't need an 'in' to talk to you, Wild. I'd already decided I was gonna hit you up later tonight once I had a free minute, got to working on this puzzle and got stuck, thought you might be able to help me out so I hit you up earlier than I was planning, but it was planned, okay?"

Wild.

I sighed. My lip twitched.

"Okay," I whispered.

"I enjoy crossword puzzles."

This got him another lip twitch even though he couldn't see it, but I was certain he heard it in my voice when I responded.

"Cool."

"Cool," he echoed, cleared his throat, then asked, "Your thinking cap do anything yet? I gotta get going."

"No, sorry. I'll keep it on, though. It looks stylish with my red hair."

I was greeted with silence.

Had my joke not landed?

"Brian?" I called into the phone.

"Red," he mumbled, and even though his voice had grown softer, I could still hear the distinct smile in it.

So I made him smile, too.

That felt *really* good.

"Red," I verified on a drop of my head. "Dark red."

I heard his heavy exhale, then the drag of a chair across a floor.

"Gotta go."

"Okay, Brian."

"Later, Wild," he mumbled.

"Later," I replied back, then quickly disconnected the call and fell onto my hip, staring down at the phone in my hand while thinking a number of things, one of those things being Brian saying I was cool and sweet, and how good it felt hearing a compliment like that at a time like this.

Another thing being the fact that he didn't have a lot of good in his life right now, and wondering what all that meant.

Maybe he had fallen on hard times. People do that. I was one of those people currently falling and falling fast.

Another thing I was thinking about being that crossword puzzle clue.

It was bugging me. I didn't like being bested.

I took another peek at the clock, slid off the bed, grabbed my phone and the mug of hot chocolate, which was now warm chocolate but still just as tasty, and carried those both downstairs with me to begin preparing one of the only four things I knew how to cook.

Tacos.

Before my run to CVS earlier, I had gone out and gotten the ingredients I needed to make my ultimate shrimp tacos, plus a few other items I wanted to keep on hand in Tori's kitchen, such as the hot cocoa mix and my favorite wasabi-flavored almonds.

They had just the right amount of kick.

And while I was getting my ingredients ready to go about preparing my ultimate shrimp tacos, my mind on that tricky crossword puzzle clue since it didn't need to be on the recipe I had memorized, it hit me.

I gasped, dropped the head of cabbage onto the cutting board, spun around while wiping my hands off on my jeans, and picked up my phone.

TAPE!

What do runners sometimes break? Tape. Starts with a T. Ends with an E.

He replied instantly.

Cool, sweet, and smart. Thanks, Wild.

I smiled. Again.

And I kept smiling while I made dinner.

Chapter Five

BRIAN

I tucked the cash into an envelope and stepped out of my Jeep, pushing the door closed with my elbow, then making the familiar walk across the dirt parking lot to the small office beside the barn.

Carolina East Therapeutic Riding was a ranch in the middle of nowhere, about forty-five minutes from Dogwood Beach, and its sole mission was to help individuals with a range of disabilities heal through a connection to horses.

I didn't get it. But apparently, the way the staff worked with people here and got them up and riding, interacting with these massive animals, it did something.

People healed, in a way. Muscles strengthened. Certain weaknesses decreased. Quality of life was improved.

Expensive shit, like everything else for people living hard lives, 'cause heaven forbid those who deserve it should catch a fucking break.

Why the government didn't fund programs like this pissed me off, and the insurance companies were no better.

They didn't cover dick.

I knew there were grants available for families concerning services like this. I'd looked into it three months ago, but allotting for the time it took to process an application and the further time it took for families to receive said grant money, which according to the person

I spoke to from one of the organizations could take sometimes up to six months, I didn't bother taking that avenue.

Plus, most parties took applications once a year, and there was always a deadline.

First of the year. I'd missed it by two months.

Didn't matter either way. I'd make sure he received the therapy no matter what I had to do.

A horse neighed from inside the barn as I walked up the ramp leading to the office doorway, kicked the dirt off my shoes on the wooden post connected to the railing, and opened the door, stepping inside the tiny office space.

Mona lifted her head at the sound of my entrance.

She was the owner of the ranch, and the only person I dealt with when I came here. Everyone else tended to the horses or the clients, worked in the riding arena or around the ranch, or did other things that didn't involve being inside the office.

I only ever spoke to her about two things every few weeks, money and progress, but I spoke to her enough to know she had a heart the size of North Carolina.

She dedicated her life to helping improve the lives of others.

Mona was good people. Straight up.

"Brian." She greeted me with a smile, pushed the glasses higher up on her nose, and set down the paper she'd been reading when I stepped inside, giving me her full attention.

"It's good to see you," she added, sounding hopeful.

She wanted me to hang around and talk. I knew this. Mona always tried putting her own version of therapy on me every time I stepped in here, the "talk about your feelings" kind of therapy I wasn't interested in, because she knew the story and, thus, felt sorry for me.

I hated the pity.

And like I said, I was only there to talk about two things.

But Mona was cool so I didn't fault her for wanting more out of me; I just never hung around long enough to give it to her.

And I wasn't about to start now.

I walked to her desk, carrying the envelope with my head down, eyes not focused on anything in particular and doing this to avoid the compassionate look I knew was in hers.

It was always there.

"Got next round's payment. It's a little more than you ask for, so throw in an extra lesson or something. Whatever he wants. Maybe let him go longer on a few days if his parents are cool with that. Your call." I dropped the envelope on the desk and lifted my head to add, "Just make sure it stays with him."

She placed her hand on top of the envelope. "Of course. It'll be put into Owen's account straightaway."

"Good," I said, nodding, then tucked my hands into my pockets and watched her slide the envelope into a drawer.

"He doing okay? Is he...improving?"

Mona folded her hands in front of her. Her eyes grew soft and she sighed.

I braced myself.

"He's enjoying it, which is the most important thing, so he doesn't realize it's work for him when it is. Some activities he enjoys more than others. There are things the therapist asks him to do that he struggles with, but he pushes through 'cause he wants to get to something he likes. That's typical. Not everything is going to come easy to him. You have to remember—in the end, this is still therapy. We want everyone to have a great time on the ranch, but if it was easy, they probably wouldn't need it. You know?"

Again, I nodded.

"But this isn't a cure. I wish it was, Brian. I wish this place had the power to change everyone's prognosis, but for kids like Owen who sustain that type of injury, we're riding on a lot of hope here."

My lips pulled tight.

I knew this. She didn't need to tell me. I knew after speaking to people in the medical field what the outcome was likely to be for this kid, but I'd also read up on this type of therapy.

People recovered. Miracles fucking happened. *Every day* they happened. After months of being on a horse, some were able to do things now that they never thought they'd be able to do, like stand unassisted or take a step, which was why I knew this was going to work.

It had to.

He deserved the life he was supposed to have, and this place was going to give it to him.

"If you want, you could stick around tonight and watch him in action, maybe talk to Mr. and Mrs. Burns and—"

I turned and headed for the door, cutting her off. Her suggestion was asinine.

What the fuck would they do if they saw me?

"I'll see ya, Mona," I said, my hand poised for the knob.

"Brian."

I stopped and lowered my arm. I didn't look behind me.

I heard the heavy roll of wheels on carpet. I knew Mona had pushed out her chair and stood up, but again, I didn't look back to confirm it.

Head lowered, I kept my eyes on the door and pulled in a breath, releasing it slowly.

"They want to know where the money is coming from," she informed me, her voice gentle but growing louder in a way I knew she was moving closer. "They appreciate it so much, you know that, but they keep asking me, Brian. A one-time anonymous donation is one thing, that's believable, but to have their bill paid in full every time with sometimes *extra* funds added to their account, it raises suspicions."

I finally turned my head.

Her eyes moved to the side, avoiding mine, then came back when she added, "I know you said you didn't want them to know, but I think they just want to show their appreciation somehow. I'm sure they wouldn't be angry."

"They can never find out, Mona," I said, my voice hard and final, my eyes burning into hers as I turned more to fully face her. "Never. They ask, you tell them you keep getting donations from local charities, church groups, or whatever the fuck you wanna come up with, I don't care, but you are to *never* tell them I'm the one paying for this. That was the deal."

"But—"

"*They can't know,*" I growled.

Her hand came up between us, palm out facing me. "Okay. Okay. I understand, Brian. I won't say anything."

I inhaled through my nose, exhaling with my eyes pinched shut.

"They won't know unless you want them to know," she added quietly, and I felt her touch on my bicep.

It reminded me of something my mother would do. Or my sister, Jenna.

Both of them were good women, too. Compassionate. Caring. Always wanting to take care of people.

Mona was just being Mona. She was looking to take care of me. She thought I deserved the recognition.

I opened my eyes.

"Appreciate you doing this for me," I said, watching as she pulled her hand back and adjusted her glasses again. "Sorry for using that language in front of you. That was disrespectful."

She stared at me. Her hands moved in front of her to clasp together.

"No sorry necessary," she replied, tipping her chin to the door, a light smile playing on her lips. "You better get going if you don't want to be seen."

"Right." I nodded once. "I'll see ya in a few weeks."

"Okay, Brian. Take care."

I stepped outside, jerked the door shut behind me, then moved swiftly down the ramp, stalking across the dirt parking lot until I reached my Jeep, pulled the door open, and climbed in, starting it up.

I would've taken off right then if it wasn't for the handicapped van pulling off the road and turning into the lot, moving slowly down the small decline and parking in the space directly across from me.

Shit.

Fucking *shit*.

I recognized that van. I had seen it in the driveway of the house I paid a visit to once a week, but this was the first time I was seeing it here.

My hands curled around the wheel. That weight I'd been feeling for the past three months pressed its full capacity against my sternum and pinned me to the seat.

I stared. I couldn't move.

I prayed to God, if he was up there, that I wouldn't be seen.

The driver's side door opened, followed by the passenger door. Mr. and Mrs. Burns stepped out, both of them congregating over on one side of the van, smiling at each other and looking eager while sliding the back door open, Mr. Burns leaning in and pressing some mechanism on the inside to activate the lift for the wheelchair.

He secured the chair while Mrs. Burns held her son's hand, grinning big as he was lowered to the ground, tapping the top of his hand with excitement.

She looked happy. They all did.

This place was going to work.

Fucking miracles every day.

It would work.

Owen maneuvered the chair himself. It was one of those powered ones, and I knew he still had some use of his hands, which enabled him to move the joystick around for direction, easing himself off the lift and onto the dirt, where he waited by the back tire.

Some use of his hands. He didn't have full use anymore, and from the watching I sometimes did, I knew he'd grow tired on occasion and his parents would take over.

He didn't seem tired right now. He was grinning and moving with ease.

I wanted to like seeing that. Smile at it, but I couldn't.

I didn't deserve to feel *good* about any of this.

I watched them cross the lot and move into the barn, disappearing into the shadows.

They never saw me.

It was time for his lesson to begin.

And it was time for me to get the fuck out of there.

* * *

I parked at the curb and grabbed a pen out of my glove box, doing what I did every time I came by here and scrawling the name on the envelope containing the remainder of what I'd earned over the past week.

It was close to a grand. I knew that would cover a handful of bills, but it wasn't enough.

It was never enough.

In-home therapy, medications, repeated doctor's visits and specialists, hospital bills, and the monthly van payments, everything added up and hardly any of it was covered by insurance.

I knew this because one of the girls I shot with on occasion had a sister working for the insurance carrier. She got me the answers I needed.

It was appreciated and she knew it. Didn't even want anything in return.

More pity.

I hated that.

I gave what I needed to give to the riding center and the rest came here, direct payment for anything outstanding, and there was a lot outstanding.

I knew *this* because of the bills in the mailbox stamped in red.

The bills I'd opened and resealed.

Overdue.

Bastards at the HMO covered jack shit, wouldn't even help with the cost of a ramp so the kid could get inside his own fucking house, and still wouldn't eat a few thousand to help a family out.

It was fucked up.

I spent an entire Sunday morning when I knew the Burnses were at church building the one they have now. It wasn't much, but it was better than watching someone struggle to enter their own home.

Pride went a long way. Taking someone's independence from them chipped away at that pride, and it was a hard fucking thing to build back up.

Owen didn't need to be carried anymore getting in and out of his own house.

That was huge, and I knew it when I saw the look on his face when they got home that afternoon.

Shock, followed by tears and embraces among the three of them.

I knew that should feel good, giving him that, giving *them* that, but I couldn't smile.

He never would've needed that ramp if it wasn't for me, so why should I feel *good* about any of it?

Guilt—it's the best thing to have. It never lets you forget when you don't deserve to.

I left my Jeep running after stowing the pen away, stepped out, and placed the envelope in the mailbox with the name side up.

Owen

Then I got back into my Jeep and took off, wondering how almost a thousand dollars in my hand could feel like nothing when placed in that mailbox, how it was never enough no matter how thick that envelope was.

No matter how much extra I gave Mona, or how many fucking ramps I built.

Almost a thousand dollars and it felt like absolutely nothing.

* * *

"Jesus Christ. I feel like I'm watching minor ball. This is ridiculous."

Jamie dropped the remote onto the couch and stood up, tossing the rest of his beer back and grabbing his empty plate.

After I got back from doing the drop, we threw some steaks on the grill and ate dinner watching the Yankees slaughter the Angels 14–1.

He was right; it was ridiculous. I'm not even sure the Angels showed up tonight.

Jamie cut his eyes to me, holding up his bottle.

"Want another?"

I shook my head, picked up the remote and cut the TV off, then grabbed my plate and followed him into the kitchen, which was right off the main living room and bigger than necessary for two men who threw everything on the grill to cook.

Everything. Even when it was raining, we rolled the grill under the deck and cooked shit out there.

I couldn't remember the last time either one of us turned the oven on. And we had two of them.

Wanting to live on the water and close to Wax, Jamie and I went in together and tossed money on the beach house two years ago, not giving a shit how big the kitchen was or how many rooms the house had but only caring that it had the sickest view. You could step off the deck and hit sand.

Life was good for Jamie. Mine had been, too, up until three months ago.

"Got Rip Pro next weekend. Winner takes home fifteen grand."

I set my plate in the sink and turned to Jamie after he spoke, watching him pull another beer out of the fridge.

"Yeah," I stated more than asked, because I already knew Rip Pro was happening next weekend. We'd talked about it when Jamie entered it last month.

Also already knew what the grand prize was.

He twisted off the cap and took a swig, then tipped the bottle at me.

"It's yours, if you want it."

"What?" I asked.

"The winnings."

I crossed my arms over my chest.

"Don't want it."

His brows rose, and he stared at me for a couple seconds before repeating back to me, "You don't want it," as if my reaction was a shock to him and we didn't have a conversation pretty damn close to the way this one was going every other *minute*.

It pissed me off.

He knew I didn't take his money, or anyone else's money. Cole being the other asshole good friend of mine who tried slipping me cash.

"Come on, Dash. Seriously, what the fuck is the difference whose money it is?"

I stepped closer.

"You know what the difference is," I bit out.

He sat his beer on the counter, then turned to face me again.

"Yeah. Some shit about how this is all on you, and it'll always be all on you and nobody else." He shook his head. "That's bullshit,

man. How long have we known each other? I'll tell you how long—
KinderCare. Fuckin' diapers and shit. We've been best friends since
we were two. We're there for each other. Always have been. You got
my back, have definitely needed you to have it on more than one
occasion, never had to ask, you got it, and I got yours. Now I'm offering to help and you don't take it? Why not?"

The muscles in my shoulders tensed.

"Were you there that night?" I asked, cutting to the fucking point
so I could end this conversation and do what I'd been planning on
doing since I drove away from that house earlier tonight, get Sydney
on the phone again.

I wanted to hear her voice. More of it. I couldn't get this woman
out of my head.

And now I knew she'd answer.

Jamie sighed and pushed a hand through his hair. His eyes fell.

I kept on chasing that point, leaning in to say, "What happened
that night falls on *my* shoulders. Not yours. *Mine*, and how I go about
attempting to make that shit right, 'cause it'll never be right, nothing
I do could *ever* make up for what I took away, all of that burden falls
right here." I jabbed a finger at my chest. "This is my fuckup. I eat
this. Not you. That being said, you know you're my brother and I
love you, and I know you're just trying to help me. I get that, but
you can't. Every dime is coming from me."

"So, what, you're gonna fuck for money the rest of your life?
Pimp yourself out until you're dead? You planning on getting married ever, 'cause I have a feeling your future wife might have a huge
fuckin' problem with this plan."

"Guess I'm not getting married then," I told him through a
shrug. That was the last fucking thing I cared about.

Jamie's eyes lowered and lost focus. He nodded as if considering
this option for himself.

"Right. Maybe I'll check out a bike," he murmured, rubbing his
chin. "Be pretty badass, you know? Getting a Harley?" He looked
up at me and let his hand drop.

I felt my lip curl.

"Go for it. Your winnings can pay for that *and* your hospital bill when you break your neck," I told him, reaching out to slap his shoulder, then turning and starting for the stairs.

"Hey, I've ridden before," Jamie called out behind me.

"You've ridden a scooter."

"Same thing."

"No, it's not."

"I'm pretty sure it's the same concept."

"It isn't."

I hit the stairs and started ascending.

"It's close," he mumbled in the distance, causing me to shake my head as I pictured Jamie getting on a bike, starting it up, after someone showed him how to 'cause he had no idea what the fuck he was doing and having experience riding a scooter gave him jack shit experience on a bike, making it two feet, then falling over or running into something.

I smiled, picturing that as I kept climbing.

"You going to bed?" he called out.

I wasn't. I wasn't even tired, but Jamie didn't need to know what my real plans were right now. I had no intention of telling him or anyone else about Sydney. Ever.

This was mine.

When I talked to her, what I talked to her about, who she was to me, it was mine.

So I lied, reaching the top of the stairs and yelling out a "yeah," while tugging my phone out of my pocket.

I stepped inside my room, flicked the light on, closed the door behind me, toeing off my shoes while pulling up my recent contacts, then sitting on the edge of my bed and hitting Dial.

The call connected after three rings. I heard a soft rustling sound, then gentle, quiet breathing.

Nothing else.

"Hello?" I asked, glancing at the clock on the wall and wondering if I was calling too late for her.

It was already after eleven.

Fuck.

"Hey," her soft voice filtered into the phone immediately after hearing mine, the tone vibrating through my ear and into some deep part of me, where it settled and warmed.

It sounded heavy with sleep.

"Shit, sorry. Did I wake you?"

"Yeah, a little." Her response broke with a yawn. She sighed, then reassured me, "It's okay. I didn't mean to fall asleep but I did. Um, hold on, let me just…" I heard more movement, rustling, then a light tapping sound, before she came back with a breathless, "Okay. Back. I was still wearing my glasses."

"You wear glasses?" I asked, settling back on a pillow, my legs swinging up on the bed and feet crossing at the ankles.

I bent my free arm and tucked it behind me, resting my head in my palm as I drew more of her in my mind.

"Only when I read," she admitted. "Or sometimes at the movies my eyes will bother me. I always carry a pair with me for that reason. You never know when you'll get a hankering for greasy movie popcorn."

"You get hankerings like that often?"

"Oh, all the time," she told me, a smile in her voice. "I've even gone to the theater once in a while without seeing a movie. Just bought the biggest popcorn they had and took it home, cued up something on Netflix, and camped out in front of my TV with a bucket the size of my head."

"You live a dangerous life," I joked.

She was silent for a breath, then she mumbled, "Oh, my God."

"What?"

"You call me Wild!" she shrieked in a quiet way that still contained every beat of her excitement. "And I've been thinking how that name doesn't fit me, like, at all, but it does! Ha! I *am* wild! I've cut the tags off my mattresses, cussed in church one time when I banged my knee on a pew and the pain was so intense, I thought I was going to throw up all over my pretty Easter dress. I didn't. Just said, 'Shit,' really loud and got looks from *everybody*. My mom pitched a massive fit after the service, but she always pitches fits so that's nothing new and not pertinent right now. I'm getting off track."

I laughed, but kept it silent so I could listen to her continue.

I wanted to hear every word she wanted to give me.

"I wear white after Labor Day. Mostly sweaters that look really cute with boots. I rarely ever use crosswalks because I'm too lazy to walk to one, and I grab some of the loose grapes when I'm at the market and eat them while I shop."

"Damn," I mumbled, grinning.

"Told you," she giggled. "*Wild.*"

She gave me a lot to focus on, but I settled for her last admission.

"You know those aren't free, right?" I asked. "The grapes."

"Um, well, actually, I'm pretty sure it's a deal we have with the supermarkets that as long as we purchase something, we're allowed to graze."

"Pretty sure that's a deal only *you* have with them, and it's all in your head, babe."

"Babe?"

"Mm." I nodded. "Babe."

"Why are you calling me babe?"

I inhaled through my nose quickly, priming to respond when she filled in our silence.

"I like it," she added softly, nearly a whisper, as if she was afraid to admit her honesty out loud. "I like Wild, too. I understand Wild, but babe? That's a sweet name, and ... really, I was *terrible* to you."

"Got another suggestion?"

"Besides Wild? Satan."

This time I didn't keep my laughter quiet.

"You aren't Satan, babe. You got sweet in you. A lot of it. Heard it in your voice even when you were laying into me, showing me your wild."

"What?" she snapped. "I was *not* sweet when I was laying into you. I was feisty and a total badass. My best friend told me so."

"You were a badass," I agreed, doing it smiling. "But you were sweet, too."

"You can't be a badass and sweet at the same time, Brian. That's like being ... I don't know, a Steelers fan *and* a Ravens fan. It doesn't happen."

"You watch football?"

Her knowledge of two teams who fiercely rivaled each other intrigued me. I didn't know a lot of women who followed sports. None of the ones in my family did.

"No, not really. My brother was a Steelers fan. My only knowledge of the sport came from him."

"Was? He wise up and start backing the Panthers? The Steelers fucking suck."

"No. He died."

Regret came like a swift kick in the chest.

"Shit," I muttered, sitting up. "I'm . . . *fuck*, I'm sorry, Syd. Jesus. Were you two close?"

I closed my eyes, realizing then how dumb that sounded.

It was her brother. Even if they weren't close, it was still her fucking brother.

Asshole.

I gripped the back of my neck, squeezing hard.

"We were, for the most part," she answered, nothing in her voice but sweet tones and light.

She wasn't upset about my offhand comment.

"He was seven years older than me so we didn't do everything together. But he was awesome. Funny and loud and just, like, a cool big brother, you know? He had all these tattoos and drove a black 1970 Charger."

"Nice," I muttered appreciatively, then slid down farther on the bed and relaxed with my head on a pillow.

"So cool," she added. "Barrett was the definition of badass. *He* was wild. Must be where I get my edge from."

"How'd he die?"

"Alcohol poisoning. Happened his second semester away at college. My mom and I flew out to California when we got word, but it was too late. He was in a coma and died pretty soon after we got there."

"Fuck."

"Yeah."

"How old were you?"

"Twelve."

"He your only sibling?"

She yawned and sighed.

I didn't want her drowsy. Not right now. I was wired and burning, restless for more words and sweet, light tones.

I wanted her to be that way, too, and to want to give me that.

Mine. This was mine. Her voice in my ear in the dark.

"Yep," she replied, sounding anxious to answer and silencing my discomfort. "Just me and him."

"Must've been hard on your parents," I commented.

"Just my mom. Dad isn't in the picture. He never was. But my mom? Yeah." She inhaled, then breathed out slowly. "She went a little crazy, which I guess is understandable. Barrett was brilliant. A good kid. Then one night he partied too hard, and that one mistake took him. It wasn't fair. You're eating popsicles on your porch with your daughter one minute and the next you're getting a call saying your boy is dying. It was too sudden for her sanity, I think. Or maybe, even if it was slow, it wouldn't have mattered. I don't know."

"She doing okay now?" I asked.

"Depends on your definition of 'okay.' She found a way to heal, a few months after it happened, and it started out great. The intentions were good. She joined this prayer group and it was really helping. I didn't see her cry as much. She smiled when I smiled. Then weekly meetings turned into daily meetings, she was always at the church and never home with me, and when I did see her, the only thing she'd talk to me about was my relationship with God and how I needed to get on the right path. She was better, happy, but different. Not the mom who ate popsicles with me. That woman was gone and far too busy with her new spiritual family to eat popsicles."

I felt something twist and wrench in my gut.

"Babe," I whispered.

"And *that* is all the sad talk you're going to get out of me tonight."

Her voice floated with a hint of laughter.

She was trying to move forward and tread with amusement, possibly into dildo territory, where our conversations stayed the farthest from serious, but all I could picture was a sad little girl and her melted popsicle.

It fucked with my head.

"You have anybody after that happened? Any other family?" I asked, fidgeting in bed, adjusting and readjusting the height of my pillow until my upper body was bent and the weight of my edginess shifted out of my chest.

"I had Tori. She's my best friend. And her family. I've always had them."

"That's good."

"Then I had Marcus."

My brows rose.

"Husband?"

"Yep."

"You wanna talk about him?"

"Nope."

I laughed. So did she.

"He hasn't called," she revealed a heartbeat later, her tone broken. "I left two days ago, packed up and walked out, and he hasn't called. Seven years together and he doesn't even bother to make sure I'm okay."

I didn't know how to respond to that.

I couldn't be reassuring. I didn't know dick about this guy or their marriage. I didn't know if silence was usual for him. I only knew what she told me, that he wanted out. He ended it. Let her walk away.

He was the dumbest motherfucker on the planet.

"Even if he *knew* I was living with Tori now, he could've called," she whispered, then with words too quiet I almost missed them, she added, "You called. Don't even know me, I cuss you out, and you ask if I'm okay."

I closed my eyes.

"You're trouble," she whispered.

I smiled in the dark.

She yawned again, sighed like she seemed to always do after revealing her exhaustion, and asked me with the smallest voice to tell her something about myself, something I've never told anyone.

Something she could keep.

"Please," she begged. "Then I need to go to bed. I start my new job tomorrow and I don't want to look like a redheaded zombie."

I was reluctant to oblige her request, to share a secret and to let her go.

I wasn't done. I wanted more.

But I also wanted to give her something. Something she *could* keep, 'cause I felt like I was taking and taking from this girl and she didn't even know it.

I rolled onto my side and stared at the wall, the phone trapped between my ear and the pillow and a smirk on my face.

I pictured her, red hair and glasses.

"I fucking love popsicles," I confessed.

It wasn't much, but I knew she wouldn't think that.

She was silent and smiling, I was sure.

And I was right.

I heard it in her voice.

"Good night, Trouble."

Chapter Six

SYDNEY

Day three, post-Marcus.

I was excited and nervous and strangely *okay*.

As long as I didn't think about the conversations I *wasn't* having.

And I didn't have a lot of time to think about those conversations. My day was jam-packed with information I needed to process, new faces and names, daily specials, menu items that were still listed but weren't technically offered anymore, since we were waiting on new updated menus to arrive, and table numbers, which for some reason seemed to be really tripping me up, due to the randomness and inconsistency of their layout.

Table 23 was next to Table 4. Booth 7 butted up against Booth 13.

I questioned this madness, earning myself a giggle and nothing more from Tori and the other two waitresses I had met when I first arrived.

Shay, short for Shayla, a cute little brunette with a brilliant smile and killer taste in hair accessories—she wore pins with jeweled crossbones on them. They were right up my alley. And Kali, a single mom whose baby daddy ditched her to pursue an affair with his boss's wife, one that was still going on and apparently not a secret in Dogwood Beach, the baby daddy being in politics and his boss running for governor, making the scandal newsworthy in a *big* way.

She was bitter when she spoke of her ex, but her face lit up when she mentioned her son, Cameron.

He sounded adorable.

I also met Sean, or Stitch, as everyone called him. He was the cook at Whitecaps and attractive in an entirely new way to me.

I had never before found rough men good-looking. Men with long hair, thick shapeless beards, and tattoos decorating practically every visible inch of skin. Men who had a pack of smokes poking out of their front pockets and who wore chains on their jeans and jewelry around their necks. I'd never looked at them twice. They were hard and intimidating.

But Sean was hot in a big way. A *new* way. And the fact that he had let the girls nickname him Stitch for accidentally cutting himself so many times and didn't seem to mind them poking a little fun, that, for some reason, made him hotter.

I was getting the hang of things, learning the absurd seating layout and making new friends, and I was doing all of this with my mind the farthest from Marcus it had ever been.

It was a great first day.

No worries. No drama. No monumental mess-ups. Nothing particularly interesting going on.

Until I heard Shay make a noise at my back that sounded an awful lot like a mix between a gasp and a squeal.

It was worthy of a head turn.

"What's up?" I asked her, watching her big brown eyes move with something behind me, her lips pulled between her teeth and her cheeks flushing red.

I was facing the kitchen now, and the back of the restaurant.

She was tuned to something at the front by the doors and looked like she wanted to climb on the bar and do backflips off of it.

Tori walked up beside me and noticed Shay's big eyes, held smile, and flushing cheeks immediately.

"You look like Tom Hardy just stepped in here, Shay. What gives?"

She turned her head at the same time as me, then muttered a soft yet unquestionably irritated, "*Shit*," under her breath.

I wasn't sure what she was seeing. I *knew* what I was seeing.

Two men sauntering through the restaurant toward a booth by the window, the one closer with short tan-colored hair and blue eyes that smiled, a shaved jaw, and sharp, muscled shoulders. He wore a white tee under an opened button-up with khaki shorts and boat shoes, and the skin on his face and neck and arms was kissed a deep golden brown.

He was all boy-next-door charm and good clean fun. Very easy on the eyes. While the man behind him screamed secret sex in your parents' bed and stolen touches under the dinner table.

Standing a head taller with limbs that stretched for days, lean but solid, this stunner had wave-tussled sandy blond hair that tickled his neck and curled at his ears, and a day-old beard you knew was rough on soft skin. He wore a loose Hurley tee that looked wrinkled from being kept in a backseat, tattered board shorts and sandals, didn't look like he cared in the least what you thought about it, and had a cigarette tucked behind his ear.

His eyes were a penetrating shade of blue, deeper in tone than his friend's and definitely *not* smiling.

And that penetrating shade turned even more intensely sexual when he slid them to my knockout of a best friend and moved his gaze from tits to toes.

"Whoa," I mumbled, shifting my weight and giving life to my legs again.

My limbs tingled.

I knew fifteen minutes into my shift this morning exactly why Tori worked here, the screaming hot locals, and why she had that mischievous shift in her eyes when she suggested *I* would love it here, again, the screaming hot locals, but now I was seeing the full effect of committing to waiting tables the rest of your life when you didn't even need a job in the first place.

Exhibit A, and his cousin with a dirty little secret, Exhibit B. B for bad-boy.

"This is so *awesome*," Shay whispered excitedly, rounding the bar and stepping beside us. "I love it when he stops in here. And he's in your section, T. As usual."

I took notice of the booth they had chosen, which was most definitely in Tori's section, and which also happened to be in *my* section since I was training and paired up with Tori, and as I was taking notice of my section and the surrounding sections, my eyes took notice of something else.

These two sun-kissed surfer boys had drawn the attention of *everyone* in the restaurant.

At least everyone with a vagina anyway.

Tori sighed, grabbed my hand, and tugged me behind her, whispering obscenities under her breath and the slapping of our sneakers against the tile.

Exhibit A had his head down and was skimming the menu.

Exhibit B was relaxed, leaned back with an arm slung along the back of the booth, his cutting, captivating blues glued to my best friend's every movement.

"What up, Legs?" he greeted her as we stopped at the hot boys' booth.

I glanced at Tori, or *Legs*, as Exhibit B had so eagerly addressed her, then back at him, swaying a little at the sight of dimples and perfect teeth.

Oh, my.

Tori, ignoring the nickname and the man who delivered it, released my hand and reached into the pocket of her apron, flipped to a new ticket, and clicked her pen open.

"Welcome to Whitecaps. My name is Tori." She paused, cutting a face-melting glare at B. "*Not* Legs, jackass."

He raised his brows, smiling with the devil's mouth while she continued.

"And I'll *unfortunately* be your waitress today along with my best girl Sydney, who is training, so try to keep the assholery to a minimum if that's even possible for you, which I realize might be a long shot and not something in your control but it never hurts to ask. We don't want to scare her off."

She bumped my hip and smirked at me.

I waved at B, and at A when he looked up, getting a smile and a wink from the former.

"Our special today is fish and chips with coleslaw, and our soup of the day is cream of crab." She looked up, pen poised to paper and profile death-stare crazy. "Now, can I get you both something to drink and possibly your tab?"

I nudged Tori's elbow.

Was she crazy? Why would she want to send them away so soon? They were so pretty.

B laughed through closed lips and tilted his head. Gritty hair fell into his eyes.

"You're extra sweet for me today. Somethin' happen between now and the last time I came in here to love on you?"

My jaw hit the floor.

Love on her?

LOVE?

What the hell was going on?

I watched, wide-eyed and clueless, as my best friend scoffed and tapped her pen.

"It's amazing, really. Even without your irritating presence for the past two weeks, I've managed to grow in my soul-consuming disgust for you."

"I see you're counting our days apart," B replied, reaching for her. "Let me take you out this weekend."

Tori stepped back.

"I'll be busy," she replied, sounding bored.

"Doing what?"

"Washing my hair."

B grinned. "You can do that at my place."

"I'd rather staple my face to the wall," she bit out with lips curling against teeth. She stuck her free hand on her hip. "Do you want a drink or not? I have other tables."

We didn't. Not at the moment anyway.

A glanced up, lifting his hand.

"I'll have a Sprite, thanks. And we have one more coming."

"Coke with grenadine for me, Legs. You know what I like." B looked at me, then tipped his head at Tori, keeping my gaze. "She talk about me?"

"Uh…"

"Get a clue, Jamie," Tori snapped, wrapping her hand around my elbow and tugging me in the direction we came, my feet shuffling backward quickly to keep up with her mile-long stems.

"What in the world was that all about?" I whispered when we reached the bar.

Shay spotted our return and slid off the back counter, where she'd been perched, legs swinging, speaking through the open rectangular window that separated us from Stitch, who didn't seem to be conversing back with her, only listening with his head down and eyes focused, and came to stand beside me, leaning her elbows on the bar.

Tori stepped behind and grabbed two glasses, lifting her shoulders and trying to appear nonchalant as she filled each with ice.

"What?" she asked.

I leaned in, my hands flat on the cool wood.

"*What?* Why was that stunner calling you Legs, and why is he coming in to 'love on you'? Did you hook up with him or something?"

Tori was the Rachel to my Monica. I didn't think she kept secrets from me, not any, and especially not ones involving a hot cigarette-smoking surfer who looked like a former J.Crew model, fired for his bad-boy image and lewd habits.

Shay giggled beside me.

"I love that he calls you Legs. Nicknames are so sweet and sexy."

I sucked in a breath, feeling warm and full and fuzzy all over.

Wild.

Babe.

Tori sat the cup with Sprite down on the bar and grabbed the bottle of grenadine. Her eyes rolled.

"*Tori,*" I urged, needing answers and gossip more than my next breath.

"Okay, seriously, first of all," she started, sounding impatient while pouring the red sticky syrup into the glass of Coke, "I did *not* hook up with that idiot. If I did, I would've told you, because I tell you everything. You're my best girl."

I smiled hearing that and stood a little taller.

"And second"—she stuck the bottle behind the bar again and frowned at Shay—"nicknames are only sweet and sexy when they aren't stupid and uninspired, like, for example, naming a girl after a body part. He might as well just call me head or toenail."

I kept on smiling, thinking about how inspiring Brian's choice of nicknames were for me, and then thinking about how much I disagreed with Tori's opinion, because I thought Legs was a pretty sweet and sexy nickname, and clearly inspiring.

Tori's legs were jaw-dropping.

But I would never admit my disagreement right now. We had each other's backs, through and through.

Tori turned her head, eyes narrowing in the direction of the only occupied booth in our section, huffed, then slid the glasses across the bar in front of Shay.

"Can you take these over there for me? I want to talk to Syd."

Shay picked up the glasses and walked away. No questions were asked.

Tori sidled up next to me.

"Okay, so here's the deal," she began, voice lowered and unamused.

I turned and gave her my full attention, pulse racing and skin warming all over.

Tori noticed my reaction and shook her head.

"Oh, my God. Could you *not* look so excited right now?"

"I can't help it!" I exclaimed, clamping a hand over my mouth after getting shushed. "He calls you Legs," I whispered between my fingers.

Her lip twitched.

"He's a loser."

"He's gorgeous," I countered.

"He's a gorgeous loser."

"With great hair and dimples."

"Looks aren't everything, Syd."

"No, but they're a nice bonus."

"He didn't care that I was with Wes."

I leaned closer. My stomach rolled unpleasantly.

"What?" I asked, no longer feeling the hurried beats of my heart against my ribs.

Tori's eyes moved over my shoulder for the briefest second, then pulled back to mine.

"About five months ago he came in here and sat in my section, flirted with me, and I mean *flirted*, asking me out and calling me Legs, saying mine would look fantastic draped over his shoulders or spread wide in his backseat."

My eyes bugged.

Tori shook her head and waved a dismissive hand.

"Who is he?"

"Jamie McCade, local surfing legend," she answered flatly, completely unimpressed as she brought one arm across her body and gripped her elbow. "He's the youngest guy ever to win so many championships in a row. He's broken world records."

"Wow."

"He's a complete dick."

"Um." I bit my lip. "How is he a complete dick again?"

I was still waiting for proof of his dickness. I wasn't convinced yet. Shay moved past us.

"I told them you'd be over in a minute to get their orders. Jamie said to tell you he misses you," she announced, the little crossbones in her hair catching in the light overhead and shimmering.

She pulled herself up on the counter again and twisted her body, her head back in the window to resume her one-sided conversation with Stitch.

Tori didn't even flinch at the mention of Jamie's sentiments, but she did lower her eyes to a spot on the floor.

"What happened?" I urged her on. I needed to know.

"I told him I was seeing someone, that I was...in a relationship and happy." She squeezed her eyes shut through a breath, inhaling and releasing slowly. "It didn't even faze him," she continued, lifting her head with disappointment in her crystal blues. "He didn't care *one bit* that I was someone's girlfriend, Sydney. Didn't even throw him off his flirting game. If anything, he went at me harder after that. I was suddenly a challenge. And that *disgusted* me. He has no respect for love."

I grabbed her hand that was hanging freely.

"And after all of it, after pushing me and throwing empty compliments and stupid little nicknames around, he still flirts with practically every girl in here when he comes in. They flock to him, and he just sits there and pats his lap. It's pathetic. I'm sure he calls them Ass or Knee-Cap, or something equally unoriginal. He's a player. And a jerk."

"And a dick," I added, now fully convinced.

She gave my hand a squeeze.

"Exactly. That's why I always ask Stitch to do things to his food."

My mouth fell open.

"Does he?" I asked, glancing over at the window Shay's face was still halfway sticking through.

Tori shrugged, kept her long, slender fingers wrapped around my hand, and suggested, "Come on. Let's go take their orders before Nate fires us."

We walked back to the booth, fingers interlocked, mine holding on a little bit tighter, and this time Tori handed me her ticket book, brushing her lips against my hair when I looked nervous and unsure and reminding me that I needed to start taking orders eventually, and also, that this would be the perfect order to screw up on.

I smiled at our secret.

She nudged my hip again and turned to the boys.

"We ready?" she asked, studying her nails.

A fired off his order of fish and chips, extra chips and hold the coleslaw, folded up his menu, and slid it to the edge, doing this saying they were still waiting on a third but were starving.

B kept his eyes on Tori, his lips curved in a smile, and requested the bacon and bleu burger, cooked medium with no pickles, a side of fries, and her phone number.

I glared at him, then scribbled down his order.

A Reuben with potato salad.

I ripped the ticket from the book and handed it to Tori when we got behind the bar.

She laughed at my chicken scratch handwriting, mumbled something about praying Jamie was allergic to eggs, then slid the paper across the steel lip of the window to Stitch, requesting with a mischief in her eyes, "Loser Special, Stitch sweetie, on the Reuben."

He jerked his chin and kept on cutting up onions.

I leaned closer to her.

"What's a Loser Special?"

"Drop the meat on the floor and let it sit there for five seconds."

I straightened in shock.

"He does that?" I whispered harshly, looking through the window at Stitch and thinking that, yes, he did look like someone who wouldn't care if he dropped meat on the floor and served it to a loser, especially a loser who deserved it, and further thinking he looked like someone who could lay a motherfucker *out* if they looked at him wrong.

The guy was straight-up edge.

I cut my eyes away before he saw me staring.

Tori smiled. That was the only answer she gave me.

Kali walked up then and joined the two of us behind the bar, coming from the employee lounge next to Nate's office.

Shay was waiting on a table and no longer hanging around Stitch's window.

"I feel *so* much better," Kali exclaimed on a rushed breath, her hands pressing her boobs through the white polo shirt we wore as uniforms. "I thought I was going to start leaking all over the place."

"Did you talk to Cam?" Tori asked.

Kali's face lit up, her brown eyes sparkling like Christmas lights.

It was beautiful to watch.

"He loves FaceTiming me," she said to me more than Tori. "He just licks the screen and babbles nonsense. It's the cutest thing ever."

My phone vibrated in my back pocket.

I slipped it out, replying, "I can't wait to meet him," and saying it sincerely.

"I'll bring him in when I'm off so you can see all his sweetness. And we should all totally hang out one night! I can get my parents to watch him if I give them notice."

"Hell yeah. Girls' night," Tori commented.

"Absolutely," I answered, head down.

"Is it Marcus?"

I kept the screen close to my body, shielded from prying eyes, and shook my head in response to Tori's question while my insides tingled with a strange energy.

"My mom," I lied, then winced *because* I lied, but I didn't know if I could tell Tori who was really texting me, or if I should.

We didn't keep secrets, but I was getting butterflies from a boy who wasn't my husband.

What would she think of me?

"They have phones on the Ark?" Tori joked, touching my arm when I giggled and moving past me. "We have another table. I'll get them started while you converse with Mary Magdalene."

I nodded and stepped back until my hip touched the counter. My thumb slid across the screen.

Wild Thing. Good first day?

I looked up and saw Tori engrossed in waitress duties at Table 4, squinted, then realized she was smiling and nodding at Table 13, all while she held a hand behind her back and flipped Jamie the bird.

He found it amusing, a giant grin plastered on his face.

I laughed while I replied, but the smile lighting me up was because Brian remembered it was my first day.

Did Marcus ever wish me a good first day? I couldn't remember.

So far so good, Trouble. What's shaking with you?
My head at that old as shit phrase.
What? What's shaking isn't an old as shit phrase. Badass redheads use it all the time.
Think you might be the only one, babe.
Think you're wrong, BABE.
You being cute?
Maybe.
Like that. Keep it up.

Giggling and feeling half my age, I glanced up at the sound of my name and saw Tori waving me over.

Gotta go. Tables to wait.
Me too. Meeting friends for lunch.
Later.
Later, Wild.

I tucked my phone away and joined Tori at Table 13, took their orders *correctly*—there weren't any losers at that table—ripped the ticket off and gave it to Stitch myself, then helped her with drinks, carrying two glasses while she juggled three.

"Fuck," I heard mumbled behind us while distributing the beverages.

I straightened and turned my head.

Jamie pushed up from the booth, his eyes heavy on his phone.

"Dash got a call. We gotta get back," he directed at A, who immediately slid across the bench and took a final sip of his Sprite.

"Shit," he muttered. "That sucks."

"Yo, Legs. We need to get this to go." Jamie cut his eyes to Tori and pulled out his wallet. He tipped his chin. "Wrap it up, babe."

Babe.

I immediately thought of Brian, pulling in breath through my nose as the phone in my pocket seemed to triple in weight.

"Whatever," Tori mumbled before she took off across the room.

I remained in place, watching Jamie toss two fifties on the table and Exhibit A a ten and a twenty, which was *insanity.*

No freaking way did the meal they were taking with them cost more than thirty dollars.

I raised my hand to bring to attention the monumental overtipping when Tori came rushing back over, bag in hand, which she wasted no time thrusting at Jamie's chest.

"There. Enjoy your Reuben."

He stared at her, looked down into the bag with a finger fishing through Styrofoam containers, then lifted his head and grinned, all crooked and rascal.

"Look at you, knowing what I like."

Tori scoffed.

Exhibit A stood and thanked us under his breath before trailing behind Jamie out the door.

I wasn't the only one watching through tilted shutter shades as the Boys of Summer climbed into a vintage sky blue Jeep with boards stacked on the roof.

It pulled to the end of the lot, dust kicking up behind the tires before it settled and cleared.

A bright yellow sticker on the bumper read, *If it swells, ride it.*

I chuckled.

Tori held up one finger while her other hand swiped the cash off the table, mumbling, "Ride this, loser."

We giggled and high-fived.

Two hours later I slipped into the lounge for some privacy and tugged out my phone during my second fifteen-minute break. I typed with one hand while my other twirled a lock of red.

Hey, Trouble. Good lunch with your amigos?

He took twenty-three minutes to respond. I read it behind the bar with my back to my best friend.

Day went to shit, Wild. Busy. Talk later.

* * *

I got home from work with Tori a little after eight o'clock.

It was a long first day and we were both starving, which was funny seeing as we worked around food all day and, thus, ate an abundance of that food all day.

After changing out of my uniform and into my sleepy pants, I took the leftover shrimp tacos out of the fridge, heated what needed to be heated in the microwave while Tori danced around me with plates in her hands, then joined her on the couch, where we ate our dinner with some wine and watched the first episode of *True Blood*, because our vampire-loving hearts were missing Eric and his fantastic head of hair.

We loved Season 1 Eric. His hair was on point.

Not that he wasn't still attractive with short hair after Pam had to cut it, because he was, this is Eric we're talking about, but we just loved it all long and free-like.

"Made for tugging," Tori snickered.

When I started yawning through Episode 4, I gave my best friend a kiss on the cheek and climbed the stairs, leaving her on the couch since she wasn't tired yet and, as she put it, "Needed more of her LaLa."

I caught the last remaining notes of my generic ringtone as I reached my bedroom. And because I didn't know who was calling me and Brian had texted me "Talk later," this being Later, I lunged for the phone and accepted the call, not bothering to glance at the name flashing on the screen before I did it.

"Hello?"

"Sydney Dawn, how are you, sweetheart?"

I fell back on the bed with a hand pressed to my forehead, the heel digging into my closed eye.

I should've checked the caller ID.

Rookie.

"Hey, Mom. I'm good. How are you?"

"You're *good*?" She sounded appalled. "You leave your husband and you're *good*? Well, I'm sorry, darling, but I don't like this. I don't like it one bit. You should not be *good*, Sydney."

"Mom."

I clenched my teeth.

"You know what scripture says. Marriage is a *binding* contract. One you do not simply walk away from. You should be sticking this out, in *your home*, not shacking up with Tori and living the single life doing God knows what. She's always walked a thin line, if you ask me."

"Mm. That's funny. I don't remember *asking* you anything."

"Don't give me lip," my mother snapped in her finger-waving-in-my-face tone. "It's disrespectful."

I bent my knees and dug my bare toes into the comforter. My calves tensed.

"Don't talk about my best friend, *Mom*. It's really uncool."

"I'm simply saying, you should be home, with your husband and dealing with this as a couple. It takes two, dear, and you're backing out when you should be fighting for your marriage."

"I'm not *backing* anywhere! He wanted out!"

My mother gasped, breathed heavily through lingered seconds, then queried, "My God. Why are you yelling?"

"Are you serious?" I sat up, punched the mattress with my fist, and cried, "You're making me crazy! *That's* why I'm yelling."

My face and neck warmed in exhausted anger.

How could she throw all of this on me? I didn't understand her. She knew Marcus was the one who ended things. I'd told her the entire play-by-play three nights ago, and it's *my* fault?

Was she serious?

"Marriage is a covenant, Sydney," she started again in a soothing but instructive tone.

I pressed my lips together so tightly I could feel my pulse against my teeth.

"An *unbreakable vow* between you, Marcus, and God. Now, I'm not saying I ever thought much of your husband, because truth be told, I didn't. Thought my baby girl could do a thousand times better, but you *chose* him, vowed *to him*, 'til death do you part, and that is not something you should take lightly and just throw away when things aren't working."

"I didn't throw anything away," I replied after taking a breath, willing my battering heart to slow.

"Well, it sure sounds like you did," my mother argued. "And divorce is not an option."

"Do you even hear yourself, Mom? What about women in abusive relationships? Or adultery? What if Marcus would've cheated, would divorce be an option then?"

"Abuse, adultery, drug use, those are all acceptable reasons for divorce if people *cannot change*. Not someone wanting out because they fell out of love with their spouse. There is marital counseling for that, which is what *you* should be seeking right now instead of living in sin in Dogwood Beach."

My mouth fell open with a gasp.

"Now . . ." My mother cleared her throat, not even missing a beat. "If you would like me to set you and Marcus up for an appointment with Father Frank, I would be more than happy—"

I disconnected the call.

My throat burned like I had been breathing fire. Tears threatened to pour down my face, but my head was the holder of the worst of my pain.

A thousand tiny needles stung my scalp, and the base of my skull throbbed so violently, my vision blurred.

Footsteps lifted my eyes as I dug the points of my fingers into my temples.

Tori appeared in the doorway with a green Christmas quilt draped over her shoulders and head.

She always wrapped up in blankets like a cocooned caterpillar when she watched television.

"You okay, hon?"

I shifted my eyes to the phone next to my knee.

"My mom," I explained.

"Again?"

Behind heavy lids, I nodded. I couldn't look at her as I clung to my lie from earlier.

It sucked.

"You wanna talk about it?"

I shook my head and stared at my eggplant-colored toenails.

"All right, well, I'm LaLa'd out for tonight. You change your mind, come get me. Otherwise I'll see you in the morning, Hookah."

I gave her a weak smile and my hazel irises, nodding when she asked in silent question with a hand on the light switch if I wanted the room dark, then I fisted my phone and slid under a heavy teal comforter and champagne satin sheets, pressing my head between two pillows and praying for reprieve.

My mouth tasted like sweet sparkling wine and mango salsa. A combination I needed to kill with Crest and mouthwash, but the throbbing in my skull kept me horizontal.

I don't know how long I lay there before my phone rang, but

it was long enough that my lips were cracked from sleep-riddled breaths bursting free.

I pulled my head out from under the pillow and flipped to my back.

The screen lit up above me. I wet my lips eagerly and answered with slumber lingering in my voice.

"Trouble. You okay?"

I heard his breathy laugh. It sounded cozy and familiar.

I wanted to watch his chest move with it, his throat and his mouth.

I wanted to see if he dipped his head or threw it back.

"Why are you asking if I'm okay?"

"'Cause you said your day went to shit," I pointed out, pulling the covers closer. "Why did it go to shit?"

He breathed slowly, then replied, "You don't need to worry about that, babe. It's better now."

I smiled against cool satin, but it didn't linger when I thought about Brian's reasoning from a day ago.

"Is this the bad in your life, Brian?"

"Yeah," he answered without pause, like a relieving breath.

"Is it stuff you can't share with me?"

"Yeah."

Again, no pause.

I rolled toward the ocean-view window and sighed, not in disappointment.

In content.

I wanted this Later.

And he was giving it to me, even after his day went to shit.

"Then we'll just talk about stuff you *can* share with me," I said after tucking the blanket over my shoulder and getting cozy.

He laughed again, light against my ear.

"Like what, Wild? What do you want to know?"

I closed my eyes.

Everything, I thought, but I started simple.

Chapter Seven

BRIAN

"I haven't had peanut butter in seven years."

I dropped my pen in the crease of the book of crosswords I was working on and closed it.

"Say what?" I asked into the phone, then kicked the chair out next to me and stretched out, foot propped up and body angled back.

Sydney and I were shooting the shit, had been since I called her up after getting home at the end of a long as fuck day working at Wax. I was listening to everything she was saying while reading and filling in answers, set on finishing out the page, but not having peanut butter in seven years had me putting my pen down and giving up on Puzzle 17.

"Crazy, right?" Wild asked, sounding like she couldn't believe it herself. "It's because of Marcus. He's allergic."

"To peanut butter?"

"To peanuts," she corrected. "And I mean *really* allergic. He can't even smell anything with peanuts in it or he'll start breathing different. It's serious. He's had to go to the hospital twice because of a reaction."

"Shit," I muttered, not really giving two fucks if this guy had to go to the hospital or not. I was more reacting to what I knew Syd was getting at.

"I love peanut butter," she whispered longingly. "I love it enough to eat it straight out of the jar, but I couldn't keep any in the house.

I couldn't even eat it when I wasn't home because I'd come back smelling like it. It lingers."

She was right. Even after brushing your teeth, you could sometimes still taste it.

"So not only did I give up peanut butter," she continued. "But I gave up peanut butter cup sundaes at Friendly's, and I loved that sundae. Whenever we got good report cards, my mom would take Barrett and me and I'd always order that sundae. It was tradition."

Christ, I hated this fucker.

He couldn't help having an allergy but it still pissed me the fuck off.

Her mom took her and Barrett there. That meant a lot to her.

Sydney should be eating peanut butter cup sundaes every fucking day of her life and keeping that memory.

"Couldn't have a dog either," she added quietly. "He was allergic to those, too."

I cracked my neck, then asked, "You want a dog?"

"I've *always* wanted a dog. A boxer. Male. They're beautiful creatures. And smart. I'd name him Sir Duke because he'd be regal and would need a regal name."

Her voice raced with excitement.

I laughed under my breath.

"Sir Duke? You serious, babe? You can't give a dog two names."

"He'd have two names but he'd go by Sir. Just Sir. Sir Duke would be on his birth certificate and I'd only yell that if he was in trouble, which would be never because he'd be perfect."

I shook my head, but I did it smiling.

She was quiet for a couple breaths.

I was about to suggest she get a dog after hitting up Friendly's when she shut me up with her speech.

"I gave up peanut butter and a pet for him, but I didn't mind because you give up stuff when you fall in love and you do it not caring *because* you're in love. You gain so much more than what you're losing, and I would've given up more than that to be with Marcus because I was in love and I knew he felt the same. There was a time he would've given up peanut butter and a pet for me, too, but you know what, Brian?"

"What, babe?"

My chest felt tight. I was no longer relaxing in that chair with my foot up. I was hunched over the table, elbows holding the weight of my upper body and my head cradled in my hand as I listened and waited, staring at the tattered pages of my book.

"He wouldn't give up anything for me anymore. Not one damn thing. Not even if I was allergic to it."

I breathed deep with such force, my nostrils flared.

I hated hearing the hurt in Syd's voice. It fucking ate at me.

I stood up and walked to the fridge to grab another beer.

It was either that or hunt down every Marcus currently living and breathing and beating the shit out of them one at a time.

"Know what I think you should do?" I asked her, holding the bottle at an angle against the counter and knocking the cap off with the side of my hand.

I took a swig.

She sighed, thinking about it. "Go buy a bag of peanut butter cups and eat the entire thing, then mail all the wrappers to Marcus in a box wrapped all pretty with a bow?"

I smirked.

"Not a bad idea, but what the fuck is the point of eating peanut butter cups if they aren't mixed with vanilla ice cream with whipped cream on top and you're not sitting at a booth eating it out of a giant sundae glass? Go big or go home, Wild. And I'd expect nothing but big coming from you."

She paused, then with a smile in her voice added, "And peanut butter sauce. They put that in it, too."

"Good. You're making up for seven years. You deserve a fuck-ton of it."

"You think that's what I should do? Go to Friendly's and eat a sundae?"

"I think you should do whatever you want to do, and if that's eat peanut butter with every meal for the rest of your life while you're surrounded by boxers with two fucking names, do it," I replied. "It's your life, babe. I get why you gave it up and respect that, I hope he respected it 'cause giving up a memory like that is heavy and not something he should've brushed aside, but if you're saying he's past the point of giving up shit for you, then fuck it."

"It's my life," she whispered, breathing a little faster like she was excited.

She was repeating what I had said, and hearing it coming out of her own mouth, *really* listening, tasting those words and getting used to the idea of living that life. For the first time.

That made me smile.

I heard the jingle of keys through the phone and turned, glancing at the time on the stove.

"Where you going, Wild?" I asked, and I did this grinning, not smiling, fucking *grinning* because I knew where she was going.

But it still felt good hearing her confirm it.

"To live my life."

Two hours later I checked up on her.

You eat a sundae?
Nope. I ate two.

* * *

What's a four letter word for the guy at Table 6 is pissing me off.
Bad day, Wild?
He's complaining about everything! And it's stupid stuff. Like his water is too cold and he wanted two tomatoes on his BLT, not one. He didn't say anything about tomatoes when he ordered and HOW IS WATER TOO COLD? I'm going to get the worst tip if he even leaves one and I'm betting he doesn't.
Maybe you need a break.
Can't. One girl called out 'cause her son is sick so we're short and it's lunch rush.
OMG he just told me the lights are too bright in here. I'm going to kill him.
Won't be able to talk to you if you're in jail.
Fine. I won't kill him. But I'm not bringing him extra napkins. So he's gonna know I'm mad.
Damn girl.
Shit just got real, B. I'm a redhead. He should know better.

* * *

I almost died just now. Our last conversation would've been about how underrated Violent Femmes are. I would've been okay with that.

I read her text and immediately hit Dial as I stepped into the back office at Wax and kicked the door shut behind me for privacy.

Cole was out on the floor. I didn't need him hearing this shit and asking me about it.

Sydney wasn't something I shared with anyone, and I was planning on keeping it that way.

"Hey," she answered with a smile in her voice. "I'm surprised you're calling. I figured you'd be working right now."

"I *am* fucking working right now."

"Uh...okay. What's up? Why do you sound mad?"

"What the *fuck* do you mean you almost died?"

I kept my voice down but didn't keep the edge from it. I wasn't sure I'd be able to swallow that back right now. I was pissed. And her nonchalant tone was only fueling my irritation.

"Oh," she answered through a light chuckle. "I was kidding. I mean, not *totally* kidding. There was a small fire but it's been dealt with. Crisis averted. But it definitely could've gotten out of control if Tori didn't have a fire extinguisher. Luckily, she does."

"Are you fucking serious?" I grated.

"Yeah," she replied hesitantly. "What's wrong with you? Are you okay?"

"*Am I okay?*" I asked harshly. "You send me a text saying you almost died and what, you're expecting me to respond with a 'That's fuckin' great, Wild,' or 'Glad you didn't kick it,' like I don't give enough of a shit about you at this point to call and ask what the fuck you mean by that. Then you're gonna get on my ass because I sound mad when I have every fucking *right* to sound mad after reading that text and further listening to you downplay it like something happening to you is one big fucking joke, and you're asking me if I'm okay?"

"Um..."

"To answer your question, babe, no, I am not okay."

She was silent for a moment, then with a quiet voice asked, "You'd care if something happened to me?"

I stared at the wall.

What the fuck?

"You serious, Wild?"

"You give a shit about me."

She stated this. It wasn't offered up as a question.

I rubbed at my face.

How the fuck could she think I didn't?

"Yeah. I do, Syd. I give a shit about you."

Exposing that about myself should've felt strange and maybe a little wrong, but it didn't. I wanted her to know. I wanted Sydney to understand why I was reacting this way and why I would *always* react this way.

If she was expecting feelings to be left out of this, whatever this was between us, it was too fucking late for that.

I heard her soft breathing in my ear as I moved to the leather chair facing the desk and collapsed into it.

"My mom sent me pamphlets on marriage counseling in the mail today," she began, this time without a hint of amusement in her voice.

I knew she was no longer smiling. In fact, I pictured her sitting on her bed and twisting a lock of hair around her finger, an admitted habit of hers, and doing this while her eyes remained downcast and her shoulders slouched.

Her mom always took the fire out of her when they spoke. I fucking hated it.

She sighed, then continued.

"Like I'd even consider counseling with Marcus at this point. So Tori suggested we put them in a pot and set them on fire, which I thought was a great idea because it would destroy all evidence of those stupid pamphlets." She took a deep breath. "We did. It got a little out of control when bits of flaming paper started floating out of the pot and onto her carpet, but Tori has a fire extinguisher so we were able to put it out."

"You didn't get hurt?" I asked.

"No. Not at all..." Her voice trailed off. "Are you mad at me?"

Now it was my turn to smile.

I dropped my head back and stared at the ceiling.

"A little. But it helps you're alive, so I'm sure when we talk later tonight, I'll be over it."

"Mm. And you give a shit about me."

She was teasing now. Doing it smiling again, I was sure of.

But I knew Sydney. I knew even though she was teasing and making me eat my confession from minutes ago, she still liked knowing how I felt. And she let me know just how much she liked knowing it with the next words out of her mouth.

"I give a shit about you too, Brian," she admitted softly. "A really *big* shit."

"Glad we're on the same page, babe," I chuckled.

"The giving a shit page? I've *been* on it. Glad you caught up, *babe*."

This time when I laughed, I didn't hold it in for the sake of being quiet. I gave it to her.

And I took what she gave me—her own admitted feelings and her sweet as fuck giggle. I took them.

With no intention of giving them back.

* * *

Famous person (dead or alive) you'd want to have dinner with. Go.

Easy. Bill Fucking Murray.

Venkman? Really?

Hell yeah. He's a legend.

I think out of all the Ghostbusters, I'd want to have dinner with Janine.

Janine wasn't a Ghostbuster, babe.

She was, sort of.

No.

She had a major role in the films.

No.

And the coolest hair in 2.

Didn't make her a Ghostbuster.

She worked with them! Guilty by association.
She have a proton pack? Flight suit?
She had the coolest hair on the show, Brian!

I laughed and dropped my head back against the Adirondack chair I was lounging in, my bare feet braced on the railing that wrapped around the deck and my eyes skyward, watching an airplane's lights blink against dark blue night.

Two and a half weeks of Wild and I was hooked on our conversations, every single type of conversation with her.

Talking. Texting. Random thoughts she'd share with me. Invading questions I avoided and ones like this that were simple and pointless and I knew, deep in my marrow and veins and ventricles, persuaded answers from me she'd never forget, because that's the kind of girl Sydney was.

A forever girl. A note-taker. A memorizer.

If it was important or insignificant, she held on to it. It didn't matter.

She held on.

She'd remember fifty years from now what movie role I would want to star in or what my last meal on earth would be. Even if we didn't still have this, she'd remember and think back, smiling with those dimples she told me she inherited from her mother, the ones she liked instead to say she inherited from her brother.

He was the coolest person she'd ever met.

We shared and laughed. Fuck, she made me laugh a lot. Talked real shit, too. Personal shit that walked the line of too personal, and if it faltered, I'd cut it down and divert her, because I couldn't...I *couldn't*.

She asked me if I lived at the beach, saying she knew I was in North Carolina because of my area code and that it was okay, I could tell her and maybe, *Trouble, oh, my God, wouldn't it be amazing if we both lived in the same town?*

She asked me what type of business I owned, because I gave vague job information to pacify her and she wanted more, she wanted everything, what and where and how long.

She wanted what I spent my days doing, because she had my nights.

Just tell me, Brian. What's the big deal?

She asked my age and what I looked like. If my hair was dark or long or soft if she touched it, if it curled fresh out of the shower or if it fell annoyingly in my eyes.

What color are they, Brian? Brown and green and gold like mine? Tell me.

She asked me what detergent I used so she could use it, too, and imagine she never had to ask these questions, because she knew me and my smell. My habits and hates. She knew my nose was poker straight and my jaw was square and clean shaven. She knew I was tall enough that her ear could rest against my heart, and my hands were bigger than hers and I liked to hold tighter, just a little tighter than she did.

I gave what I could, and only what I could, my fingers itching to type more, *just tell her, fuck it*, and my tongue pressing against my palate to prevent speech.

She couldn't know too much. She could never know.

Never.

I gave her enough so I could still have her, but I took everything.

Every fucking thing. It was mine and she wanted me to have it. She gave it up. She was perfect that way. She was perfect in every way.

Red hair. Hazel eyes. Moles she hated, two on her face and two on her neck. The scar that ran in the bend in her elbow from a bicycle accident when she was eight and the piercing on her belly she got on a dare when she was sixteen, lying and saying she was eighteen to get it.

How she loved to cook but couldn't do it well enough, leaving her with four recipes she held dear and perfected.

How she drank Godiva Milk Chocolate Hot Cocoa every night with whole milk, nothing less, adding her own mini marshmallows so she could control the sweetness and liking it that way, and drinking it no matter what the temperature was outside.

How she loved a winter sky and the first signs of spring, and how she donated blood every year because it was important and everyone should do it.

If you could save a life, what's stopping you?

I took it all and it was good. So fucking good.

But I took only what I could handle.

I knew if I let her tell me where she worked, I would go there no matter how far away it was and I would look at her closely and openly where she could see it, where she could see *me*, and I didn't know if she was the type of girl who watched porn. We talked about everything but we didn't talk about shit like that. It didn't seem important. But I couldn't risk her recognizing me and reacting, ending this when I wasn't nearly finished.

If I allowed her to tell me her last name, I'd search. If I allowed her to tell me where she lived, I'd move.

My world was one miserable mistake-shaping second after another, except for the breaks in my misery that belonged to her.

And no way was I ready to give that up.

Best two and a half weeks of my life came from a girl who was never meant to give me anything.

And she was giving me everything.

I was still smiling with the sounds of waves and wind surrounding me as I focused on the life in my hands, typed my question, and waited.

What about you, Wild? Who do you want to have dinner with?

That smile vanished the second I read her response.

Alive? You. Dead? Barrett.

Because what the fuck was worth smiling over. She'd never get her shot at either.

Chapter Eight

SYDNEY

Girls' nights are awesome just being what they are, getting together with your friends and getting loud and laughing a lot, but throw in a theme and a very creative wardrobe courtesy of your best friend and they become a whole new level of awesome.

And tonight's theme was eighties night.

I was in luck. Red hair teased out and sprayed stiff looked totally kick-ass on me.

I felt wild. I liked feeling wild. It made me think of Brian.

And I *really* liked thinking about him.

Kali got her mom to keep Cameron so she could come out with the girls, which included myself, Tori, and Shay, who looked like she stepped straight out of a Madonna video with her black mesh top concealing little of her black lace bra, a black tutu over black tights, spiked black pumps, and bangles covering her arms, all in black and metal. Her hair was teased high enough to reach heaven and she had star earrings dangling from her ears that touched her shoulders.

She looked rocker chic and could totally pull wearing stuff like that daily if she wanted to.

I told her that and she said she'd consider it, joking how much her tips would probably increase if she did just that.

Kali kept it simple with a *Flashdance*-style oversized sweatshirt that hung off her shoulder, black leggings, and leg warmers. She said she couldn't fit into cute stuff yet because she still had fifteen pounds to lose from being pregnant with Cameron, which the three of us argued.

She looked hot and had great curves. And the men in the bar were taking notice of those curves every time she stood up, so she stopped hating what she was wearing about fifteen minutes into our night.

Tori and I stuck to similar looks—neon tanks and bright-colored tutus over fishnets, multicolored bangles on our wrists, and the highest heels we owned, mine being hot pink Jimmy Choos I'd purchased at the Nordstrom sale last year and cherished with all of my heart.

They were patent leather and made my calves look amazing.

And when you find heels that make your calves look amazing, you cherish them.

We were the only ones keen to eighties night at The 13th Floor, but we didn't care how badly we stood out. We were having a great time, talking and laughing while drinking lemon drop martinis.

They were delicious, and I was sipping my second one while staying in the conversation going on around me and the one I was secretly having in my lap.

They're sweet and sour. And I think Oprah's favorite drink if I'm remembering that episode correctly.
2nd one?
Gearing up for 3rd.
Get a cab.

I smiled because I liked Brian worrying about how I was going to get home. I wanted him to care and he did, and he didn't keep that from me either. He wanted me to know it.

I *really* liked that.

But I kept that smile on the inside as I looked up at Shay, who had just brought up Stitch for the second time tonight.

Once was a coincidence. Twice and you knew it *wasn't* a coincidence.

She was thinking about him.

"Is there something going on with you two?" I asked, keeping one hand in my lap concealing my phone and the other on the stem of the martini glass in front of me.

Shay was always hanging around that window, leaning in and conversing like she and Stitch had loads to discuss, and Stitch didn't look like he minded it too much even though the man was harder to read than a Chinese Bible and could've absolutely minded it. I just wasn't reading him correctly.

He never showed much emotion and barely spoke two words if you asked him something.

"You say no and I'm calling bullshit," Tori threw out, doing this pointing a finger at Shay.

Shay shook her head. The star earrings sparkled in the light when she did it.

"It's not like that. He just lets me talk as much as I want and he doesn't tell me to shut the hell up when I do it. It's a nice change. I know I talk a lot. It annoys my brothers."

"What do you two talk about?" Kali asked, disbelief in her voice.

"Whatever. Work stuff. Things I'm dealing with at home. The weather." Shay shrugged and sipped her drink, then added, "And it's just me doing the talking most of the time. He listens. He's good at that. Sometimes he'll comment on what I said or ask me something, but that's rare. Most of the time he just keeps cooking while I ramble. It's sweet of him."

Kali looked at Tori. Tori looked at me. I looked from Tori to Kali to Shay, then questioned, "He's *sweet*? Stitch is *sweet*?"

The man was edge and hard looks. *Anything* but sweet.

Shay looked between the three of us as if we'd all lost our minds in thinking Stitch was anything *but* sweet.

"He is. You talk to him enough, you'll get it. His eyes are the warmest shade of copper I've ever seen."

Kali looked at Tori. Tori looked at me. I looked from Tori to Shay to Kali, watching the lip curls on everyone minus Shay.

Oh, we all got it all right. Stitch could have the hardest looks and the most edge of any man living and breathing and Shay would've still had that opinion.

She liked him. She might not admit it right now, but it was clear.

"Well, in that case," Kali chuckled. "I mean, copper eyes on a man who looks like he's done time is seriously sweet. I guess I just don't get to look at him close enough to see it. You're always hogging that damn window and blocking the view."

Shay crumpled up her cocktail napkin and chucked it at Kali's face. They both giggled.

"You find another job yet, Sydney?"

I looked at Kali after her question, doing this shaking my head.

"There's nothing available right now. I've only applied for one and never heard back. I'm thinking they found someone to fill it already."

"Well," Kali started, then pressed her lips together while looking at the other two girls and told me on a rushed breath, "I really don't hope you find anything. Sorry. I know that's awful but I'd hate to see you go. I love working with you."

"Me, too," Shay echoed with a warm smile on her crimson-painted lips.

I smiled at both of them, hoping to convey how much I enjoyed working with them as well, because I definitely enjoyed it, then I looked at Tori, who was remaining silent and had her head turned.

"Is that Nate?" she asked.

The three of us followed Tori's gaze across the bar.

Dancers had wandered and were no longer obstructing our view of everything on the far side of the room, which was where Nate sat on a stool with a glass in front of him, his head lowered and his eyes either focused hard on something behind the bar or unfocused on anything.

He looked deep in thought, either way.

"Why does he always look so sad?"

I threw out my question to the girls not only because Nate currently did look sad in the middle of a kick-ass bar with great tunes, Beastie Boys currently playing overhead, which I was tapping my foot along to against the leg of my stool, but because he always looked sad every time I saw him, and even though that wasn't a lot since he stayed shut up in his office more than he wandered the floor, his sadness wasn't lost on me.

I knew he was looking sad behind that door, too. I knew it in my bones.

Tori looked down at her drink. Kali took a sip of hers, but her eyes were lowered to the table.

They were avoiding.

I looked across the table at Shay with expectant eyes and she read them, sighed, then gave me a look I knew meant I wasn't going to love what I was about to hear.

But I still wanted to hear it. I was curious.

"I really don't want to ruin this fantastic evening with a sad story, but I have a feeling you're just going to keep asking me," she said, dipping her head.

She was right.

I nodded.

"It's really sad, hon," Tori threw out. "Are you sure? I almost cried after I heard it the first time."

Hearing that warning, again, I nodded.

"I want to know."

Shay prepared herself to deliver this sad story, and she did that by finishing off the last bit of her lemon drop, then grabbing the attention of the nearest waitress and pointing at her empty glass.

Tori did the same and lifted hers, silently requesting another.

Shay then gave me her full attention again and did it most likely feeling the rush of the alcohol she'd just consumed.

I guessed it was going to help.

"Nate didn't always used to be like he is now. Up until about a year ago he was really present around the restaurant and rarely ever spent time in his office. His wife was really present, too. Sadie. She was always stopping in and chatting up the staff even though she worked a lot herself. It didn't matter; she made time. Then she got pregnant and was still coming around a lot, but we knew it was because she was so excited about being pregnant and wanted to show off her baby bump every second she got. Nate ate that up. He was crazy about her and even more crazy about her carrying his kid. It was really cute to see."

I smiled but I did it cautiously because I didn't want to get too comfortable with the idea of Nate being happy. This was a sad story, and when a pregnant wife is involved, I could only imagine how sad it was about to get.

Shay took a deep breath and continued.

"Marley was born, or Mo as we call her. She's the prettiest baby ever. Seriously. Full head of blond curls and the biggest blue eyes you'll ever see, holding so much expression it steals your breath. She looks just like Sadie."

Kali shifted beside me, and I saw that her attention was now on Nate instead of where it was at the beginning of this story, the table.

Tori was studying Shay as I was, looking sad.

"Nate didn't know. He was working all the time and doing anything he could to make the money they were losing with Sadie being out on maternity leave. I'm not even sure he noticed Sadie's absence when she stopped popping in as much, then not at all because he was so busy. We all noticed it but honestly I figured Sadie just wanted her mommy-daughter time and I couldn't blame her for that. Those baby years are important. But apparently Sadie was in a rough way and no one knew it. She was suffering and she was doing it alone, not confiding in Nate when she should've been and then it was too late. He couldn't help her."

"What happened?" I asked, my voice sounding tight like I needed to clear my throat.

"He went home after work one day and found Mo asleep in her crib and Sadie in the bathtub with an empty bottle of sleeping pills."

I clamped a hand over my mouth, my breath bursting warm against my palm.

"Oh, my God," I whispered, cutting my eyes to Nate.

She had killed herself. Nate came home and found his wife dead and their baby girl asleep, completely oblivious to the state of her momma.

Pain circled my heart and folded in on it.

"I hate hearing that story," Kali declared quietly, picking off chunks of the napkin in her hand. "I miss seeing Sadie around. It feels like yesterday she was showing us all her first ultrasound photo."

"It's been almost a year, hasn't it?" Tori asked.

Shay nodded.

"Next month. I think that's why he's been locked in that office more than usual. He's hurting."

I looked from Shay back to Nate.

His head was still down, eyes still unfocused while his mind was on something heavy, I'd decided.

"What about Mo? Do you guys get to see her at all?"

"Nate's mom brings her in sometimes. She watches her while he's working," Kali answered. "She still looks just like Sadie."

"Prettiest baby ever," Shay professed, smiling gently when she said it.

I couldn't imagine Nate's pain and the enormity of the pain Mo would feel when she got old enough to learn about her mother. It was almost too much to even think about. Adding on the pain Sadie no doubt was feeling and feeling it silently, suffering alone and having this beautiful life she created with her while she was suffering from it, most likely not experiencing those mother-daughter moments the way they're meant to be experienced because she couldn't let herself experience them; it was all too much sadness.

But Nate, his pain I felt deep and there was no option but *to* feel it. He was right in front of me.

"Gosh," I breathed, pulling my eyes back to the girls. "That is such a sad story."

Tori shot me a look.

"Told you."

I stuck my tongue out at her.

She slapped the table, declaring enthusiastically, "Subject change!"

Shay made a motion with her hand that she wanted to be the one giving us our next topic of discussion. She looked across the table at me.

"Have you spoken to your husband yet?"

Tori groaned and shoved Shay's shoulder.

"That is a terrible subject change," she snapped.

I couldn't have agreed more.

"We don't have to talk about him in detail!" Shay argued while leaning closer to Tori. "I was just wondering if he'd done the *right thing* and reached out to her yet. It's been, what, three weeks? He can't call her and see how she's doing since pulling the rug out?"

Shay looked at me after she was done speaking.

So did everyone else.

I didn't want to talk about Marcus. I didn't even want to think about him.

It hurt to do it.

I dropped my eyes to my glass, collecting sugar off the rim with my finger.

"Haven't heard a peep," I answered Shay, hearing irritated tongue clicks and a quietly muttered "asshole" I was certain came from Tori.

I lifted my head and looked around at the three of them.

"And I've decided I'm not reaching out to him. Ever. I don't need to talk to Marcus for any reason besides what needs to be done to get this divorce final, and that hassle falls on him. This was his doing. He wanted this, so he can do all the work in getting that shit started if he hasn't already. I'm not dealing with lawyers and spending *my* time getting paperwork together or paying costs if there are any. Let him eat it. Three weeks and he doesn't even reach out *once*? No." I shook my head, breathing heavily through my nose. "There is nothing I need to talk to him about anymore. Our finances have always been separate, so that's not an issue. I took everything I wanted to take when I left so there's nothing there I need to get from him, and whatever we bought together under the false pretense of sticking through thick and thin, for *life*, he can keep. I don't want it. If it's tied to a memory of him, I don't want anything to do with it."

Tori touched my hand. "Hon."

"He lied to me," I went on. "He said he'd love me forever, no matter what. He promised I'd never walk alone and then he walked away, and for whatever reason he had for doing this, one I still don't know since he hasn't reached out to me *at all*, I can't for the life of me imagine that reason being big enough to treat someone who was in your life for seven years like a complete stranger. Like *nothing*. So no, I'm done. I'm not going to sit around and wait for Marcus to call me anymore. I'm going to live my life how I want to live it, and even though I'd already decided I was going to do this a week ago, I'll say for effect that I'm doing this starting *now*. And you three are my witnesses."

Tori squeezed my hand.

"Good for you," Shay said, smiling favorably.

"Yeah, Sydney. I think that's the right move," Kali agreed. "Screw him. He doesn't deserve you. You're, like, the sweetest thing ever and he's obviously a jerk. I'm sure you'll find someone who deserves you when you're ready."

As if he knew how perfect his timing would be, my lap vibrated at that exact moment.

My hand curled around the device. I watched Tori get to her feet and snatch her glass off the table.

"I'm getting us all another round since my best girl just declared she's living the life she *wants* to live now, and that's worth celebrating, and also since our waitress sucks ass and decided she doesn't want to serve four hot chicks who look better than she does on her *best* day."

"Ouch." Shay laughed.

Kali giggled and stood up, too, grabbing her almost empty glass. "I'm joining."

I watched the two of them walk away, then watched as Shay tugged out her own phone and started messing with it, giving me the go-ahead I was grateful for.

You get a cab?
Nope. I'm getting drink number 3!
How late you staying out?
Why? Miss talking to me?
Yeah.

I blinked and read that message twice. Then I read it again.
My belly warmed, flipped, then twisted.
God, that felt *good*.

I could slip outside and call you real quick.
Can't talk now. Out with my boys.
Oh.

I didn't hide my disappointment. I didn't think it was fair since he didn't hide wanting to talk to me.

Call when you get home. I'll be up.

And just like that, my disappointment vanished.

He'd be up, waiting to talk to me. *Wanting* to talk to me. That felt better than two going on three lemon drops, and those felt *good*.

OK.
Get a cab.
We're calling an Uber.
Good.
Glad you approve.
You being smart?
I'm being WILD.

I typed this smiling so big my cheeks hurt.

Right. Be Wild and call an Uber.

I giggled and looked up just as Tori was walking back over with Kali, both of them laughing about something while Tori carried a tray like I'd seen her do a million times at work, kept close and perched beside her shoulder and doing it with ease, this one covered in drinks ranging in size from the four lemon drop martinis to tiny shot glasses filled with different-colored liquids.

I was confused as to why she was carrying it. I was also confused as to why it was covered in shot glasses when I thought we were sticking with lemon drop martinis tonight.

She slid it onto the table and wasted no time explaining herself.

"That guy in the suit over there wanted to buy us drinks because apparently we look like a bunch of women who can't buy our own drinks and needed his big manly wallet to come and save us," she started, doing this while distributing a martini glass and a shot in front of everyone. "So I decided to buy us a shit load of drinks to show him none of us need a man to buy us *anything*, and I did this while also explaining to him that this is girls' night and on girls' night we buy our own drinks."

She lifted her shot and turned her head.

The three of us followed, Shay even spinning around to look, and saw the guy in the suit staring at us with wide eyes like he'd just been told to go fuck himself.

I wouldn't have put it past Tori to deliver that message.

"To girls' night!" Tori cheered.

We all toasted to girls' night before shooting it back, and we did it *loud*.

* * *

"Oh, my gosh. Where is this guy? My feet are *killing* me!"

Kali stopped walking on the sidewalk and held on to the lamp-post, tugged off her heels with a groan, then continued the trek down York Street barefoot with her heels in one hand and her clutch in another.

We'd left the bar ten minutes ago after calling Uber twenty minutes before that, expecting to see our ride waiting by the curb since that's where he said he'd be.

He wasn't. Apparently the man who drives for a living got lost.

So now we were walking down the block a little ways in hopes of spotting him so we could all get home, which I was dying to do since I knew Brian would be waiting up for me and I couldn't wait to talk to him more about anything and everything.

I loved our conversations. And now I knew he missed them when we weren't having them.

The flip and twist was happening constantly as I thought about that.

"Maybe you should call him again," Shay suggested beside me, giggling and dropping her head on my arm.

She was completely loaded. I was pretty certain we were all some level of drunk, but Shay was definitely leading the way with the most shots thrown back.

I felt great. Warm and a little numb all over. I wanted to lie on the sidewalk and gaze at the stars.

"He might be in front of one of these other bars and be waiting for us, like an idiot," Kali pointed out, bringing us to a halt in front of a nameless bar I couldn't focus on because the neon lights were too bright for me at the moment.

I squinted away and watched Tori slip out her phone and study it for a minute before dialing.

"Yeah, it's me again. Where are you?" she clipped into the device, looking down the street and across it while she spoke.

"Are you kidding me? When? We stood out there for ten minutes waiting for you!"

I dropped my head back with a sigh.

"I'm drunk. I can't track your location on a map! And *you* were supposed to text me when you arrived!"

"I really hate to pump and dump," Kali admitted quietly, grabbing my attention and pulling my ears off Tori's conversation. She bit her lip. "Do you think I'm a horrible mom for going out tonight?"

I shook my head. "No way. You're so pretty."

She smiled.

Shay giggled either because of us or something else. The girl was laughing at everything.

"Just head north on York Street and we'll walk back. You can't miss us." Tori ended the call looking irritated as all get-out, then motioned for us to spin around and instructed, "Go back. He's been waiting for us."

"Ugh! What a jerk. He was supposed to text!" Shay hissed.

"Men are such idiots with technology," Kali commented.

I pinched my lips together so I wouldn't scream at the top of my lungs about Brian being awesome with technology.

It was torture keeping his awesomeness a secret.

We were walking back in the direction of the bar with Tori leading the way when she stopped dead without warning.

Shay and I stumbled a little, bumping into each other since we were the two walking mostly behind her. Kali was off to the side.

"What?" I asked, then moved in front of Tori when she didn't react to my question, not with a response or even a jerk of her head. "What's going on?" I pressed further.

I followed her gaze to the parking lot we were standing in front of, and I couldn't be sure because I was drunk and also because there were a lot of vehicles filling that lot, but it looked like Tori was shooting daggers specifically at a sleek red sports car that was taking up two spaces.

Rude. I couldn't stand it when people did that.

"Tori!"

My assumption was validated when I watched my best friend bolt down the sidewalk a few feet and follow the bend that swept into the parking lot, take to the asphalt and sprint in her four-inch heels to where the sleek red sports car was parked. She stood beside it and looked it over for a whole two seconds before attacking the passenger side window with fists flying.

She must've thought it was *really* rude.

"Oh, my God!" Kali screamed.

"T! What are you doing?" Shay called out.

I took off running after her and heard the girls on my tail. Shay's heels mainly, but I knew Kali was with her. We got inside the parking lot and over to the car, and I wasted no time in grabbing on to Tori's shoulders and yanking her away from the window.

"Sweetie! What are you doing? Stop!" I yelled.

Tori fought me, twisting in my arms and then leaping for the window again.

"Tori!"

"Let me go, Syd!"

I yanked her back again and maneuvered around her, putting myself between her and the window and holding my hands up to keep her back.

Tori rubbed the edge of her right hand like it was stinging. "Move, hon."

"No way."

"Sydney." Tori stepped closer. It was then I saw the tears in her eyes. "Move out of the way."

I kept my hands up and I didn't move.

"Not until you tell me what the hell you're doing and why you're doing it."

"It's Wes."

"What?" I asked, then it hit me.

"Oh, God," Kali whispered.

"Shit," Shay muttered.

I lowered my hands and looked over my shoulder at the car.

It was sleek. It was expensive. And it belonged to the man who broke my best friend's heart.

"First, I'm busting out his windows. All of them," Tori started, bringing my head around. "Then, I'm going to drag my heel across his door and carve *Douche Bag* into the paint." She moved closer. Her hands were balled into fists. "Then, depending on my mood, I may set fire to it."

"Hell yeah!" Shay cried. "Let's do it!"

Kali stayed silent, but she was nodding her head approvingly. She knew Tori's motives behind this and she felt they were justified.

Tori looked from Kali to me, tilting her head. "What do you say, Syd?"

I watched a tear drop onto my best friend's cheek. I didn't need to think about my decision regarding giving Wes some hurt.

I'd made it three weeks ago.

I spun around and started pounding my fists on the window and doing it with all my strength, screaming and hollering because this was crazy, and not to mention illegal, but fuck it, Wes deserved to walk out and find his car demolished so I was giving it my all.

Tori joined me a half a second later, then it was Shay's turn.

I beat that window with everything I had. I was determined to break it, bullheaded determined, so the longer it stayed intact, the madder I became and the harder I beat on it.

"I hate you! I hate you! I hate you!"

Tori was yelling at the top of her lungs, her arms flying with the punches she wasn't landing either, but still flying all the same.

Shay was getting creative and ramming her shoulder into her window.

"Hey!"

I heard a man's voice but I kept punching, smacking, and clawing at the glass.

"Hey, what the hell are you doing?"

Someone tugged on my shoulder and pulled me away from the car. I looked back and saw it was Exhibit A from the restaurant a couple of weeks ago.

"You want to go to jail?" he asked me, dropping his hand.

I shook my head with wide eyes, then watched him stalk around the car and grab Shay. She giggled, not giving him much of a fight.

He deposited her next to me and moved behind us, falling in beside Kali.

He looked at her. She looked at him, smiled hesitantly, then shared, "I have a son."

He stuck his hands in his pockets, then muttered an indifferent, "Cool."

"Legs! What the hell, babe!"

Jamie had his arms wrapped around Tori and was dragging her away from the window, her legs flailing about and her body thrashing against his.

"Calm down!"

"Get off of me! Let me go!"

Tori's feet were kicking in the air and she was twisting her head frantically.

"Quit trying to bite me and I will! Shit!"

He put her down and stepped back, getting between us and the vehicle to block us, a hand pushing through his hair, and his chest pulling in deep breaths.

"Now, what the fuck?" He stared at Tori. "What are you doin'? Are you tryin' to get the cops called on you?"

"What I'm doing is none of your business," she hissed. "So move out of my way."

"Not a chance."

Tori stuck her hands on her hips.

Jamie took this moment to really look at her, letting his eyes wander the length of her body and then doing it again, finally pulling back to her face to ask, "What the *fuck* are you wearing?"

"It's eighties night," she snapped, leaning closer. "And it's girls' night so if you don't mind, go the fuck away."

I jerked when I felt my phone vibrate from its keeping spot in my bra.

Oh, my. That felt nice.

I watched Jamie cross his arms in defiance.

"Not going anywhere 'til you tell me why you're attacking this sweet ride. You better have a good reason, and by good, I mean it better be something on a government level and involving al-Qaeda, since this is a brand-new Corvette and costs a fuckin' mint."

"I know what kind of car it is, *loser*," she replied. "And I know *exactly* how much it costs, considering I was there when he fucking paid for it."

"So you know it costs a mint."

"I know you better move out of my way." Tori inched closer.

"Not happening, Legs. Not without your reason."

My phone vibrated again.

This time I felt it all the way down to my knees and practically hummed.

"My reason doesn't involve you, but you can rest assured knowing it's the *best* reason, and that's all you're gonna get."

Jamie tilted his head. "Not good enough."

"Move," Tori seethed.

Jamie bridged the gap and came right up on Tori, bent his head to get closer, and ordered, "Tell me and I'll move. Why are you doing this?"

I watched Tori take in a breath. I watched the hands at her sides go from fists to slack and submissive.

"Hey!" another voice yelled from a distance. "You need me?"

Everyone, including me, turned around and saw where the voice was coming from.

A man was standing by the vintage Jeep I recognized from the other day. It was idle and clearly not in a parking spot, which I assumed was because of the guys spotting our act of vengeance and throwing the gear into Park to rush over and stop us.

I couldn't make the man out too well, thanks to the distance and it being dark, but I could see him leaning against the passenger door and looking in our direction with his arms crossed over his chest.

He appeared tall and had really short hair if it wasn't completely shaved. That's all I could make out.

"We're good," Jamie yelled back. "Be ready in a minute."

The guy heard him, clearly he did, but he kept watching from where he stood. He didn't get back in the Jeep.

"Now," Jamie started again, drawing my head around.

He was still standing just as close to Tori as he was a minute ago.

"You tell me why you're trying to get yourself arrested and I'll move, but not until you tell me, Legs. And you're not getting past me so don't even waste your energy."

Tori shook her head.

"You need to just go and pretend you didn't see me."

"Yeah." Jamie studied her for a minute, looking her over like he was admiring a piece of art, then continued, saying the tiniest bit quieter, "That's not fuckin' happening."

My right boob vibrated and sent a shiver up my spine. I ignored it and watched Tori roll up on her toes to get into Jamie's face.

He didn't move back. I didn't think he minded her getting that close to him.

"Fine," she grated out. "You want to know? I'll tell you. That *sweet ride* belongs to my ex who became my ex when I ran into him and his perfect little family at the mall a few weeks ago, including his drop-dead gorgeous wife and their super-cute daughter who couldn't have been more than two, this perfect little family *not* being something I was aware of but became not only aware of but acquainted with when he decided it was best to introduce me to them as an old friend from high school."

Jamie leaned back, blinking.

"*Fuck*," he muttered. "You serious? He did that to you?"

"Do I *look* like I'm serious?" Tori asked rhetorically. "Now if you don't mind, I'd appreciate you moving out of my way so I can finish destroying something precious of his since he went about destroying everything precious of mine."

I moved then and stepped up beside Tori, taking her hand and wrapping it up in my own.

"So *we* can finish destroying it," I corrected her, looking at Jamie.

Tori gave my hand a squeeze.

Jamie looked only at Tori, not even flinching when Shay stepped up and took Tori's other hand.

"I'd like to say that even though I am not participating in the destruction of that vehicle, I am with her one hundred percent."

"Thanks, babe," Tori replied to Kali, keeping her eyes on the man standing in her way.

Jamie kept on looking at Tori, but he was doing it differently now than when he first yanked her away. His eyes were soft. Tender.

He understood.

Then he did something that shocked the hell out of me and everyone else standing there.

He spun around and moved beside the vehicle, pulled out a pocket knife, flicked the blade open, and jammed it straight into the back passenger tire.

I jumped and whispered, "Oh, my God."

"Holy shit," Tori breathed.

Shay started giggling and Kali gasped.

We all watched Jamie yank his knife out and heard the sweet hiss of air being released into the night.

He didn't look at us. He repeated the gesture and popped the remaining three tires, doing it quickly, then slid his knife away and came to stand in front of Tori, bent to get his face close to hers again, and whispered, "Get out of here."

Tori tightened her grip.

"Let's go!" Shay yelled, tugging on Tori, who then tugged on me.

Then we ran, leaving Jamie and his knife skills, quiet Exhibit A, and the mystery man at the Jeep behind us.

And we all did it laughing.

* * *

My entire body was still trembling with energy when we finally got home after tracking down our Uber idiot.

Shay was dropped off first, then Kali. Tori announced she wanted to take a shower the minute we walked in the door to strip the gunk out of her hair, so she left me in the kitchen, where I went about making my mug of hot chocolate while reading the missed texts from Brian, which were all versions of him asking if I had called Uber yet or if I was still drinking. Seriously, his concern for my whereabouts couldn't have been any cuter. Then carefully carrying that mug up the stairs while my ear was pressed to the phone, listening to it ring.

I couldn't wait to tell Brian about my night.

"What's up, babe?" he greeted me, all smooth and warm sounding.

I wanted to slide inside his voice and live there. He made my skin tingle.

"Trouble, oh, my God, you are not going to *believe* what happened tonight! I was Wild to, like, the thousandth degree!"

I kicked the door closed and carried my mug over to the bed, sat on the edge and toed off my heels, then scooted back and took a sip of my drink.

"Yeah? What did you do? Steal a car?"

"No. I beat the *crap* out of one!"

He was soundless while I chewed up a marshmallow.

Obviously shocked and wanting to hear more information, I obliged his silent request and elaborated, bulldozing through my recount of the evening and not stopping to pause for questions, only for a sip of my beverage when needed because my mouth was dry.

Brian quietly listened. I was sure he was silent because he was anxious for more, this was such a good story, so I continued on, not wanting to make him wait.

"*Then*, and oh my God, this is the craziest thing *ever*, Brian, these two guys showed up to stop us and pulled us away from the car. The one guy who is a total loser because he always hits on Tori and calls her Legs, he hears why Tori is attacking this car and pulls out a knife and *slashes the tires*! It was *so* badass! Then he tells us to scram so we did. I nearly fell into a bush 'cause of my heels but I didn't care. It was the coolest thing that's ever happened to me!"

More silence. A lot of it, which was odd now that I was done recounting the events and I was sure he'd have questions or comments.

I worried we got disconnected.

"Hello? Brian?" I called into the phone.

"What kind of car was it?" he finally asked, his voice a lot quieter than it normally was when we talked.

"Uh…oh, a red Corvette. Apparently it costs a mint."

"A red Corvette," he repeated.

"Mm-hm. Yep."

"You were trying to bust out the windows of a red Corvette and two guys stopped you, one slashed the tires, and you were all in eighties gear."

"*Yes*," I stressed, confused as to why he was recounting the events for me when I lived them. "God, it was such a rush!"

"Unfuckingbelievable," he mumbled.

"Right? I've never done anything like that before in my life." I laughed. "We totally could've gotten arrested. Jamie *definitely* could've gotten arrested. I hope he wasn't caught."

I sat my mug on the nightstand and fell back on a pillow, legs reaching. I rubbed my heels against the comforter.

"Was I wild, Brian?" I asked when his silence was killing me.

"What?"

"Was I wild? If you'd seen me tonight, would you have thought I was wild?"

"Why are you asking me that?"

I attempted to twirl a lock of my hair but the hairspray prevented it. I pulled at the bottom of my tutu instead, twisting my fingers in the tulle.

"There was this other guy there and I saw him watching us, and I wondered if he saw me and thought I was wild going after that car like I did."

Brian was quiet for moment, then answered, "I'm sure he did."

I smiled at that.

"I missed you tonight," I told him, feeling a little bold from the alcohol and the rush of adrenaline still scratching in my blood. "Thought about you the whole time I was with my girls."

"Yeah?"

"Yep. You think about me the whole time you were with your boys?"

"What do you think?"

"I think you did, but I don't know if you thought about me the way I thought about you."

"And how's that?" he asked, and I couldn't tell if he was smiling or serious. His voice wasn't giving anything away. There were no familiar tones to it. Nothing I'd normally take comfort in *knowing* that voice and loving that I knew it.

It was different but I didn't care. I wasn't being cautious. I didn't feel the need to be.

This was Brian. I knew him.

I *knew* him.

"I thought about what your bottom lip might taste like," I confessed, pulse racing and stomach clenched.

He inhaled in my ear. It was sharp like the cracking of a whip.

"Yeah?" he asked, but I heard him beg.

Yeah. Keep going.

"And I thought about what your skin would feel like under my hands and against my thighs. Um, you know...if you were between them."

He didn't say anything. He was breathing, just breathing, slow and heavy in my ear. It was simple, an essential action he *had* to do to stay alive. It had absolutely nothing to do with me or this conversation.

Still, it was the hottest noise I'd ever heard in my life.

I became bolder. Something was happening to me. Attacking Wes's car was a rush, but this felt like someone had cut me open and filled me with a thousand heartbeats. My bones vibrated excitement. I was breathless. It was like I was being chased.

And I wanted to be caught.

"I thought about your fingers," I continued. "What they would feel like. If they would pull and grip and if you would want to keep them in my hair or move. If you liked to kiss or if you liked to bite. The sounds you make when you're close. God...Trouble, I thought about everything. Honestly, I've thought about it a lot."

I dipped my hand between my legs, under hot pink tulle and over black satin. I wasn't being cautious about this either.

I was burning up.

"Brian," I moaned, moving with eyes closed so I could imagine I wasn't the one moving. "Did you think about me that way?" I asked anxiously. "*Do* you?"

"*Fuck*," he hissed. "Wild, what are you doing?"

"What do you *want* me to be doing?"

I hadn't done this in months. I couldn't remember the last time I was touched or I touched myself. My fingers felt foreign, but sure-fire. Aware. This was just like I remembered.

But it was so much better with the sounds and the voice in my ear.

A self-induced orgasm was a chocolate brownie.

A self-induced orgasm persuaded by Brian was a chocolate brownie covered in ice cream and sprinkles and whipped cream, heated so it was all gooey and sloppy.

I made a noise in my throat and spread my legs wider. The tulle scratched the back of my hand.

"Come on, Brian," I coaxed through a quiet laugh. "You don't want me to stop, do you?"

"Fuck no." I heard the soft rustling of clothes. "What are you thinking about?" he asked.

"You."

"Doing what?"

"Everything."

"Touching you?"

I nodded and licked my lips. I didn't answer. I didn't have to.
He knew.

"Kissing you?"

"Yes," I moaned.

"Where?"

"Right here."

I dragged my finger over my clit and shuddered.

"Your pussy?" he asked. "Is that where I should kiss you, Wild?
With your thighs against my ears so tight I can't hear you scream?"

"God, yes."

I wiggled against the onslaught of my fingers.

"Would you kiss me there?"

"I would," he answered raggedly. "You'd have problems stopping me."

"I...I wouldn't stop you. I'd never stop you."

"What about my dick?" he suggested, and just the mention of
that word had me arching my back and panting. "Filling you. Fucking you. Have you thought about that?"

"Have *you*?" I asked, grinding my palm against my clit and pressing my fingers against the barrier of my tights, picturing just that.

His dick. Filling me. Fucking me.

"You wanna know what I've thought about?"

"Please," I begged.

The pressure was building. The muscles in my legs and arms and
belly tensing and twitching and tightening.

I wanted to explode.

Brian made a noise then, deep and tortured in my ear, and I knew,
I *knew* he was getting off, too.

"I've wondered how sweet you'd really be on my tongue and
how wild you'd get around my cock," he said, low and smooth and
wicked. "Your ass and the color of your cunt."

"Oh, my God," I whispered.

"How tight you are and how wet you'd get just from my fingers.
Your tits...touching them. Tasting them. If you liked to watch or if
you'd keep your face buried in my neck while I fucked you."

"Brian," I groaned, fingers sliding faster. "K-keep going."

"I've thought about fucking you for *hours*, Wild. Only stopping so I could eat you or to watch you suck me off, then fucking you again and again...*and again*. Every way. Everywhere I could take you, I would." He panted in my ear. "You need to know, Syd..."

"What? Tell me. *Please*, I'm so close."

"Fuck."

He hesitated for a moment, allowing me to focus on all of his other sounds, and God, I wanted him to keep going and tell me, tell me everything, but I didn't want to miss the noise his hand made moving over his cock or his eager breaths, growing more and more desperate by the second.

"I get so hard just from hearing your voice," he admitted. "I think about you all the time. More than I should. If I ever got the whole thing..."

"Oh, God. Oh, shit...Oh, *oh*," I gasped. "Brian...*Brian*."

Blood rushed in my ears as I came hard and heavy limbed, toes curling and eyes rolling and so wet I could feel it against the tips of my fingers through my panties and tights.

It was exquisite.

I felt weightless and warm on the fall down, maybe a little drunker than I was at the start of this conversation, and my eyes shot open when I heard Brian moan my name and "Fuck, fuck, fuck" over the quiet slapping of skin.

He was coming.

I bit my lip.

God, I would've given my right arm to see that. I bet he looked beautiful, because he was.

I *knew* he was. In my blood, I knew it.

We were both silent for a moment, then I had to ask. I *had* to know.

"What would happen if you got the whole thing?"

He exhaled brokenly.

He wasn't going to give me that last little piece. The moment had passed. I could feel it, could sense him pulling back and allowing uncertainty to creep in and settle, tainting what we had just shared.

I wasn't going to allow that to happen. But he spoke before I could.

"I should go," he suggested.

"Brian, wait. Don't." I sat up and tucked my knees close to my belly. "I wanted that to happen, okay? I've wanted it for a while now. Maybe since the beginning."

"Syd..."

I didn't let him finish. I had to get this out before I *couldn't* get it out.

"I think about you all the time, too," I rushed. "More than I probably should because we've never actually met, but that's the *only reason* why I shouldn't think about you this much. It doesn't make sense. I've never laid eyes on you, but I don't care because I like thinking about you and I *love* talking to you, and what we just did together." I closed my eyes and softened my voice. "I really *really* liked that, too. It wasn't a mistake, and...and I won't let you think it was. I won't."

I stared at my knees and waited. I fought the urge to crawl under my bed and hide until winter.

"Your husband is a fucking moron," he growled seconds later.

I sat up straighter and pressed my fingers to my lips. I felt them curl.

Oh...*wow*.

He just totally said that. Brian's never said anything about Marcus before. He's only listened to me bash him or retell our history, commenting to let me know he was with me and listening, but that was it. That's all he'd ever given me.

Until now, when he just totally said *that*.

I was grinning so big I was afraid my lips were going to stretch out and never fall back looking right again.

Too bad I totally didn't care if that happened or not.

This felt great!

"Gotta let you go, babe," Brian said.

My grin turned into a pout, and I quietly pleaded, "Not yet."

"Not gonna sit here and talk to you with jizz on my stomach."

"Oh."

I blushed and slid back down the bed, covering half of my face with my hand.

"Yeah, *oh*," he repeated with a hint of humor. "Talk to you tomorrow."

I was suddenly grinning again.

We would talk tomorrow, and maybe do more of *that*.

I couldn't wait.

"Okay, Brian."

"Later, Wild."

"Later."

I disconnected the call and fell asleep in full eighties gear without stripping the gunk out of my hair or anything. I didn't care.

I'd have Brian again tomorrow.

Chapter Nine

BRIAN

Things were different with Sydney now. Different in a way I knew we'd never go back to what we had before she came both soft and savage in my ear.

Three times now I'd stroked my dick to her sounds while confessing my own desires. I didn't give a shit, and I told her. Straight up. She knew what I was thinking about, and it drove her fucking wild, spurring her own indecent thoughts and the courage to share them with me, thoughts that were getting filthier and filthier with each passing day.

She shared them. All of them. She didn't give a shit either.

"Brian," she whispered, her breaths growing quicker and heavier. "I'm so little down there. Do you think you could fit?"

And, *"What does your dick look like? Describe it to me."*

And, *"I want to taste it after you've fucked me."*

"God, Brian...Brian."

"Please. Yes. Yes. Yes."

And, *"Fuck...oh, fuck!"*

Not participating in our phone sex wasn't an option, not unless I suddenly became deaf. I'd die from lack of blood flow to my brain if I sat there and ignored my throbbing cock. And truth be told, I was experiencing the best orgasms of my life with Sydney moaning in my ear.

Give that up now? Fuck that.

I didn't want to go back to what we had before. I wanted both, her sweet laugh and the way her voice hitched when she came. Our random conversations and unguarded desires.

I *needed* both, but I had two major fucking problems that could and were causing serious issues for me the longer I ignored them.

First, Sydney was here, in motherfucking Dogwood Beach, where I could see her anytime I wanted, and I *wanted*.

God, I wanted. It was torture denying myself.

I saw her that night we first slipped over the line dividing friendship and more so I knew *exactly* what I was missing.

Temptation personified, with luminous eyes, a killer fucking body, and hair that looked tangled and worked from my hands.

I was concealed in the dark waiting for Jamie and Cole to handle whatever bullshit they felt was their business. I stood there growing impatient while the two of them dragged three strangely dressed women away from a beautiful vehicle any man would appreciate owning, even if they were like me and didn't give a shit about sports cars.

I called out when I was ready to move the fuck on and find out where Syd was, which in hindsight was pretty damn ironic. All heads turned in my direction but I focused on one, not only because of the weird as hell getup she was wearing, but also because she had a body I knew would look damn good in anything, including the weird as hell getup she was wearing, had eyes that practically swallowed me up they were so wide and wondering, and red hair I immediately pictured belonging to someone else.

I continued picturing this until my girl leveled me with information I was half wishing I never knew.

My life would be a lot fucking easier, that was for damn sure.

But I knew it now, and there was no giving it back.

And what I knew had me fighting it every second and with every breath I took.

I wanted to go to Whitecaps and watch her, see and study her in the daylight.

I wanted to be close enough to count the freckles I knew spotted her nose and admire the moles she hated, press my lips to them and tell her they were mine and they were beautiful.

I wanted to fuck her discreetly or in public, bend her over one of the tables she was waiting on because I couldn't wait a second longer to get inside her tight wet pussy, live out every lewd act we'd confessed and finally satisfy the hunger that itched in my veins and watered my mouth.

Taste and touch and suck and fuck. I wanted to do everything.

But I couldn't. I couldn't *do* anything. She was right in front of me, a mere ten minutes from my store and fifteen from my house, and I couldn't do a damn thing about it.

She watched porn, not heavily but she did on occasion watch it, a fear I had confirmed two nights ago when I got the balls to ask her straight out, thinking we could go ahead and breach the topic since I'd just made her come by explaining in detail all the ways I wanted to fuck her.

Tits. Mouth. Cunt. Ass.

Not much seemed off-limits now.

I didn't ask which ones or what sites she visited. I didn't want to bring any more attention to it, and honest to God, I was afraid she'd elaborate and give me shit I didn't want to hear like who her favorite porn stars were or what titles got her off the most.

If it was me or one of mine, this would be over. I knew that.

I'd eventually break and go see her at work, reveal who I was and watch her rip everything we had away from me.

I could only fight this for so long.

If it *wasn't* and I knew the fuckers, or hell, even if I didn't, I'd find them and wind up in jail for assault.

So here I was, stuck. I couldn't do anything.

Torture.

I hadn't known the definition of the word until three days ago. Now I was living it.

There was something else, too, another fucking problem I was dealing with, only this one I could *deal with*. I could manage it.

And that was exactly what I was doing strolling into Xstasy on a day I didn't need to be there.

Shit had changed. There was no going back to the innocence we shared before. Syd and I both knew that.

But I had obligations. Guilt I couldn't turn away from.

I also had a plan.

I crossed the dank studio on Tuesday afternoon, using my lunchtime to handle this shit after Jamie had returned to Wax following his lesson, my eyes locked ahead of me on the office door and my ears indifferent to the crude noises echoing off the walls and ceiling.

I fucking hated this place.

I knocked twice and waited to enter only when I heard the go-ahead. Getting that, I pushed inside.

Mike was sitting behind a metal desk littered with papers. Across from him perched on the edge of her seat sat a young blond woman, face coated in a thick layer of makeup and tits pushed up and in.

I didn't recognize her. She must've been new. I knew all the girls.

Her eyes moved to me and widened in favor.

I looked from her to Mike and tipped my head, asking, "Got a minute?"

He grinned like the Joker.

"For the man responsible for lining my pockets with enough cash my ex-wife has shut the fuck up about the child support I owe her and is currently all over my dick, keeping it wet 'cause she wants me to buy her new titties for Christmas?" He slung his feet up on the desk and linked his hands behind his head, leaning back and doing it still grinning. "Fuck yeah, you can have a minute. Sit down, Dash." His eyes trailed to the woman as she slowly stood. "Talk later, sweetheart. I'll call you."

"Okay. Thanks, Mike."

I stepped aside so she could slide around me and get to the door.

Her hand grazed my hip as she moved.

I knew it was done deliberately. She had plenty of space to get past. I made sure of that.

"Excuse me," she whispered with sex and opportunity in her voice, batting her lashes before turning and stepping out.

The door shut behind her.

I slumped down in the chair she'd vacated and rubbed at my face.

Mike chuckled, shaking his head.

"Jesus Christ. How much pussy does your dick see on a daily basis? Shit, man." He looked at the door, then back at me. "You wanna work with her, 'cause I can make that happen. She's interested in the job. *Very* interested. Willing to do anything. I can arrange it so you're the one breaking her in."

"I'll pass."

His eyebrows rose.

"You sure? I offered eighteen-year-old virgin ass to Shane, he'd be all over it."

"Then offer it to him," I growled, driving home my point. "I'm not interested."

Mike dropped his arms to the chair and shrugged.

"Suit yourself."

"Need to talk to you about something."

"Figured that's why you were here. What is it?"

I pulled in a deep breath and sat my right ankle on my knee.

"I want to switch to solos starting immediately," I informed him. "Just me and the camera. None of your girls. I'm done with that. And I want to make close to what I'm making now."

Mike gaped at me, didn't blink for what felt like a solid minute, then started cackling like he'd just been told the funniest shit he'd ever heard in his life, head thrown back and hand slapping his thigh repeatedly.

I stared at him and didn't even crack a smile.

After longer than I had patience for, he righted himself and stared back, taking notice of my annoyance.

"You serious?" He suddenly looked affronted.

"Very."

His expression hardened as his eyes narrowed.

"You, Dash Savage, Internet sensation and the biggest fucking draw I have here, bringing me more traffic than two of my other fucking stars *combined*, want to keep your dick to yourself all of a sudden and jerk it on camera. That what you're telling me?"

"Yep."

"No fucking way," he scoffed. "Your videos get the most hits because of you and the way you fuck, Dash. Not how you pull your taffy. Jerk off on your own time. I'm not paying for it."

I'd expected this reaction from Mike. He was a transparent piece of shit on a good day, and I was prepared for it.

I smiled and flicked the laces on my shoe.

"The hell you smiling at? I said no."

"You'll say yes," I countered. "This isn't negotiable."

Mike pulled his feet off the desk and dropped them to the floor, propped his elbows on whatever papers he had in front of him, and glared at me.

"Say again?"

I glared, too, but did it still smiling, repeating slower this time so he wouldn't fucking miss it.

"You'll say yes. This isn't negotiable."

"And how the fuck do you figure that?"

"You said it yourself. I'm the biggest fucking draw you got here. Things are good with your ex and you wanna keep it that way, meaning you gotta keep pulling in the kind of bank you're pulling in now. That won't happen when I walk." I leaned forward then, mimicking his position with my elbows on my knees, then continued, "And I will walk. You don't agree to this, I'm done with Xstasy. Give you another two, three months before your ex realizes she won't be getting her Christmas present, hops off your dick, and gets in front of a judge. How many kids you got, Mike? Three?" I shook my head. "Two years of not paying a dime for them, I'm guessing your pockets are gonna be emptying pretty fucking fast."

Mike smirked.

I fucking hated him.

"You're forgetting all the uploads I already have of you, Dash. That one of you and Jayden got over ten thousand hits."

"Yeah. The day you streamed it. How many hits it get yesterday?"

He lost his smirk.

I cocked my head and explained to the idiot, "Depreciation. Shit's only hot when everyone who subscribed got notice of the stream and logged on. Stayed hot for a few days thanks to word of mouth. Now?"

I let that question hang in the air between us.

I knew the answer. So did Mike, based on the agitation shadowing his face.

He was barely making jack-shit off dated uploads. Nothing compared to the new stuff. It was why he always pushed getting me here every chance he got.

I had a motive, giving that kid as much money as possible. That's the only reason I obliged him.

Otherwise I would've told him to fuck off.

"See you're understanding me now," I said after he refused to offer up the answer, knowing I'd like what he told me. "You wanna keep me here? Keep pulling in the kind of money you need to be pulling in? You're gonna let me switch to solos and pay me close to what I was making already."

"How *close* are we talking?" he snarled.

The shit bag was pissed.

Too bad I didn't give a fuck.

I leaned back and stretched my legs, replying, "Six."

"*Six*," he repeated as he cracked his knuckle. Laughter built in his throat and erupted on a breath. "You want me to pay you six hundred dollars to step in front of a camera and whack off when I was paying you eight to fuck someone? Do I look like an idiot to you, Dash?"

I smiled.

"Absolutely."

Mike didn't find any humor in my response. If anything, I think it pissed him off even more.

Again, I really didn't give a fuck.

I was taking a pay cut but I really wasn't if I played this how I was planning on playing it, coming in on my terms and filming more than I had been. It'd be just me, so I wouldn't have to wait on a call when Mike had a girl lined up, and I was jerking off every day at this rate anyway, so what the fuck?

This would work.

Mike wasn't as enthusiastic about the change as I was. His eyes darkened.

Flashing a smile, I reminded him, "Biggest pull you got."

I watched him breathe tight through his nose and shake his head.

"*Fuck*," he growled, shoving papers off his desk before slamming himself back in his chair.

He pulled out a pack of smokes and stuck one in his mouth, smacking his pockets looking for a lighter.

"You're an asshole, man," he mumbled around the cigarette, lit it, then took a drag. "Get the fuck out before I start giving a shit about my kids and tell you where you can shove this new arrangement."

I stood up and turned, ignoring his pathetic little tantrum, and walked over the scraps of white and yellow that had floated to the cement, heading for the door.

"I'll be in tomorrow to shoot. After six sometime," I told him behind my back.

"Whatever."

I slammed the door shut.

Yeah, Mike was pissed. And yeah, I still didn't give a fuck. I belonged to someone. This girl fucking *had* me.

Craziest shit I'd ever felt.

She didn't know it. She might not ever know it, but the second this changed between us, the night Sydney gave herself to me in a way I will never fucking let go of, that was it.

Fucking *it*.

She came.

And I was a fucking goner.

I wouldn't give Syd what I was giving her now and have this shit going on behind her back. Fuck no. Never.

No matter if she found out about this or not, I wouldn't betray her like that. I wouldn't taint what we had or spit on what she gave me.

It was everything. From the start, from that first mistaken phone call, it was *everything*.

Everything I had and wanted and needed.

I'd do this new arrangement and get the cash for the kid, help his family the way I needed to be helping them, and I'd have my girl in my ear at night.

Fuck yeah. This would work.

It had to. I didn't have any other options.

* * *

Balancing the two boxes on one hand, I took to knocking after ringing the doorbell once and not getting an answer, hoping the pounding of my fist would grab someone's attention.

It did.

The door swung open seconds later.

A round face with big brown eyes framed in blue glasses and freshly bathed hair, wet and wild looking, drew my attention down from where it was fixed to greet my sister.

Oliver, my nephew, filled the doorway instead, standing in his *Star Wars* pajamas and the dog slippers he got for Christmas last year.

"Hey, Uncle Brian," he greeted me with his crooked smile, then immediately slid his eyes to the boxes in my hand, where they went wide and stayed wide as he pumped his fists in the air and jumped up and down, chanting, "Pizza! Pizza! Pizza!"

"Pizza?"

I heard another little voice calling from inside the house, then not two seconds later Olivia came rushing up to stand beside her brother, grinned big when she saw me and even bigger when she saw the pizza boxes I was carrying, pumped her fists in the air but did it by alternating them in time with her knees drawing up as she bounced from one dog-slippered foot to the other, also chanting, "Pizza! Pizza! Pizza!"

"You guys eat yet?" I asked over their chanting, stepped inside, and closed the door behind me.

"Nope! Momma's making a roast and it smells like feet. We don't want it," Oliver answered, scrunching up his nose after.

I kept my laugh silent.

"Feet?"

"It really does, Uncle Brian," Olivia assured me, reaching out and tugging on the bottom of my shirt. Her hair was wet, too, and fell in two long braids past her shoulders, making damp spots on her flower-covered pajamas. "Can't you smell it? She put onions in there and those green things we don't even like! She's trying to poison us."

"Now we're having pizza."

Oliver held up his hand and his twin high-fived him.

"Yes!" Olivia whispered excitedly.

They were seven. Got along great for siblings, which I figured had to do with them being twins and sharing something regular siblings didn't share.

Regular siblings fought, at least occasionally. These two didn't. Siblings also liked having breaks from each other, alone time, but not Oliver and Olivia. They mourned each other if they were ever apart. Even for a night.

My sister Jenna moved into the room then from the direction of the kitchen, wearing an apron and wiping her hands off on a towel.

"Uncle Brian brought us pizza, Mom!" Olivia shrieked, pushing her matching blue glasses up her nose when they started sliding down. "Can we have it?"

"But I made roast," Jenna replied, watching both kids drop their heads. She gave me a wink, then shifted her gaze between the two of them. "Yes, we can have it. I'll save the roast for tomorrow."

"Yes!" Oliver pumped his fist into the air, then spun around and took the boxes from me.

Olivia followed behind him into the kitchen, hooting and hollering.

"Big brother," Jenna greeted me, coming over for a hug. "It's good to see you."

She was two years younger than me, which kept us tight growing up, petite like our mother and barely came up to my chin. Her dark hair tickled my jaw as she squeezed my waist.

"You, too," I said, reciprocating the affection. "Figured I'd bring food since I haven't made it over in a while." I gave her an apologetic look as she pulled away. "Sorry. Work shit."

I was including getting called to Xstasy in the "work shit" excuse. There was nothing shit about Wax, and nothing Wax related ever kept me from coming over here.

"It's okay. I get it. I'm just happy you're here now." She gave me a smile. "Come on. Let's eat before the two of them put all that food away and leave us with nothing but roast that apparently smells like feet."

Laughing, I followed behind Jenna and got some of the pizza.

After dinner and cleanup, I stood in the kitchen while Oliver and Olivia played the Wii in the living room.

Jenna was putting away the roast and the vegetables now that they were completely cooled, and she was doing this after warning her kids they'd be having roast and Brussels sprouts for dinner to-morrow.

Bellies full of pizza and soda, they didn't give her any lip over it.

I stood with my hip to the counter finishing off the last of my second Coke, taking in the surroundings of my sister's small but cozy apartment and the two kids in the other room, absorbing their laughter and triumphant squeals when she nudged my side.

"You seem better," she whispered from beside me. "That's good, Brian. Really good. I'm happy to see that."

Shit.

I didn't want to get into this. I never did. Especially not with Jenna.

I moved a little so I was ahead of her and kept my eyes to the living room when I spoke.

"Come on. Stop."

"Stop what?" she asked, moving with me, *fucking typical*, only this time spinning when she reached my side again so she could look up at my face. "I'm just saying it's good to see you laughing and smil-ing again. You *should be* laughing and smiling, Brian. None of it was your fault."

I sat my can on the counter and rubbed my face with both hands, then kept avoiding her deeply compassionate eyes, which I knew she had on me, and remained staring into the living room when I replied.

"Not getting into this with you, Jen. Had a nice dinner with you and the kids and I'd like to leave here still thinking it was a nice dinner and not a pain in my ass 'cause you're hitting me with this bullshit again. I don't want to hear it." Then I looked down at her to say, "You weren't there. You don't get to weigh in. And you're wasting your breath anyway. We both know that."

She touched my elbow, her cool fingers wrapping around it.

"I was just commenting on how nice it is seeing you this way again. I've missed it." She bit her lip. "And I thought maybe you had come around to thinking what I know is to be true."

"That's not it," I interrupted.

"*Or*," she continued, letting go of my arm as the lip she was biting started twitching. "If maybe you're happy because of something else..."

I raised my brows.

"Like?"

"Like, a girl maybe?"

Arms crossing over my chest, I moved my eyes up and over to the living room again, huffing out a breath.

"Oh, my God," Jenna whispered.

"Not talking about this with you."

She popped up on her toes and leaned closer, pointing at me.

"I don't even care. You're totally admitting to me right now there *is* a girl and *she's* the one making you happy."

I shook my head, but I did it smiling.

Big mistake.

"Brian!" she squealed, jumping up and down while gripping my biceps.

Oliver's head popped up from in front of the couch.

"What's going on?"

Olivia's followed.

"Yeah, what's going on in there?"

"Nothin'," I answered, stepping back and out of Jenna's grip, then swatting at her hand when she reached for me again.

Jenna smiled up at me, baring white teeth ready to sink in for the kill.

"Uncle Brian has a girlfriend and he loves her."

I glared at my sister.

She smiled bigger.

"Never said that," I growled.

"You smiled," she shot back arrogantly with a cock of her hip. "And I didn't miss it."

"Cool," Oliver muttered before sliding down the couch and disappearing again, the game on the TV unpausing.

"Super cool!" Olivia yelled, with a grin matching her mother's. "She pretty?"

Jenna was nodding like she fucking knew the answer to that question.

It was time for me to go.

"I'll see you guys later," I called out as I made for the door, hoping I wouldn't upset Olivia for ignoring her.

"Brian, wait!" Jenna yelled behind my back. "You're still babysitting for me next week, right? I have that date."

"Yeah, Uncle Brian!" Olivia shouted. "We're coming over to play, remember?"

"Yeah, Liv," I said, looking back at her and then turning to give Jenna a smile. "'Bout time, too."

She scrunched up her nose and made a face.

After waving and saying my good-byes, I got into my Jeep and drove home, where I called my girl the second I cut the engine.

With her in my ear, I smiled some more.

And I let her have it.

Chapter Ten

SYDNEY

My mother used to tell me not to get comfortable being happy.

She said this a lot after Barrett died. To herself and to me, although I think it was mostly to herself when she would sit on the couch and stare off at nothing.

Don't get comfortable being happy, she would say. *It'll only hurt worse when it's gone.*

I didn't understand the truth to her statement then. My twelve-year-old mind couldn't understand it. I just sat there and squeezed her hand or pressed closer, wishing and praying she would get better soon and want to eat popsicles on the porch with me again.

Lime was my favorite. Hers was cherry.

I would've eaten cherry every day if it meant getting that back.

Now I realized what my mother meant twelve years ago. And just how true her statement was.

It was Thursday, and it was my day off this week.

I'd worked six straight days and would've worked seven, no problem, considering how much I loved my new job and the tips I was getting, the kick-ass, laid-back atmosphere, the cute little uniforms that were super comfy, the people I worked with, okay . . . *everything*.

I loved everything.

It felt more like hanging out with my closest friends than work on most days.

I was even starting to consider Stitch a friend now that we'd spent a lot of shifts together and I'd gotten used to his big bad bearded ways, which included him being silent 99 percent of the time while I gabbed about my life and about Brian, figuring he wouldn't mention it to anyone since he never spoke unless *really* provoked, those times being few and far between and normally coinciding with something Shay did or said.

She was still all over that window and was always sharing with him.

He was still letting her share and listening like he did with me and the other girls, but appeared to be listening harder and taking more in when she spoke.

All hard looks and edge, drove a motorcycle, and smoked like a chimney on his breaks, fingers, hands, forearms, and I'm betting the rest of him covered in tattoos, plus the whole not speaking thing, which made him a tiny bit scary.

But twice now I'd seen him smile.

Not much of one. Barely a lip spasm behind his blanket of a beard, but it was there and both times appearing after Shay said or did something cute with her back to him.

Stitch had a soft spot, and Shay filled it. I was certain of that.

It felt good telling him about Brian. Telling *anyone* about Brian, when I wanted to tell everyone and everything, living or not, because if I was being honest, I had already confessed my secret to numerous objects around Tori's house, and to just about every blade of grass surrounding Whitecaps when I'd step outside on my break.

Even confiding in a stupid blade of grass felt good.

But the one person I really wanted to tell, my best friend, my partner in crime, and the one person I didn't keep anything from *couldn't* know. I couldn't tell Tori.

For a number of reasons.

I was scared she wouldn't approve.

I was scared she'd tell me I shouldn't be feeling the things I was feeling for Brian when I was still technically married to Marcus, and boy oh boy, was I feeling things.

Lots of things.

Tickling butterfly wings and a runaway heartbeat. Goose-bump-giving thoughts and toe-curling desires.

I felt them all the time.

I was scared Tori would tell me it was too much, too soon, too fast.

I was scared I'd start believing her.

I was scared she'd be right.

So I confided in coffee mugs and my bedroom ceiling, her favorite Christmas quilt wrapped around me and my shower-fogged reflection.

And now Stitch.

I had no idea what his thoughts were on the matter, but his silence didn't bother me. It just felt good telling someone.

Anyone.

Stitch would do for now. Maybe in a month I'd feel better about telling Tori.

And maybe she wouldn't hate me for keeping it from her.

Maybe.

God, I really hoped she wouldn't hate me.

Guilt, I was feeling it. And I was feeling it hard, which led me to spending my day off cleaning Tori's house from top to bottom, set on making it sparkle. I even cleaned the oven, got a little dizzy from the fumes and had to sit for a minute and regroup myself, then heard the buzzer go off on the dryer and went about folding a mix of our clothes.

I was being stupid. I knew deep down cleaning wouldn't help me feel better about keeping my secret from Tori, but it did distract me and I appreciated the distraction.

It also wore me out.

By four thirty I was slumped on one arm of the couch in my cleaning sweats and baggy tee, my hair a hot tangled mess and my eyes closed as I curled into the soft leather cushion.

The front door swung open, hinges creaking.

I peeked my eye open and watched Tori do a little spin and hip shimmy in the entryway after closing the door, find my one eye peeking and lock on to it, smile big, then continue popping her hips as she threw her hands into the air and swayed them like trees blowing in the wind.

Someone was in a good mood.

"Good lunch with your dad?" I asked, popping my other eye open and lifting my chin to see her better over the armrest.

"Good? No. *Great* lunch. Check it out."

She stopped dancing and pulled something white and rectangular out of her back jeans pocket, held it out in front of her as she closed the gap between us, doing this while sliding her fingers smoothly, separating the objects and displaying two of whatever it was as she came to a stop in front of the couch.

I stared at the objects, not getting what I was supposed to be checking out, then lifted my gaze to hers.

"What's that?"

She smiled, slow and devilish with wine-colored lips.

"Get up, get in the shower, and put yourself in something fierce, hon, because you and me are spending the night with"—she turned the objects around and thrust them in my face, yelling— "GAGA!"

I sucked in a breath and sat up, blinking between her and the tickets in her hand.

"What?" I asked, my breath hitching excitedly. "You got us tickets to see Lady Gaga? Where?"

"The Pier," Tori stated casually, handing me a ticket and fanning herself with the other. "They sold out in eight minutes, but Daddy pulled some strings for his little princess. Surprised me with them at lunch today. He's the best."

I couldn't begin to think how much these probably cost Mr. Rivera. I knew he had connections, but Gaga connections?

Holy shit!

"This is awesome!" I leaped off the couch, tugging the waistband of my sweats when they started sliding down, and stood in front of Tori after she took a step back. "How much do I owe him for this? Oh, my God. I can't believe we get to see her! We're her little monsters!"

"Yeah, we are!"

"No, but seriously." I touched her arm. "How much were these? I don't want your dad paying for me."

Tori waved her ticket in the air dismissively.

"It's on him. He said he's proud of you for staying so strong right now and finding your happiness. I filled him in the other day on the phone."

I pulled my lips between my teeth, fighting tears.

God...

Sweetest man ever.

And the closest thing I'd ever had to a father.

Tori shook her head at my reaction, then leaned in so we were touching foreheads.

"You're his other princess, hon. You know that."

"I know," I whispered, thinking back to my thirteenth birthday party, which Tori's parents threw for me, renting out a hall and hiring a DJ and caterer, going all out for their daughter's new best friend when they didn't have to and filling that room with so much love I forgot why my own mother hadn't done a thing for me that day.

She was off finding her peace over Barrett. Peace she didn't think included me.

Thank God for Tori and her family.

Thank. God.

Breathing deep and shaking off all sad thoughts right now, because this moment was seriously kicking ass and I wanted it to continue kicking ass, I pulled back an inch and slowly lifted my ticket between us, smiling brightly around it.

"I'm so excited I might pee myself," I admitted.

Tori threw her head back with a laugh, linked her arm with mine, and pulled me in the direction of the stairs.

"Keep it in, will ya? These floors look *bangin'*."

I giggled as we walked side by side up the stairs, asking, "Think you can hook me up with something to wear tonight? I don't have anything fierce."

"Gotcha covered on that."

We separated at the top so I could cut a right and Tori could cut a left.

I was fishing through my top drawer for some panties when she popped into my room and deposited an outfit and accessories on my bed.

Little black dress with mesh across the top, revealing the tops of your breasts when worn, and big silver studs clustered in a thick stripe going down both hips to the hem. It was short and sleeveless and breathtakingly expensive, by the looks of it.

Next to it on the bed was a studded cuff bracelet, two choices of choker necklaces, and black sling-back heels.

Fierce. I loved it.

"What are you wearing?" I asked Tori, halting her at the door.

She gave me a wink behind her overgrown blond bangs.

"You'll see."

I showered and shaved, slathered on my favorite sweet-smelling body lotion, slid into the dress after deciding on a thong and no bra, thanks to the mesh, and curled and teased my hair, giving it body and height that looked kick-ass paired with my outfit.

I also went to town on my makeup job, keeping everything heavy but the kind of heavy that screamed fierce concertgoer and not back alley hooker.

Dark, smoky eyes, false lashes that flared at the ends, and warm cerise lipstick.

I felt pretty. *Really* pretty.

The kind of pretty a girl had to commemorate with a selfie, and there was only one person in the entire world I wanted to send that selfie to.

I bit my lip while swiping my phone off the bed and pulling up the camera mode.

I was nervous.

Understandably so. This would be the first time Brian was going to see me.

Like ever.

Heavy stuff right there.

I'd thought about sending him pictures before, but got sidetracked with conversation and his sweet as warmed honey voice I wanted to taste, and all thoughts of pictures would slip my mind. Considering he never asked to see a photo of me didn't help either.

Since he wasn't bringing it up, I was hardly thinking about it.

But right now, standing in my bedroom with my makeup done up and my hair looking prettier than it had on prom night, sending Brian a picture of me was suddenly all I could think about.

And before I could think or whisper talk myself out of it, I reversed the camera so I could see myself on the screen, held the device out in front of me and off to the right a bit, pursed my stained lips into a kiss, other hand poised at my chin to blow it, and snapped the picture.

Then I attached it to a text and hit Send.

Feeling WILD.

I wanted to put my phone down. Really I did, especially since I had to snap on my studded cuff bracelet and that required use of both hands, furthermore because Tori had given me a fifteen-minute warning close to fifteen minutes ago, but I couldn't let the damn thing go.

I couldn't stop looking at it either.

My stomach was clenched. I was biting my fist and pacing the length of the bed, head down and eyes anxiously focused.

But when the little bubbles floated in teasing intervals on my screen and I *knew* Brian had seen my photo, that's when the real panic set in.

Would he like how I looked? Would it be how he had imagined and confessed to imagining countless times late at night to me, or better, would my photo exceed the limits of his imagination and paint a more pleasing image in his mind?

Or would he hate it *and* me for sending it to him, shattering his dreamed-up spank-bank material and ruining every orgasm I ever gave him?

Shit.

Shit!

Which was it and why the hell was he taking so long to type? Didn't he know this was killing me?

"Hurry up!" I whispered against the screen.

It started ringing in response to my plea, startling me and nearly slipping out of my hand.

Oh, God, he was calling.

Brian was calling after looking at my picture.

I was going to have a heart attack and never live to see the Pacific Ocean.

Damn.

I held my breath and hit Answer.

"Hey there, Trouble." I spoke lightly, forcing a smile I wasn't sure I was going to keep, depending on which way my photo swayed him.

"You fuckin' shitting me with this, Wild? What are you thinking right now? Huh?"

He was swaying a hard right into Suck Land, where he hated me, the photo, and was most likely regretting all those orgasms.

I felt sick and gripped my dresser for support.

"Um . . ." I stammered, swallowing hard. "I was thinking I'd send you a photo, of me, you know, since I hadn't yet. That's me in that photo."

"No shit," he growled. "What I'm asking right now is, what are you thinking sending it to me?"

"I was thinking I wanted you to see it," I answered honestly.

He exhaled slowly then spoke, still sounding pissed off but doing it softer.

"You shouldn't have done that."

My stomach unclenched, only to lurch and twist uncomfortably.

He wasn't attracted to me.

I closed my eyes and whispered, "I know."

"You know," he echoed unconvincingly.

"You don't like it. You . . . it's not what you thought I'd look like and you're wishing you never would've seen it." I shifted over to stare at my reflection in the mirror. I suddenly felt the farthest from pretty. "That's why you're mad."

"You don't know," was all he replied, and he said it firmly. Resolutely.

"What?"

"You. Don't. Know."

"What are you saying?" I asked.

"I'm saying, the reason I'm pissed isn't because I was sent a photo of a gorgeous girl, *my* gorgeous girl, and I wasn't liking what I was looking at. That ain't it. You're beautiful, Syd. Knew it before I saw the photo and that opinion damn sure hasn't changed now that I have seen it. If anything, it's become more solid."

My stomach wasn't lurching and twisting anymore. Those pesky little butterflies were back, enjoying their favorite flip and twist.

My gorgeous girl.

Oh, wow.

Brian totally just called me his girl.

And he thinks I'm gorgeous!

I wet my lips, careful of my color.

"Okay," I replied gently.

"What I *am* pissed about is the fact you sent that photo to me."

I cocked my head in the mirror.

I was officially confused.

He liked the photo, thought I was gorgeous in it, but he was mad I sent it to him?

Why would he be mad? He liked it.

"You lost me there," I admitted. "Why are you pissed again?"

"You ever meet me, Wild?"

"Um, in person? Or—"

"Yeah, in fucking person, you know, to verify I'm not some psycho looking to find out where you live so I can kidnap you and do all kinds of messed-up shit, 'cause there's people out there in this world who are like that, babe, and sending your photo to a guy you've never physically met is probably the dumbest fucking move ever. You don't know me."

Okay, that hurt. I didn't think it was a dumb move.

And he was wrong.

Next to Tori, Brian had become the most important person in my life. We spoke daily, sometimes multiple times a day, for hours and hours.

I knew him.

"You're not a psycho, Brian," I said, stepping back and waiting until I felt cotton comforter against my legs before I sat down on the bed. "And I *do* know you."

"No, you don't," he argued, his voice rising. "You don't know me, Syd. You'll never fucking know me. I'm a voice to you. That's it. I could be *anybody*."

"No you couldn't!"

My own voice shook now. I could feel the tears threatening, I was so angry and confused.

Why was he saying this?

"You're not anybody, Brian. You're *you*. I sent that photo to *you*, not just anybody. We've talked every day for the past month."

"And that's all we're ever gonna do, don't you get that?"

"Why?" I practically shouted, grateful for the closed door. "Why is that all? Why should *that* be all? Is it, do you think I won't like how you look? Is that it? Because I *would*. I *know* I would."

"Christ," he groaned. "That is the farthest thing from it, okay? I'm not worried about that."

"Then what is it?"

I was becoming agitated now. He wasn't the only one getting pissy and ruining the mood.

"What is it, Brian?" I pressed, teeth clenched.

"I don't want to know you! I can't, all right?"

Breath pulled from my lungs as if someone were sucking it straight out of me.

I blinked at a knob on my dresser, body stilled. Deadened.

He didn't want to know me.

God . . . that hurt.

Worse than Marcus pulling away. How was that possible?

My head snapped right when Tori knocked sharply on the door.

"You ready?" she called from behind it.

"Fuck, Wild," Brian breathed in my ear, heavy and sad sounding. "I didn't mean it like that. Okay? That's not—"

"I'm done talking to you right now," I cut him off and stood, walking over to my shoes and stepping into them. "I need to finish getting ready for the Lady Gaga concert, and Tori is ready so I need to finish now. You don't want the picture I sent? Delete it. Problem solved."

I bent down and slid the straps behind my heels.

He was being a total jerk. I didn't like it one bit.

Tori knocked again.

"Hon? Time to go."

I gathered my purse and studded cuff off the bed and gripped the phone tightly.

"Good-bye, Brian," I said curtly.

"Syd..."

I disconnected the call and switched my phone to vibrate mode, already feeling it shudder to life inside the confines of my purse when I took the steps to open the door and got a look at my best friend.

She wore a black sleeveless leotard with fishnets and combat boots. And she was rocking that red lipstick like a pro.

Totally fierce.

"All good?" Tori asked, stepping back so I could move into the hallway.

I hid my bleeding heart behind a smile, nodded, then took her hand.

"All great."

* * *

The concert was amazing, jam-packed and theatrical.

It was also incredibly distracting.

I stopped thinking about my conversation with Brian five minutes in and danced without a care between sweaty bodies, screaming lyrics at the top of my lungs with my hands raised and my head thrown back.

I seriously needed to send Mr. Rivera a gift basket or something.

Most fun I'd ever had in a little black dress.

We were floor level, standing room only, so when a slower song cut on halfway through the show, Tori and I leaned into each other, arms wrapped around hips and bodies angled, supporting weight.

It was the start of the second verse when I felt the vibration at my thigh from where my purse dangled off my shoulder.

I debated not looking for the whole second it took me to pull out the phone and check the screen, expecting another message or missed call from Brian, he had racked up four in total, but seeing Joyce's name flashing rhythmically instead.

She was an old co-worker of mine at my job back in Raleigh. Nice woman. Baked the best cherry-almond cookies at Christmastime.

It was strange she was calling me, though. Maybe something terrible had happened to someone I used to work with.

God, I hoped not.

I slid out of Tori's hold, motioned to her I needed to take a call, then pressed Answer but didn't speak into the phone until I pushed through the crowd and made it up the stairs, past security at the fence and onto the gravel parking lot surrounding the outdoor arena, where the chances of hearing her seemed most promising.

"Hey, Joyce," I finally greeted her, feeling the pop of gravel beneath my feet as I meandered aimlessly.

"Hey, sweetie. Um...look, this might not be any of my business, but I just wanted to give you a heads-up. You know, woman to woman. This was a bitch move if you asked me."

"Okay," I chuckled, ignorant to where this conversation was headed.

She pushed out a breath.

"I saw Marcus picking up Christine after her shift."

Christine was another one of my former co-workers, though we never officially worked together. I was day shift. She was night.

The most communication we'd shared was a friendly smile at the time clock during shift change.

Still...

"What?" I stopped meandering aimlessly. "When?"

"This morning. Wanted to call you sooner but I was running late and we've been slammed thanks to a ten-car pileup. I spotted his truck at the emergency entrance when I was parking, thought maybe you were back and things with him were patched over, gotta admit, that excited me. Between you and me, this place is now seriously lacking in decent techs, but then I saw Christine getting into the passenger's seat and she was doing it smiling. He leaned over and kissed her before taking off. I saw it."

I started breathing differently, quick bursts of air escaping as I locked my knees and focused on remaining upright.

"What a shit, right?" Joyce asked. "Her and him. You don't dip into your ex's company ink. That's just low."

"He's...do you know how long they've been seeing each other?" I asked, but in my heart I knew the answer to that question already.

It was his reason. Why he wanted out.

Marcus had an affair.

"I don't know, sweetie. You know I don't talk to her since we're on opposite shifts. This could've been going on for years for all I know." She paused, then quietly added, "I'm sure it wasn't that long."

I was going to puke all over Tori's designer dress.

Years?

"I have to go," I told her, speaking fast, my legs carrying me somewhere, I had no idea where, it felt directionless. I just needed to move. "Thank you for calling me, Joyce. I appreciate it."

"Sure thing, Syd. You know I got your back."

"I know. Thank you."

I hung up the call and scrolled through my contacts until I landed on the most deceitful name in the English language, didn't hesitate to dial even though I wasn't entirely sure I was strong enough to handle this conversation right now, but found the strength I needed in my anger and homed in on that as I pressed the phone to my ear and paced at the front of the darkened lot.

"You finally broke," Marcus answered after two rings, sounding all too pleased with himself. "Took you long enough, Syd. Jesus."

"What the *fuck*, Marcus!" I shrieked, uncaring of any audience I might have.

He was silent for a moment, then under his breath, I heard him mumble, "You know."

I felt his teeth tear into my heart and rip it open.

Pain replaced rage. Tears for temper.

"Joyce called me," I said brokenly with wet eyes. "She saw you two this morning, saw you kiss her. God, Marcus, you are such an asshole. It had to be someone I *knew*? Someone I *worked with*?"

"Hey, I didn't do shit with her until I ended things with you so get off my ass. I did right by you."

"You did *right* by me?" The hand at my side curled into a fist. "How? You cheated!"

"No, I fucking didn't!" he growled. "I waited, Syd. Saw Christine a few months back when I was visiting my mom after her surgery, Christine just happened to be doing an x-ray on her, got to talking a little and, yeah, I may have flirted but I didn't touch her until *after* you left. I wouldn't do that to you."

"Oh, you're such a decent guy, Marcus," I snapped. "You still *looked* at her."

"I had to look at her. She was working on my mom."

"That's not what I mean and you know it."

"Don't give me a fucking attitude like everything was perfect between us. You know it wasn't. We were drifting, Syd. We barely spoke anymore and we sure as hell weren't fucking. Things weren't good. The time we were spending together we spent bickering over bullshit. Christ, come on," he pleaded. "It wasn't fun anymore. You know it wasn't. Neither one of us was happy. So when a pretty girl showed me attention after I'd gone months without getting it from my own wife, I noticed, and I gave her that same attention back. It felt good."

"I can't believe this," I whispered. "You're saying this was *my* fault?"

"I'm saying I wasn't happy. You weren't either," he stated indifferently. "Found someone who could make me happy and I'm not about denying myself when shit at home wasn't worth being miserable over. We were done."

"We could've worked things out," I murmured, then blinked and sent the tears free-falling. "Fought for it."

"I was tired of fighting, Syd. So were you."

I closed my eyes.

He was right. I couldn't dispute it.

I had been tired, mind and heart exhausted in my marriage. I wasn't happy with the way things were but that didn't mean I was considering a life without my husband. I wasn't at that point a month ago.

But he was. He'd been there for God knows how long.

Reached that point and gone farther. He put it into motion.

He wandered.

"You weren't supposed to see anyone but me, Marcus. You promised, in our vows, remember? Only me." I inhaled through shattered breaths and spoke with tear-soaked lips as my eyes lost focus on a streetlamp. "But you looked at her. You looked at her when you were mine. How could you do that?"

"You weren't looking at me anymore," he answered guiltlessly. "I was just the first one of us to realize there was somewhere else to look."

I swallowed down the sick creeping up my throat.

This was cheating in my eyes, no matter how hard he disputed it. I knew how I felt and how much it hurt knowing the truth.

Ten minutes ago I hated my husband for cutting me loose without an explanation.

Now I hated him for not doing it sooner.

"Got the papers for you to sign. I'll put them in the mail tomorrow. Overnight them."

"You know where I am?" I asked, the backs of my fingers catching a tear.

"Tori's," he replied. "Christine said she heard you moved to Dogwood."

"Right." I rolled my eyes. "Thanks a lot for checking up on me, by the way. Nice to know you cared enough to make sure I was all right after seven years."

"We weren't happy together, Syd. Knew you'd be good once you got away. Same as me. I'm better now."

"Not gonna lie and say I'm glad to hear that, 'cause I'm not," I huffed.

"It's better for both of us. You'll see."

"Whatever. Send the papers. I'll sign them, then I don't ever want to hear from you or see your face again."

Marcus sighed. "This doesn't need to get ugly, Sydney."

Seriously?

Seriously...

I sucked in a breath.

"It got ugly the second you *cheated* on me, Marcus."

"I didn't cheat," he argued. "Lookin' and flirtin' ain't cheating."

"You're an idiot if you think that's true, and honestly? I'm glad I'm not tied to you anymore if these were your beliefs all along. God knows how much *lookin'* and *flirtin'* you've been doing behind my back over the years."

"Never hurt you, did it?"

My breath caught somewhere between my chest and my throat.

He'd been looking and flirting. All these years, he'd been doing it.

Oh, God...

Hand cupping my mouth and body trembling, I listened as he continued on enlightening me of his ways.

"Way it is, Syd. As long as it's not taken a step further, nothing wrong with it."

Nothing wrong with it.

Those were his thoughts, ones he never felt the need to share with me.

This conversation was over.

"Send the papers," I whispered with fresh tears in my eyes, lowered the phone while hopefully disconnecting it—I couldn't know for sure because I couldn't see anything through my veil of watery suffering—pushed the device into my purse, and spun around on weak footing, moving with devastated purpose to get back under the pavilion and to my best friend before I collapsed right there in the middle of the parking lot.

Tears were falling steadily now. My body jerking with each cry-filled breath I took.

I could barely see.

It was dark. My makeup was running and hindering my sight and I was moving faster than my heels safely allowed.

I needed Tori.

Between a blink and a sniffle, I slammed straight into a wall of a chest, large and unmoving, not seeing it come out of nowhere if it did or maybe I ran at it unintentionally when I could've avoided it, I had no way of knowing.

I was dizzy with sadness. Pain and hurt and shock filled my veins and twisted my awareness.

The man didn't speak. I didn't either, because I couldn't.

I fell, hand to mouth into him as his arms swallowed me up and his presence surrounded me then folded in, bringing me closer at the same time as I burrowed deeper and broke into a thousand tears.

It wasn't awkward. I didn't pull away. Neither did he.

Makeup smeared and saliva soaking. He didn't seem to care.

He held on.

And I pressed closer.

Marcus ate my heart, piece by hope-filled piece during a five-minute phone call.

I couldn't feel its beat anymore, and I was finding comfort in this stranger's arms; his shape and smell and size became my security and safe place. I was taking what he gave and he was giving it selflessly, holding on as I held tighter, my one hand clutching his shirt as his soothed in slow movements up and down my spine.

The harder I cried, the firmer his hold became.

The more my body shook with sadness, the stronger he stood.

I never saw his face. I never even looked up.

I fell apart and he held me through it. Then I left him without uttering a word.

* * *

An hour later Tori and I were back at her place, even though the concert was still going strong and we both knew it wasn't ending before midnight. It didn't matter.

She saw my face when I got back under the pavilion, heard what Marcus did from my lips pressed to her ear, and ended our night.

Best friends knew when it was time to leave.

I told her I just wanted to be alone, that I needed the quiet of my bedroom and the warmth of my bed, promising we'd talk about everything tomorrow.

She agreed only after my promise, kissed my cheek, and cued up HBO after stretching out on the couch.

Bedroom door closed and best friend occupied, I pulled my phone out of my purse and dialed Brian's number.

There were several things motivating what I was about to do, but one thing stood out and rippled awareness over and under my skin. I couldn't ignore it.

This was going to suck. Bad. There was no doubt in my mind. It was going to hurt, too.

Really bad.

But it had to be done.

"Wild," Brian answered gently.

That was all I could take of his voice.

"I can't do this anymore," I said, lip quivering.

I heard his pull of breath and knew he was about to speak, protest, plea, and I couldn't hear it so I kept going.

"I can't keep hoping and holding out, waiting for you to give me what I need, Brian, because I'll never stop waiting. You know? You said it yourself. You're just a voice and that's all you'll ever be to me and I can't, I'm not okay with that. I'll never be okay with that little of you."

"Send me pictures, Syd," he begged urgently. "Okay? You wanna send me pictures, send them. Send one right now. I wanna see you."

"This isn't about the picture," I stressed. "How many times have I asked where you live? Or if we could meet up? *That's* what I want, Brian. I want to see *you*. I want to see how you smile and feel your hands against mine. I want to lie next to you and dream with you and I *can't*. I'll...I'll never have that."

"I lie next to you every night. Don't you know that?"

I sobbed hard into my hand. My devoured heart reached for him.

"You got me, babe. Fuck...you've *had me*. When I was Wes, you had me."

When he was Wes...

I wiped tears away and spoke through broken breaths.

"Tonight, you know what I did?" I asked. "I let some stranger hold me and comfort me and I let myself *think* it was you. I imagined your arms and your breath in my hair and it was perfect, it was exactly what I needed because I *needed* it to be you, Brian. But it wasn't. It will never be you holding me or catching me. I'm gonna fall and you're not gonna be there."

"Syd..."

"No...No!" I dug my nails into my palm and held it at my side. "This is over. It's over, Brian. Don't call me again. Don't text me. I won't answer. I swear, I won't."

"Don't do this," he shot in, quiet and quick. "Please, Wild, don't...don't do this to me. To *us*."

"You did this, Brian," I shot back. "You did it, because I'm here. I'm *right here*, waiting, asking you for more like I've always asked you and I'm not gonna wait anymore."

"Sydney..."

"Good-bye, Brian."

"It was me!"

I blinked at the wall.

"What?"

"Holding you tonight," he explained, voice tight and anxious and filled with desperate, lying words. "It was me. Okay? It was *me*. No one else holds you."

I shook my head.

He wanted to believe it, too. Too bad that wasn't enough.

"Don't call me again," I whispered.

I held the power button down until the phone went black, let it drop out of my hand, and hit the floor, breaking, I hoped. I didn't want it anymore. Then I crawled in heels and washed-away makeup onto my bed and collapsed on my side, face pressed to the pillow and hand over my mouth.

It was over.

I didn't stop crying until morning.

Chapter Eleven

BRIAN

Hand moving furiously over my dick, knees bent and spread with muscles strung tight, I arched my back off the bed and came in four shots onto my stomach, grunting with jaw clenched and nostrils flaring.

Eyes closed and mind focused on one person. One image.

Wild.

She was beautiful, a chaos of crazy red and pale skin disguised.

Perfection that tortured and teased me.

My girl.

My *fucking girl*.

"Cut!"

My eyes opened. I exhaled irritation and hatred for this place.

Fuck them all. I wanted to burn this building to the fucking ground.

"Nice work, Dash," someone commented. It sounded like Eddie, the cameraman.

Slimeball. He'd jerk off half the time while filming, didn't care no one wanted to see that shit.

Fucking degenerate.

I ignored him and pushed my legs out, stretched, sat up, and wiped off with a towel someone had thrown on the bed, then swiped my clothes off the floor and tugged boxers, shorts, and tee on, arms sliding through the sleeves as I shoved through the crew hanging back to wrap up.

I never stuck around.

I came, collected, and got the fuck out of there.

Not bothering to knock on Mike's door this time 'cause I was on day two of no Wild and I was losing my goddamned mind over it, I pushed the door open and stepped into the office, ignored his whining protest of my disturbance and whoever the fuck else was in the room with him, snatched the cash he had laid out for me on the corner of his desk, counted it, turned without a glance in his immoral direction, and made for the door.

"Don't gotta be a dick about it, Dash," Mike tossed out at my back.

"Fuck off," I growled, slammed the door shut behind me, and crossed the room to get to the exit.

Demetrius was headed to the office, caught my eyes as we passed, and tipped his chin.

"Didn't think that shit was going to cut it, but you're killing it on the site, man. People love watching you whack off."

I ignored him, too. Didn't give a shit about hits on the site or anything else Demetrius had to tell me.

Didn't give a shit about anything except getting gone.

"Dash, you hear what I said?" he called when I reached the door.

I shoved it open and stalked outside, silent, exchanged the phone in my pocket for the wad of cash and scrolled to my recent calls, hitting Dial as I got to my Jeep.

My ass hit the leather the same time Sydney's voice mail kicked on.

Her phone was off. Knew it was and had been since Thursday night. I'd called it enough to know. Left plenty of messages for her, not knowing if she was getting them but figuring not, doubting she wanted to hear my voice if she was refusing to hear direct from me.

I was in hell.

Worse off than I was a month ago because I'd gotten a taste of something good and I'd forgotten what good tasted like, and worse, the good Sydney gave me was better than everything I'd had stripped away the night I fucked up.

Sydney's good filled my head and my heart. Blood warming and soul soothing. It pushed the deserving bad into a place I couldn't focus on or feel because she held my attention in the tips of her fingers and the ridges on her tongue. She made things sweet and right with her laughter and sleepy sighs, her stories through those stupid emojis she somehow made cute and charming and the way she'd whisper my name and pleas to God when her hand moved between her legs.

Her good was better. Better than I was worth and she knew it. *I* knew it.

Didn't change the fact I wanted her more than I could remember wanting anything. Ever.

How fucked up is that? I knew I didn't deserve her.

Didn't stop me from wanting, though.

The device cracked in distress when it struck the inside of the passenger door.

I started up the Jeep, pulled out of the lot with dust spilling off my tires, and headed to the one place I'd been fighting going to because I knew stepping foot in Whitecaps could seriously end it all for me, but I was desperate and stupid and *gone*.

Day two into my madness. I no longer gave a shit about consequences.

Throwing the gear into Park, I cut the engine and got out, the slam of the door still echoing in my ear as I ascended the stairs and tore inside the restaurant with eyes scanning for red.

It had been months since I came here. I couldn't remember the last time. Jamie frequented and Cole tagged along when he was free, but I usually kept to eating at the shop or picking somewhere within walking distance.

Once I found out Sydney worked here, I definitely stayed away.

"Hello, welcome to Whitecaps."

Not spotting who I was here for, I turned to the woman standing in front of me with a menu poised at the ready.

She was tiny. Chin-length dark hair held out of her face with a skull and crossbones bandanna, bright red lips, and black-lined eyes.

Vaguely, I thought I recognized her as one of the girls Wild was with the night she went Mike Tyson on a Corvette.

Her name tag read *Shay* in swirled purple and black marker.

"Sydney here?" I asked, watching her eyebrows slowly knit together.

"No, sorry, she called out. I think she's still sick." The woman drew the menu against her chest. "Are you friends?"

Still sick.

She wasn't sick. Not in the way this pocket-sized pixie was referring to. I knew that.

And knowing what happened between us was keeping Syd from a job I knew she loved more than her last one; on top of everything else I'd been feeling recently, I started feeling *sick* right along with her.

"Sir?"

I sighed and squeezed the back of my neck, then looked at the woman.

"No," I answered firmly.

We weren't friends. We weren't anything.

She smiled politely.

"Just one of you? Or are you waiting for people?"

I was already turned around and halfway to the door when I mumbled an obvious and unnecessary, "Not staying."

* * *

Beer number two in my hand, I leaned with elbows on the rail of my deck and stared out at the sunset-kissed waves over the light crowd settled on the beach.

Gorgeous night. Still hot as shit out, making the water a good temperature, I imagined.

Wasn't like I was getting in it and enjoying myself.

Called Syd three more times since I got home from Whitecaps an hour ago between doing a whole fuckuva lot of nothing else, and believe it or not, I was growing sick of the sweet voice I never thought I'd get enough of.

If she asked me one more fucking time to leave a message after the beep, I was going to kill someone.

I inhaled deep, searching for calm but coming up short.

I was on edge and standing out here wasn't helping. I should've known. Tried it yesterday and found no relief doing it, but I didn't have anything else, so here I was doing it again.

If I wasn't calling Syd, I was staring at her picture, and if I wasn't doing that, I was out here, phone inside and a safe distance away from the water, because I knew if I dialed her standing on the deck and she hadn't turned her shit on, I'd leave my message and then toss that fucker into the ocean.

Couldn't have that happen, could I?

Movement stirred my awareness, and I slid my eyes to it. I spotted Jamie walking back to the house with his board under his arm.

"What up?" he yelled from below, propping his board against a post and taking the stairs rapidly.

I shook my head with the bottle to my lips, swallowed some Corona, and kept looking out at the water.

Jamie hit the planks below my feet and strolled my way.

"Fuck, Dash. You get some incurable STD from one of those bitches or somethin'? Shit."

I turned my head to Jamie. "What?"

"Look at you." He came to a stop a foot away, jutted his chin at me, then pushed salty wet hair out of his eyes. "You're making *me* depressed, man, and I don't even get remotely sad, you know that, but I'm on the brink. The fuckin' brink, Dash. What's up with you?"

I cut my eyes away.

"Nothing," I mumbled.

"Bullshit," he shot back, sounding a second away from throwing a punch and, thus, earning my eyes again. "You've been moping around the past two days, barely speaking to anyone including customers at work, who even after that shit went down four months ago, you still kept it professional and did your job, spoke to *everybody* who stopped in and acted like you wanted to be there. Now you're barely doin' that. If it keeps up, me or Cole are gonna have to start droppin' lessons so we can hang around and make sure shit is gettin' sold."

"You sayin' you have to babysit me?" I asked, straightening then and facing him head-on.

Might be me throwing the first punch.

I was bigger than Jamie. A little thicker in the arms and shoulders, but he was quick like a fucking feral cat and the same height as me.

It'd be a good matchup.

Jamie didn't waver when I changed my stance and kept my gaze as he spoke.

"I'm sayin' something's up with you and it's different than what's *been up* with you the past four months. Shit, you were getting better. And I wasn't the only one noticing. Cole brought it up last week sayin' you were acting like the old Brian and you might be ready to paddle out soon."

"That's not fuckin' happening," I bit out.

"Yeah, I figured," he replied, arms crossing over his chest, still dripping water. "Not that I agree with that decision but I fuckin' get it."

"Great. Glad you get it."

I took another pull of my beer while Jamie stared at me, saying nothing for a solid four seconds.

Probably a record for him.

"It's a girl," he stated, head cocked, still staring.

I stared right back, not uttering a word.

He smiled.

Shit.

Asshole and his fucking gut instinct. Never failed him in the water or on land.

I should've stayed inside and kept on hitting Redial.

"It's a woman," Jamie clarified, finger pointed at my face. "You're fucked up over some pussy, that's what this is. Who is it? One of the girls you've shot with? Jayden? I bet it's Jayden. You've been seeing her?"

I glared at my idiot best friend.

"Do me a favor? Stay off the site my dick is visible on."

"Whoa." His brows drew together as he leaned back. "I'm strictly there for the lesbian love. Never seen your dick. Don't plan on seeing it. Videos are labeled, so thank fuck for that. Knew you shot with Jayden a couple weeks ago and put two and two together. That's all."

"It ain't Jayden. Ain't none of the ones on the site," I informed him, eyes narrowing to add, "You call my girl *pussy* again and I'll beat the shit outta you."

His face relaxed.

"Damn." He blinked several times, a laugh crackling in his chest. "You're hard up. Who is she?"

I exhaled slowly.

Didn't see the point in keeping this shit to myself anymore. Not when I no longer had it.

"Think you know her," I said, setting my bottle on the rail. "That girl you're always going to see at Whitecaps…"

Jamie stepped closer, halting me.

"You're fuckin' *seeing* Legs?"

"I'm talking about her friend, jackass. Back up."

He backed up, but he did it looking ready to tear my flesh off if I didn't explain quick who I was specifically talking about, conclusively eliminating Legs as an option.

I wasn't the only one pining for someone.

"Girl's name is Sydney. She works with Tori. Lives with her, too."

"Who?"

"Legs," I grated impatiently.

"Not her," Jamie snapped. "Christ, I know her fucking name. Just 'cause I don't call her by it doesn't mean I don't hear it every time she shoves it down my throat. I'm talking about yours. Which one is she?"

"She just started a month ago. Red hair…"

"Oh…yeah, okay." His mouth twitched. "I know who she is. Bit nicer than her friend, though she kinda sucks at waitressing. Woman is constantly messing up my order." He lost the smile and studied me. "How'd you meet her? You never go to Whitecaps."

I hesitated answering and turned back to the water, took another swig of beer, this time finishing it off, swallowing, then held it over the railing and dropped it into the trash can we kept below for such purpose.

I hesitated for one reason I wasn't sure I wanted to disclose.

I was gone for a woman I'd never fucking met.

Pathetic?

Maybe.

Did I give a fuck when that shit was kept personal?

Not one damn bit.

But I was about to blow the lid off and air it out, confide in my friend, who could very easily bust my balls over this indefinitely.

I stayed silent for a minute, then decided to hell with it. Again, what the fuck did I have left to lose at this point?

Let him talk shit. Let everyone.

Like I said before, I no longer cared about consequences. So I told him everything about Syd. Every fucking thing. I didn't leave nothing out.

And he listened, taking it all in while remaining silent and looking surprised at some of the shit I was saying, but also looking like he got some of it, too. He understood.

I knew that when I reached the end and Jamie finally spoke.

"This girl was healing you," he offered quietly.

I shrugged.

She was. Didn't know how it was possible coming from a girl I couldn't even get to, but she was.

"Know what you need, man?"

"Yeah? What's that?"

He gripped my shoulder, attracting my attention then, and once he got it, he grinned with self-satisfaction brightening in his eyes.

I glared. "What?"

"Saturday night. We ain't got shit to do." He dropped his hand and shrugged. "Might as well throw a party."

That was the last thing I needed.

"I don't want a bunch of assholes in my house."

"You need a distraction and a bunch of assholes is a good distraction," he argued. "We'll get some kegs, play some beer pong, I'll get laid a couple times." He smiled. "It'll be good for everybody."

I shook my head.

"Not in the mood for this," I said, giving him a hard look. "Seriously, man."

Bastard wasn't hearing me. Knew he wasn't—he was grinning like an idiot and already planning shit in his head. I could tell.

Once Jamie had his mind set on something, that was it.

I was going to have a bunch of assholes in my house.

"It's happenin', Dash. Gonna be a fuckin' blast, too. You'll see." Jamie took a few steps backward in the direction of the slider, hit me with a chin jerk, then turned his back on me, speaking as he walked toward the house, "I'll get Cole on invite duty. He'll get the word out. BYOP."

I shook my head.

Bring Your Own Pussy.

Fuck.

Chapter Twelve

SYDNEY

I felt the couch dip near my feet.

Tori's hand found my ankle through the Christmas quilt covering me and gave it a squeeze.

"Just wanted you to know," she began in a gentle voice, hand still wrapped around my ankle. "I'm seriously debating driving to Raleigh and setting your old house on fire with Marcus trapped inside, so speak now if you got any attachment to that house or the things in it because once I light the match, I'm following through."

Tori was reacting to the vegetative state I'd adopted since Thursday night, fetal position on a comfy surface, which I switched up every few hours, going between the couch and my bed, thinking it was stemming from the phone call with Marcus and thinking that because it was the only thing I informed her of when she crawled beside me in bed Friday morning and we had our talk. She still had no idea about Brian, our history, or our ending, so the blame for my depression was fully and solely on Marcus and now she was getting creative in her act of retaliation against him.

Yesterday morning she wanted to chew him out on the phone. Last night she thought about sending a hateful letter.

Today she wanted to burn him alive.

Knowing Tori, it would only escalate from there, though I wasn't sure how you could go bigger than killing someone and doing it painfully, but I was sure she'd come up with something.

My lashes brushed the fibers of the quilt as I stayed blanketed and curled up on my side.

"I don't think there's anything in that house I'd miss," I replied honestly.

Hell, I'd even light the match myself.

"Just wait until next weekend before you kill him," I requested. "I'd like him to see my signature on those separation papers first and they won't go out until Monday."

I got the envelope in the mail today. Marcus overnighted the papers like he said he would and I signed them without hesitation.

We were now officially separated.

If I had it in me, I'd do a little dance in celebration of that fact.

I did not have it in me.

"I can do that," Tori obliged. "I'm thinking we need to drag out his death. Make it last as long as possible. I'd hate for Marcus to suffocate on the smoke before the flames hit him so that'll require me going in there and putting some sort of a cover on his face, a mask or something, like the military use. I bet my dad could get his hands on one for me."

"He's the best."

"Right? I just love him." Her hand gave me another squeeze.

I closed my eyes and breathed deep.

"I am seriously pissed off, hon. Nobody does this to my best girl," Tori added, the couch dipping more as she leaned closer, putting pressure on my feet. "You were upset when you first got here, understandably so, but you were getting better. You know? You *got better*. Being away from Marcus and all his negativity, you were my silly, fun-loving Syd again, laughing and playing and smiling all the time. Finding *your* happiness and living *your* life. Now that dipshit has taken my girl away from me again, and I'm so mad I am actually planning out my last meal in prison 'cause I know I'm gonna get the death penalty after I take him out, but doesn't matter. I'm doing it. He deserves to pay and pay good. I mean, really, Syd, look at you. I haven't seen your head since Thursday night. You're constantly being swallowed up by a blanket."

"I'm fine."

Lie. I was the farthest from fine I'd ever been. I knew it and so did Tori.

"You'll *be* fine," she argued. "I know you will. Being here, away from him, just like before, you'll be fine. It just might take a little longer but you'll get there."

Tori thought she had it all figured out, that I'd found my happiness on my own, and since I did it already, I could do it again, but that was just it.

I hadn't found my happiness on my own.

I had Tori, and yeah, being with her every day helped, my new job and the friends I'd met here, Shay and Kali, but I'd had someone else, too.

And since Tori hated Marcus now to the point of death plotting and most likely wouldn't have an issue with me feeling things for someone else, it was time I crawled out from behind my secret and shared it with her.

I was numb enough. If she ended up hating me for a few days, I might not even feel it.

I sat up and let the blanket slip down over my shoulder, gathering the cocoon I'd inhabited around my waist as I twisted on the couch and sat knee bent, foot resting beneath my thigh, and body angled to face her.

She looked super pretty in a soft yellow strapless sundress and a red lip, her hair twisting loose in beach-water waves.

I was wearing leggings and a UNC hoodie, hadn't brushed my hair since yesterday, and my eyes were swollen from tears shed.

Sweet blues roamed my face, shining upbeat.

"There you are," Tori said, smiling lightly. "Forgot you had all that red under there."

I quickly finger-combed my hair.

God, I needed a mirror.

And a toothbrush.

Tucking chunks of tangled red behind my ear and swiping my

tongue over my teeth, I prepared myself for confession, taking a few deep breaths and reaching for Tori's hand.

"I need to tell you something," I began, watching her scoot closer and feeling her hand tighten around mine.

I held on tighter, wet my lips, and got on with it.

"I've felt different over the past month. Happier. You saw it. I was just...better in a lot of ways I think, and I know a lot of that had to do with being here with you and meeting everyone at work, but there was something else helping me, getting me there a lot quicker than I was expecting and making me feel things I haven't felt in a *really* long time. Maybe ever."

"Oh, God," Tori whispered, suddenly looking concerned. "Are you hooked on something?"

"What?"

She pulled my hand into her lap, jerking me forward.

"I watched this Lifetime movie a couple months ago about a woman who was down on her luck, recently divorced due to the loss of a child; and it being too much for her and her husband to handle together, they split up. Then one night, she went out to this club and got hooked on smack."

I pulled my hand back, taking hers with me and keeping them between us.

"I am not hooked on smack," I hissed. "I don't even know what that is. What is it?"

"I think it's a combination of crack and crank. Or it could be heroin." She moved to get off the couch. "I'm gonna Google it."

"Wait a minute." I tugged her back down.

My best friend was crazy.

"I am not taking any drugs. That's not what I'm trying to tell you."

Tori studied me, soundless for a second.

"I've been talking to someone," I finally admitted.

"Like a therapist?" she asked, eyes lighting up. "That's great!"

I blinked heavily and sighed.

"No, like a *man*," I replied, watching her brows slowly knit together. "I've been talking to this guy and not in a billing your insurance type of way, okay? We've been...sort of dating, exclusively on the phone, I guess, just talking a lot but it's done now. We're not anymore. It all ended Thursday night."

Because he didn't want to know me.

I fought tears, slumped sideways, and fell into the couch, resting my heavy head on the cushion.

"I miss him so much," I whispered. "If Marcus hadn't eaten my heart I'd swear it was breaking."

Tori's mouth dropped open.

"You've been dating someone?" she asked, shocked voice barely above a murmur. "Who is it? And when did you have time to meet him? All you do is work."

I wiped at my face with my sleeve.

"You're not mad at me?"

"What? Why would I be mad at you? You were happy."

My lip twitched. I loved this girl. Seriously.

Tori dropped her head on the cushion beside her shoulder, mimicking my position, then continued on to say, "And I'm sure whatever reason you had for keeping this to yourself was a good one and not something I would be mad at you for. That being said, you owe me a month's worth of details and you're not allowed to skip over anything. That means I get to hear *everything*, juicy stuff and all, starting with who this guy is and how you met."

She had a point. I owed her a lot, and since I did the shitty thing by keeping this from her, the least I could do was share a few details.

Even the private ones.

"Remember that guy I accidentally dialed thinking he was Wes?"

Her eyes widened.

"Him?"

I nodded.

"He texted me the next day and it just...went from there. Quickly. Texting and talking, every day, sometimes multiple times, for hours."

"You gotta be kidding me," she murmured.

"It was fast but it was easy," I continued. "Like, *really easy*. I could talk to him about anything. He knew about Marcus, I told him, and he was good about taking my mind off of it, making me laugh and stuff. And the things he would say to me, Tori, it was like he really cared about me, like he wanted me to be happy more than anything and it just *got* to me. You know? I started really caring for him, thinking about him all the time, what he looked like, where he was, if he was thinking the same way about me. I know I had feelings for him. A lot of feelings, especially after we started doing stuff on the phone together."

I gave her a look then, indicating my meaning, and it came across loud and clear, Tori's mouth pinching together thinly and her cheeks flushing.

"It was sudden and probably too fast, I know it was, which is why I kept it from you, but I really wanted to know him. Like...*know him*. Talk to him in person and do all the other stuff we were already doing but *really* do it. More than anything, I wanted that. More than I wanted to patch things over with Marcus." I swallowed thickly, eyes lowering. "But Brian didn't. Told me so Thursday night. Said he didn't want to know me. That's the last time we spoke."

"He actually said that to you? That he didn't want to know you, he said those words?"

"Yep."

"Did he have a reason?" she asked, tugging my hand a little and raising my eyes.

When I caught hers, I replied, "Did he need one?"

She frowned.

He didn't. Tori knew it and so did I.

Having a reason wouldn't change anything. It could be the noblest reason on earth and it wouldn't lessen the pain I was feeling or make any of this better. Besides, whatever it was, if Brian had something driving his decision to keep me out, it still had *everything* to do with me.

He didn't want to know *me*.

Tears filled my eyes as I mumbled, "I really *really* liked him, Tori."

"Oh, hon. I'm sorry." She gave my hand a squeeze. "I really wish you would've told me. I never would've thought anything making you *that* happy would've been wrong or too fast. Not ever, okay?"

I gave her a weak smile, sniffling.

"That being said, you know how crazy this is, right? I mean, aside from the fact you've been engaging in phone sex with a man you've never met before, you totally asked him during that first conversation if he liked to get fucked hard and deep, not to mention requesting he take the dildo out of his mouth you figured he was sucking on, and he *still* wanted to talk to you again." Her eyes bugged. "You must've really made an impression, Syd."

I had. In hindsight I believe Brian thought I was amusing, even though I was going for total badass bitch that night, one who shouldn't be messed with.

Tori thought I was badass, so I felt good about it.

"I don't think he'd been talked to like that before," I offered. "I'm guessing it intrigued him."

"I don't think *a lot of men* have been talked to like that before," Tori countered. "Seriously. You were scary." She twisted her body a little until her back was touching the cushion.

Eyes directed at the bay window, she let out a heavy breath and kept hold of my hand, resting the pair of ours between us.

"He made you my Syd again," she murmured.

I nodded, even though she wasn't looking at me, curled my fingers around the back of her hand, and tightened my hold.

"Since we're sharing stuff, I guess I should share with you a decision I made yesterday that I kept to myself because you were so sad over Marcus, which"—Tori turned her head and looked at me—"I'm guessing now, your sadness might've had more to do with the other guy and not the man I've been plotting to kill?"

"Probably," I answered, blinking tears away.

Definitely.

My marriage was over, yet I was mourning the loss of Brian's voice more than my united in holy matrimony relationship.

He had the best voice. Hands down, best I'd ever heard.

And he chose the most perfect words to manipulate with it.

"Should've told me," Tori stressed. "I could've been plotting two murders and saved myself the time. Now I have a dilemma on my hands because I kind of like the other guy, seeing as he gave me back the old you and, thus, has potential. Marcus never had any potential so his death is an easy choice."

I smiled faintly, watching her turn away.

"What's the decision?" I asked her.

"Still deciding it," she answered. "Sheesh, give me at least five minutes."

"Not that." I tapped our conjoined hands against her thigh. "The one you decided yesterday."

"Oh." She cleared her throat, twisting the fingers of her free hand in the hem of her dress.

Uh-oh. Tori was anxious.

This was big. It had to be. Tori never showed signs of nervousness. Not even in her pageant days.

And my assumption was only confirmed when she played it down with the first thing out of her mouth.

"Well, it's really not a huge deal or anything. I was just doing a little thinking regarding my no more boys rule and thinking that was probably a hasty decision considering my state at the time and, um, you know, Wes isn't *all* boys. He's one horrible, worthless piece of shit, but does not sum up the entirety of the male race, even though there are several others who fall into that category, Marcus included. Also, that kid Jace I was *talking to* in seventh grade who dumped me at the Valentine's Day dance. I'm sure he's still a winner."

I pulled my lips between my teeth and let Tori continue on without any interruption, even though I was on the brink of giggles.

"Anyway, my point is, I've gone about a month without any boys and I miss them, my girl parts *really* miss them, and it's about time I did something about it."

"You're gonna start dating again?" I asked, watching her head snap my way.

"Dating? No. I'm just talking about getting laid." Tori smiled a little, appearing excited. "And I've already picked out lucky bachelor number one."

"Who?"

"Jamie McCade."

"*What?*" I peeled away from the couch. "Hello! You hate that guy, remember? He doesn't respect love. I've been screwing up his order for weeks."

Not to mention getting Stitch to do god-awful things to his food, things I didn't ask about because I was almost too afraid he'd take me out to eliminate any possible incriminating evidence linking him to whatever illness Jamie contracted after eating at Whitecaps.

Now Tori wanted to fuck him?

"I know, but he's *stupid* gorgeous, Syd. The hair, the dimples, that look he had on his face slicing Wes's tires that night and not giving a damn about going down for it."

I kept my mouth shut. Couldn't really argue with any of that.

Jamie had a really good look that night.

Tori's phone started ringing in the distance. It sounded like it was coming from the kitchen.

"And besides," she continued, standing from the couch and turning to face me. "*I am using *him* for sex. I will have the upper hand the entire time, and when it is over, I'll never look at his stupidly gorgeous face again. One and done. That's all I need."

She moved around the couch quickly, darting in the direction of the kitchen.

One and done? With the ex-J.Crew model who yielded a switchblade like a greaser and defended Tori's honor?

Yeah. I wasn't holding my breath.

"I hope you know what you're doing," I shouted out, then collapsed back on the couch, slid down onto my hip with my knees pulling up and my arm bent, head resting on the inside of my bicep.

I started pulling up the quilt, getting ready to return to my former cocooned position, when Tori's animated shriek coming from behind yanked me upright again, head spinning around so I could watch her strut back into the living room with her phone in her hand and a brilliant smile on her face.

"Looks like it's gonna happen a lot sooner than I thought," she stated, twirling and fanning out her dress.

What in the world?

"Huh?"

Tori wiggled the hand holding her phone in front of her and stepped closer.

"That was Shay. She got word on a massive party Jamie is having at his beach house, which I've heard is ridiculous. Not that I gave a damn about it before, but since I'm planning on bedding him and he's giving me an opportunity to make that happen tonight, I give a damn about seeing it now. And you're going."

I shook my head and pulled the quilt around me.

"I'm really not in the mood for a party, Tori."

I wasn't in the mood for anything besides this quilt and a comfy surface I could burrow into.

She tilted her head and dropped her hand.

"I need my wing woman, hon."

"No you don't," I argued. "Jamie will totally want to have sex with you the second you walk in his house. You won't even have to speak."

She pressed her hands together in a praying position the best she could, given she still had hold of her phone, stuck her bottom lip out, and pleaded.

"Please. You're my best girl. I need you."

I wasn't budging. Tori saw it.

I drew the quilt over my head, making it so my face was the only thing showing, and blinked at her.

Tori sighed and looked at the ground beside the couch.

"Okay, but you're gonna be missing out on seeing Shay and Stitch together for the first time outside of work..."

"What?"

Her eyes sliced to mine.

"Stitch and Shay are making their debut appearance together as a couple at this thing?" I asked, building height on my knees and letting the quilt slide down my back.

They weren't a couple. Not officially, and if you asked Shay or had the nerve to ask Stitch, she denied it and he ignored you, but Kali, Tori, and myself all knew better.

They were totally into each other.

"Sort of," Tori replied, her shoulder lifting with a jerk. "Shay invited him and she's hoping he shows. I'm thinking since this is the first time she's invited him to anything and he's probably been chomping at the bit waiting for such an invite, he's gonna show."

My decision was made. I knew I couldn't miss an opportunity like this for the world.

I sprung from the couch and let the quilt fall to the floor.

"Okay, I'm in, but I'm not changing," I told Tori, tugging on the bottom of my hoodie. "I'm not going to impress anybody so I don't see the point."

She grinned big.

"You look super cute and comfy in that so I agree, don't change."

"Great."

"But maybe comb your hair a little." She cringed through her suggestion. "It looks like rats were building a nest in the back."

My eyes widened as I reached back and felt the tangled mess Tori was referring to.

I could barely feel my scalp.

Needless to say, I combed my hair before we left for the party.

* * *

Tori was right. Jamie's beach house was ridiculous, at least from what I could tell from the outside.

It had to be the size of at least three of her houses, and in my eyes, Tori always had the best of the best.

This was crazy big.

And absolutely stunning.

Two stories and right off the beach, so close you could hear the waves crashing—it was like having your ear pressed to a seashell— the house looked front cover of a magazine worthy or something you'd rent for the weekend with twenty of your friends.

A gorgeous wraparound porch made of white worn wood seemed to be the home for multiple multicolored surfboards, all propped against aged earthy green siding and, above it, another porch for the second level, this one acting more like a deck for the front of the house.

I couldn't imagine having my own deck access from my bedroom. I was just thrilled to have a window facing the ocean.

The driveway was filled with vehicles, and so was the yard, for that matter. People had pulled right off the road and onto Jamie's half-sand, half-grass terrain, including Tori, who drove us.

I followed her up the front steps and inside, the door swinging open freely. Bodies filled the wide-open entryway. The house somehow appeared bigger on the inside, with rooms off to the right and left, one looking like an office I imagined didn't see much use and the other possibly a formal dining room, except in place of a standard table, a pool table sat in the middle of the floor.

A game was going on while girls in bikini tops and jean cutoffs danced to some bass-heavy tune off to the side, dropping low and popping their hips.

I was slightly overdressed in my hoodie and leggings but it didn't matter. I wasn't planning on dropping low or popping anything.

Straight ahead was an extra-wide staircase leading up to the second level. You could walk around it and enter another part of the house, which was the direction Tori was headed as I followed close behind her.

"Is Shay here yet?" I yelled over the music as we walked past a speaker, tugging on Tori's wrist.

"She texted when we got here. Stitch stood her up so she isn't coming."

I halted in the hallway, which in the process halted her.

"You got a text before we left the house. Not five seconds ago," I pointed out through a hiss.

Tori turned her head to look at me.

"Same difference," she said, smiling a little.

Damn it!

"Tori!"

God, I could kill her. She knew I didn't want to come to this.

Tori twisted her arm, broke out of my hold, only to grab my elbow and give it a jerk, pulling me behind.

"Come on, Syd. You needed to get out of the house anyway. You were starting to attach to the furniture."

"I was not," I snapped but I did it weakly.

I kind of was. Or at least I was on my way to attaching to the Christmas quilt. I was starting to drag that thing around everywhere like Linus with his blanket.

We moved around the staircase and stepped into a large room that seemed to span the length of the house, with floor-to-ceiling windows giving view to another deck that also ran the length. A huge, open kitchen was off to the left, one I was certain Martha Stewart would cut a bitch for. It was gorgeous even from a distance. I thought I spotted two ovens, *two ovens*, before my eyes moved through the rest of the room, occupied mostly by a large seating area—a comfy-looking sectional and two recliners facing a giant flat-screen TV mounted above a fireplace.

I was calculating how rude it would seem if I curled up on that sectional and stayed there the rest of the night when Tori nudged me with her elbow, grabbing my attention.

"There he is," she said.

I followed her eyes across the room.

Jamie was standing at a rectangular table littered with red plastic cups, a game of beer pong going on, which he appeared to be participating in. He was focused on it, his arm around the waist of a scantily dressed blonde, all tits and ass hanging out of a bikini, no shorts, who was up on her toes pressing kisses to his neck.

Or at least she was.

Eyes lifting from the game, Jamie spotted Tori a second after I spotted him, released the neck kisser like she was on fire, and grabbed a cup before moving purposely through the crowd.

I might as well have been attached to a piece of furniture at that point. He didn't notice my presence at all.

"What up, Legs," he greeted Tori with a sexy, all-knowing smile, hair tussled and a cigarette tucked behind his ear, coming to a stop when he entered her personal space. "Surprised you're here. Thought you hated me, babe."

Tori plucked the cup out of his hand, brought it to her mouth, and downed it, thrusting it against his chest when she was finished and licking the residue off her lips.

"I do," she replied, but she said it over her shoulder as she walked away and in the direction of the kitchen, giving Jamie eyes that screamed, *Come and get me*, with hips swaying heavily.

"Fuck yeah," he mumbled, and was about to follow her when someone yelled behind me, turning his head and then, on his own, lowering it, spotting me for the first time.

His sexy smile turned soft and slow lip-curling, like something was jogging his memory.

I waved and attempted a smile, though I was sure it came out looking more like a quirky frown.

I wasn't much for smiling these days.

"It's you," he said, eyes roaming my face. "Sydney, right?"

I gave him an odd look.

Idiot.

I waited on Jamie every time he came into Whitecaps because Tori refused to do it, and every single time, I went through my standard greeting, politely introducing myself, yet here he was, acting like I hadn't told him my name at least ten times before.

Why were pretty boys so stupid?

"Uh, yeah," I replied, awkwardly cutting my eyes away because he was now full-on staring. "Nice house. Seems like a lot for just one person."

"I have a roommate," he replied, undisclosed humor in his voice. "You should meet him. He's around here somewhere, sulking over some girl he's completely fuckin' gone for. Messed up big with her and now he's miserable, killin' the mood and shit."

Why was he telling me that? What did I care about his room-mate's relationship issues?

Idiot.

"Bet you could cheer him up," he added.

I cut my eyes back to Jamie.

He was still smiling, doing it more obvious now.

Bet I could cheer him up.

Yeah. I knew exactly what that meant.

Random sex with a stranger was the last thing on my mind.

I shoved my hands into the front pocket of my hoodie and twisted my fingers together.

"I think I need a drink," I said, wetting my lips.

Alcohol, the curer of all heartaches.

Jamie held his arm out and, with his other hand holding the empty cup, directed me toward the kitchen with it pressed to my lower back.

"Help yourself. I'll be busy with Legs the rest of the night, so if you need anything, like I said"—he smiled down at me—"find my roommate."

"Right. Thanks."

I moved into the kitchen and over to the island, where every combination of girly beverage was on display.

Daiquiri mix in a blender, wine coolers, wine, Jell-O shooters.

I grabbed a cup and filled it with the cream-colored slush I assumed was piña colada flavored and took a sip, confirming that while my eyes scanned for Tori.

She was missing. So was Jamie.

I had a feeling he had either found her and they were off doing something together, naked and heavy breathing, or he was still trying to find her and hadn't gotten to his bedroom yet, which I imagined was where she was waiting, naked and on the verge of heavy breathing.

I cringed when someone cranked up the music.

The room was noisy without the extra background effects. Over the music, people were hollering and squealing, some were even singing along to song lyrics, and all of it was pressing on my brain and making my eyes hurt.

I moved to the slider and stepped outside onto the deck.

It was quieter and nowhere near as crowded as the inside of the house. A small group of people were sitting on lounge chairs and smoking. They were talking but they weren't hollering, so my head was already thanking me. Below, I could hear voices of people walking to and from the beach, which I got a better view of when I moved to the railing and looked out.

The view was beautiful. Salt water seasoned the air, and the shades of the setting sun painted the water in oranges and muddied reds.

I'd been in Dogwood a month and had been down to the ocean only once. Insane, right? I lived at the beach and I wasn't experiencing it.

It hadn't been a priority, and honestly, I didn't have a lot of free time on my hands.

When I wasn't picking up shifts at Whitecaps, I was talking on the phone to Brian, shut up in my room or doing it lying on the couch if Tori wasn't home.

Now I wasn't shut up in my room or lying on the couch, quilt-covered and heart-shattered. I was no longer talking on the phone to Brian and I wanted to see the ocean. I wanted to feel the sand beneath my feet and skim the waves with my hand.

I had tons of free time tonight while Tori got laid. Might as well make the most of it.

I took the stairs down a level and stepped out beneath the deck.

A couple was sitting on a hammock going at it like their boat was sinking, sloppy-suctioning kisses and need-filled moans spilling into the air.

There had to be a handful of empty rooms in that house. They couldn't pick one and save me the surround sound?

Gross.

I followed the sand-covered path down to the beach, taking small sips of my drink as I went. Deep voices grew louder the closer I got to the water. I wasn't paying much attention to them. I was looking ahead and forward to feeling the temperature of the ocean and maybe even finding a couple of pretty shells when the voices grew loud enough to hear clearly.

Very clearly.

That's when it happened.

I stopped, feet frozen and ears alert when one of the voices not only grew loud enough to focus on but also registered in my mind as a voice I'd possibly heard before.

"Don't know why I gotta keep repeating myself. It wasn't like that," the man said, sounding irritated. "She was sweet and good to talk to. Funny and cute about shit. Real cute. The fact that she was also a stunner didn't surprise me. I heard it in her voice. But for the last fuckin' time, and I mean this, I'm not saying it again, that's not what got me. I was fucked before I even saw her picture."

"You saying you were gone for a girl you never fucking met, Brian? Not possible," the other guy replied.

I sucked in a breath.

Brian.

A phantom heartbeat fluttered in my chest.

No way...

With gentle steps, I moved closer to the voices, reached the end of the path, and peeked around an overgrown bush, spotting the two men standing on the beach.

I watched the one guy, taller than the other, who had his back to me, cross his arms over his chest and say to his friend, "Yeah, that's what I'm saying. You talk to Sydney one fuckin' time and you'll know where I'm coming from. It was that fuckin' good."

I squeaked then. Not a gasp but a squeak I tried to conceal with a quick hand to my mouth, cup hitting the sand, but it was too late.

They both heard it.

Two pairs of eyes sliced in my direction. I stared back at the one pair coming from the one voice I *knew*, in my blood and my bones and the breath filling me, I knew that voice and the man it belonged to.

He stared back, eyes narrowing to focus better, focusing enough to make me out where I stood then going round and filling with surprise.

Pain lanced through me.

I wanted to run. To him or away, I didn't know which urge was stronger, and it felt like I was being pulled in both directions by forces I couldn't fight so I stood there, staring back as my hand uncovered my mouth and skimmed my throat.

"Brian?"

He was moving before I spoke, long legs closing in fast, and before I could blink, he was right in front of me, close enough to smell and *feel* if my eyes were closed but I definitely couldn't test that theory right now.

I stared unconsciously into his face, tilting my head back to do so and taking in every inch of him.

Dark hair buzzed close to his scalp, thick eyebrows and deep green eyes, several days' worth of stubble coating his jaw, which appeared sharp beneath it and full, perfect lips, parted as he breathed slow and heavily.

Beautiful.

I knew he was.

"Oh, my God," I whispered. "It's you."

He blinked, breath shuddering.

"You recognize me?" he asked.

I bit my lip to suppress a moan because, *God*, that voice. It melted my insides when it sweetly assaulted my ears and turned my bones to jelly. It always had but now, seeing the man behind it and the mouth responsible for it, watching it shape and twist those words so perfectly, I was *done*.

Done.

Toast.

A goner.

I blinked when he stepped closer.

"Syd," he pressed, eyes desperate as they searched mine.

"Holy shit. Are you the girl?"

The other man moved beside us and slapped his hand against Brian's back, who was keeping his eyes focused on me.

I looked to the friend and recognized Exhibit A from Whitecaps, who I now knew went by Cole.

"Uh," I answered.

I was in shock. Was he expecting me to speak?

Cole grinned.

"Small world," he chuckled, looking between us. "Small fucking world. I'll leave you two alone since you probably have a lot to talk about."

He gave me a wink then shuffled past me and disappeared down the path, doing just that. Leaving us alone.

I was alone . . . with Brian.

Oh, God.

Oh...*God*. Now what?

I looked up and met pleading greens, filled with desperation I could feel against my skin.

Questions and confusion swirled in my brain. My stomach was doing nothing but flips and excited little twists.

It was Brian. My body knew Brian and it was acting up impulsively, reacting to that smooth familiar voice and more, and when he reached out and held my face, thumb sweeping over my cheek as his lips whispered, "Wild," soft and ache-filled, I stopped thinking and feeling altogether and sprang, launching myself at him and into his arms, which curled instantly around me, drawing me nearer and higher until our mouths met in a kiss that hurt and healed so deeply my soul cried out.

Beautiful.

Knew it would be.

He kissed hard and I kissed harder, exploring every inch of his mouth as I whimpered with moaned-filled breaths that vibrated with hunger.

Brian was a great kisser. The *best* kisser, sure and practiced, and even though he was only the third guy I'd kissed in my entire twenty-four years of life, I was certain no lips matched up to this pair.

No tongue.

No teeth, knowing expertly when to nip and drag and *sink* until I cried out.

Strong hands moved down my back to my ass and gripped, lifting me until my legs wrapped around his waist and I felt him *there*, hard and heavy.

"Please," I whispered across his mouth.

Brian groaned, head tilting to kiss me deeper.

One hand settled on my ass and dug in so hard I thought he might shred my leggings while the other pushed through my hair, twisted into a grip, and held on at the base of my neck, his legs carrying us somewhere quickly while I raked my nails over his scalp and across his shoulders through his tee.

The light changed above us. I felt it on my eyelids, and opening them, I saw we were now under a pier, hidden from sight and more alone than we were a minute ago.

"We should talk," Brian suggested, pressing me against a post with lips grazing my jaw and lower, where he sucked openly on my neck.

"We will," I answered, and maybe it was the assurance I gave that we would have *something* after we fucked because that was absolutely what was about to happen, we both knew it, and it was enough of a promise to pacify and allow him to focus on latching his mouth back onto mine and using it to kiss instead of suggest differently.

Or maybe he felt as crazy as I did in that moment, Wild in every sense of the word, and he couldn't stand another second of missing my taste, setting me on my feet as our hands ripped and tugged and stripped each other of clothing then pressed and felt, touching everywhere for the first time. Breasts, hips, chest, waist, ass. We were frantic.

"God," I moaned, my head dropping back as he sucked on my nipple and around it, wetting my entire breast before moving to the other and teasing it unhurriedly with his tongue.

His hand moved surely between my legs, slowly finger-fucking me, and I felt his grin against my neck when I started grinding my hips, down and out, chasing something I wasn't sure I wanted to catch yet.

This felt too good. Too perfect to end but it got better the closer I got, the faster I moved and his hand, *God*, his hand was so much better than my hand it was almost unfair.

"Want you this gone when I fuck you," Brian said against my ear, sliding his thumb over my clit until I shook and gripped at his shoulders. "The whole time. So close I can feel your heartbeat *right here* like I do now."

Sweet Jesus. I was going to pass out.

"Okay," I breathed, licking my lips anxiously. "Not a problem, but can we get to the fucking now?"

He leaned back to look at me, eyes heavy and heated and lowering to my mouth.

"I should get something," he said, and I knew he was talking about a condom.

My legs tensed. I shook my head.

I was fucking crazy.

"Don't. I . . . I wanna feel you. It's okay."

I felt his body stiffen.

"Fuck," he rasped, looking into my eyes again. "You have any idea what you fucking do to me, Wild? Do you even have a clue?"

"I, I think so. I . . ." My breath caught with a moan when Brian moved his hand out from between my legs to the back of my thigh, where he gripped and lifted, sliding his hold to my knee as it wrapped around his hip.

He slid closer, dipped until I felt his cock glide through my wet and waited.

"What, babe? Finish telling me."

I bit my lip.

God, he was right there, teasing me, killing me, owning me.

"Wild," he urged.

The tip of his cock pressed hard against my clit.

I opened my mouth with a gasp and squirmed in his arms.

"I make you insane," I told him, quietly, shyly, as my body did the opposite and pushed out, silently begging for it.

"Yeah," he murmured, low and dark in his throat. He kissed the corner of my mouth, his breath hot and wanting when he asked, "Know why you know?"

I did. I knew, but I still probed.

"Why?"

Brian moved his hand between us, positioned his cock and slid in slowly, stretching me on a groan as my mouth fell open and my body shook in pure, perfect bliss.

"Oh, fuck," I whimpered.

"'Cause I make you insane, too," he answered finally, the answer I knew already in my heart, then pushed in the rest of the way and did it roughly, jarring my body and filling me with every inch of him, sliding out then slamming back in, over and over.

It was all I needed. It was everything I needed.

It was beautiful.

It was us.

And he was mine.

"Oh, God, yes. Fuck me," I cried out, grabbing on to his face and pulling it to me so I could suck that sweet, full bottom lip into my mouth, my other leg hitching up to his waist on its own but then being held there when he clutched on to it and rammed me hard and fast, driving my back into the post.

The wood scratched and burned my skin but I didn't care, and honestly, it felt good.

Everything felt good.

Every throb, every pull, every pinch or bite of flesh.

I'd never been fucked like this, pounded into with such raw, shocking, beautiful force my teeth chattered and pieces of my soul broke off, reaching out and seeking the very person I was clinging to. Plus, Brian was bigger than Marcus, thicker and longer by what felt like a mile. I wasn't used to someone this size, but I was so wet and hot and ready, he made sure of that, and with each thrust I grew not only accustomed to Brian's cock but tighter around him, building to that perfect point of madness without any trying on my part.

Everything he gave, I took, and I did it *begging*.

I was his girl.

"More," I whimpered. "Please. Please...oh, God, *please*."

I took his thrusts and his hands bruising as he fucked harder, giving me it all.

Out. In. Out. In.

Harder...

Harder...

God...

My breath hitched.

"Fuck, you're right there, Wild," Brian said, brushing my hair out of my face and kissing me deep. "I've got you," he whispered. "I've had you, Syd. Let go."

He had me.

Even when he was Wes, he had me.

One last swipe of my tongue against Brian's and I cried out, head snapping back and eyes rolling, every muscle in my body tightening as I came apart and exploded in his arms, feeling weighted and weightless at the same time.

Feeling *everything*, all because it was Brian and he was giving it to me.

And I fell, knowing he was catching me.

There wasn't anything more beautiful than that.

Him and me.

He kept it up, hips pumping faster and his noises growing louder and deeper as my world drifted back together and I opened my eyes.

I knew Brian was close. I could feel it in the way his breathing changed against my cheek and his hands and fingers on my skin repositioned then gripped, readying to pull back and out.

"Don't," I pleaded, tightening my legs around his waist and my arms around his neck.

Brian leaned back, straining. "I'm gonna come."

"I know. Do it."

His eyes flashed.

Crazy.

Beautiful.

Gone.

I pulled him back and kissed him as he poured himself inside me, stilling as deep as he could go and holding it there, jerking between my legs and moaning into my mouth, then changing the kiss to something soft and sweet and quiet, no tongue, only lips and panting breaths.

Something like a first kiss.

He gave it to me slow and shy, maybe knowing deep down I'd imagined this moment with him a thousand times and a thousand different ways in my head and wanting to give that to me, or maybe needing it himself.

It didn't matter and I didn't ask because it was perfect.

And you don't question perfect moments. You let them happen.

So I did.

Only when the kiss broke naturally did I move my hand to his cheek and pull back an inch, looking into his eyes.

He looked back.

We stared, breaths catching and eyes capturing.

"Hey," I said shakily.

He licked his lips.

"Hey."

"It's so good to meet you." I closed my eyes at how stupid that sounded. "Uh, I mean, officially anyway. Sorry. That was dumb."

His chest shook with a soundless chuckle.

"Nah, it was cute," he said, his arms giving me a squeeze.

I opened my eyes and smiled.

"I can't believe we're at the same party." I laughed a little. "Seriously, what are the odds. It's crazy enough you're in Dogwood."

"I live here."

I tilted my head.

"Here...Dogwood?"

He lifted me off his cock and lowered me to my feet, saying, "Here, this house. I live here."

I blinked up at him.

Holy...

"*You're* Jamie's roommate?" I asked.

Oh, my God. He *knew*! That's why he told me to go find Brian. He knew I was the girl his roommate was messed up over.

I could kill him. And hug him for not saying anything. I wasn't sure I would've reacted to seeing Brian the same way I did if I'd have known he was here before I found out on my own.

And I really liked the reaction I had and what followed.

Brian bent down and snatched up our clothes, handing me my items before shaking the sand off his shorts.

"Yeah," he answered, looking into my face to state, "And you don't recognize me."

It took me a second to understand what he was saying as I stepped into my panties and slid them up my legs while he pulled on his boxers and shorts, then I remembered his question before we attacked each other, a question I didn't really think about at the time, but now that I was thinking about it, I got what he was asking and *why* he was asking it.

It hit me.

"It was you," I said quietly, watching his chest puff out with an inhale and his body grow stiff. "At the Corvette that day. When Jamie sliced those tires, it was you by his Jeep, wasn't it? I saw you."

Brian visibly relaxed, then nodded.

"Did you know it was me?"

"Not until you called me that night," he replied, pulling his shirt over his head. "Couldn't fuckin' believe it either." His eyes moved between the pants in my one hand and my bra and hoodie in the other, then rose to mine. "You gonna get dressed?"

"Why didn't you say anything if you knew it was me?" I questioned, keeping hold of my clothes instead of putting them on. "And why did you get so angry when I sent you that photo? You knew I was here. You'd sort of seen me already."

He scrubbed a hand down his face.

I stepped closer, getting ready to ask something else or plead for an answer, when he spoke, head down and voice quiet.

And what he said changed everything.

"Gone for you fast, Wild," he began. "Can't explain it. Don't know how it happened or what it was about you specifically that got to me, but you fuckin' got to me, babe, and it was good. Best I'd felt in a long time, maybe ever. Didn't want to risk anything messing that kind of perfection up. It was too good the way we had it, your voice in my ear, what you'd give me every time we spoke. I was living for that."

Oh, God.

I was wrong. His reason totally mattered and I completely understood it.

He lifted his head to look at me.

I could barely see him, my eyes were flooding fast with emotion, but I heard and registered his sudden movement then felt his hand on my face and the other on my hip, pulling me close.

"Wild," he whispered, thumb catching a tear.

"It—it *was* perfect!" I cried out, agreeing, letting it all go and clutching at him with my head tipping forward and dropping on his chest. "I don't know how either, Brian. I don't understand what it was about you, but since that first day, that first text you sent me, it was perfect and everything I needed and you *knew*." I lifted my head to look at him. "You just knew the right things to say and the right times to call. You healed me. You didn't know it but you did!"

"You were healing me, too, babe."

Oh...*God*.

I started crying harder.

His lips touched the top of my head, and his breath fluttered as he chuckled.

"Healing me is a good thing, Syd. You know that, right?"

"I know," I whispered between sniffles.

"Then why are you crying?"

"Because that's the sweetest thing anyone's ever said to me!" I explained, blinking away my tears. "And I'm mostly naked and feeling vulnerable right now, plus, we've just had the best sex of my life and I'm still processing all of *that*, and also"—I got on my toes and pressed closer to stress—"I've just really *really* missed you. This is a lot to handle all at once."

His mouth jerked with a smile.

"Missed you too," he said. "Past two days have been Hell."

I nodded in agreement, grabbed his face with both of my hands, inhaled deep, then spoke.

"I learned after losing my brother that you shouldn't wait to tell someone something you're really feeling, that you never know how much time you have with them, and in a second, they could be gone and you regret everything you never told them."

His eyes held mine, sure and steady. He didn't even blink.

I swallowed and continued on.

"That being said, I know what happened between us happened fast and it happened in a way neither one of us can explain, and at the start of it, I wasn't even legally separated from my husband."

His jaw flexed under my palm.

"Which, by the way, has changed," I assured him. "I signed the papers today and they're going out Monday. In the eyes of the law, I am now legally separated and free of Marcus."

"That's good, babe," he told me.

"Thank you. I agree," I said, pulling my bottom lip into my mouth and sucking on it while I stared up at him.

He quirked an eyebrow.

"Thought you were leading up to telling me something with that speech, Syd."

I released my lip.

"I was. I'm just...wondering if now is the best time to say it."

"This ain't a good time?"

I looked down at myself, then back up at him.

"Well, I am naked. Mostly." I glared at his tear-soaked shirt, then wiped my hand across his chest, hoping the friction would dry it while I muttered, "And I totally cried all over you. I'm sorry."

"Wouldn't be the first time."

Hand stilling, I lifted my head and tilted it.

"Mm?"

He smiled.

"Nothing." He bent and gave me a soft kiss. "You won't? I'll say it."

I gasped against his mouth, watched him lean back an inch and slid my other hand to his chest to join the one I already had pressing there.

"Told you I was gone for you," Brian started. "Think you know what that meant. Think you might be feeling me the same way and that's what you were wanting to tell me." He ran his thumb along my jaw down to my neck. "Am I right?"

I nodded. "Yes."

"Good," he said, smiling. "That's ours, Wild. What we have, how we build on it, and I don't give a fuck if it makes sense or not. It was fast but I don't care. People might not get it like we do but again"—he dipped closer—"I do not *fuckin' care*. What I do care about is you, everything that involves you, and right now, getting you covered up enough so I can get you inside to my room and into my bed where I've dreamed about getting you, and straight up, Syd, in case you didn't know, I've dreamed about it a lot."

My eyes were round, had been since Brian said what we had was ours.

I liked knowing something was ours.

I liked it a lot.

I also was as anxious as he was to get me into his bed.

"I've dreamed about it, too," I admitted softly, watching his smile reappear.

It was beautiful and something I wanted to stare at and study for hours, but first I needed to put on pants.

I went about doing that and doing it quickly, letting Brian help me when he insisted on sliding my leggings up and over my ass, taking that hands-free moment to wipe at my face with my hoodie sleeve before slipping my bra on, Brian also helping with that, and finally, pulling my hoodie over my head.

I tugged awkwardly at the hood strings as I stepped into my flip-flops.

"I wasn't coming here to impress anyone so I just wore this," I told Brian, feeling the need to explain my wardrobe selection. "I normally dress a little nicer."

He finished tying his shoe, stood, and looked me over, slow and purposefully.

"You're beautiful," he said, green eyes sweet and filled with honesty.

I really didn't want to, but damn it, I couldn't help it.

Head falling into my hands, I burst into tears again.

His arms curled around me and drew me close as his lips pressed to my hair.

"Didn't know my girl was so sensitive to compliments," he said, laughter touching his voice.

His girl.

My chest warmed as it continued vibrating with my cries.

I took several minutes to collect myself, wrapped up in Brian's arms while I did it.

Then I let my boy lead me back to the party.

Chapter Thirteen

BRIAN

I walked with Sydney tucked against my side down the sandy path that led to the house, my arm over her shoulder, keeping her close, and her arm around my waist, pressing closer.

Even when we took the stairs to get up to the deck, we stayed like that.

I wasn't pulling away and neither was she. I'd waited too damn long for this moment.

Way too damn long. And I never thought I'd get it.

Knowing that, I held on tighter.

Nothing else mattered but this girl. Nothing. And I was planning on keeping her by my side for as long as I could.

I'd been close to beating the shit outta Jamie for going through with tonight, so close I had to step outside, get away from all the motherfuckers filling my house and get some air, hoping to do it alone but gaining Cole's attention when I slipped out; and getting locked into a conversation on the beach I didn't fucking feel like having.

I just wanted to be left alone so I caved. Figured telling him would get him off my back. Also figured I could talk about Syd, brief as fuck, then drop it. I wouldn't think about her again the rest of the night.

I was delusional.

And she was there. Right fucking there, listening and looking at me, *really* looking at me, and I didn't know what she was seeing— Dash or me. She wasn't speaking and I had no idea how to interpret that.

Wild typically spoke a lot.

Then when I was close to losing my fucking mind, she launched into my arms, giving me that sweet mouth and wild pussy and I took it.

All of it.

I was gone for this girl before I came inside her. Now I didn't know what the fuck I was but it was more than gone. Way past it. There was no going back to what we had before.

Then we talked and even that surprised me. I wasn't sure how it was all going to go down, but this was Syd and she deserved answers. Knew she'd want to know my why and I didn't want to hurt her.

I would never fucking hurt her. I'd die first.

That's how far past gone I was.

And her knowing what I'd been doing before we had whatever the fuck it was we had *could* hurt her, in some way or another, so I gave her my why and it was nothing short of the truth.

I just held on to the one piece she didn't need to feel. I did it to protect her. She didn't need to know that ugly, and I was done with it.

All of it.

I'd make good of that as soon as I could. And maybe one day I could tell her everything, but I needed this to be solid first. I needed to make sure I had Syd in a place where, when I did tell her, she'd understand why I did it. Getting there might take a while, but I wouldn't keep this from her forever.

She was my girl.

And this was the craziest shit I'd ever felt.

The deck was vacant, no assholes I had to deal with, so we moved together to the slider. I opened it and eased Syd inside with my hand on her back, stepped in behind her, closed the door, then threw my arm back over her shoulder and pulled her close, looking above her head and scanning the packed room to yell, "Party's over! Everyone get the fuck out!"

Wide eyes hit me, some annoyed, some looking startled, those belonging to the chicks, then shifting quickly to annoyed.

I wasn't playing. If every single one of these pricks didn't make their way out of my house in a minute, I'd be removing bodies myself.

Someone cut off the music. Muffled voices moved about the room.

"Brian," Sydney whispered, looking up and fighting a smile with her hand pressing on my stomach. "That's kinda rude."

"Don't care," I replied flatly. "Want to get you alone and I'm not doing it with these motherfuckers hanging around. They need to go."

She thought that was some sweet shit, too. I saw it. The way she melted closer and her hazel eyes got soft.

Then with her lips pinched together, she turned to face the crowd, got up on her toes, and hollered over the commotion, "Thank you so much for coming! We loved having you!"

Some of the annoyed eyes stayed annoyed. Others turned amused, those belonging to the chicks.

"Jesus," I mumbled through a laugh, then grabbed her chin, tilted her head back and kissed her, starting sweet with that, too, but then feeling her tongue on my lip, hot and ready, that feeling shooting straight to my dick and forcing me to take it dirty, my tongue sliding across hers and into her mouth and my hands gripping at her with impatience, roaming down her spine to the top of her peach-shaped ass, where they held back from going lower and shook.

She moaned around my tongue and found my skin beneath my shirt, gripping my hips with her warm fingers.

"Uh, hon. There's a boy attached to your face."

We both pulled away, Syd panting for breath before she turned to the voice who just spoke, my eyes slowly following after being transfixed on how wet and swollen Wild's lips had gotten.

Perfect. Fuck, she had a perfect mouth.

Legs stood in front of us in a short yellow dress, arms crossed and eyes curious, going between Syd and me.

Knew it was her. Sort of recognized her from the night with the Corvette, but it was my best friend's infatuation that had me *knowing* this was Legs.

"Oh, hey, Tori," Sydney greeted her and grabbed her hand, keeping her other hand on my hip. She tugged her closer. "Um, so, this is Brian," she said, then leaned in to add, *"Brian* Brian."

Tori looked up at me. Her mouth fell open.

"No way. You're in Dogwood?"

"He's not just *in* Dogwood. He's Jamie's roommate," Syd answered for me.

Tori's mouth fell open farther.

"No freaking way!"

I smiled, slid my arm over Sydney's shoulder again, and tugged her until she couldn't get closer to me unless I picked her tiny ass up.

I considered doing it. Missed her legs wrapped around my waist.

Tori watched this happen and she did it looking happy, her mouth closing and then twisting into a grin and her eyes shining with approval.

She was so happy about it, she jerked forward, careful of my girl, threw her arms around my neck, and gave me a squeeze.

"You have so much potential, you have no idea," she said quietly against my ear.

Syd giggled next to me.

"Uh, thanks," I replied, reciprocated by patting her back with my free hand, and then giving her a nod when she released me and stepped back.

"So much," she added, then frowned to say, "Your roommate? *Not* so much."

"Oh, my God. Did you sleep with him?" Syd asked.

I wasn't interested in sticking around to hear this conversation. Didn't care who my friend fucked, who Syd's friend fucked, or if they happened to fuck each other, but Sydney cared.

"God, no," Tori said, appearing disgusted. "And that ship has sailed, will never turn around and look back in his direction even if his ass is in the water drowning, which is why I've been looking all over this stupid, not even the least bit impressive, house for you. I'm ready to go." Her eyes sliced to mine. "No offense."

"None taken," I told her.

Tori looked back to Syd, asking, "You ready?"

My grip around her tightened.

Sydney felt it, inhaling sharply. Tori saw it happen and reacted her own way by lifting her eyebrows and assessing the two of us, not looking pissed but instead looking interested and pleased she got to witness what just happened.

"Or . . . are you *not* ready?" Tori corrected, eyes fixating on Syd.

I watched Syd look up at me, suck on her bottom lip, then turn her head back to Tori.

"I'm gonna stay here . . . for the night." She added that last part quickly, looked back up into my eyes then lower, seeing my contented smile and giving one back, bright white teeth and dimples.

"Yeah, I kinda figured that," Tori chuckled, then released Sydney's hand only to pull her into a hug and doing it awkwardly, considering the permanent grip I had and my close proximity.

I could've let go, stepped back, and given Syd some space.

I didn't.

No matter. It didn't seem to faze the two of them and they hugged it out anyway, whispering words to each other then waving after they pulled away.

"See you tomorrow," Tori told Syd, then looked at me to say, "Later, Potential."

She said it wearing a smile that matched my girl's, content and a little excited.

"Later," I replied.

Tori spun around, blended in with the crowd heading out of the living room and toward the door, and filed out with the rest of them, a few lagging behind thinking I meant, *Get the fuck out, but do it at your own pace.*

Wasn't what I meant, and the second they saw me glaring at their slow-moving asses getting off my couch, two guys and a chick, they picked it up and moved out, doing it swiftly.

We were alone. Finally.

Sydney turned in my arms, wrapped hers around my waist, rested her chin on my chest, and blinked up at me, sighing

"He must've done something *really* bad for Tori to pass on bedding him for good." She squinted, thinking. "What do you think he could've done? I mean, he clearly wants to get with her. Why would he risk screwing up his chances? Unless he had no idea he was doing something stupid. I bet that's it. Idiot," she huffed, rolling her eyes. "Is he really as dumb as he is pretty? Because I'm convinced he's getting by life solely on looks."

"Babe." I dropped my forehead against hers.

"Yeah?"

"Sorry. Gotta be honest."

"Of course," she said, smiling a little.

"Don't really care what happened between the two of them," I told her.

She scrunched up her nose.

I studied how cute she looked with her nose like that, then explained. "The only thing I care about is my girl and the fact I finally got her. I'm gonna let that soak in. Part of taking the time to do that involves getting you upstairs now that everyone has cleared the fuck out so I can eat your pussy."

Her eyes went wide.

"Oh," she whispered.

"Yeah, so if we could, can we stop talking about why other people aren't fuckin'?"

She nodded enthusiastically.

Sweet and cute.

Laughing and pressing a kiss to her hair, I turned her and moved us together across the living room and into the hall, making her go in front of me up the stairs so I could stare at her ass and not keeping that from her, making my motives known, then directing her to the last door on the right with my hand on her lower back.

I reached in, flipped on the light, stepped inside, made it almost to the bed, then turned back to see her halted in the doorway.

"You coming?"

"I can't believe this is happening," she said softly, appearing almost nervous with her hands knotting together in front of her.

"You can't believe what's happening?" I asked.

"This." Her eyes cut away. "I'm about to walk into your bedroom. Touch what you've touched. Feel where you've slept. I've wanted to do this so bad and for so long and I, I wanna go slow and just savor it. I don't want to rush this moment."

"Babe."

She lifted her eyes.

"Come here," I told her.

"Let me savor it."

"You can savor it after I kiss you for being so damn sweet about something as insignificant as my bedroom."

Her brows pulled together.

"It isn't insignificant, Brian," she argued, moving closer then but only by a foot. "It has to do with *you*, and anything that has to do with you is important to me and something I want to learn about. How many times have you talked to me while sitting in this bedroom?"

I smiled.

"A lot."

"Right." She tilted her head, brows lifting. "See? We have history here. You thought about me in this room. You said some of the sweetest things to me in this room, and I listened, imagining where you were and what this room looked like. I've dreamed about this room."

I moved then, closing the gap since she wasn't, and grabbed her face, kissing her slow and deep.

She sucked a little on my tongue and moaned into my mouth.

"There," I said, pulling away and leaving her breathless. "Now you can savor it."

She licked her lips.

"Just so you know, I'm totally going to savor that, too," she told me through a slow blink, looking half-drugged. "You kiss like a dream."

I laughed and watched her step back, press her fingers to her

mouth, then turn and move around, looking at and touching everything, studying posters on the wall and pictures I had framed and
displayed on my dresser, staying silent and taking it all in while she
absentmindedly twirled a lock of her hair.

I stayed silent, too, not wanting to interrupt this moment for her,
knowing how important it was.

I let her savor it.

She lifted the crossword book off my nightstand and smiled, then
set it down and turned, walked up to my old board I had propped in
the corner of the room, and ran her hand over it.

"Do you surf?" she asked, looking back at me.

I shook my head.

"Used to. Not anymore."

"Not at all?"

I stared at her.

Sadness passed over her face. She lowered her hand and moved
around the bed to get to me.

"This the bad stuff in your life?" Sydney guessed, her hand circling my wrist.

"Part of it," I answered.

"Are you ever gonna tell me about it?"

I exhaled and pressed my hand to her breast, rubbing my thumb
over the tight nipple I could feel through her layers.

She arched into me and closed her eyes.

"Not tonight," I whispered, bending to kiss her jaw and moving lower. "You wanna stand when I eat you or you wanna lie on
the bed?"

I felt her pulse flutter against my lips.

"Bed," she answered shyly.

One last kiss to her cheek and I moved away to take care of the
door, shutting and locking it. I reached back and grabbed my shirt,
pulled it over my head and tossed it on the floor as Sydney peeled her
pants and panties down, only getting about a third of a way down
her thighs when she stopped with a squeak.

I looked between her stilled hands gripping black and light blue
lace and the top of her head as she kept it tilted down.

"Something wrong?" I asked.

"Oh, uh." She lifted her head but stayed bent. "I'm kind of leaking you."

Breath caught in my throat.

She was leaking *me*.

My cum.

Fuck yeah. That was hot.

First time a girl had ever said that to me, and I couldn't hide how much I liked hearing it. My mouth lifted into a half smile as Syd kept hers unsure, twisted into something between a pout and a goofy-looking frown.

Could've stood there and continued appreciating what she was dealing with but realized she needed something and that's why she was frozen and not continuing to remove her clothes.

I wanted her to continue removing her clothes. And I wanted to be the man getting that something she needed and taking care of it for her.

I lost the smile and looked into her eyes, saying, "Be right back," then I stepped into the bathroom and grabbed a washcloth, got it damp with warm water, and carried it back out into the bedroom, kneeling in front of her with it.

Syd had removed her pants, panties, and hoodie now, standing only in her bra while pinching her legs together tight.

"You want to do it?" she questioned in disbelief when I slid the washcloth between her legs, forcing them apart.

"Yeah," I answered, catching her timid smile before I focused on cleaning off the inside of her thighs and, once that was done, moving the cloth higher.

She held on to my shoulders and breathed heavily.

"Feel good?" I asked.

"Yes," she replied, spreading her feet wider. "No one's ever done this to me before and it's, well, honestly it's kinda crazy you're doing it."

Syd was talking about her ex not taking care of her, I got that, but she was also referring to me and her, fucking without a condom, and I knew she was wondering if that was shit that happened regularly with me or not, and she was justified in wondering.

We'd never talked about it before tonight or the second I had to think before I slid inside her bare.

Also, I thought a small part of her might be wondering if I'd ever taken the time to do this for someone else before or if this was just for her.

The answers were simple and I didn't have a problem giving them to her.

I lowered the cloth and looked up.

She was studying my face with anxious eyes while sucking on her bottom lip.

"Never done this," I confessed, watching that apprehension slide away with the breath she expelled. "Never wanted to, but that being said, never had to either. I've always worn condoms, and thank fuck, haven't had any mishaps. Also got tested a little over a week ago so you're good."

Even though I'd always wrapped it up when I shot for Xstasy, I'd still gotten tested often. I wasn't risking shit.

Syd smiled a little.

"Okay." She nodded and tucked some hair behind her ear. "I'm clean. I've never had anything, but I haven't always used condoms. Marcus and I didn't. I get the Depo shot so we're good there, but if you want me to get tested before we do it again like that—"

"You planning on getting tested in the next ten minutes?" I asked, cutting her off.

She tilted her head.

Christ, it was cute when she did that.

"I don't think places are open this late," she said softly. "Or on weekends."

"They aren't. Even if they were, you'd have trouble getting results back that quick and I'm feeling pretty impatient right now."

She looked bewildered. "You are?"

I tossed the cloth on our pile of clothes and gripped her hips, pushing her back until she had no choice but to sit on the edge of the bed.

"Yeah, Wild, I am."

"But we just had sex."

I pushed between her legs and felt the heat of her pussy against my ribs, rested my hands on her hips while hers slid to my arms, gripping me there as her face dipped close.

"And?" I asked.

Her cheeks flushed.

I ran my thumb over one. "Wanted you again the second I finished coming, Syd. Thought about this for weeks, and I'm not the type of man to be satisfied with just one hit of something I've thought about this much. Not if that hit's you. Because of that, I'm gonna drag it out this time, eat you before I fuck you slow. So unless you can find a place open right now and convince someone to rush results, I'm thinking we can just go off you knowing you've always been clean and trust that your dick of an ex was being honest and didn't mess around with that girl you used to work with until after he fucked up by letting you go."

Her grip on my arms tightened and her breath caught.

"How do you know about that?" she asked, eyes searching. "Did I tell you? I don't remember telling you."

"You didn't," I assured her, dropping my hand. "But you were yelling pretty fucking loud that night outside the concert. Got the gist of it. Unfortunately, didn't get to give you my input on the situation considering how the rest of the night played out, but just so you know..." I held her eyes to stress this next part. "Your ex is a fucking piece of shit and never deserved you."

Wild sucked in a breath, pressed her lips together, and looked on the verge of tears.

"Oh, my God. It *was* you," she whispered, voice straining. "I thought you were lying."

"Said no one else holds you but me," I reminded her.

She shook her head quickly, eyes cast down as she pleaded, "Please stop being so sweet to me. I don't wanna spend our first night together crying, Trouble. You'll think I'm crazy."

Trouble.

Loved when she called me that.

I kept my laugh silent, lifted her chin, leaned forward, and kissed her soft.

Her hands glided up to my neck and held on. Those tears never fell.

"Lay back, babe. Wanna taste you."

She whimpered against my lips then she did what I asked, stretching out on her back and lifting her feet to rest them on the edge of the bed, knees bent and spread for me and that tight little cunt glistening.

She was ready, hot, and wanting, needing this as much as I needed to take it.

Perfect.

Her hands fidgeted restlessly by her sides, gripping and releasing the comforter, and her stomach dipped in anxious breaths.

I leaned over and dropped my head to press soft kisses to her ribs as my hands squeezed her tits through her bra then slid down and pushed under the wire, filling my palms with her heavy flesh as I dragged my tongue across her navel and flicked her piercing. I moved lower with lips dragging over creamy skin to her hip, sucking there before pressing my mouth to the top of her pussy and lifting my eyes.

Her breath shuddered as our gazes locked and I held on to that sweet, willing look she was giving me as I dipped my head and swiped my tongue through her pussy.

"Oh, *yes*," she moaned, thighs tensing reflexively against my ears then pulling apart, unsure.

I grabbed her legs and pushed them back, pinning my head between them so I only heard muffled cries and muted breaths while I ate her roughly from cunt to clit and back down, fucking her with my tongue until she dripped down my chin.

She slipped off her bra and tossed it.

I sucked the smooth skin around her pussy, teasing her until she whimpered and then diving back in.

Her nails raked over my scalp to the back of my head, where she gripped and held on, then her hips started pushing off from the bed and she rocked into me, riding my tongue in hot little jerks and then melting, body warming when I moved to her clit and pulled there.

"Brian," she gasped. "Please, don't stop."

"Knew you'd be this sweet," I told her, head lifting so she could watch me give her a long, slow lick. "Fuckin' knew it."

"Yeah," she said, shaking and breathless, lips parted and eyes heavy, maybe agreeing with me or maybe just feeling it, that pull I was building in her and being so close to coming she'd agree to anything right now just as long as I didn't stop.

I wouldn't stop. I couldn't.

I drew her clit into my mouth and sucked hard.

Her head dropped back, chest heaving, and she peeled my hands off her legs and held them beside her, linking us together and pressing with fingertips and blunt nails, threatening to bruise bone and break skin.

Mark me, I thought.

I wanted her all over me.

Her scent, her flavor, her desperation, and she was right there, a suck or a lick away from falling.

I jerked up then, keeping her on edge and panting as she whined and reached for me with fingers and feet wrapping around my legs and hips, wanting my tongue back.

"Brian," she begged.

"Scoot back," I told her, and she did as I shoved my shorts down and my cock sprung free, slapping against my stomach then bobbing heavily as I climbed on top of her and in between her legs, pushing one to her chest and holding it there as I drove in, filling her on a moan that shook in my throat and tasted like fire, and the second I bottomed out, she came, air leaving her as she arched off the bed, crying out then reaching, pulling me down until our mouths fused and I swallowed her shallow, sated breaths.

I kissed her and pumped my hips through her orgasm and she rode it, hands roaming down my back to my ass and gripping, urging, pleading.

"Brian, my *God*," she whimpered, staring into my eyes.

I released her leg and guided it around me, thighs squeezing my hips and fingers tensing on my stomach as I started building it in her again, measured and exact through heavy drags of my cock that were promising and punishing.

She closed her eyes with parted lips and shook with desire.

"That's it, Wild," I said, bending to kiss the corner of her mouth, then leaning away to watch her take me.

My pace was deliberate. She both loved and hated what I was doing.

And I loved it. All of it.

I'd make it last as long as I could.

I stayed slow when she begged me for faster.

I pinned her hips to the bed when she tried grinding down.

I fucked and fucked and fucked, mad with the need to keep her and our crazy, the smell and taste and feel of Wild spreading through my veins.

I kept off my release and her next one, sweat dripping and limbs shaking, her pussy so wet I could slide my finger between her cheeks and press with lubrication.

She pressed back, liking it.

I'd fuck her ass another time and I didn't hesitate sharing, which got her nodding desperately and even asking for it, wanting it now because I was offering and she was so wound up she'd come the second I slid past that tight ring of muscle, I knew.

She knew.

But I had other plans.

"Yes, yes, please," she begged, lips pressing to my ear. "Do it, Brian. Fuck me there. I want it."

"Need you coming on my cock tonight, babe," I said, thrusting in and out, in and out with my spine burning and my legs and arms trembling.

"I will. I will," Syd assured. "Let me. Just *let me*. I will."

"A little more," I told her.

She closed her eyes, bit her lip, and moaned.

"Just a little longer," I soothed.

Fingers dug into my back and sank between my ribs.

"Give me everything," I pleaded.

Wild opened her eyes and nodded, saying, "Take it. Take all of it," then reached above her head and pushed against the headboard, bearing down on me and sending heat through my limbs.

"Fuck," I gasped, the need to pump faster clawing at my skin and I broke, slamming into her while keeping hold of her waist. "Syd...babe, get there."

She pulled me down and kissed me hard.

"I'm there," she moaned. "Brian, please, *God*, I've been there."

She broke apart first, a beautiful chaos of fire and light in my arms.

Dirty and delicate.

Then my orgasm ripped through me and I came on a growl that vibrated in my chest, shooting deep inside her pussy with hips thrusting frantically, back straightening, and head thrown back then tipping forward and stilling to watch her milk my cock with the last bit of her climax, tiny squeezes I felt all the way in my spine as her moans turned to adoring little mews I wanted to eat.

She was so damn soft after she came.

I loved her soft.

With heavy limbs and breath, I collapsed on top of her, head buried in her neck and beating heart against beating heart.

"Damn," I mumbled.

How could I feel broken and whole at the same time?

"Uh...yeah, damn. That was seriously crazy," Syd declared through a small voice, her hands rubbing up and down my back soothingly. "I think that's what people call tantric sex, you know, when you hold off that long."

"Yeah?" I asked, lifting my head and scanning her neck until I found those two moles I knew she hated, dead center on her throat, one beside the other, then pressing my lips there and saying, "Don't know nothing about that weird shit. Just felt like fuckin' you for a while."

"Mission accomplished." She laughed, her shoulder jerking when I kissed that spot again. "What are you doing?"

"Kissing my moles," I informed her.

She turned her head.

"I hate those moles."

"They're beautiful."

"They're moles, Brian," she giggled, wiggling to try and get me away from them. "Moles can't be beautiful. They're an imperfection."

"Gotta disagree, babe," I argued.

I pushed back onto my knees, watching the look on her face as I slid my cock out, mouth open and eyes heated, *fuckin' needy*, loved that, then climbed off the bed and got another cloth from the bathroom, got it damp, and grabbed a hand towel, wiping my dick off with that while I carried the cloth to the bed and went about taking care of her.

She spread her legs for me and bit her lip, then yawned and sighed sleepily when I was done.

I froze.

Fuck.

That noise.

How many times had she made that noise in my ear at night and I'd wished she was doing it in my arms?

Too many times to count.

"What?" she asked when she caught me staring.

I shook my head, leaned over her looking like I was going in for a kiss but at the last second ducking, tilting her head back with my hand and kissing her moles.

She made a grumbling sound in her throat but didn't push me off.

I got rid of the cloths and pulled the covers down, got Syd under them and comfortable, then climbed in beside her, rolled to my side, and with an arm snaking around her waist, pulled until we were touching, my front to her back, my legs pushing hers into a bend and my head dropping, mouth pressing to the soft skin between her shoulder and neck.

She folded into me and threw her arm on top of mine, letting me know she liked where I put her.

"We fit perfectly," she stated. "I knew we would."

I closed my eyes and breathed deep.

"Want me to run out and get you that hot chocolate?" I asked, knowing that was her pattern at night, even though I didn't want to move considering how phenomenal her ass felt against my cock, but I'd move if she asked.

Her hand pressed down on mine.

"I don't want you to go anywhere."

I smiled and gave her a squeeze.

"Fuckin' beat. You got plans tomorrow, or can we stay here all day and only get up when we need to recharge with food?"

"You don't have to work tomorrow?"

"Nope."

"Wait...what is it that you do again? You never said."

No. I avoided that topic. Definitely never said.

"Co-own a surf shop with Jamie," I informed. "Wax. Not far from here. And we never work on Sundays. Those are always for surf."

"Except you don't surf anymore," she replied.

My arm tightened around her.

I was prepared for questions I'd dodge for a later discussion. Wasn't in the mood to get into all of that tonight, but Syd didn't press.

"Well, I would love to stay here with you, but I *do* have work to-morrow," she replied, sounding sad about it. "And I need to be there. I called in sick the past two days and I felt horrible doing it. Nate seemed understanding about it but I still felt bad. He's got a lot on his plate and he didn't need me leaving him short-staffed."

"Sure if it wasn't manageable, he would've said something to you," I suggested.

Her shoulder jerked.

"Maybe," she said quietly. "Maybe not. It's Nate. He's like a ghost around there a lot of the time. It's so sad."

I remembered Syd telling me about her boss and the shit he was dealing with after finding out about it herself.

Not just shit. Sad shit. Wife committing suicide and leaving him a single dad to their newborn.

Not a conversation I wanted to have after experiencing what I'd just shared with my girl.

Luckily for me, Syd appeared to feel the same way and instead turned in my arms so we were facing each other and started shifting closer.

I took over.

Hand forming to her waist, I pulled until she was flush up against me, tits to ribs, her head resting half on the pillow and half on my arm, her hand sliding over my cheek to my hair and down to my neck and shoulder, and my leg slung over and behind her knees, locking us together.

I twisted a piece of messy red around my finger, feeling her eyes on me.

"What's your last name?" she asked.

My hand stilled.

That was definitely not something I would've shared before, fearing she'd search it online to find me and see shit I didn't want her seeing, my last name possibly linking her to something, but I didn't have that same fear anymore so I didn't mind sharing with her.

Why would she search for me now? I was right here.

And she had me.

"Savage," I replied, finger moving and looking into her eyes. "Yours?"

Her nose scrunched up.

"Well, my married name is Paige."

My hand stilled again.

"You aren't married anymore," I told her, and I did it roughly, not being able to help my tone because, *fuck*, I hated everything of that motherfucker's that touched Syd, his last name included.

Stupid to feel that way since it was what you fucking did when you got married to someone—you took their last name or you gave them yours.

Still.

I wasn't seeing reason on this subject.

I forced myself to settle, watched her nod in agreement with me, face relaxed, then continued on to say, "And you sure as fuck deserve better than that last name. It's not good enough for you. What's your maiden name?"

She smiled.

"Whittaker."

I tucked the red I'd been twisting behind her ear, draped my arm over her waist, then replied.

"There you go, babe."

She smiled bigger.

I slid my hand to her neck and gripped her there, rolled to my back, and pulled her down on top of me.

"Like you here," I whispered.

Her breath held and her fingers stilled against my chest as her eyes brightened with an emotion I hadn't seen yet, then she relaxed and smiled lazily, shifted down a little, and dropped her chin to the top of her hand, staring at me.

Her hair was a mess from fucking and her cheeks and lips were bitten red.

One hand forming to her ass and the other twisting in the ends of her hair falling on her shoulder, I stared back, feeling the haze of exhaustion sweeping over me and asking, "Any more questions tonight or can you hold off until tomorrow, the next day, the day after that, and every other day I'm planning on seeing you so we can both get some shut-eye before I need to be feeling you around my cock again."

Her lips turned up, stare brightening a little, then she twisted her neck and lay on her cheek.

"I can hold off," she replied quietly.

I gave her a squeeze and shut my eyes.

Not a minute later did I open them again when moans crept under the doorway.

Syd's head shot up with a gasp.

"Oh, my God," she whispered, looking around in a panic. "Is that..."

"Jamie," I answered irritatingly, shutting my eyes again and hearing another moan, then two more, all three of lighter pitch and distinctive between each other.

"And friends," I hissed, jaw flexing.

Motherfucker.

Thinking it was time he soundproof insulated his bedroom.

"That's...I think he has three women with him," Syd guessed.

"Sounds like it."

She made a noise in her throat, a cross between a grunt and a gag, then I felt her head hit my chest again.

My arms tightened around her.

"Night, Wild."

"Idiot," she murmured. "Knew it was something stupid. He totally blew it with Tori."

I gave her another squeeze.

She sighed, squeezed me back, then gave me a sweet, "Night, Trouble."

It was just as cute as it had always been all those nights she'd give it to me before we hung up, but in my arms it was better.

The best.

I felt her fall asleep as I lay there, mind heavy and working out the plan I needed in order to keep Sydney here with me.

Only when I had it did I finally drift off.

* * *

Sipping my coffee, I flipped the bacon I was frying when movement over my shoulder turned my head.

Jamie walked through the living room and entered the kitchen wearing unbuttoned shorts and nothing else, rubbed his hands down his face and back up, looking exhausted, then acknowledged me with a jerk of his chin as he went straight for the coffee.

"Hell yeah. You makin' breakfast? What's the occasion?" he asked, grabbing a mug out of the cabinet and pouring himself a cup. "I'll take my eggs over easy. And make sure you cook them in the bacon grease. Don't waste that shit."

I focused on the pan in front of me.

"You'll take your eggs to go at fuckin' McDonald's, unless you plan on making them yourself," I replied, turning to look at him. "This is for me and Syd whenever she wakes up."

His eyebrows lifted.

"No shit," he said, smiling as he hoisted himself up on the counter, mug in hand and legs swinging like a fucking elated child waiting up for Santa on Christmas Eve. "She found you, I take it. How'd that go down?"

"She's in my bed. How do you think?"

Jamie took a sip of his coffee, nodded, then shared, "Happy for you, man. Straight up."

"Thanks."

"Seriously. That's great for all of us. Means I won't have to put you on suicide watch and take shifts with Cole. Just so you know, pretty sure it was coming to that."

I glared at him, got a smug grin in return, then went back to the bacon, pulling out pieces that were on the good side of being burnt and putting them on a plate covered with a paper towel to soak up the grease.

"Fuck. Last night was crazy," Jamie muttered next to me. "Think I might need a cast for my dick."

"Not that it's any of my business and, please, let's keep it that way. Only sharing this 'cause it was shoved upon me last night and I had no choice but to hear it. Now I'm figuring I can pass it off and maybe I'll forget I ever heard it in the first place, which would be fuckin' great." I cut my eyes to him, continuing on to say, "You fucked up with Legs. Pretty sure she wants to kill you."

Mug in his hands resting in his lap, Jamie looked irritated as he asked, "What the fuck for? She shows up at *my* party looking like straight-up pussy on a fuckin' platter, flaunts that shit in my face knowing I want it then disappears on me like a fuckin' ghost, making me tear this place apart looking for her hot ass, which I did for a solid fifteen minutes, passing up opportunities left and right, and she wants to kill *me*? Why?"

"Don't know. She didn't say," I replied, then studied him hard to ask, "Wait, who the fuck did you have in your room last night then? I know you had more than two."

Jamie shrugged.

"The Baker sisters," he answered casually.

"That's weird, man," I told him.

He looked affronted.

"They're stepsisters. It ain't that weird."

I shook my head while looking away, pulled the rest of the bacon out and turned down the heat, then grabbed a bowl and slid the carton of eggs in front of me, cracking a few in and whisking them quickly with a fork.

"Need to talk to you about something," I said after draining out most of the grease but leaving enough in the pan so it would flavor the eggs.

"Shoot."

I checked over my shoulder, making sure we were still alone, then turned to Jamie.

"What's happening with me and her upstairs is something I want permanent. I'm not fuckin' around with her. Never was."

He smirked. "Pretty sure I got that."

"Good, then you'll get why I'm asking you to buy my share of Wax from me."

Smirk vanishing, Jamie stared at me long and hard, eyes unblinking, looking like I'd just confessed to murdering someone he hated and wanted dead, but wasn't sure if he should like the idea of me murdering someone or not.

Figured this reaction was coming. Hoped for something less complicated like an easy nod and a pat on the back so I could get to finishing Syd's breakfast, but I've never been lucky.

I cut the heat on the stove, not wanting to burn the grease, stepped back until I hit the island, and leaned against it, arms crossing on my chest.

"You... want me to *buy you out*?" Jamie asked. "What the fuck? Why?"

I pulled in a deep breath to explain.

"Figured I'd continue doing what I was doing at Xstasy, the solo shit, until I could give that kid enough to get by for *years*, taking some of that burden off and letting that family breathe easy. I need that for them. It's important. I think you know that."

Jamie nodded, letting me know he understood.

"That being said," I continued, "there is *nothing* more important to me than that girl upstairs. Not one damn thing. Can't explain why she has me like this but she fuckin' does and it's good, the kind of good you'd change your life for. So solo or not, I won't have ties to something that could hurt her. I won't chance her feeling this, which puts me in a fuckin' bind 'cause I need that money and doing shit like I was doing for Xstasy was the only way I could think of to get it fast like I needed and in that quantity without risking getting arrested."

Jamie shook his head.

"It's not lost on me what this girl's doing. I see the good she's giving you but there's gotta be something else," he said. "Another way you can get them that money. A loan or something. *Fuck*, Dash, this was our dream, owning Wax. It's something we've worked our asses off for and you wanna sell out?"

"No other choice, man."

Jamie clenched his jaw, nostrils flaring as he looked down.

He was upset and I got that. Appreciated where he was coming from, too. This wasn't an easy decision for me, but at least I'd still be connected to Wax somehow. I'd still work there.

I wouldn't have to give up that dream completely.

I watched Jamie set his mug down and hop off the counter, then take a step toward me, hands raised seeking peace.

"Hear me out," he requested. "There's another option and it's one you can take without giving anything up."

"No," I said, shooting it down before hearing him because I already knew his suggestion. "It's not going down that way. I'm not taking your money unless I sell."

"Come on. What's the difference?"

"Don't fuckin' ask me that again," I hissed, impatience burning in my throat. "You wanna help me? This is how you can help me. Buy me out."

He lowered his hands.

Silence settled between us.

Jamie wasn't going to give me this. He didn't understand. I could tell by the look on his face.

I shook my head through an inhale, jaw tight and shoulders tensing.

"Forget it," I mumbled, moving back to the stove with heavy steps. "I'll figure something else out."

What the fuck that was gonna be, I had no idea. Last night this seemed like my only option.

I stared down at the pan, hands braced on either side of the stove and head down.

Maybe I could sell everything I had. Might get a little over ten grand for my Jeep. Not as much as selling my share of Wax, but it was better than nothing. I could take the bus or bum rides, that or walk everywhere. Getting the exercise wouldn't hurt.

"I'll do it."

I slowly lifted my head and turned my neck.

Jamie held my eyes when he said, "I'll buy you out. Get the figure and let me know."

Tension poured out of my limbs. I breathed a sigh of relief.

"Thanks, man. Seriously. Means a lot," I told him, straightening my back.

He nodded once, twisted to grab his mug, then took a sip.

I could get in touch with our accountant today, no problem. The guy worked seven days a week. As for Xstasy, that shit could be handled with a simple text. I'd get on that as soon as I got Syd back home in case Mike decided to be one dumb motherfucker and call me to discuss.

There would be no discussion.

And this was going to work out.

Thank *fuck*.

"But your name is staying on all the promotional shit. I don't care if you want it removed, it's not happening," Jamie informed as I was clicking the burner on. "It would be a pain in my ass getting it changed so deal with it."

I kept my head down and focused.

"I'm good with that," I said through a smirk.

"Not asking your permission," he replied shortly under his breath.

My smirk twisted into a smile.

I was feeling good again.

We talked more about the party and some work shit while I cooked the eggs. I was on my second cup of coffee, keeping the food warm in the oven, when I heard quiet footsteps on the stairs and I stopped listening to Jamie, turned my head, and watched Syd step with sleepy eyes and finger-twisted hair into the room wearing nothing but the shirt I was wearing yesterday.

I'm sure she looked slamming in a lot of things, but that might've been a top look for me.

She froze, bare feet and pale limbs pressing together and her hands tugging on the hem of my tee, which was funny since it almost reached her knees hanging loose.

"Mornin', Wild."

I smiled at her, sat my mug down, then made my way across the room.

Her eyes danced between me and Jamie.

"Uh, mornin'." She settled on me. "Should I go put something on?" she whispered when I reached her.

"No. You look sweet," I said, bending to kiss her mouth.

She broke it fast and shyly, explaining, "I haven't brushed my teeth yet."

"And?"

"My breath isn't kissable right now. You'll keel over."

Her one hand acted like a barrier between our lips as she blinked up at me.

I laughed and kissed her forehead instead, which she allowed and seemed to enjoy, moaning quietly as I did it, then tucking close when I draped my arm around her and moved us back into the kitchen.

Jamie smiled at Syd, lifting his mug.

"What's up, Sunshine? Sleep good?"

I looked down and watched my girl shoot daggers at Jamie.

Right. Legs.

Syd had her girl's back.

"You got a problem?" Jamie asked with humor in his voice.

"Nope," Syd snapped, looking away sharply, making her point known that she did indeed have a problem, possibly several, but she wasn't interested in hashing it out right now.

Her attitude was another cute thing about her.

Jamie didn't seem to care. He laughed under his breath while pouring himself a second cup of coffee, then moved to the pantry next to the fridge, pulled out a pack of Pop-Tarts, closed the door, and turned, winking at Syd as he walked around the island.

"Gotta head upstairs and wake up my guests," he said on his way out of the room. "Ten o'clock is checkout."

Sydney made a soft grunting noise.

"That's disgusting," she commented quietly when we were alone. "I can't believe not one but *three* women wanted to have sex with him. They must've been paid off."

"Probably an easy transaction, considering the one bank account."

She tilted her head adorably and gazed up at me.

"Mm?"

I smiled, choosing not to elaborate, then turned into her, grabbed her waist, and lifted, hoisting her up onto the island and pushing her knees apart, shoving between them.

"You hungry?" I asked, lips moving over her cheek.

I felt her nod.

"Eggs?"

"Yummy," she replied softly.

"Bacon?"

"Oh, my God, yes!" she whispered excitedly. "I *knew* I smelled bacon."

I leaned back, grinning.

She was all dimples and bright eager eyes with fingers dancing on my neck.

"Get you set up."

"Okay."

I left her on the counter to pull the plates out of the oven, grabbed some forks, napkins, an extra plate, asked if she wanted ketchup or anything for her eggs and laughed at the face she gave me, nose wrinkling in disgust, then moved back to the island and set everything beside her hip, handed her a fork and the extra plate which she set aside, we were sharing, then gripping my own fork and digging into the eggs while she went straight for the bacon.

"How'd you sleep?" I asked.

Her eyes smiled.

"Perfect. You're a very comfy pillow," she replied, snapping into her bacon and moaning while she chewed.

I shoveled eggs into my mouth.

"Pillows are soft, babe. I ain't soft."

She smirked. Heat bloomed in her cheeks.

She was thinking about my cock.

Fucking *loved that*.

I'd show it to her right now if I didn't think there was a slim chance Jamie would walk back in here after kicking out his trio.

"No, but you're cozy and snuggly and warm. And you smell really nice," she clarified. "Think I might like you better than Tori's Christmas quilt."

I didn't know what that meant but it sounded like a good thing, so I didn't question it.

"What time you gotta work today?" I asked, snagging a piece of bacon off the plate.

She chewed up a bite of eggs and forked some more.

"Eleven. So I should probably get home no later than ten thirty. I need to shower."

I nodded.

"Gives us forty-five minutes to eat and fool around," I said, popping the rest of the bacon in my mouth.

Syd's eyes slowly lifted from the plate, then she shrugged nonchalantly and looked back down.

"Think I can make that work," she replied, voice even and accommodating.

"Glad to hear it."

She looked up again, this time doing it smiling.

I gave her one back.

Then we finished eating and left the dishes, making it halfway up the stairs before we got started.

* * *

After dropping Syd off at Tori's house, which was a mere ten minutes away from mine, go fucking figure, she'd been this close to me the entire time, close enough to walk to and I never knew it, I pulled my phone out of my pocket after I slid back into my seat and shot Mike a text.

Done working for you. Don't expect to see me again.

His response came seconds later, and I'd predicted it.

FUCK. YOU.

I didn't reply. There was no need to.
It was over.
I slide my phone away and headed home to get that figure for Jamie.

Chapter Fourteen

SYDNEY

After breakfast with Brian followed by an even yummier dose of morning sex, including him eating me out from behind then taking me hard and fast up against a wall, a rough fucking that ended in me leading in orgasms for the day 3–1, Brian dropped me off at Tori's with two minutes to spare and a promise of later.

I loved his laters. I'd loved them when they'd consisted only of phone calls or texts, but now his laters were different.

Better.

Because they consisted of *him*.

And knowing I'd get Brian with that later had me in one of the best moods of my life, two hours into my shift and smiling so much the patrons were starting to give me odd looks because who smiled when they lagged on getting refills for a table?

This girl.

I couldn't help it and I didn't care.

I was over the moon happy and nothing, not one thing, was ruining that.

Plus, I had put the signed separation papers in the mail before I left Tori's house so I wouldn't forget to do it tomorrow. Another reason for my elation.

Bacon. Multiple orgasms. Sweet kisses and legally freeing myself from Marcus.

This day just kept getting better and better.

I was in the middle of explaining the reason for my elation to Stitch through the window that separated us, figuring he'd want to know why I'd been absent from work and the amazing coincidental sequence of events that followed, not that he'd asked, and I'd just gotten past the part where I'd overheard Brian talking to Cole about me on the beach when Shay came up beside me and nudged my hip.

"You have someone requesting you," she said in my ear, then turned her head, looked at Stitch through the window, which he must've sensed because he chose that exact moment to finally look up after I'd been talking his ear off for the past ten minutes and he didn't so much as lift his head once.

He locked his hard gaze onto hers with so much heat, I felt it on my skin.

Shay broke that connection immediately, saying nothing before she quickly cut her eyes away.

Apparently she was a little upset at him for bailing on their plans last night.

A harsh banging noise turned both Shay's and my heads again.

Stitch stalked out of the kitchen with a cigarette tucked in his mouth, lighter poised at the ready, but waited until he'd kicked the back door open with his black boot and stepped outside before he lit up.

The door slammed shut behind him.

Apparently he was a little pissed at Shay for being upset with him.

Shay muttered something but I didn't hear it because I was busy turning around and scanning the restaurant with curious eyes now that I was remembering what she'd interrupted me for, looking for who was requesting me, then I stopped paying attention to everyone else in Whitecaps.

The flip and twist happened. It was quite possibly my favorite feeling in the entire world.

Brian sat at a booth next to the window by himself. He was smiling at me warmly in a teal blue shirt with a pair of sunglasses hanging on the collar, and *he looked good*, let me tell you, better than any other man I'd ever seen sitting at that booth.

Or in this restaurant.

Or walking around the state of North Carolina.

I was about to sprint across the room and launch myself into his arms like Baby from *Dirty Dancing* when Shay took a hold of my elbow.

"He's, like, unfairly hot, Syd," she commented appreciatively. "Who is he? He came in here looking for you yesterday but acted a little weird about it. Said you two weren't friends when I asked."

I looked from Brian to Shay.

That puzzled me but only for a moment. It was understandable he didn't tell Shay we were friends. For two days we weren't anything.

I gave Shay a reassuring smile.

"It was complicated but now it's not. He's... well, I guess he's my boyfriend. We're dating." My brows pulled together while hers slid behind the bangs she had tickling her forehead. "At least I think we are. Hold that thought."

I left Shay giggling, no doubt amused at my unsureness of this newly developed situation, which I couldn't fault her for. I mean really, why I hadn't taken a moment to ponder this myself was beyond me. Now I had no idea what to label us.

Brian was definitely my boyfriend. I just wasn't sure what I was to him.

I stepped out from behind the bar and walked with determination across the room, weaving between tables before reaching the booth.

"Hey, Wild," Brian said, all smooth and perfect boyfriend material like.

I needed to get to the bottom of this immediately.

"Trouble." I crossed my arms under my chest. "Can I ask you something?"

"Is it what'll I have to drink? 'Cause straight up, I think I need another coffee. This cute little ass kept rubbing against me all night and I barely got any sleep." His eyes lowered to my breasts. "Those didn't help."

"Oh?" I flattened my hand on the table and leaned down, giving him a better view. "And who do these belong to?"

His eyes took their time lifting to my face, which was now only inches from his.

"You?" he asked unsurely. "Odd question, babe. You tired, too?"

"Nope. I feel very energized actually. Three orgasms will do that to a girl. I'm just wondering what this girl is to you exactly."

His eyebrows lifted.

"You don't know."

I opened my mouth then closed it because I thought it was sweet how he made that sound, more as a statement than a question and one he couldn't quite understand.

Brian thought it was obvious what I was to him and maybe it had been obvious for a while. That I was getting. However, the simple fact was, I didn't want to risk any misinterpretations that would lead to my heart getting damaged, which was why I was being a smidge confrontational and wanting him to spell it out, right here and right now.

Before I went and got his coffee.

Brian pulled his sunglasses out of his shirt and set them on the table, then leaned forward, his face serious as he studied me.

"You don't know," he stated again, this time a little quieter and worry-filled, like he should've done better to make sure it was obvious for me, too.

God…

I was feeling his sweet all the way down to my toes.

"I've never been good at picking up on clues," I explained quickly, figuring he should know the reason behind my foolishness.

He smiled.

"And how would you like me to spell this out for you?"

"I think we need to lock down a title."

"Lock down a title?" he questioned.

"Yes. Like, what is this exactly? I know what you are to me. And if I'm being honest with myself I think I've known for a while, but I'm not sure what I am to you, which makes it incredibly difficult to answer questions about who you are because I can't be telling close friends of mine that you're my boyfriend if I'm not your girlfriend. The two go hand-in-hand. So I think before I introduce myself, run through the daily specials, and get you your coffee, we need to go ahead and lock something down."

Brian smiled bigger. Then he quickly reached out and grabbed my arm, which was bracing me on the table, and pulled gently, twisting me until I fell into his lap with a squeak and my feet kicking out.

He ran his nose along my cheek as his arms wrapped tight around me.

Trouble had the best arms. Biggest and safest I'd ever felt.

"You wanna lock something down, Wild?" he asked playfully, the tone of his voice and the feel of his breath breaking goose bumps on my skin.

I dropped my head closer and nodded. Nerves pricked in my throat.

It was strange. I suddenly felt incredibly anxious and considered sliding off Brian's lap and curling into a ball underneath the table. I wanted to hide.

Even in the safety of his arms I felt vulnerable.

What if he didn't *want* to give me a title?

Or worse, what if he thought all this time I didn't need one? That I was easy and didn't see this as anything title-worthy?

This was why people should have formal discussions before they fuck like wild animals on the beach and then slip into a sex-induced coma where bacon is cooked perfectly. Eliminate all confusion while you're still of sound mind and there's no distraction of hard bodies.

Brian moved his lips to my ear.

My hands tensed in my lap. I closed my eyes.

Please tell me I'm your girlfriend. It's all I want.

"Never been this way for me," he said in a low, gentle voice. "Had a lot of girls growing up. Some serious. Some I just had because they wanted to be something and I liked them enough they stuck around for a little while, but I never called one of them my girl, serious or not. Girlfriend? Yeah. But never *my girl*, and I've been calling you that since the beginning, Syd. Since before I probably should've. That puts you somewhere no one else has ever been. On top of that, done some things with you I've already explained were a first for me, so that should tell you how serious this is. You wanna lock something down? Say we're seeing each other or dating or whatever? You don't need to ask me, babe, 'cause I'm locked down. Whatever you wanna call us, I'm good with. Just know I'll be saying you're my girl 'cause that's what you are. That's yours."

He pulled back, allowing me to turn my head and look at him through tear-soaked eyes.

I was no longer wanting to be his girlfriend. This was so much better.

"That spell it out for you?" he asked.

I didn't get to do the Baby thing because I was already in his lap and the table wouldn't allow for any launching, but I did throw my arms around Brian in an equally dramatic way, a sob catching in my throat and my chest quaking with broken breaths as I buried my face in his neck and hugged him with every ounce of strength I had.

"I love being your girl. I think it's my favorite thing in the entire world," I said, feeling his arms tighten around me. "And you're my boy."

"Your man," he corrected.

I shook my head against his.

"Man doesn't go with girl. If you're my man, then I'm your woman."

"I'm not changing what I've been calling you for weeks, Wild. You're my girl."

"Then you're my boy."

He leaned back, pushed the chunk of hair out of my face that had fallen out of my pretty jeweled clip and was now damp with tears, tucked it behind my ear, and held me there, fingers curling around the back of my head and neck.

Brian stared at me, looking ready to argue.

I stared back, feeling a million different things, but the predominant feeling was love and it was blooming so quick inside me, I was certain the word was going to start sprouting from underneath my skin.

I cleared my throat, prompting him to speak.

"Just told you some things that meant a lot to me so I don't feel like fighting you on this and ruining the mood," he started. "That being said, you call me your boy and I don't answer to that, you know why. It's not 'cause you don't got a hold on me, Wild, so don't go thinking that."

I blinked away more tears.

"Okay," I said.

"You wanna call me your man? I will *always* answer to that."

I closed my eyes, loving the idea of Brian being my man, smiled, and probably did it looking all doped up on something but I didn't care, then I looked at him with that same smile and said, "I'll answer to anything you wanna call me. Just don't call me late for dinner."

Brian stared at me, face serious through several blinks, then breaking into his own slow smile and laughing quietly through a shake of his head.

"Jesus. How long you been wanting to use that, babe?" he asked, arms squeezing me. "Honest."

"Forever," I confessed, laughing a little. "But I swear, no one ever set me up for it. It's torture having a joke cued up and never being able to use it."

"It's a really bad joke."

My eyes narrowed.

"It is not," I argued. "It's hilarious. You totally laughed."

"I was laughing at you for using it, nut."

"Don't call me nut. I'm your girl." I tilted my head. "Or Wild or babe."

"Nut," he added.

Eyes narrowing again, I leaned in close to whisper, "You might not know this, but over the past month I've thought a lot about sucking you off, Brian."

His brows lifted in interest.

Knowing I had his attention, I continued on just as quietly.

"And I'd love to make that a reality, maybe even later on tonight, but you should know, I can go from wanting to suck you off to not wanting to suck you off in a second if you keep calling me nut. There are women out there who aren't into that, the sucking-off part, and I don't think you want me to become one of those women."

I was feeling powerful in my speech. My chest was even puffed out a little.

Too bad I forgot how badly I wanted to suck Brian off, that being something else I'd dreamed about frequently, and the urge to see it through being something Brian was apparently well aware of, giving the triumphant little gleam flickering in his eyes as he stared back.

It was possible he was a mind reader and was watching me work out this predicament in my head.

It was also quite possible I'd spilled the beans on this dream of mine one night when we'd been getting each other off over the phone and I was so far gone, I'd shared my deepest darkest desires with him.

Brian smiled, licked his full, soft lips, then uttered, "Only way you're keeping that sweet mouth off my dick is if I keep you off it, babe. We both know you're hard up for it."

My shoulders slumped in defeat.

Damn. He knew.

"But I'll drop the nut," he continued. "Doesn't have the same ring to it as the other shit I call you."

My chest puffed out a little again.

"Thank you," I said. "I appreciate your sensitivity on this matter."

He smiled bigger.

"Anytime."

A door shutting at my back had me craning my neck to see behind me.

Tori was coming from the direction of Nate's office with Nate on her tail, her eyes finding me and filling with approval once she took in whose lap I was sitting on.

She headed in our direction, smiling at Shay, who was avoiding the kitchen window and hanging out at the bar instead, filling salt and pepper shakers by the looks of it.

Nate was headed for the coffeemaker behind the bar, it appeared. He wasn't looking my way yet.

Probably not best for your boss to see you canoodling with patrons the way Brian and I were canoodling. His hand was currently squeezing my ass and his other was settled between my legs, holding firm to the inside of my thigh.

I *really* didn't want to move.

I also *really* liked having a job, and I needed this one considering the awful luck I was having finding an x-ray position locally.

Before I could be spotted and possibly fired, I slid off Brian's lap and stood, spun around to face the booth, smoothed out the tiny apron I was wearing, then pulled out my ticket book and clicked open my pen.

"Good afternoon, sir. My name is Sydney and I'll be your waitress today. Our specials are lobster linguini and the smokehouse burger. They are both super yummy. I eat them all the time."

I smiled pleasantly and professionally at Brian, who was leaning back casually in the booth with one hand resting on the table.

He grinned beautifully.

I fought off the urge to molest him with my lips and fingers.

"Afternoon, kids," Tori greeted, stepping up beside me.

She smiled at Brian and wrapped her arm around my waist.

"Potential, you had my best girl floating on cloud nine this morning. I kinda love you for that."

I love you, too, I thought, so loudly I swore the words broke out through my ears and floated around me in little hope-filled bubbles where he could read them.

Brian looked to me and kept his eyes on my face. It appeared the words hadn't slipped free.

I breathed a little easier and continued loving him quietly.

Tori gave me a squeeze. I turned to look at her.

"Schedule is up. Nate has you off on Tuesday, then on Sunday. He said depending on Kali, he might not need you on Saturday but to be prepared. She might not have a sitter that day."

"Okay," I replied, smiling.

That meant I could possibly have two days off in a row but I wouldn't count on that. Normally if Kali wasn't sure about a sitter, it meant she wouldn't have one.

"You working with me any of those days?" I asked, sounding hopeful.

Tori nodded.

"All but Thursday. I'm on Tuesday."

"Cool," I replied.

Tori smiled, opened her mouth, and began echoing back a "cool," but lost it when her eyes lifted and focused in on something behind me, then narrowed to tiny slits of fury at the same time as her mouth snapped shut and her lips curled in distaste.

Her "cool" came out sounding more like "crud."

I turned my head and saw Jamie standing behind me.

Crud indeed.

His hair was damp and salt-water messy, and he was wearing tinted aviators.

Indoors.

Idiot.

I was still mad at him for screwing up his chances with Tori, especially after finding out exactly what happened this morning.

She walked in on him engaged in a threesome.

I almost threw up in my mouth hearing that. And even though I wanted to root for the best friend of my boy, I was having a hard time seeing any good side of Jamie to root for now that I knew he passed up an opportunity with my best friend to have a foursome.

Anyone who passed up spending *any* time with Tori was an idiot in my book. She was the best.

Jamie removed his sunglasses and tucked them in the front of his light gray tee, which I supposed was acceptable timing to remove sunglasses after entering a building, but I wasn't admitting that, considering what I now knew, and went ahead thinking he was stupid for wearing them inside.

"Sunshine," he greeted me, barely looking at me before he found Tori at my back. His hand lifted in question. "What the hell, Legs? You turn invisible or something last night? I looked all over for you."

I turned to look at Tori.

She still had her eyes narrowed, but now had her hands on her hips and was leaning her weight on her right foot, looking sassy.

"Well, I'm not sure why you thought I'd be up some girl's snatch, since that seemed to be the only place you were *lookin'*," she tipped forward and hissed quietly, respectful of patrons but still delivering her cut with venom.

"Say again?" Jamie asked at my back.

"You heard me," Tori replied with boredom.

"Yeah, I heard you, babe, but what I'm asking is for you to repeat it." He stepped closer, forcing me to step back so I wouldn't be squished between the two of them. "You come lookin' for me?" he pressed.

I swore I heard hope in his voice.

Tori tilted her head back and held his eyes. Her shoulders lowered and the fingers at her hips eased their tension.

She was losing her fire. I could see it, but she wouldn't let that on.

"I'd *never* come looking for you," she whispered, then rolled up on her toes to add, "Not. Ever."

"Right," Jamie muttered. "You came lookin' for me. That's what this is about."

"Nope. Sorry."

"You did."

"Didn't."

"Then how come you know I was buried in pussy?"

"Lucky guess," Tori snapped. "It was between that or your own ass. I had a fifty-fifty shot."

Jamie smiled and crossed his arms over his chest.

"That's cute, Legs. Real cute, and I gotta be honest. I'm digging you being jealous."

Tori scoffed.

"I am *not* jealous."

"You are."

"Am not."

"Are."

"God, are you *that* conceited? Seriously? Not everyone wants you, Jamie."

He bent down, getting closer and forcing Tori to rock back onto her heels.

"You do," he said, his voice dipping lower. "You're hard up, babe. As bad as me. Admit it. How long'd you stand there watching last night, wishing you were one of them?"

Tori's eyes rounded to the size of dinner plates.

I peered around Jamie to look at Brian, indicating with my head and knowing eyes for him to step in and break up this back and forth before it got any worse.

Brian shrugged casually.

"Told you before, Wild. Unless it's getting pushed on me, I stay out of it," he reminded me.

I glared at him to show my disapproval.

I could tell by the smile tugging at his mouth that Brian thought my glare was cute and not at all threatening.

That made me glare harder.

"Anyone working today?" Nate asked at my back with a tone that screamed unemployment for all of us.

I lost the glare, quickly spun around, and waved my ticket book in front of me.

"I am!" I said enthusiastically, grinning at his hardened face.

Nate was a good-looking guy even when he looked angry. It was the dark hair, dark eyes, dress shirt rolled at his forearms, and Clark Kent glasses.

Nerds were right behind hot boys who used to surf, in my book.

"I was just getting ready to take down orders," I further explained when Nate looked unconvinced.

He kept his face hard as he cut his eyes to Tori, his coffee steaming in his hands.

She was already moving away and toward a table on the other side of the room, greeting a four-top with that small town girl charm she radiated and everyone fell in love with. The two couples ate it up, and if they'd been waiting long, they forgot all about that wait the second Tori started talking.

I looked back at Nate and saw his approval. His face was marginally less angry, and he turned that face on Jamie and relaxed it further to ask, "You being helped?"

Jamie nodded, choosing not to get Tori into trouble, which I could've seen as sweet but I chose not to because I was still holding on to the knowledge Tori shared last night, then he moved in front of me and took the seat across from Brian.

Nate stepped away and took his coffee to his office. The door shut loudly behind him.

"Dude is hurting," Brian observed, pulling my eyes to his. He jerked his chin. "You can see it. That wasn't just about you girls standing around and not getting to work."

I thought it was sweet he noticed Nate's pain, thinking most guys wouldn't pick up on something like that and would only see a boss getting on his employees, and I chose to show my feelings about Brian being in tune to that by leaning over the table and kissing him quickly.

It was soft and sweet and tasted like spearmint gum.

I *loved* spearmint gum.

Then I pulled back, readied my ticket book, and looked between Brian and Jamie, asking, "Do ya'll need time or are you ready to order?"

Brian chuckled.

Jamie slid the menu that was already set out on the table closer to me, keeping it closed.

"Not sure I should bother," he said. "You seem to get some crazy idea of your own every time I come in here and bring me whatever you're feelin'."

"Well, you could always eat somewhere else if you're unhappy with the service," I suggested, forcing my lips into a smile that was one hundred percent fake.

The smile Jamie hit me with in return was one hundred percent genuine—heart-melting dimples and all.

"Nah. I like the view here," he told me, winking. "Just bring me a Coke with grenadine if you feel like it."

I looked at Brian.

His smile warmed my belly and melted other parts of me, not just my heart.

"Southern stuffed shrimp, Wild. And that coffee."

"Got it."

I scribbled down his order and my choice of the day for Jamie— a bucket of clams—swiped the menu off the table, and deposited it back at the hostess booth, then ripped the ticket off and carried it to the kitchen window.

"Is there a way to do the Loser Special on the bucket of clams,

Stitch?" I asked, sliding the ticket across the cold steel. "Or is it a waste of time to drop clams on the floor?"

Stitch was standing at the grill with his back to me, stirring up something in a sauce pan.

He turned his head after hearing my question, registered it with a jerk of his chin, then went back to staring at the sauce pan.

I leaned my elbow on the steel.

"I have no idea what that little chin jerk means, you know that, right?" I asked.

Stitch said nothing.

I turned my head to look at Shay.

She had moved on from filling salt and pepper shakers at the bar and was now passing time between tending to her patrons by sitting at a vacant table and rolling extra sets of silverware.

No one ever volunteered to roll silverware. You only did it when Nate asked you to.

I looked once again at Stitch, rolled up on my toes, and added for only him to hear, "She's upset with you and she has reason to be. You bailed on her. And when girls are excited about something and that one thing they're excited about falls through, they get disappointed and sometimes get quiet."

I watched the silent man, all messy edge and lawless looks, leave that sauce pan and turn to face me. His eyes were hard and his nostrils were flaring with irritation.

"Never said I'd go," he clipped, saying more than he'd ever said to me at once before, and if that didn't make me highly interested in listening, it was the topic and tone of his voice that kept me invested and not ducking behind the bar. "She just assumed 'cause I didn't say different when she was talkin' about it, and that's on her. I got no business bein' at a party like that and she knows it, just like she's got no business invitin' me to one. What the fuck would I do there?"

I was staring and I was doing it with my eyes wide and my mouth dropped open.

Whoa.

Stitch had an extremely sexy voice hiding behind that beard.

Nice.

"Uh," I stammered, then stated as if it was obvious, "You could've hung out with Shay."

He shook his head and looked down at the prep station.

"Got no business doin' that either," he muttered. "Girl like that with that kinda light..." His voice trailed off, then he lifted his eyes, tensed his jaw, and said curtly, "Not talkin' about this."

My brows shot up.

I absolutely wanted to keep talking about this. What Stitch was saying was incredibly interesting and something I would definitely share with Shay.

He thought she had light. He also thought he wasn't good enough to touch that light. I was hearing that loud and clear.

Shay was right. Stitch *was* sweet.

I wanted to jump through that window and hug the crap out of him.

But before I could do that or urge him into further conversation, he reached out and slammed his hand down on the steel, swiped the ticket, read the order quickly, then tacked it up along with the others before he turned around and supervised the sauce pan.

"Not much I can do with the clams," he informed, facing away. "Droppin' them on the floor ain't gonna do what you're lookin' for it to do."

I nodded at his back, deciding to be generous and letting Jamie off easy today. Mainly because Stitch seemed in the mood to get creative if I asked and I was scared to think what he'd come up with while standing back there alone and pining over Shay.

"It's okay, don't worry about it," I told him, rocking back onto my feet. "But if it's not too much trouble, could you make those Southern stuffed shrimp extra yummy for my boy? He's here."

"Whatever," he muttered, his arm moving as he stirred.

"With lots of love," I added. "Not that I'm telling you how to cook, but maybe slip in an extra hush puppy?"

Stitch shook his head through a noisy exhale.

"Jesus Christ, I need a new fuckin' job."

I left that remark alone and stepped in front of the coffeemaker, grabbing a mug for Brian.

As long as Shay worked at Whitecaps, I had a feeling Stitch wasn't going anywhere.

* * *

I was running my tongue along the underside of Brian's cock as I knelt between his knees on the floor of his living room in front of the couch.

He'd dropped calling me "nut" so I was making good on my promise to suck him off, starting on that as soon as I got to his place after my shift ended.

I was moaning and taking him deep while fighting off the urge to press my fingers between my legs, knowing the second I did that I'd go off, enjoying the feel of his long, thick cock in my mouth so much that I was getting there without even trying. And Brian was fisting my hair and thrusting his hips, saying some of the hottest stuff to me as I worked him.

"Wild," he groaned.

"*Fuck*," he snarled.

"Jesus, babe. Never been sucked this good," he confessed.

Hot.

We had the house to ourselves for the rest of the night because Jamie went to look at some bike he was interested in buying two hours away, an investment Brian found hilarious for some reason he hadn't shared with me yet, which led to the fooling around on the couch instead of in the privacy of Brian's bedroom.

I loved it. I wanted to be out in the open with Brian everywhere.

Let everyone see our crazy.

Rising up on my knees, I swallowed him until my lips touched the top of my hand squeezing his base, then I started sucking and jerking in slow, wet strokes, twisting my wrist and keeping pressure.

"Shit," Brian muttered as his legs tensed. "Wild, get up here."

"Un-mm."

I shook my head a little and kept sucking and jerking as my other hand cupped his balls.

"*Syd*," he growled.

Concentrating on the head, I swirled my tongue and flicked it as my hand pumped firmer and faster.

I wanted him to come. I wanted to taste Brian and I knew he was close, but before I could push him over the edge, hands gripped with impatience under my arms, lifting me off and then up until I was on my feet, standing in front of Brian and gripping his shoulders for stability as he tore savagely at my uniform shorts. He peeled them down my legs along with my panties, tossed them on the floor, then gripped the back of my thighs, took my weight, and somehow spread my legs and lowered me at the same time until I slid down onto his cock in one perfect, fluid, *oh, my God, how am I this wet* motion.

"Brian," I gasped as he stretched me.

His hand slapped my ass and I yelped, lurching forward until our bellies and chests were touching and I could feel the rapid pounding of his heart against mine.

"Ride me 'til I come," he ordered with fire in his eyes.

"I wanted you to come in my mouth," I shared, leaning back and settling in his lap.

"I was getting that." His lip twitched, then he held my hips and started shifting them, urging me to move with his hands and pressing me, "Come on, babe. Fuck me. Let me see what my girl can do."

My skin tingled.

His girl.

No way was I saying no to that.

I started taking over, grinding down and forward while my hands gripped the back of the couch, going from slow to fast to slow again, then circling my hips instead of rocking them, pulling deeper, dirtier noises out of Brian.

"*God*, Wild."

"So good," I moaned, popping my booty and bouncing in his lap. "You feel...*so* good."

His hips started driving off the couch as his fingers dug into my back under the white polo I was wearing and quickly peeling off so he could get to my breasts. The second the material hit the cushion beside us, Brian had my bra pushed down and his mouth latched around my nipple, sucking it hard and hungry when the doorbell sounded with a charming pitch.

I gasped and froze like a stone.

Brian froze, too, releasing my nipple but keeping his mouth against my flesh, his arms tight around me, waiting.

If we didn't move or make a sound, they'd leave. This was apparently the train of thought we both shared.

Seconds passed.

"False alarm?" I guessed, then felt my spine tighten when the unmistakable sound of metal sliding against metal and unlocking alerted us of someone entering the house.

"*Fuck*," Brian hissed, shifting me off his lap until I fell backward onto the cushion beside him.

He grabbed my shorts and panties off the floor and tossed them at me, both of us frantically pulling on and sliding up clothes, tucking and zipping and covering as best we could before the door pushed open and little excited voices filled the house.

"Uncle Brian!" a boy yelled.

"We're here! We're here!" another voice cried animatedly, this one sounding like a girl. "And we brought our iPads! Wait 'til you see my Minecraft now, Uncle Brian. It's *so* awesome!"

Uncle Brian?

Panic raced through me.

"Oh, my God, your family is going to see me naked and know *exactly* what we were doing. My first impression is going to be *horrible*," I whispered, pulling on my polo now that my shorts were fastened, which turned out to be a chore doing on my back but I had no other choice. It was the only way I could stay concealed.

This was so embarrassing!

"Did you know they were coming over?"

Brian stood to zip his shorts.

"I forgot," he replied quietly, looking me over while pressing a hand to the front of his shorts. "Fuck, I was so close."

"Get over it," I snapped softly, struggling to get one arm through my shirt. "And hold them off from coming in here. I still have a boob out."

Brian smirked, which I totally could've slapped him for but he looked really cute doing it so I let it go. He moved around the couch to hold off our company but halted only a couple of feet away when quick footsteps padded into the room.

"Uncle Brian!" the little girl shrieked. "Guess what? I chopped down Ollie's tree!"

"Livvy! Why did you do that?" the boy asked, sounding angry. "I just put that up."

"Because it was the only other tree I could find," she replied meekly. "I'm sorry, Ollie. Don't be mad. You can chop down my tree."

"Would you both stop talking about Minecraft for five seconds and go give your uncle a hug?" a woman suggested.

Teeth clenching, I finally got my arm through the second hole and pulled my shirt down, double checking I was covered then sitting up slowly and stretching my hands above my head while forcing a yawn.

"Oh, wow. That was the best nap *ever*," I lied, then rubbed my eyes and blinked fake sleepily between the two kids who were peering around Brian's arms wrapped around them and the young woman standing a few feet away who I assumed was their mother.

She had Brian's high cheekbones and full lips, which she was turning up into a knowing smile as she looked at me.

I didn't think she was buying my nap story.

"Uncle Brian, who is that?" the boy asked.

The girl blinked with round eyes the color of melted chocolate.

Brian released them, stepped back, and turned his body halfway, giving them full view of me as I stood from the couch.

Both with blue-rimmed glasses and dark hair that looked playground messy, they were the same height and looked to be the same age.

Were they twins?

"This is Syd," Brian said.

The girl took a step closer and tilted her head.

"Are you Uncle Brian's girlfriend?" she asked, giving me a once-over and, when she was done, smiling big. "I know you are. He said you were super pretty and you are *so* super pretty. Your hair looks like Ariel."

My cheeks warmed.

"Thank you," I replied, moving around the couch and stopping in front of her. "I'm Sydney. I go by Syd, too. Is your name Livvy?"

She shrugged.

"That's what Ollie calls me. It's Olivia. You can call me Livvy or Olivia. Uncle Brian calls me Liv sometimes. He also said he loved you."

My eyes widened. I turned them to Brian and watched him pinch his shut and drop his head, shaking it.

"*Olivia*," the woman hissed behind her. "He didn't say that, *I* said it." She lifted her eyes to me and softened them, adding, "Not that it isn't true. If my brother told you already, then I'm sure he means it."

Brian groaned, clearly uncomfortable.

"Why did I give you a key?" he asked, turning his head to her.

The woman smiled, telling him, "Because I used to live here, remember?"

"Duh, Uncle Brian," the boy, Oliver, added, looking up with tight brows.

Olivia spun around, her pretty dress fanning out as she giggled.

"Yeah, duh," she echoed.

Brian's sister turned back to me, keeping that smile but notching it up in brightness as she stepped forward and offered me her hand.

"I'm Jenna, by the way. It's so good to meet you, Sydney."

She knew about me, I was sure of that, but I didn't know the extent and I really wanted to know what all had been said about me.

Especially the whole love business.

"It's good to meet you, too," I replied, dropping her hand and looking down at her shoes. "Cute booties."

Really cute.

They were camel-colored leather with a chunky wooden heel that had to be four inches.

I wondered what size she wore.

"Thanks. I have a date tonight and he's six-five. Needed some height." Jenna turned her head and looked at Brian. "Did you forget?"

Brian shoved his hands in his pockets.

"Nope."

"You forgot." Jenna sighed. "It's fine. I can reschedule."

"No way!" Olivia cried, stomping her foot.

"Oh, man. This sucks." Oliver crossed his arms over his chest and huffed out a breath. "I don't wanna go back home. It's boring there. I wanted to walk on the beach."

"Oliver, don't say sucks. That's not nice," Jenna scolded.

"Well, it does," he whispered, ducking his head.

"I don't care. You're not allowed to say that word."

"Fine. This is stupid."

"You aren't allowed to say that either," she snapped, sounding on the verge of losing her temper. "Do I need to take away your iPad privileges?"

Oliver looked up at her, quickly shook his head, and muttered, "No, ma'am."

I decided to cut in before the poor thing said something out of panic and got his iPad privileges taken away. I felt bad.

"You don't have to reschedule. We didn't have plans tonight. We'd be happy to watch them," I told Jenna, seeing her smile then looking over at Brian to confirm and watching his brows lift in surprise. "Right?"

He stared at me, face stuck in that expression.

"*Right?*" I probed.

"We didn't have plans?" Brian asked incredulously. "'Cause I thought we were sorta in the middle of somethin'—"

"That can be pushed back until later," I cut in, bringing my hands to my hips. "Obviously."

He cocked his head.

"Not sure it can, babe."

"It totally can."

"You understand what I'm dealing with right now?"

"Um, should we step out?" Jenna asked hesitantly.

"No. Please stay here," I replied, eyes narrowed as they sliced back to Brian.

Brian narrowed his back.

This was so not the time or place to have this discussion, and seriously, how painful were blue balls anyway? I was certain men played that shit up.

"Really?" he asked.

I nodded hard. "Really."

Brian looked to the ceiling and breathed in deep.

"Well, it was a good run. Sweet while it lasted."

He was talking about our relationship.

"Very funny," I quipped, catching the smile he was fighting before looking between the kids. "You two wanna hang out here for a while?"

"Yes!" Oliver punched his fist into the air and jumped off the floor. "Thank you! Thank you! Thank you!"

Olivia shook her hips with a little dance, then cutely high-fived her brother.

"Are you sure?" Jenna asked, concern in her voice. "I don't wanna put you two out."

"You won't be. Go enjoy yourself. We got this."

She smiled again.

"I like your girlfriend, Uncle Brian. She's cool," Oliver said, taking the two small duffles out of his mother's hand and giving the one decorated with pastel circles to Olivia. "And I guess she's pretty."

"She's super pretty!" Olivia shouted, looking up at me and clutching her duffle against her chest. "Wanna play hair salon? I brought my accessories."

I smiled big.

"Absolutely. I love accessories."

"Awesome," she whispered excitedly, then turned her head. "You hear that, Ollie? Syd is gonna play hair salon with me, and she loves accessories, too!"

"Yeah, whatever. Me and Uncle Brian are gonna play Road Blocks."

Oliver rounded the couch with his duffle and climbed on, heaving the bag up on the cushion and unzipping it.

Olivia scrambled after him.

"I have my cell if you need me. We shouldn't be that late so you won't have to put them to bed," Jenna said, stepping in front of Brian and laughing quietly at the frustrated expression he was still holding, then wrapping him up into a hug. "I love her," she whispered, loud enough for me to hear. "Don't mess this up."

"Don't you have a date to get to?"

She leaned away and stuck out her tongue, then gave me a wave, smiling.

"Have fun!" I said, waving back.

Her heels slapped against the wood floor as she exited the room, then the front door closed behind her.

I stepped in front of Brian and grinned up at him.

"Hey, Trouble."

He didn't grin back.

"Wild."

I rolled up on my toes and whispered a promise. "I'll make it good."

His cheek twitched, then he wrapped his arms around my back and pulled me close.

"Countin' on it, babe," he said against my hair.

I gave him a quick squeeze, then turned my head to ask the kids, "Did you guys eat?"

Oliver looked up from his iPad.

"No. We weren't hungry before we left. But I'm starving now."

"Me, too," Olivia said, keeping her eyes focused on what she was playing and not turning around. "Can we order pizza again, Uncle Brian?"

"Why don't we make them instead?" I suggested, both pairs of eyes drawing to me with interest. "You can both make your own how you like it and we can even do a dessert one. It's easy and super yummy."

"A dessert one?" Olivia sat up taller and licked her lips.

"Yep. We can put chocolate or peanut butter sauce on it and chocolate chips, marshmallows, M&M's—"

"Let's do that!" she shrieked, cutting me off and spinning around completely so she was hanging over the back of the couch. "I love marshmallows and chocolate. We can do a s'mores one with graham crackers, right, Ollie?"

"Yeah, totally. Can we eat them on the beach?" he asked, mimicking his sister's position and looking a milder form of excited.

I looked up at Brian.

He was staring down at me in a way that made my toes curl against the wood.

"Wanna have dinner with us on the beach?" I asked, pressing my hands to his chest. "I think the kids will really like the pizza. I make it all the time, and I don't mind running out and getting ingredients."

"Sweet of you," he said.

I shrugged.

"I've been told I can be sweet sometimes."

His eyes dropped to my mouth.

"Yeah," he breathed.

"Are you guys gonna kiss like they do on TV?" Olivia questioned through a small, excited voice.

"That's disgusting," Oliver muttered. "I can't watch this."

Brian's chest shook with a laugh, breaking him out of his fixation.

I tipped my chin back and waited with eyes closed and lips puckered.

He gave me a very G-rated kiss, sending Olivia into a fit of giggles while Oliver groaned uncomfortably, apparently he lied and totally watched it happen, then Brian pulled back only to press another kiss to my forehead.

I moaned and melted closer.

Forehead kisses from Brian were the best.

"Make a list for the store," he ordered. "I'll go."

I smiled, then turned to Olivia, who was still watching us, and gave it to her.

"Ready to play hair salon?"

She was ready, and she showed that by dropping her iPad on the couch like it was on fire and trading it for a bubblegum pink case she pulled out of her duffle, holding it above her head with both hands and nodding frantically.

I wanted to eat her up. She was the cutest.

After making Brian a list of ingredients, I sat on the floor in front of the couch and let Olivia brush, twist, braid, pull, and tease my hair, accessorizing me with nearly every clip she had, all while listening to her gab about Minecraft, some show about a gumball, and her brother, who was older by ten minutes.

Then we switched places and I made her hair super pretty, as requested.

* * *

The kids loved making their own pizzas, which both ended up being extra sauce and two types of cheese after Olivia heard what Oliver wanted and changed her mind from her original plan, lots of pepperoni.

It was sweet how she wanted to keep with what he had, and according to Brian, it happened a lot and Oliver was the same with her.

I wanted to eat Oliver up, too.

Seriously, these kids were the sweetest things in the world.

We had our slices of pizza on the beach, picnic style on a blanket, then the two of them ran around for a bit and got in the water but only up to their knees, keeping their clothes dry.

When it was time for dessert, we headed back inside and I popped the s'mores pizza into the oven while Brian sat on the couch between the kids and cued up a movie on Netflix.

I could see the top of Olivia's wildly accessorized head. It was resting on Brian's shoulder. Oliver's wasn't but he was sitting close enough I knew he was leaning against him, too.

It looked natural. All three of them cozying together. The scene struck deeper than witnessing a doting uncle spending time with his niece and nephew. It warmed my heart so much more than I was expecting, blooming unfamiliar hopes and dreams and wishes inside me. I stood next to the island for long silent minutes, taking shallow breaths and staring at the three of them as fear and longing spread through my soul.

I wanted kids.

For the first time in my twenty-four years of life, I wanted kids.

I, Sydney Whittaker, wanted to be a mom.

Holy...*shit*.

I was either going to pass out right here, throw up, or start crying. One of those three things was bound to happen.

Brian turned his head and peered at me over the couch.

"Coming over?"

I sucked in breath through my nose, feeling it tingle as my eyes watered.

Option three. I was going to start crying.

Brian noticed my change in demeanor and craned his neck farther to question it.

"You all right?"

I needed to get a handle on my emotions. This was a happy night, and I didn't want my newfound desire for kids bringing down the mood in the room.

But seriously, this was life changing and warranted a minute of freak-out, at least.

Just not right now.

Needing to find my composure since I had eyes on me, I turned my head and looked at the wall by the slider, focusing my gaze on the eight-by-ten picture that hung there of Jamie on the beach, sun beaming down on him, board in hand and a shiny gold medal around his neck.

My nose stopped tingling and my eyes dried up.

Idiot.

"Syd?"

"Perfect," I answered, calmed and confident, then walked across the room and rounded the couch. I smiled at Brian, gave a little of it to Oliver, then shined it all on Olivia as I sat down next to her. "I'm perfect."

She smiled back and giggled when I shook my hair and made the clips clack against each other.

I hadn't taken all of them out yet.

"Can you turn the fireplace on, Uncle Brian?" Olivia asked, tilting her head up. "My toes are cold."

Brian stood from the couch, walked over to the wall next to the slider, and flipped a switch. The fireplace made a clicking noise like a burner on a stove, then roared to life seconds later.

Olivia hopped off the couch as Brian reclaimed his seat and moved to the floor so she was closer to the fire, stretched her legs out in front of her, and wiggled her feet. Then she looked over her shoulder at Oliver and pushed her glasses higher on her nose.

"Ollie, come down here and watch."

He joined her without protest, sprawling out on his stomach and tilting his head back to watch the movie, knees bent and feet kicking the air.

I looked from them to Brian, holding on to a smile.

He patted the spot next to him.

"Hey," I whispered, burrowing against his side and breathing him in.

He smelled like salt water and spring meadow detergent.

"Hey," he whispered back, throwing his arm around me and holding on to my waist as I leaned on my left hip, dropped my head against his shoulder, and bent my knees, resting my bare feet on the couch.

Olivia giggled at the TV, looked at Oliver when he laughed at the same thing, then turned back and giggled some more.

"They used to live here with you?" I asked quietly.

The thought made me smile. I could picture tiny feet jumping on the bed in the morning and rousing Brian awake.

I felt his head turn and the heat of his mouth against my hair.

"Two years ago. Moved here from Denver and stayed with me until Jenna found them something. It was only for a couple months."

"Denver? Jeez. That's crazy far away," I replied. "What were they doing out there?"

"My parents live there," he said. "We grew up in Emerald Isle but my dad's job took him to Denver when I was a senior in high school. Didn't want to go so I moved in with Jamie and his family. Liked the idea of staying near the water. I'm not much for snow sports. Jenna was fifteen so she didn't have a choice. My parents took her with them."

Jenna looked young, maybe close to my age, and I knew the kids were seven.

"How old is Jenna?" I asked.

"Twenty-six."

I did the math, then sat back to look at him, forcing his arm to slide to my back.

"She had the kids when she was nineteen?" I questioned with shock in my voice.

He nodded.

"Oh, my God. That had to be insane. I can't imagine two babies at nineteen." I looked to Oliver and Olivia, then turned back to Brian and leaned in to ask quietly, "Where's the father?"

His face hardened.

Uh-oh.

"Asshole signed over rights when they were barely a year," he spat. "Didn't want Jenna to carry them. Told her to terminate the pregnancy."

My eyes went round.

"What? Her boyfriend asked her to do that?"

"They weren't together," Brian clarified. "Hooked up at a party once and that was it. Jenna wanted something to come of it but Derek didn't want anything to do with her. Couldn't even man up and be a dad to those kids." He shook his head with a clenched jaw. "Good thing I wasn't living there. Probably would've killed him if I ever met the shithead. Know it was tough on her doing it alone but she didn't have to for long. My parents stepped in and took some of the load off. Watched the kids while she finished school and got her degree. Once she was done, she wanted a fresh start, for her and the kids. Told her to come out here and I'd help out as much as I could."

I placed my hand on his chest.

"That was sweet of you."

Brian shrugged, then looked at the floor where they were sitting.

"Wanted to know them. Be someone they could rely on. They're good kids who got dealt a shit hand."

"That's not true."

He turned his head to me.

"You saying they aren't good kids?" he asked.

"Of course not. They're terrific kids. I love them so much already," I replied, seeing his mouth twitch. "I'm saying they weren't dealt a shit hand."

He cocked his head.

"How'd you figure?"

I got close again, pressing against his side as my hand slid up his chest to his neck and jaw, where I held him there.

"They have a mom who loves them enough she knew she'd be facing a hard road and she took it anyway, doing it because she wanted them," I explained. "She fought for those kids and she fought alone, and I have no doubt in my mind they aren't missing out. I only had one parent."

Brian's eyes went soft and the hand holding me tensed at my side.

"Up until she couldn't be a good one anymore, my mom was all the parent I needed," I continued, sliding my hand down to his shirt. "That being said, I also had a nana who gave me the kind of love only a grandparent can give, which those kids also had, only they had both your parents. That's a lot of love, Brian. Then they got you when they moved here. I see what you mean to them. The way Olivia smiles at you and Oliver absorbs what you're doing and watches you closely. Their hearts are very full. In no way did they get dealt a shit hand."

Brian reached out and snagged one of the butterfly clips dangling at the end of my hair and held it between his fingers.

"You act like you've been watching me with them for years," he said, sliding his eyes to mine. "Only been a couple hours, Wild."

I swallowed against nerves crawling up the back of my throat.

"It has," I agreed softly. "But I could watch you with them for five minutes and still come to the same conclusion I've come to."

"That we're close?"

"Yes."

He smiled.

"And that I'd very much like that someday."

Brian chuckled softly.

"Pretty sure we're close, too, babe."

"No, not that."

He released the clip, let his hand drop to my thigh to hold me there, and with eyes curious and calming, searched my face.

"What then," he pried, dipping closer until his lips touched my temple. "What do you want, Syd? Name it. I'll get it for you."

God...

I sucked in a breath, mouth opening to answer just as the timer on the oven buzzed behind us.

I leaned away. "I should get that." Then I scurried off the couch, moving quickly into the kitchen.

"Is it ready?" Olivia called at my back.

"Maybe," I answered. "Let me make sure the marshmallows are all gooey."

"Yummm. Gooey marshmallows," she moaned, and smacked her lips.

After silencing the buzzer, I fitted my hands with oven mitts so I could grab the tray the pizza was cooking on.

"Here."

Brian was at my back, easing me to the side so I was no longer standing in front of the oven.

He slipped one of the mitts off my hand and fitted it on his right, then opened the oven and pulled out the tray, holding it up for me to examine.

"Done?" he asked.

The chocolate was melted. The graham crackers looked toasted. And the marshmallows were definitely gooey.

It looked and smelled delicious.

"Done," I answered.

Brian set the tray on top of the burners, turned off the oven, took his mitt and grabbed the one I was still wearing, and tossed them on the counter. Then grabbing my hips, he pulled me against him and stared intently into my eyes.

"What do you want?" he asked again, this time sounding more urgent.

"Uh."

"What conclusion did you come to after watching me spend five minutes with Oliver and Liv?"

"Well, maybe a little longer than five minutes."

"Syd."

"Mm?"

He squeezed my hips and bent to get closer.

"You want somethin' from me?"

I slowly released my breath and, on the last bit of that exhale, admitted a quiet, "Yes." Then I went on to explain after hopefully pulling in a nerve-calming burst of air.

"I was with Marcus for seven years and I never thought about having kids with him."

Brian didn't say anything. I wasn't sure if he was even breathing, but his fingers were definitely holding on to me a little tighter.

I swallowed down hesitation and went on.

"Never. And that's what you do when you get married, you think about if you want a family or not, and you talk about it together, but that never happened. I never brought it up and neither did he. I spent practically every day with Marcus and not once did I look at him and want him to give me that. *Not once.* Then I see you sitting on that couch with Oliver and Olivia, and for the first time in my life I want it, and I want it in a way I know I'll never go back to *not* wanting it, and that's just after one actual day with you. One day, Brian. What am I gonna want in a week, or a month? What other hopes am I gonna have? I've missed so much of myself being with Marcus. Not just peanut butter and puppies. I wanted kids and I didn't even know it. You showed me that."

Brian was definitely breathing now. I felt it when he hauled me closer, moving his hands to my back and taking my weight until I was up on my toes and my legs and hips and belly and chest were all pressed against his and our faces were almost touching, lips almost kissing as we shared the same air.

I thought he was going to tell me I was crazy, because I was. *This* was.

I thought he was going to say we needed to slow down, get to that week or that month before we talked about stuff like this.

I thought he was going to say no.

But Brian didn't say any of that.

He breathed, slow and steady, then uttered a stilling, "Okay."

My eyes blinked wider.

Just okay.

That's it. That's all he said.

One word that held so much and sounded so loud, and if it was written, I could read it forever.

"Okay?" I asked.

"Yeah."

"Really?"

"Really."

Wow.

"Okay," I whispered anxiously back. "This is crazy, Brian," I pointed out, laughing a little. "We're talking about kids and neither one of us has said...you know...*it* yet."

Brian smiled, moved his hands to the top of my ass, and dropped his head until it was touching mine.

"It?"

"Yes."

"What's *it*?"

I fake glared at him.

"You know..."

"Does it count if I wrote it?" he asked.

Losing the glare, I blinked as he leaned away, then released me, watching him move to the kitchen table and pick up the crossword book I spotted in his room last night. He carried it over, head down as he flipped to a page near the front.

When he reached me, he kept hold of the pen and held out the book for me to take.

I took it and my eyes began scanning the page he indicated with a tap of his finger.

Most of the answers appeared to be filled in and there was nothing written along the margins. I wasn't sure what I was supposed to be looking at or what I was expecting.

Perhaps "I LOVE SYDNEY" in bold capital letters?

Or "Sydney and Brian forever"?

Yes. That's what I was expecting.

I liked stuff spelled out for me, remember?

"Um. Sorry, where am I..."

"Sixteen across," Brian stated.

Top-right corner. The word "WILD" was written in bold capital letters.

It was the only answer written that way.

I appreciated the tribute to his nickname for me, but I was still expecting something different.

"Um..."

"The clue, babe. Read it."

I found the clue for 16-Across.

And I read it.

Zero, on a court.

"Love." The answer was "love." I knew this one. I played tennis in high school.

But Brian hadn't put "love." He'd put "WILD."

"WILD" was his four letter word for "love."

I slowly lifted my eyes.

"Filled that in two weeks ago," Brian confessed, catching the tear that was falling down my cheek with his thumb. "Only puzzle in that book I can't finish 'cause I wrote my answer and it ain't the one they're looking for, but it's mine."

I blinked up at him, trying to see through the emotions flooding my eyes.

"It is?" I whispered, pulling the book against my chest and holding it there.

He nodded, looking down at the book then back up at me.

"Never felt anything like this. Told you I didn't care how crazy this was. Still don't. I love you."

"Brian," I whispered.

He took my face between his hands.

"I love you, Syd," he repeated, eyes serious. "Fuck it, all right? Fuck our crazy. I want it."

A laugh bubbled in my throat.

"I love you, too," I said. "You're the best mistake I've ever made."

Lazy smile and sweet eyes soft, Brian ran his thumb over my cheek and breathed easy.

"Feels good saying it."

He had no idea.

"Yeah," I agreed. "Really good. I've been whispering it in my head for weeks."

Brian smiled bigger and caught another tear with his thumb.

"How many you want?"

I knew he was talking about kids. I tilted my head as Olivia giggled in the background and thought for all of two seconds.

"Two. A boy and a girl." I pressed closer to ask, "You?"

"Whatever you want, babe."

Whatever I want.

It didn't matter to him either way. Brian was going to give it to me.

I had the best boy in the world.

He bent down, pressed his full lips against mine, and kissed me breathless.

It was not G-rated. There was a lot of tongue and gripping hands involved, mainly his since I wouldn't let go of the book.

I had plans on getting it framed.

"Is the s'mores pizza ready *yet*?" Olivia called out impatiently from the living room. "What's taking so long?"

"Gross," Oliver muttered. "Don't look. They're doing it again."

Olivia gasped.

"I wanna see," she whispered excitedly.

I laughed inside our kiss.

Brian broke away laughing, too, then wrapped his arms around me and held tight, and even though I wasn't holding him back, it felt like I was holding him tighter.

Turning my head and leaning, I peered around him to see the kids.

They were standing now. Olivia was staring at us with her fingers covering her mouth, looking so happy she could burst.

Oliver was shielding his eyes from the scene in front of him.

"It's ready," I proclaimed from the cloud I was floating around on. "We were just waiting for it to cool."

Both kids came running into the room.

They told me about a hundred times how good that s'mores pizza was.

I liked hearing that, and I promised another pizza and movie night soon.

I also made good on my promise to Brian.

An hour later, after Jenna had picked up the kids, we were back at it on that couch, only this time I stayed on my knees.

I sucked him off like I wanted but I stopped when Brian got the impulse to take me from behind. I didn't protest.

When you love someone, you compromise.

And boy, did I love him.

Chapter Fifteen

BRIAN

I was circling another ad in the classifieds on Tuesday when Jamie stepped inside Wax with a black duffle slung over his shoulder.

I looked at the time on the computer screen. It was just after eleven.

"What are you doing here?" I asked, watching him walk toward me. "Thought you had lessons this morning?"

He lifted the bag off his shoulder and heaved it up onto the counter.

"Had to move them to tomorrow. You wanted the money, right?"

Jamie unzipped the duffle and pulled on the flaps, showing me the contents in the bag; bundles of hundred-dollar bills, all wrapped and labeled.

"Holy shit," I muttered, leaning over to see.

There was a lot of fucking money in that duffle.

"It's all there. Had to hit up four different banks this morning to get it so I knew I'd be pushing the lesson times. Figured this was more important." He zipped the bag and shoved it in front of me. "Also cleaned out my safe. Sucks if I get the urge to go Pacman Jones up in a strip club now. I'm out of ones."

I placed my hand on the duffle.

"Probably for the best," I told him. "That didn't end well for him."

"Only 'cause that dumbass wanted it back," he shot back. "If I make it rain at The Golden Horse, those bitches can keep it. Once you commit to something like that, you need to follow through."

Laughing under my breath, I slid the duffle off the counter and sat it underneath, tucking it behind a box of hats I still needed to tag with a price before putting out on a shelf.

"Thanks," I said, straightening up and catching his eyes. "Means a lot, you doing this. Appreciate the cash, too. I didn't want to have to write them a check."

Jamie nodded as he leaned his elbows on the counter.

"Figured. Not gonna lie, felt cool carrying that bag around, like I was doing a drop or something," he replied, grinning. "Smell of all that green got me hard."

I stared at him, shaking my head.

"There's something wrong with you," I observed, eyes firm. "Seriously. You need help."

He started laughing.

I wasn't sure if Jamie was telling the truth or not, and I didn't care enough to ask. In fact, the sooner we got onto another topic, the better.

I had something else I needed to talk to him about anyway.

"Thinking about moving out and getting a smaller place," I shared. "Something that'll work long term, room for kids when that happens."

Jamie's brows lifted.

"You being serious?" he asked.

I nodded with hands spread and braced on the counter.

"Makes sense to do it now," I explained. "The way things are moving with Syd and with the pay cut I'm taking now that I'm not part owner, can't afford that house every month. Want something I can easily swing that'll work down the road, too. She wants kids. I wanna give them to her. Three bedrooms should be plenty."

"Jesus," he mumbled, shaking his head in disbelief and lifting his eyes from the counter. "Knew you two were serious, but shit, not gonna lie, I didn't think you were talking about moving in together yet. Not sure this is normal, Dash."

"Normal for us." I shrugged. "Don't give a fuck what anyone else thinks."

"I can see that," he joked, then straightened to ask, "You telling me this so I can get my dad on it?"

Jamie's father was in real estate. Most successful Realtor in North Carolina. He was pretty famous because of it. You couldn't drive along the coast without seeing his face on one of those giant bill-boards off the highway.

It was how the McCade family made all their money before Jamie started competing and getting sponsored.

"Think he'd mind?" I asked.

"Fuck no. You kidding? Pretty sure Dad gets a boner every time he pulls up a listing." Jamie tugged out his phone and started mess-ing with it. "Need to know specifics. You want beach front? Big yard? Sex dungeon?"

"Doesn't need to be beach front but keep it local. Good-size yard would be nice. Nothing less than three bedrooms and it needs to have a porch."

Jamie lifted his eyes.

"You gonna take up knitting or something?" he asked dryly.

I cocked my head.

He shot me a dumbfounded look.

"Why the fuck else would you need to have a porch? You're not an eighty-year-old woman."

"Syd used to eat popsicles with her mom on her porch growing up," I said, defending my request. "Lost that when her brother died and her mom stopped being much of anything to her anymore. Know that's something she wishes she still had and I'm gonna make sure she gets it."

He stared at me as I spoke, listening as if I were speaking another language, then continued staring when I was done and not saying anything back. Just slowly started grinning and looking too fucking pleased for his own good.

Great.

He was going to give me shit.

"If it doesn't have a porch, tell him not to bother showing it to me," I stressed, hoping to move on.

"You're fucking adorable, Dash."

I closed my eyes.

He wasn't ready to move on.

"Jesus Christ." Jamie laughed. "Anything else for Sunshine and her golden pussy? She want a white picket fence and a golden retriever with a bow around his neck sitting at the door?"

"Boxer," I corrected, eyes opening.

"Say again?"

I looked at the classifieds sitting on the counter, then lifted my gaze to Jamie, stepped back, and crossed my arms tight against my chest.

He wasn't getting that shit.

"Nothing." I shook my head. "Make sure it has a fucking porch," I insisted. "Three bedrooms. Good-size yard. Sex dungeon is optional."

"Optional. We're so different," he muttered quietly, then looked back down at his phone and started typing.

The front door chimed open.

I lifted my head and watched Syd step inside, bright smile on her face as she waved excitedly, wearing white cutoffs that were tiny as fuck and showing all kinds of leg, a peach-colored tank that stretched over her tits and flat stomach, and cowboy boots that in no fucking way possible were sexy unless they were attached to my girl, making them the sexiest goddamn pair of shoes I'd ever seen in my life.

On top of all that, her hair was down and looking just-rode-my-dick messy.

Fuck.

Fuck.

I pulled in breath through my nose and fought off punching a hole through my shorts.

"She doesn't know," I said quietly to Jamie before moving out from behind the counter and standing next to it to see her better.

"Got it," he mumbled as he continued texting.

Jamie would keep the house shit between us. He had my back and knew this was important.

Syd would find out when I was ready.

"*Wow.* Look at this place," she said with wonder in her voice as she moved farther into the shop, head tipped back and eyes scanning the room. "It's *awesome* in here! So bright and beachy. If I knew anything about surfing, I would probably buy one of everything." She turned her head to look at me all sweet. "No matter. I'm planning on buying one of everything anyway. I gotta support my boy."

Her boy.

Christ.

I laughed and shook my head.

"Come here," I ordered.

My hands were itching to touch her.

She took off running straight at me, dodging a rack of shirts, got within arms' reach, then leapt into the air with a squeal, gripping on to my shoulders as I took her waist and lifted, my hands moving to her ass and holding there as her legs wrapped around my hips and linked at the ankles, squeezing tight.

"Hey, Trouble," she whispered, running her nose along mine and then rubbing them together.

"Wild." I kissed the corner of her mouth. "Thought you were stopping by after lunch?"

She pressed her chest out, held on to my neck, and leaned back to look at me.

"I was going to but I couldn't stand it any longer. I've been twiddling my thumbs waiting to come see you and there's only so much Food Network I can watch before I start eating everything in the house," she admitted. "I had to get out of there while I could still fit into my shorts."

I squeezed her ass.

"Like these shorts, babe."

Her lips curved up.

"Why the hell were you watching Food Network?" I asked.

Shyness dipped her head.

"Because I was hoping to get a new recipe to try out tonight when I make you dinner."

My brows lifted.

"You're making me dinner?"

"Yep. At Tori's house."

"And it's something you've never made before?"

"Yep."

I slid my grip farther around her so she was pressing closer and I was holding tighter.

There was a chance she'd try and push away after I finished getting my point across. I was eliminating that chance.

She wasn't going anywhere.

"You sure that's a good idea?" I asked carefully. "Straying from the four things you know how to cook? I'm good with pizza again."

Her face tightened in annoyance as she lifted her chin.

"I know how to read a recipe, Brian," she returned.

"Pretty sure you don't, babe."

"Excuse me?"

"You can't read a recipe. You told me the story of how you almost burned your house down trying to make cavatini," I reminded her, thinking back to that night. "Said you set the oven temperature wrong, forgot to cook the noodles before you baked them, and after tasting it, realized you'd put in too much garlic, thinking one clove meant the entire head."

Her eyes lowered to my neck.

"It wasn't *that* serious. I pulled the dish out before it burnt up completely. Also, I was fine with that measuring mistake. I just so happen to like a lot of garlic."

"You put in eleven cloves of garlic in a recipe that called for *one*. No one likes garlic that much."

Not sure how it was possible but her face tightened more, gaze threatening as it squared off with mine again, and this time, her cheeks were flushed with embarrassment and her lips were curling against her teeth.

"Know you're trying to look mad, Wild, but you just look cute as hell," I informed her.

"God, you two are precious," Jamie commented from where he was standing. "If I stick around and hear any more of this shit, I might get my period."

Syd shot daggers at Jamie, then narrowed her eyes on me and ducked to get closer.

"That's exactly the look I was going for, thank you very much," she clipped. "And I'd appreciate it if you would see my look as intimidating and allow me to do this for you, because I really want to. It's important to me."

I heard the subtle change in her voice, the way her tongue lost that edge and her speech grew softer and withdrawn.

It wasn't just important to her. It meant a whole fucking lot.

"You really wanna cook something for me you've never made?" I asked, dipping my head. "'Cause you don't need to. I don't mind cooking for us or eating the same four meals you know how to make for the next fifty years. Your pizza was damn good and I'm guessing I'm gonna like the other three things. Really don't want you stressing over this."

She sucked her bottom lip into her mouth.

"Wild," I urged.

"I won't stress. I promise."

I lifted my shoulders. "Right," I conceded. "Can't fucking wait to try it then."

She wiggled her hips excitedly with a little dance. Then her phone started ringing in her back pocket, and she reached back to grab it while telling me, "It'll be perfect. You'll see. What I got planned is gonna blow your mind, Brian. You're never gonna want to get rid of me."

I smiled, admitting, "Already there, babe."

Her cheeks pinked up again, this time with the kind of embarrassment I liked seeing on her, and without looking at her phone, she hit a button and pressed it to her ear.

"Hello?" she answered, smiling at me, then losing that smile and the pink in her cheeks after whoever she was speaking to responded. Her face hardened. "What are you doing calling me? I told you, I never wanted to speak to you again."

My jaw clenched

"Babe," I said, my voice carrying warning, because I knew who was calling Syd and I also knew I was a second away from taking that phone and laying into that motherfucker for calling my girl.

Syd ignored me and kept on at him.

"I'm happy now, Marcus. Happier than I ever was with you 'cause I have a boyfriend who is *amazing*, and if you're calling me to try and get me back, you are wasting your time. I'm—"

She stopped laying into him, met my eyes and widened hers, then looked down at a spot on my shirt.

"Oh. Yeah, I forgot to do that," she said with a softer voice. "I'll take care of it next week." She listened for a second, then added, "That's fine. Thank you for letting me know. Okay. Bye." She ended the call and slipped her phone away.

"What's that piece of shit want?" I asked.

Syd looked at me. Her hand slipped around my neck again, joining her other one.

"He was just reminding me to change my address with the post office," she said. "My mail is still going there."

"Oh."

"Yeah." She sucked on her lip. "But I was ready to tell him all about how amazing you are if he was calling for other reasons, and I would've had a lot to say, meaning that phone call would've lasted hours. You're *that* amazing. Also, I would've given examples and gone into detail."

I smirked.

Syd's cheeks pinked up again when she leaned closer and shyly added, "A lot of detail."

I chuckled.

"Come here." I shifted her ass in my hands, pulling her until her tits pushed up against my chest and her arms wrapped around my neck instead of her fingers, then I turned my head and pressed my mouth to her jaw and the smooth skin below.

"Seriously. Think I just became a woman," Jamie said.

Syd's growl vibrated against my lips.

"Do you have the authority to fire him?" she asked quietly. "He's ruining the moment."

I chuckled, shifting her back until her legs released and her feet dropped to the floor, then sliding my arm over her shoulder, I tucked her against my side as we moved together in front of the counter.

Jamie grinned and slid his phone away, shook the hair out of his eyes, and remained leaning on the counter, fixating his gaze on Syd.

"See you're off today. Is my girl workin'?" he asked, cocking his head. "Fuckin' starved for a burger and her smart-ass mouth."

"I really think she'd prefer it if you went someplace else to eat," Syd replied, sliding her hand around my back.

Jamie grinned bigger.

"Beautiful. She's workin'. I'm headin' out." He shifted his eyes to me as Syd sighed heavily in response. "You good?" he asked, straightening. "Should be back around four."

I nodded, answering, "No problem."

Jamie looked at Syd again. His brows pulled together.

"What kind of flowers does she like?"

Silence turned my head. I looked down at my girl and saw disbelief etched on her face.

"You . . . want to know what kind of flowers Tori likes?" she questioned slowly.

"That's what I'm askin'."

"Why?"

"Why the hell do you think? I wanna get her some."

Syd's expression changed from disbelief to straight-up shock. She stared at Jamie with her mouth slack and hanging open, eyes rounded and refusing to blink.

"You *do*?" she pressed, tipping forward. "But . . . you're an idiot."

Jamie flinched. "What the fuck?"

"I'm just saying, that's thoughtful and you don't strike me as a thoughtful person," Syd quickly clarified. "Now you wanna be *that guy* who takes her flowers?"

"No. Honestly? I really fuckin' don't," Jamie said, crossing his arms and appearing irritated. "I wanna be the guy who fucks up a car owned by some worthless motherfucker who did her wrong and gets to see that soft look on her face after I do it."

Syd sucked in a breath. The hand gripping my waist held tighter.

"Unless you got a list of names of people I can pay a visit to, I'm shit outta luck with that," he added. "So are you gonna help me out? Or do I need to buy one of every flower and hope for the best."

Syd slid her other hand over my stomach, body turned so I could feel her tits against my ribs.

"Tori only likes dahlias," she said. Her voice was softer. "That's it. Coral ones if you can find them, but if you can't, she likes every color. And she likes displaying them so make sure you put them in something, not just with the stems wrapped up."

Jamie nodded, looking hopeful, then started flipping his keys around his finger and heading for the door, calling back, "Thanks, Sunshine. Appreciate it," before disappearing through it.

Syd tipped her head back to smile up at me.

"I'm kinda rooting for him now. Don't say anything."

"Who the hell would I say anything to?" I asked, bringing my other arm around her. "Feel the need to stress again, Wild. I don't care who Jamie fucks, who Tori fucks, or if they finally end up fucking each other. That's their business. Only person I care about in terms of fucking is you."

She got up on her toes and, with excitement racing through her voice, said, "Then you better give me a tour of this place and do it fast, 'cause I'd really like to get to the fucking part."

I leaned back.

"Here?"

"*Yes*," she strained. "It's the entire reason for this outfit I'm wearing because these shorts make my butt look really nice and I know how much you like staring at my butt. So..." She released her arms from around me, wiggled out of my hold, and grabbed my hand, tugging. "Give me a quick tour and then take me to your office. And every time you go in there, I want you thinking about me and what I looked like with my legs spread wide on your desk."

Fuck yeah. That was one helluva visual.

Wild pulled me along the counter, and without her seeing, I slid the classifieds underneath a magazine then cut my eyes back to her and lowered them to her ass.

She was spot on with my obsession and my dick was hard before we reached the other side of the room. The tour lasted all of thirty seconds before I started moving my hands over her tits and between her legs and she started grinding back and grasping at me. Then our mouths took over and I somehow managed to keep kissing and touching and building it for her while taking the time needed to lock the front door and flip the sign to *Closed*.

We made it to the office a second before her limbs started shaking and she was tightening around my fingers and moaning in my mouth.

Then I fucked her while I sucked her tits, shot my cum onto her stomach when she told me to, and watched her rub in it with that heavy look in her eyes like having me all over her was the biggest fucking turn-on, leading to me getting hard seconds after finishing and taking her again, eyes on her ass the whole time she bent over the desk with her arms braced. I pounded her to another orgasm and rooted deep when I couldn't hold off, filling her pussy as she cried out and clenched around me.

She was right. I'd never look at this desk the same again.

* * *

Bag in hand, I crossed the parking lot of Carolina East Therapeutic Riding, climbed the ramp, kicked the dirt off my feet when I reached the top, then yanked the door open, stepping inside the small office.

I was in a hurry. I needed to get this done so I could get to Tori's and have dinner with Syd. She was expecting me right after work and I was hoping Mona wasn't going to keep me long or give me shit about this.

I didn't have time to argue, and it wouldn't fucking matter anyway. I was going through with this, and nothing she could say would change that.

Mona was seated at her desk on the phone. She glanced up at the sound of my entrance and greeted me with a quick smile, then whispered something into the line, listening and disconnecting a second later.

"Brian, it's good to see you," she exclaimed with her usual kind voice. She pushed out of her chair and stood to round her desk but halted behind it when she saw me making my way across the room. "Though it's a little unexpected. You were just here."

"I know," I muttered, lifting the bag off my shoulder and setting it on the desk. I looked her in the eyes. "Need you to do one last thing for me, Mona. This is it."

Her shoulders slumped.

"I'm sure whatever it is, it's unnecessary, Brian."

I ignored her comment, it was typical and expected, then I pushed the bag in front of her.

"Need you to make sure Owen and his family get this," I told her. "Can't leave it at their house like I've been doing. Someone could take it."

She stared at me, then lowered her gaze to the bag.

"What is it?" she questioned while sliding the zipper open. She pulled the flaps back and peered inside, her breath catching on a gasp. "Brian," she whispered, looking up with caution flooding her voice. "Where did you get this money?"

"It's mine to give," I assured. "Didn't do anything illegal to get it. Know that's what you're thinking and you don't need to be thinking that. That's clean money. I need you to make sure it gets to them."

"It's too much."

"It's not." I shoved my hands into my pockets. "Not even close."

Mona kept her hands on the duffle as she closed her eyes and breathed slow, conflicted, and pitying breaths.

I could argue with her for years over this, force my understanding onto Mona and will it to stick, and she'd still come back telling me I was wrong and this was excessive beyond reason. It was who she was.

Like Jenna and Jamie and Cole, she didn't understand my fault or the guilt I carried with me. She couldn't. No one could.

They weren't there. They weren't responsible.

They would never understand.

I could never give enough. I could never give them back what I took but I could do this.

I needed to do this.

"Mona," I prompted, watching her eyes slide open. "Please."

Her hands fisted the duffle.

"I just...I don't know if you realize what this will mean to them or if you will ever know because you won't allow yourself to feel that, Brian, and that breaks my heart and makes me incredibly angry at the same time. I could hit you with this bag for being so disjointed."

Relief pulled across my shoulders.

"You'll do it then," I verified.

She shook her head in exasperation, answering, "Of course I'll do it. My God, I wish I could do this for all of my families. This is an incredible gift."

"Just make sure they don't know it's from me."

Her lips pressed into a tight thin line.

Fuck.

"I don't like doing that," she informed quietly. "And I really think they should know where this kind of money is coming from. They will want to thank you—"

"They can thank me by taking the money," I cut in brusquely.

"Brian," she pleaded. "I really think—"

"*Please*," I growled through my teeth. "*Do not tell them.*"

Mona flinched at my tone, closed her eyes, and nodded quickly.
Fuck.

I hated getting on her like that. She didn't deserve it.

I reached out and placed my hand on top of one of hers and squeezed, prompting her eyes to open.

"Appreciate you doing this and everything else. Means a lot," I said. "Knowing how you feel about what I'm doing, that means something, too."

Her mouth relaxed and lifted softly.

"You're a good man, Brian. I hope one day you'll believe that."

I gave an easy smile to appease her. I needed to get going and I had zero fucking time to argue that one.

Pulling back, I dropped my head into a nod.

"Thanks again," I said.

Mona gave me one last smile.

Then I turned without giving that bag another thought and got the hell out of there.

* * *

I knocked again on the front door, this time a little louder, and stepped back, waiting to be let inside.

A muffled yell came from Tori's house. I couldn't make out what Syd was saying and I knew it was Syd since she was the only one here, her car being the only one in the driveway, so I tested the knob and it turned willingly, allowing me to ease the door open and step inside.

"Syd," I called out, shutting the door behind me as my eyes scanned the room.

Tori's house was fucking impressive. On the smaller side, but you could tell there was a lot of money in it and not just because of the ocean view.

The decorating was some fancy shit.

It reminded me of Jamie's parents' house. Everything was either dark oak or leather, and the art hanging on the walls looked like something Oliver or Liv could've painted, which meant it wasn't just fancy shit, it was expensive shit.

"I'm in here! And I'm stressing out so just get back in your car and go home! This was a *huge* mistake!"

Laughing, I moved through the living room and around the corner where the noise was coming from.

It couldn't have been that bad.

Syd was in the kitchen at the stove, bent at the waist with her head in the oven as thick smoke billowed out around her and into the air.

It was that bad.

"Shit!" she yelled, pulling a dish out and sitting it on the burner. She kicked the door closed and waved her hands over the charred remains, murmuring, "No no no no."

"Babe."

The smoke detector sounded loudly from the hallway.

"Oh, God, not again," Syd groaned, covering her face.

Jesus. She was definitely stressing.

I fought a smile as I grabbed a dish towel off the counter, moved out of the room, and stood below the detector, reached up, disabled it, then took the towel and fanned the air to clear the smoke so it wouldn't go off again.

When I stepped back into the kitchen, Syd was still standing at the stove, facing it with her head down, only now she was massaging her temples.

I came up behind her, wrapped my arm around her apron-covered waist, pulled her back against me, and dropped my head beside hers, breathing in the apple-scented shampoo she used in her hair.

"I don't know what I did," she admitted in a small voice, lowering her arms and gesturing at the dish, which at this point was unrecognizable, blackened, and still smoking.

I couldn't make out what she was going for.

"I followed the recipe perfectly, double-checking my steps and the ingredients before mixing everything together, and I *know* I set the oven temperature right. I triple-checked that."

I kissed her temple.

"What were you making?"

"Homemade chicken potpie with all kinds of yummy veggies and spices, all beautifully contained in a made-from-scratch pie dough."

Shit. That sounded really fucking good.

She sighed in defeat, then said on a whisper, "I wanted to do this for you so bad, and I've messed it up."

I gave her a squeeze, let her go, then moved to the counter where she had mixing bowls, cutting boards, and measuring spoons laid out, found the recipe she had printed, and picked it up, reading the cooking instructions.

"You take it out after forty-five minutes?" I asked, looking over at Wild.

She slowly turned her head.

"Forty-five minutes?" she echoed with a suspicious pout. "No. Why would I do that?"

"'Cause that's the cooking time."

"What? No it isn't!"

She eliminated the space between us in three quick steps, yanked the recipe out of my hand while pulling a pair of red-framed glasses out of the front pocket of her apron and sliding them up her nose, then began scanning the paper frantically.

Glasses like that would be cute on anyone else.

They weren't cute on Wild. They were sexy as shit.

"Like those," I observed, watching warm hazels lift and peer up at me through the lenses.

She gave me a small smile and a sweet, "Thanks," returned her gaze to the paper, and continued scanning.

I bent closer. "Want you wearing them the next time we fuck."

With a gasp, her eyes snapped to mine again, this time going round.

I leaned back.

"Oh," she breathed, swallowed, then added a quick, "O-okay. Yeah, that's totally doable."

Smirking, I jerked my chin at the paper.

"Back to it. You said forty-five minutes isn't the cooking time, babe."

With a frown, Syd resumed scanning the paper.

"There *was* no cooking time. It says right here, look"—she pointed at the bottom of the page—"put it in the oven, walk away, completely forget about it, and come dangerously close to burning the crust." She looked up at me. "I did exactly those things."

My eyebrows rose.

"Think you went a little further than coming dangerously close to burning the crust. I had no idea that was potpie."

Her eyes narrowed. She stood on her toes and tipped her chin up.

I bit back a smile.

Fucking *loved it* when she challenged me like that. Her sass made my dick hard.

"It told me to walk away and forget about it. I was just following directions," she snapped.

"Not all of them."

I grabbed her hand and moved her finger to the top of the page, indicating where I'd been reading.

She gasped. "Look how tiny that is! Who can read that?" Her head whipped around and she glared at the stove. "I can't believe this. I followed the recipe *perfectly*. It took me ages cutting up those vegetables. I cut myself twice, but I recovered. Everything else was simple. I even brushed egg wash on the crust so it would golden up and made a pretty design with a fork around the edges, and you can't even tell. I'm not even sure it *has* edges anymore."

I slid my hand to her hip.

"Wild."

"I can't believe I didn't see the time, or question what I was doing." She looked up at me with pleading eyes. "There's something wrong with me. I let myself forget about what I was making. That's insane! Who does that?"

Before I could answer, Syd lowered her head and crumpled up the recipe, holding it tight in her fist.

"I am so mad at myself," she whispered brokenly.

Fuck that.

I moved her over so I could grab a spoon off the counter, stepped in front of the stove, leaned over it with a hand bracing on the granite, and dug into the burnt potpie. I got to the meat and vegetables baked inside, heaped a spoonful of them, and ate a mouthful.

I'd eat this whole fucking thing if it made her feel better.

"What are you doing?" Syd questioned at my back, her voice growing closer.

"Eatin'." I scooped out some more, shoved it in my mouth, and said around the steaming bite, "Not into wasting something my girl took time to make for me. I'm finishing this."

"Brian, don't." She wrapped her hand around my bicep and pulled. "It's ruined. Look at it."

I kept eating.

She pulled harder, laughing when I went in for a fourth spoonful.

"That can't be good. Seriously. Stop. Come on."

I swallowed my bite and dug around for more.

"Not bad, actually," I said. "Once you get past the bitter, it's good. I like the chicken." Lifting the spoon to my mouth, I turned my head and peered over my shoulder, letting her watch me eat it. "Hope you made something else for you 'cause I'm eatin' this whole thing and not into sharing."

Syd laughed harder, tossed the crumpled recipe onto the counter, reached up, and covered my mouth with her hand as her other wrapped around the front of my waist and pulled me back, forcing me to leave the spoon in the dish and turning me away from the stove.

"Okay okay okay. You've made your point."

I moved willingly this time, waited until her hand slid off my mouth so I could speak, then asked, "And what's that?"

"That you're incredible."

I blinked, chewed up the rest of my mouthful, then swallowed it down.

She slid her hands up my arms to my shoulders and linked them around my neck, pressed her front against mine, and tipped her head back.

"You make everything better," she admitted softly, running her tongue over her lips to wet them while coming up on her toes and getting closer, further admitting, "You make my entire world better."

My hands, fitted around her waist, tightened. Warmth spread out from the center of my chest.

I dropped my head until it touched hers and closed my eyes, holding her and breathing easy, concentrating on every part of Wild's body I could feel against mine and the sound of her living—shallow heartbeats and expanding lungs pushing life through her.

Best thing I'd ever felt.

Best thing I'd ever held.

Best girl period.

"Like hearing you say that," I murmured, opening my eyes.

Her hands gave my neck a squeeze.

"Like saying it," she whispered back.

I smiled, then pulled away but only because a phone started ringing and it wasn't mine.

Sliding her hands down and off me slowly, Syd spun around and picked up her phone off the counter by the sink, looked at the screen with a curious tilt of her head, mumbled something about not knowing the number, then pressed a button, answering it and bringing it to her ear.

"Hello?" Her shoulders pulled back and her eyes lit up with alertness. "Yes it is. Oh, yes, hi, how are you?"

I watched and listened with interest, noting the mood this call was putting my girl in and appreciating whoever it was on the other line.

Syd answered a few yes and no questions, speaking quickly the way she did when she was excited about something, while she moved along the counter back and forth, finger twirling a lock of red and anxious eyes capturing mine every few steps. This only lasted a couple of minutes, then she was telling the caller to hold on so she could open a drawer and pull out a piece of paper and a pen, telling them to continue when she was done and jotting something down while pinching the phone between her ear and shoulder.

"Great! No, that works perfect. I can absolutely do Monday morning," she said, straightening and holding on to the phone again. "Yes. Okay. Thank you so much." She disconnected the call, set the phone down, and turned her head, smiling big as she walked over. "Guess what?"

"What?"

"That was the job I applied for at NHC. The one that had been open for eight months and I thought for sure was filled already. They want me to interview for it."

"That's great. You can get back into x-ray." I picked up the lock of hair she'd been twirling and I tucked it behind her ear, watching her mouth twist into a pout. "You want that, right?"

She hesitated, then answered, "Yeah, I do, I just...I love Whitecaps," she replied, pressing her hands to my chest. "And I don't want to short-staff Nate. He's got so much going on. I'd like to keep working there if I can." She looked down for a minute to think, sucked on her bottom lip, then looked back up to add, "Once I find out the hours on Monday, I can see if something is manageable."

Grabbing her hips, I told her, "If it isn't, if your hours at the hospital don't allow for you to keep helping out at Whitecaps, you don't need to worry over it. Nate will understand. Knew it was a possibility you'd be leaving."

Syd lifted her chin.

"I won't worry over it," she whispered.

"Good." I pulled at the tie on her apron. "Take this off. Wanna take you out to celebrate you getting a new job. This calls for Italian."

She obliged me and slipped the apron over her head, doing it wearing a look of confusion.

"I didn't get it yet," she corrected, tossing the apron on the counter.

"You got it, babe. They'd be stupid not to hire you."

Syd's cheeks pinked up again and she gave me that, letting me see it before turning around, grabbing that same paper she'd written on, and quickly jotting something else down.

"Want to make sure Tori doesn't eat that potpie," she said while her hand scrawled. "She'll be home soon from the hair salon and I doubt she's had dinner."

I thought Syd was in the clear with Tori leaving that potpie alone, but I kept my mouth shut.

I loved her sass but I wanted to hold on to her sweet right now.

Chapter Sixteen

SYDNEY

Licking peanut butter sauce off my lip, I dug my spoon into the giant sundae glass in front of me while I sat across from Brian in a booth at Friendly's.

He'd remembered. Coming here after dinner at La Tavola was his idea.

My boy was amazing.

I took another spoonful of vanilla with hot fudge melting into my mouth and moaned with my eyes closed.

Brian chuckled. It was a beautiful sound.

He wasn't eating anything. Just watching me enjoy every bite, and I was definitely enjoying.

Any minute now I was certain I'd hear a "I'll have what she's having" from someone close by.

I blinked my eyes open and smiled, dipped the spoon for another heaping taste, this time mixing ice cream with the whipped topping and also getting chunks of peanut butter cup along with the gooey sauce, making this bite the best bite ever, raised the spoon, and held it out across the table.

"Never shared one of these with anybody," I confessed through a bat of my lashes. "Wanna be my first?"

I watched Brian's eyes go soft and absorbing, liking what I'd just said, then I watched him lean forward and take the bite, his full lips pulling slow across the silver and removing every drop, swallowing it after a short savor.

Is it possible to be jealous of cutlery?

Yes. Absolutely.

"Good?"

He nodded, sucking vanilla off his lip.

"Yep."

"Sure you don't wanna get something? I don't mind sharing, but they have other good choices too. Look." I dropped my spoon into the glass and grabbed the dessert menu, opening it on the table and pointing at it. "Sometimes Barrett would get the Jim Dandy. That's sorta like a banana split. He didn't like it as much as the peanut butter cup but he liked changing it up sometimes."

Brian nudged my foot underneath the table.

I lifted my eyes.

"Wish I could've met him," he said gently.

My belly dipped.

God . . .

I wished that, too. So much. I wanted to share Brian with everyone who meant something to me. Brag. Gloat. Even show him off to my mother, who I currently wasn't speaking to.

But Barrett . . . that would've been amazing.

"Me, too," I replied softly, reaching out and taking the hand he had resting on the table. "Barrett would've liked you."

Brian smiled, twisted his wrist so he could hold my fingers in his palm, and questioned, "Yeah? Why's that?"

"'Cause you're trouble and he was a badass, just like me. He would've appreciated that."

Brian laughed deep in his chest.

"And 'cause you make me the happiest I think I've ever been," I added. "I think he would've appreciated that, too."

His grip that was already holding firm grew firmer, putting pressure on the bones in my fingers, but nothing I couldn't stand so I held back and stared, letting him see my happiness and taking his for my own, admiring his warm, contented smile until it was fading and he didn't have it anymore, not even a shadow of it because his eyes had left mine and were now focusing hard on something behind me.

He grew taller in the booth. His shoulders and arms tensing with flexed muscle and his chest moving air more powerfully.

"What's wrong?" I asked, starting to turn my head when his grip went from tolerable pressure to unbearable stress and I gasped, struggling to pull away when my fingers started aching.

"*Brian*," I urged through a tight voice.

"Get up. We gotta go," he grated, sounding urgent.

He released my hand and stood quickly, pulled some cash out of his wallet and tossed it on the table, then moved beside me, grabbed underneath my arm, and yanked me out of the booth.

"Brian!" I yelped, startled, gripping his bicep for balance. "What—"

"Now, babe. Move."

He spun me around and then his strong arm was pulling me close and hurrying us through the restaurant toward the door.

"What's going on?" I asked as my feet struggled to keep up, looking from his unyielding profile to the room ahead and searching for understanding, some mad person wreaking havoc because Brian was panicked, that was clear.

There was nothing unusual about the scene in front of me. No one being held at gunpoint. No hysteria.

Families sat eating at tables or booths, the waitstaff tended to their duties, and as we made it to the front of the restaurant, I saw the hostess who seated us standing at the podium, greeting what appeared to be a family waiting to be seated.

A husband and wife and their young child, a sweet-looking boy with messy blond hair and anxious ice cream eyes that roamed the room.

His father's hands were holding the grips on the wheelchair he sat in.

"Brian," I tried once more over my shoulder when the arm around me became nothing more than a cold push at my lower back, urging me without affection faster to the door.

He said nothing. His hand on my spine trembled as we moved

closer to the podium and the sweet-looking boy, the hostess, and the mother and father, whose head turned and eyes noticed our escape, finding not my own face but the man beside and slightly behind me.

It was not an unfamiliar glance or a passing scan your eyes did out of reflex. The fleeting meet of gazes in a crowded room, that wasn't this. Not even close.

The man saw Brian and recognized him, the shadow of familiarity passing over his face and holding there.

Those eyes of his widened. He knew Brian.

Maybe not well and maybe not enough to be friendly, but my boy was no stranger. That was certain.

Brian didn't slow or acknowledge this man or his family. He didn't even glance in their direction, not once, and then they were behind us and we were leaving.

I was too confused to speak.

What the hell was happening?

With unyielding fingers pressing to the right of my spine, Brian steered me left and farther forward, shoving the front door open with his other hand and then forcing me outside and into the night.

"Brian, stop! What's going on?" I yelled, finally finding my voice, twisting away but being captured in his arms again, arms so strong they lifted me without effort and carried me when my spine went rigid with protest and my feet started dragging gravel.

"What are you doing?" I shrieked, trying to see behind me.

"Get us out of here. Then I'll explain," he grumbled against my hair, crossing the parking lot in quick strides with his long legs while I stayed pressed against his body.

I struggled in his grasp.

"Syd," he said in warning, tightening his hold.

"I don't understand. What happened? Why are you acting like this? Was it that man?"

I asked that last question but I already knew the answer.

My boy was scared. He was scared and he was running.

"Talk to me," I pleaded, hearing my own voice shake with worry.

We reached the Jeep before another word was said, then the passenger door was opened, and because he must've known there was no way I was climbing up willingly without hearing an explanation first, my choice was eliminated for me and I was *put* in that seat like some helpless child.

"Brian, please. You're scaring me."

I felt tears sting my eyes and the rattle of my whispered words battering my throat.

He paused at the door, ready to shut it, then his eyes lifted to mine and I saw the panic there in his wide irises, but I didn't know if it was because of whatever he was taking us away from or because of what I'd just said.

I didn't have a chance to ask.

Brian leaned inside the car and reached for me, sliding his hand to the base of my neck and gripping me there, then gently tugging me forward until he was so close I could count his lashes.

If he'd been in a trance before, he was out of it now. If he'd been too focused on his own trepidation and leaving to hear my voice or feel my struggle, I was now the only thing that existed to him.

"Don't be scared of me," he urged in a stressed voice, putting a firm but calming pressure on my neck. "Don't ever be scared of me, Syd. I'd die before hurting you."

I swallowed his words and locked them inside my heart.

He would. Brian wasn't lying. He'd never hurt me. I knew that.

"I know," I whispered, curling my fingers around his arm. "I just need to know what's going on. I need you to talk to me."

"I will," he promised. "Let me get us outta here and I will."

"Okay."

He heard my reply but he waited before letting go, keeping hold of me and looking into my eyes while taking his other hand and brushing his thumb across my cheek.

It was a soothing gesture. This was Brian taking the time to make sure my okay really meant okay. That I wasn't just saying it to get answers. That I wasn't scared.

I wasn't. Not of him.

Of what he might tell me? Yes, but I was good at hiding that.

He let me go.

I buckled my seat belt and watched through the windshield as

Brian hurried around the front of the car. He climbed inside, started it up, and pulled out onto the main road.

My hands stayed tangled together on my lap as I waited for Brian to start talking, willing my anxious breaths to stay quiet so I wouldn't miss even the slightest sound from his direction. I didn't know how far he needed to take us before I could get any answers, but I promised myself I'd be okay with however far that needed to be, that I could wait until he was ready because he would be ready. He promised me he'd talk and I believed him.

Five miles felt like five hours. My foot tapped restlessly against the floorboard and I cursed red lights like I hated their very existence and whoever the bastard was who invented them.

So much for patience. I was ready to crawl out of my skin and scream into the night. My palms stung from the bite of my nails and my stomach twisted.

Then it was over and the only thing I felt was relief.

I didn't know if it was coincidence that made Brian pull over at the exact moment I contemplated throwing the gear into neutral and forcing him to stall, or if he had meant to drive us here, to this exact spot.

Brian shifted out of gear and cut the engine.

Seconds passed. The silence in the car threatened to swallow me up.

I unbuckled and turned in my seat, hoping to tempt conversation.

Brian's chest heaved with slow, filling breaths and his shoulders pulled back while he stared ahead out the windshield, clenching his hands nervously in his lap.

I sucked on my lip and waited. He didn't make me wait long.

"Got hit hard in February with snow this year," he began in a low voice. "Don't know what it was like in Raleigh, but I'm assuming it was the same as it was here. Seemed like every week we were getting slammed with another storm. Sun would come out during the day and melt it, making the roads a fuckin' mess; then at night temps would drop and that shit would freeze."

"It was the same in Raleigh," I told him, remembering back to last winter. "I was scared to drive in it."

"I wasn't," he mumbled tightly. "Had a truck before I got this.

Made getting around easy, especially in bad conditions. I always went out. Didn't even mind sliding a little."

I swallowed uncomfortably before saying, "That can be terrifying."

"I was fuckin' stupid," he hissed, turning to look at me then. "Had no business being out on the roads when they were like that but I wanted the rush. That feeling of nearly losing all control, the one that terrifies you, babe, I fuckin' loved that. I chased it. It's why I surfed. Which is why I can say without a doubt that I would've been driving in that last storm no matter what."

I knew what storm Brian was talking about. It was the very one that kept me at work because of the warning of black ice. The ER was slammed that night from accidents.

My stomach knotted.

"Brian..."

He turned away with a cold laugh and resumed looking out the windshield again.

"You're feeling sorry for me already and you have no idea what I've done."

"I love you. I'll love you no matter what it is," I confessed, watching his eyes pinch shut as if hearing that caused him pain. "It's true."

"You won't," he said quietly. "Not like this. It'll be different." He looked at me once more and whispered slowly through a thick voice, "I don't wanna tell you."

Tears fell onto my cheeks.

Brian was afraid. He was afraid hearing this would change how I felt about him, that this would change us.

This was the bad in his life he held on to, the bad he never spoke about.

The bad I was healing him from.

I reached across the console and grabbed his hand, squeezing it between both of mine.

"Tell me right now so I can tell you I love you," I pleaded. "Just like this. Just like how I do now. Tell me."

He held my eyes for a long second, smiled a little, and said, "You're really fuckin' pretty when you lie, Wild."

I leaned closer.

"I'm not lying."

"How much do you love me right now?" he asked, face deadly serious. "Scale of one to ten."

"Eleven."

"That man back there at Friendly's, you saw him looking at me?"

I nodded.

"I'm the reason his son is in that wheelchair. How much do you love me now?"

I sucked in a breath and blinked.

"Twelve," I whispered with a broken heart.

"Liar," he whispered back through a smirk, reaching out and running his thumb across my cheek. "So pretty, babe. You should've been a lawyer." He turned away and looked ahead, breathing deep like he was trying to calm himself.

"What happened?" I asked, giving his hand a squeeze.

Brian kept his eyes on the windshield as he spoke.

"I was already driving home when they issued the state of emergency. I was going about forty and I most likely pushed it faster hitting the incline. Like I said before, my truck got around fine in bad conditions. Didn't have a problem getting up the hill." He paused, and I felt the muscles in his hand tighten. "Wish I would've. Wish I would've hit that black ice on my way up and slid off the road instead of hitting it at the top like I did. Maybe it'd be me in that chair instead of the kid."

Agony pinched in my chest.

"Don't say that."

"That hill, it's as steep on the way down as it is on the way up," he continued, his voice hard and unforgiving with himself. "You can't see what's over it until you're at the top and I knew that. I've driven this way for years. I should've slowed down, especially with the conditions, the visibility, the fucking ice, it was everywhere, but I didn't. I pushed up that hill like I always did and I lost control."

I looked out the windshield then, finally turning away from Brian's profile, and squinted, tilting my head down to see the top of the hill.

"Were they driving this way?" I asked. "Did you cross lanes?"

"They were on this side, stopped about a third of the way down the hill but not out of the road completely. Their back end was still in it. That's what I hit."

I looked at him again.

His eyes were cast down on the wheel.

"I was going too fast to slow down. I didn't have time to react and it was too late anyway. I slammed into their car. Crushed the back end so bad it looked like a fuckin' two-seater. Police had to use the jaws of life to get the doors open and get to the backseat. That's where their son was sleeping."

My hands tightened around his.

"Did anyone else get hurt? Did you?" I asked softly.

His eyes sliced to mine. They looked as cold as his voice sounded.

"Yeah, I had a few cracked ribs. My knee was a little banged up, but I could *fucking walk*. It was nothing. Same with the parents. They had minor burns from the air bags, a few bruises. But the kid? Owen? He was unconscious for a *week*. A fucking week! For seven days his parents didn't know whether their kid was going to live or not, and then when he finally did wake up, they had the pleasure of telling him he'd never walk again. How fucked up is that?" He paused, shaking his head and breathing a choked laugh. "That kid fell asleep able to do everything. Then he wakes up a week later and he's paralyzed. He'll never walk again because of me. He'll never do anything."

"But you said you hit ice."

"I did. It's why I lost control."

I studied him hard, reading his guilt and his blame and not understanding any of it.

"Then...Brian, it's not your fault," I told him, wiping the tears from underneath my glasses then regripping his hand. "You would've lost control no matter how fast you were going if there was ice. It was an accident."

He sighed, rubbed at his face with the hand I wasn't clutching, then dropped his head against the seat and stared out the window.

"Christ, you sound just like them."

"Who?" I asked.

"Jamie. Jenna. Cole. Everyone who doesn't fuckin' know better."

"Well, do you think maybe that's because we're all right and you're wrong?"

His eyes cut to mine.

"I think it's because none of you were there," he growled, tilting his head up and leveling me with a scowl. "I was the one driving that night. I was the one going too fast coming over that hill, knowing I should've slowed down 'cause I couldn't see *shit*, but I didn't, my truck could handle the conditions so what the fuck did I care, you know? That was *me*." He jammed a finger at his chest. "I was the one who smashed into that car. I was the one who saw the looks on those parents' faces when they finally climbed out and saw what I'd done, and I was the one they looked to for blame. Their agony, their fear, their hate, they turned that right on me and they should've. I got it because *I* deserved it. They were screaming and crying because of *me*. Because of what *I* took from them."

I shook my head and grabbed his wrist, trying to ease his finger away.

"They don't hate you. I'm sure they don't. It would've happened anyway," I said. "It could've been anyone driving."

He flinched.

"What?"

"That boy, what happened to him, it would've happened anyway even if you weren't on the road that night. He would still be paralyzed, Brian."

He looked completely dumbfounded, his eyes narrowed and his mouth slack.

"It would've," I pushed.

"Get the fuck outta here." He yanked his hands out of my grip and shook his head, then looked at me like he was struggling to see me in focus. "That's...*Jesus*, that's fucking crazy, Syd. Most of the time everyone just tells me it was an accident and I shouldn't take the blame so I gotta give it to you for being original. Haven't heard that one yet, but straight up, that's some seriously fucked-up way of trying to make me feel better."

"I'm not just trying to make you feel better. It's true." I leaned back and held on to the console, sitting taller in my seat.

I needed a stiff spine for what I was about to say. I hated even thinking about it.

"Whatever you say, babe," he mumbled, looking away.

I took in a deep breath, wiped once more at my face to collect any stray tears, then spoke evenly and carefully, making sure I was heard.

"You know my brother died. You know how he died, but you don't know the part I played in it."

Brian slowly turned his head. His brows furrowed.

"What are you talking about?" he asked.

I felt my spine bend, just the slightest give in my strength, but I gathered it back up before replying.

"Barrett had two choices he was looking at when he graduated," I said. "UCLA and Boston University. Had scholarships from both, so it was just a matter of where he preferred going. One night I was playing in my room and he came in, carrying the brochures he had from the two schools and laid them out in front of me. He asked me where I thought he should go. Said he was having trouble deciding and wanted my opinion, a twelve-year-old's opinion, so I gave it to him. I picked up those brochures and studied them for the time I needed to make my decision, which lasted all of three seconds because the brochure for UCLA had pretty palm trees on it and a picture of the Pacific Ocean. I thought it was beautiful so I told him to go there, and he did. Four months later he died."

Now it was Brian who was turning in his seat a little to face me, his thick shoulder bracing his weight on the backrest.

"You don't blame yourself for that, do you?" he asked, face tight with worry.

I shook my head and closed my eyes through an exhale.

"No. But I could," I replied, looking at him. "I could very easily feel guilt over Barrett dying. Let that consume me like your guilt's consuming you."

"It's not the same thing."

"What's the difference?" I asked. "My brother died because he went to a school that I picked. Maybe if he went somewhere else, it wouldn't have happened. I was driving that day. It was my fault."

"Syd—"

"*Or*," I interrupted. "My brother died because no matter what school I would've chosen, he would've gone to UCLA anyway because it was where he really wanted to go. He was just humoring me by letting me pick. It didn't matter what I said. If I'd chosen Boston, he still would've wound up at UCLA."

I sniffed and pushed my glasses back on my nose. My other hand was being held tight in one of Brian's.

"Or my brother was never meant to live past his nineteenth birthday," I continued. "He could've gone anywhere and he would've died. It didn't matter. It didn't matter what school I picked or where he got scholarships. It didn't matter if he even went to college at all, he would've died anyway."

Brian stared at me.

I held my breath and my tongue. I wanted him to ask me the question I needed him to ask me. I couldn't say any more until he did and the words I had to say were so important I wanted to write them down so Brian could hear them while I spoke and read them whenever he needed to and carry them with him always, so he'd never feel this way again.

He leaned closer and held my cheek, and a breath of relief filled my lungs and burst on his wrist as I said a silent prayer because I knew the question was coming.

"You really believe that?" he asked. "You think he'd be dead no matter what? No matter where he would've gone?"

I felt my lip tremble.

"Do you think I killed my brother? Do you think he's dead because of me? Because I chose palm trees and a pretty ocean for his place to die?"

"No," he answered quickly and firmly and on what sounded like a full breath. "No, I don't fucking think that."

"I have," I confessed. "I've thought all those things at one point. The last one is just the easiest. I'm not as sad when I believe that one."

He closed his eyes and lowered his head, whispering my name one time.

He was sad for me. I needed him to feel sad for himself, too, instead of angry, so I kept going.

"What happened wasn't your fault. It was an accident, and if you hadn't been driving that night, it would've been somebody else. That little boy's fate was already mapped out, Brian, just like Barrett's."

He shook his head once. "Someone else could've been driving, fine, but you know what?" He glanced up. "Maybe they wouldn't have been speeding. Maybe they would've been going slow enough to get control of their car and they could've avoided—"

"No." I leaned closer and took his own face in my hands when he let go of mine. "I've driven on this road. I've gone down that hill, which means I know how steep it is, and I can tell you knowing in my heart that it's true, it didn't matter how fast you were going that night. You could've been doing the speed limit and you would've still lost control when you hit that ice, and given how sharp that drop is, you would've sped up, Brian. You would've sped up and you still would've hit them. Anyone would've hit them."

"I could've controlled it."

"You couldn't, honey. There was nothing you could've done."

He blinked hard and I felt the muscles in his jaw tense.

He was hearing me. I was getting to him.

I had to keep going.

I looked between us, at the console and his body pressed against it to get closer to me and my body pressed against it to get closer to him.

"What are you doing?" he asked, leaning back and gripping my waist as I put my weight on my left foot and carefully brought my other leg over to his side.

"Getting closer," I replied.

I slid over him and straddled his lap.

"Syd..."

My hands moved from his shoulders to around his neck. I pressed closer until I could feel his breath on my mouth.

"I'm gonna say some things to you and I want you to listen," I said. "Can you do that?"

His hands glided to my back.

"Do I have a choice?" he asked.

"No, but I thought I'd be polite and give you the option."

He looked to my mouth, then back to my eyes, replying, "Sweet of you."

I shrugged, found the words I wanted to say, and said them quickly, speaking fast because I didn't want to be interrupted and because I believed them so much I couldn't keep them to myself another second.

"You're a good man, Brian," I started, feeling his neck pull as he tried to look away but I kept a tight hold so he couldn't. "*Amazing*," I continued, bending closer. "I needed you, but I didn't know I needed you until you reached out to me and made sure I was okay. You told me to focus on you, remember? When I said I felt lost and scared, you wanted to talk to me. You comforted me. You didn't need to do that but you did, and I don't care if your reasons were selfish in the beginning. I don't care if you wanted to know the girl who had to be a little crazy for going off on you the way she did. You made me laugh and live and you helped me find the person I was without Marcus, and you did that carrying this guilt inside of you that you didn't deserve to carry. You were hurting so bad but you shut that out so you could heal me. You kept that locked inside and you made sure *I* was okay. That's... I mean, my *God*, how amazing of a man can you possibly be? Who does that?"

"Syd," he tried, interrupting when I paused to take in a shuddering breath.

I was a mess of tears and a quivering voice, but I pressed on. I didn't stop.

"You are a dream, Brian Savage," I repeated, dropping my head until our foreheads touched. "You're my dream. The most amazing person I've ever known, and I'm going to heal you. I am, and you're not going to be able to stop me so don't even bother trying. This is happening. It's my turn. You healed me and now I'm healing you. I'm going to do it. I'm going to make sure *you're* okay, and I'm not going to stop until there is none of that guilt left inside of you. I'm not going to stop until you're the one telling me that accident wasn't your fault. I promise. Forever." I dipped closer. "I'm going to give you Wild for the rest of your life and so much of it you won't have room to feel anything else."

His eyes flickered wider.

Then on a growl he wrapped his one arm around my waist and slid his other hand to the back of my neck, gripped me there, and yanked me down until he could take my mouth in a kiss that tasted like love and felt like madness, that was so hard and violent my lips burned and bruised, but it was good. So good I went harder and took him deeper, holding him so tight my hands shook.

We were a chaos of tongues and teeth and hurried breaths. I matched his fire. I matched his depravity.

He pulled and I pulled. He bit and I bit. He loved and I loved.

I was already spinning a second into it and by the time Brian broke the kiss on a moan that rattled in his chest, I felt mindless and melted into him, sank lower, then dropped my head on his shoulder as his arms coiled around me.

We were silent for minutes but it was strange. I said so much and heard him so loudly, the words that made up his heartbeat and mine, it became my favorite conversation.

My eyes were closed when I felt his lips press to my temple, and a second later, I heard him quietly ask, "You'll never let me believe it was my fault, will you?"

I breathed deep and shook my head.

"No. And you'll never let me believe it was mine."

Brian's arms held me tighter, and that was all I needed because I knew.

He was going to let me heal him.

* * *

It was Sunday evening and I was excited.

No, scratch that, I was beyond excited. This was excitement on a whole new level because I had accomplished something I had never accomplished before, to be more specific, something I had *ruined* to the point of no return five days prior.

The homemade potpie with made-from-scratch pie dough.

I wasn't going to let some recipe with misleading instructions knock me down and keep me from cooking again. No way. I was determined. And I had an entire afternoon to tackle that recipe and get it perfect for Brian.

We spent the morning together since we were both off work today, but Brian said he had something he needed to take care of around one o'clock for his sister, he'd be gone several hours and wouldn't get home until after five, and even though my throat stung with disappointment because I wasn't invited to whatever it was he was taking care of, nor was I informed of it, I quickly swallowed that disappointment and focused on the opportunity I was given.

I wanted this to be a surprise, a good one this time, and now I had my chance.

I hit the market on my way home, pulling up the recipe on my phone so I didn't have to go off memory and risk missing an ingredient, then I studied that recipe for a good hour after I got home before I even got started. I was not missing *anything* this time.

Thirty minutes of prep and forty-five minutes of bake time later, I had a golden delicious potpie cooling on my stovetop and the biggest grin on my face.

No more burned-up dinners for my boy. He deserved the best.

And now that I was currently carrying that pie plate in my hands and walking up the drive to Brian's house, that grin I had on earlier didn't hold a candle to the one I was wearing now.

I couldn't wait to show him what I'd made. The pretty design on the edge of my piecrust looked *awesome*.

"Hello?" I called out as I entered the house, knocking once but not waiting for an answer because Brian told me never to wait for an answer, just to walk in as long as his Jeep was there.

"In here," Brian yelled from the direction of the kitchen.

I shut the door, kicked my sandals off and scooted them up against the wall, then padded down the hallway with a bounce in my step.

A sound came from upstairs. It was light and quick like a snap, but sounded an awful lot like a yelp...or a muffled bark.

"Oh, gross." I shivered with disgust as I moved around the staircase. "I better not see Jamie walking around here collared on a leash," I mumbled to myself.

Brian was leaning over the counter when he came into view, staring down at what I knew had to be a crossword book. He flicked a pen between his fingers and tapped it rhythmically against the granite.

Pen not pencil. He was *that good* at crosswords.

"Hey, Trouble," I greeted him as I crossed the room, watching his head lift and his eyes smile.

"Hey, Wild." He dropped the pen in the center of the book, straightened, then noticed the plate in my hands. He cocked a brow. "You did it again, didn't you?"

"Did what?"

"Told you, babe. I'm good with four recipes and that looks like a fifth. Is it?"

"Nope," I replied cheerfully, liking that he remembered what my four trusted recipes were. I came to a stop in front of him and held out the plate proudly. "Well, it is but it's not a *new* fifth. It's the same one I burnt up before, but now it's not all burnt up. See?"

He took the plate from me and admired the dish.

"Damn," he mumbled appreciatively. "This looks good. *Really* fucking good." His eyes lifted to mine. "Like your designs along the edge. Nice touch."

Ah! He noticed!

I wanted to pirouette around the room but instead I chose to satisfy my need to celebrate with a less obnoxious bop of my shoulders.

"Thanks! And it should taste just as good as it looks. I left all the bitter out this time."

A laugh rumbled in his chest. His eyes warmed.

"Didn't need to do this," he said, leaning in and kissing me quick. "Appreciate it, though."

"Anytime, babe."

He gave me a slow smile as he pulled back.

"Ready to eat?" he asked, setting the pie plate down next to his book, opening up the silverware drawer, grabbing two forks, then coming back over to stand next to me. "Need to taste some of this," he murmured to himself, not bothering with a plate and sticking his fork into the crust like he was starved, digging out a heaping bite that needed to be warmed but apparently he wasn't bothering with that either, and shoveling it in, chewing and moaning in potpie heaven.

"Savage," I joked.

He gave me a wink.

"I'm a lady so I'm using a plate."

I went to move around him to get to the cabinet that held the dishware when that quiet barking sound came from upstairs again.

I slapped the counter.

"Seriously? How do you put up with that? Aren't your ears bleeding?"

Brian slowly turned his head.

"Huh?" he asked through a mouthful.

I gestured at the ceiling conveniently after another Jamie kink bark sounded.

"That!" I snapped. "How can you stand here eating homemade potpie while your best friend is upstairs acting like a house pet?"

He shrugged, swallowed, then stated matter-of-factly, "Really good potpie, babe."

"That's..." I lowered my hand and joined it with the other, knotting my fingers together. "Really?" I asked softly, leaning closer.

Brian nodded through a smile.

I inhaled sharply and curled my toes against the wood floor.

The urge to do another celebratory dance was stronger than ever, but I kept myself composed.

I'd wait until he went to the bathroom or something.

Brian dropped the fork in the dish, wiped his mouth with the back of his hand, and reached for mine, tugging me to follow behind him as he led us out of the kitchen.

"Come on. I'll show you the house pet," he said, heading up the stairs.

Panic tingled up my spine.

As if the weird, freaky bastard could hear me, he barked again.

I pointed up the stairs, then turned that finger on Brian and waved it in his face. "No thank you."

Brian shook his head through a laugh, grabbed the hand I had suspended in the air, and resumed tugging me behind him as he continued climbing.

"I'm not sure why I gotta keep saying this but you seem to keep forgetting, don't care what the fuck Jamie is doing or who, not my business and I never want it to be my business, which eliminates the possibility of me ever wanting to *show you* anything he's doing in there."

"Well, that's a relief," I commented on a sigh, reaching the top of the stairs and being led to the right, down the hallway where Brian's room was located, not Jamie's.

Thank *God*.

Brian stopped in front of his door, turned the handle, and pushed it open.

"Good thing this guy here's keeping guard, 'cause you even thinking that makes me wanna throw you on the bed and spank the shit out of you."

My eyes widened for two reasons.

One, I was turned on. Immediately. *Really* turned on and absolutely wishing he'd go through with his threat. The way Brian spanked had me begging for it and I wasn't ashamed to admit that.

He was really *really* good at it.

And two, I didn't miss the first part of his sentence, which led to me investigating with searching eyes what guy he was referring to that was keeping guard, leading me to spot only a second later the metal crate in the corner of the room next to the dresser and the puppy leaping around inside of it.

Not just any puppy. A boxer puppy.

No ... *fucking* ... way ...

"Oh, my God!" I shrieked with more excitement than I'd ever felt in my entire life, jumping into the air repeatedly with my hands covering my mouth while the puppy shared in my enthusiasm, barking and whining for attention.

I bolted across the room and fell to my knees in front of the crate.

"Look at you, you sweet thing. Were you the one making all that noise up here?"

The puppy pushed his nose through a slot and started sniffing and licking the air while his paws kicked out and slid along the metal floor.

"It's a boy," Brian said behind me as I offered up my fingers for playful nibbles. "Hope you don't mind but I named him already. He seems to like Sir."

I turned my head with my eyes stinging.

Brian was leaning against the frame, arms crossed, watching me intently. He tipped his chin at the crate.

"He's yours, Wild."

Oh, *God*...

Brian bought me a puppy. That's where he went today and why he didn't inform or include me in it, but not just any puppy. The puppy I'd wanted most of my life.

I was going to start bawling. I knew it.

This was too much and too perfect all at once.

Nodding, I wiped wetness off my face with the hand not being licked and nibbled.

"He's ours," I whispered, and Brian's eyes melted into warmth hearing that. "And he's beautiful," I added, turning my head back around.

He *was* beautiful. Fawn, with an all-black nose and white markings on his chest, big paws, and a docked tail.

Regal.

I giggled through my tears and stuck more fingers through the metal slots, allowing for even more playful nibbles.

"Thought about it," Brian began. "Figured I can take him to work with me so he doesn't need to be crated all day if we're both gone. Let him hang out at Wax."

"One of the boys," I murmured, smiling and stroking Sir's nose.

"Breeder gave me a bag of puppy food for him but it'll only last a couple of days. We need to go out and get him some more."

"Absolutely. We can go after dinner," I suggested. "We need other stuff, too. Collar, leash, bowls, comfy bed for when he doesn't want to sleep with us. Chew toys. A brush for his coat."

"Syd..."

"Maybe one of those training books. And he absolutely needs teething sticks. Dental health is very important." I leaned closer to the crate. "Right, Sir? We need to keep that smile pretty. Don't we?"

Sir shook out his coat and went back to biting at my fingers.

"Wild."

"Hmm?"

"You gonna let him out or are you just gonna keep torturing him?" Brian asked with a smile in his voice. "Had to crate him so it could be a surprise when you got here. I'm sure he wants to play."

Sir's little tail started wagging like crazy.

Of course. What was I doing?

"I'm sorry. Do you want to play, sugar bear? Let's get you out, okay?" I whispered anxiously, then sat up tall on my knees and scooted back a little, unlocked the two latches on the crate, one high and one low, pulled the door open, and fell back with a squeal when Sir barreled out and slammed straight into my chest, pawing his way up my body so he could lick all over my face.

"Sir!" I laughed, tilting my head back and laughing harder.

He had that fantastic puppy smell I thought came in the top five of best scents ever, and the softest coat.

I didn't know what Brian's plans were but I'd already decided Sir wasn't sleeping in the crate tonight.

His place was at the foot of the bed, or sharing my pillow if he preferred.

Scrunching up my nose, I turned so he could nip and lap at my ear.

My eyes locked with Brian's.

My boy did this for me. He was making sure I was living that life we talked about weeks ago.

He didn't know just by having him, I was already living it.

It was ours.

Thank you, I mouthed, feeling so happy I feared my heart would pop.

Love you, he mouthed back.

I closed my eyes, dropped my head back, and kept on laughing.

And that life? It was perfect.

Chapter Seventeen

BRIAN

Two Weeks Later

Standing outside of the emergency entrance at NHC, back pressed against the door of my Jeep and arms crossed, I turned my head toward the driver's side window where Sir was hanging out and let him sniff and lick the side of my face when he started whining.

"Getting impatient myself," I told him, then reached up, scratched behind his ear, and turned back to look at the sliding doors.

Syd got the job she'd interviewed for. Her schedule at the hospital ended up being four ten-hour days, and even though I thought that was plenty of time for her to be working every week, she didn't agree and told Nate she'd stay on a day at Whitecaps.

She was dead set on helping him out any way she could.

I thought that was sweet. I also thought it was unnecessary and knew Nate could figure shit out without her, but I kept that opinion to myself.

I figured as long as the day Syd helped out didn't end up being a Sunday, I could agree to it. I wanted my day off to coincide with hers, and I wasn't shy about telling her that.

She didn't argue and kept that day clear. She wanted Sundays with me, too.

Life was fucking good.

Had my girl, who was holding true to her word and healing me just by being who she was, giving me so much good I didn't have the space to feel anything besides what she was putting out.

Her light and her sweet and that fire that burned inside her when she loved. I'd never felt anything like that.

Never felt anything like her.

Syd handed me her heart and pressed her lips to my chest, whispering promises to mine.

She made sure I woke up hearing that accident wasn't my fault and I went to bed believing it a little bit more.

She said she would love me loudly, and she did. Every second.

Sydney Whittaker was my fucking dream. Soft and Wild and *mine*.

Life wasn't just good.

It was perfect.

Waking up to her sexy little body sprawled across my chest and feeling her press back against me at night, ass to cock, my arm over her waist holding her there and hers keeping pressure on top of mine, locking us together.

Fucking heaven.

We'd talk for hours. We'd fuck for hours.

I fell in love with Wild's voice in my ear. Now I had her in my arms while she was giving it to me, and I was out of my fucking mind lost for this girl. There was no turning back.

I'd be anything she needed. I'd be everything she needed.

And I'd spend the rest of my fucking life making her happy.

She said it was her turn to heal me but I wasn't done healing her.

Not even close. Not until she had it all.

And after tonight, hopefully she'd be one step closer to getting it.

I pushed off the Jeep as the emergency room doors slid open and Syd walked out, wearing light blue hospital scrubs that hid her curves more than the outfits she normally strutted her softness around in, plain white sneakers, and her ID badge clipped to her front pocket. Her hair was pulled back out of her face and she had a black and pink Adidas backpack slung over her shoulder.

She looked tired but perked up when she spotted us, a look of

surprise washing over her, holding for a second then slowly morph-
ing into the dimpled smile she was always giving me as she quickly
made her way down the sidewalk.

"Trouble, what in the world?" She paused to stand on her toes and
gave me a brief kiss. "What are you doing here?"

A chunk of red had fallen out of her ponytail. I tucked it behind
her ear and rubbed her cheek with my thumb.

She wasn't wearing any makeup. I could see every freckle and
mole and the natural flush of her cheeks she'd claimed was an unfortunate side effect of being a redhead.

Assholes paid money to stare at beauty like this and I had it in my
hands.

"Wanted to show you something. Thought we could go for a
drive, then come back here and get your car." I slid her book bag
off her shoulder and tipped my head at the Jeep. "Sir's been going
fuckin' nuts waiting for you."

Syd smiled bigger. She gave me another quick kiss before moving
in front of the window, where she started petting and kissing Sir.

"Sweet boy, did you have fun today at work?" She scratched behind his ears and let him sniff her face.

Syd was referring to Wax.

I'd been taking Sir to work with me so he wouldn't have to stay
crated all day and hadn't run into any issues so far. In fact, kids got
a kick out of him when they came into the shop. Happy kids meant
happy parents.

And happy parents bought a lot of shit.

Sir turned out to be a smart business investment.

"Good day?" I asked.

She shrugged, replying, "Busy day. I barely got to sit down. Made
the time go by fast, though." She turned to look at me. "So, what did
you want to show me?"

I nudged her hip gently with my hand.

"It's a surprise. Get in so we can get going. I want you to see it
before dark."

With wide eyes full of interest, she walked around the Jeep.

"I love surprises," she said.

"Know that, babe."

I tossed her book bag in the back and climbed in the driver's seat, taking a hold of Sir and holding him out for Syd to take after she got in and buckled.

"Tell me what it is, sugar bear, and I'll give you some peanut butter when we get home," she whispered against the top of his head as I pulled away from the hospital.

I breathed a laugh, shot her a quick glance, and asked, "You really want to know? I can tell you."

She sat up tall in the seat and shook her head, fighting a grin.

"Nope. Surprise me. I want to be wowed."

I smiled at the road.

Fuck yeah. I'd wow her. She had no idea this was coming.

Fifteen minutes later, I pulled up in front of the house I signed the papers for an hour ago, parked in the driveway, and cut the engine.

Syd sat forward in her seat and peered through the windshield.

"Is this where your sister lives?" she asked, looking around. "It looks empty."

"That's 'cause it is empty. Come on."

I grabbed the leash from the backseat, stepped out, and met Syd around on her side.

She looked from the house to me.

"What's going on? Why are we here?"

I attached the leash to Sir's collar and took him from her, letting him down so he could sniff around the yard. Reaching into my back pocket, I produced a set of keys and pressed them into Syd's hand.

"Go in and check it out, Wild," I told her.

Her eyes moved between the keys and my face.

"What?"

"The house, babe. Go check it out for me."

She tilted her head, blinked up at me, then asked, "Why would I do that?"

I smiled.

So fucking cute.

Bending down, I kissed her while Sir was tugging on the leash.

"'Cause I'm renting it for us, and if you hate it, I need to know. Ink is still wet on the contract. Got time to back out if I have to."

She gasped against my lips.

"What?" she whispered, pulling back and staring up at me as her hand lightly held on to my hip. "You got us a house?"

"Yep."

"You...you want me to move in with you?" She leaned closer. "Really?"

"Yeah, Wild, really," I replied, almost laughing at her shock because I thought where this shit was going between us was pretty damn obvious. "Want a lot of things with you and living together is one of them. Needed our own space and figured the way we're moving, I'll be giving you kids sooner rather than later and I want us to be settled somewhere before that happens. Somewhere you want us to be. You don't like it, I'll back out. You do? We have an option to buy down the road when we're ready." I swatted her left ass cheek and tipped my chin at the house. "So go check it out."

She stared at me, mouth hanging open and eyes blinking rapidly.

"You want us to *live together*?" she repeated, leaning even closer and higher when she rolled up on her toes to stress, "*For real?*"

"Jesus Christ," I muttered. "We're together every night, Syd. Practically live together already, babe. I'm just making it so we're living together someplace that's ours."

She fell back on her heels. Her eyes were watering fast and her lip started quivering.

Syd cried every time I did something for her. No matter what it was.

The first night I made the hot chocolate she liked and surprised her with it while she was waiting for me in bed, it took an hour for her to calm enough to actually drink it.

She couldn't believe I remembered. I made her suck my dick for thinking I'd forget.

And by "made," I mean she liked it so much her first orgasm hit with my cock down her throat and her fingers between her legs.

I had to reheat her drink twice that night.

Grabbing my face, Syd declared through a trembling voice, "You are way too sweet, Brian Savage." She tipped her chin up. "*Way* too sweet."

"Only to you," I replied, looking at the house then back at her, asking, "You gonna go check it out or do you hate it?"

"I'm gonna go check it out."

Fighting a smile, I bent to take her mouth, murmuring, "Good."

She wrapped her arms around my neck, smashed her tits against my ribs, and took the kiss harder, sucking on my tongue and moaning a little before pulling away breathless, steadying herself then spinning around and taking off toward the house in a sprint.

I moved closer to the grass so Sir could do his business, watching my girl climb the stairs and step up onto the porch.

She walked the length of it slowly, taking everything in while running her hand along the railing, made it to the end, and stopped in front of the white wooden glider the previous owners had left behind and I kept there knowing Syd would like having a place to sit. She studied it like she was studying a piece of art in a museum, taking her time to appreciate it. After several minutes she turned her head to look at me and gave me a smile I felt all the way in my fucking gut.

Then she blew me a kiss and spun around, walked the length again and stopping at the front door, slid the key into the lock, opened it, and stepped inside, giving me one last look and a cute wave before she disappeared.

I breathed deep and turned to Sir.

"Think she'll like the rest of it?" I asked.

He found a blade of grass he liked and took a piss on it.

I kept Sir in the yard for close to ten minutes then led him to the house, pushed the door open, and moved inside, letting him off the leash so he could roam around now that he'd done his business and I trusted he'd be good to go for a while.

He took off down the hallway, slid into a wall, shook it off, then disappeared into one of the three bedrooms.

"Syd?" I called out, dropping the leash by the door. After not getting a response, I moved through the empty house in the direction of the kitchen.

The house was a rancher-style home with three bedrooms, a kitchen, a living room, and two bathrooms all on one level. The basement was unfinished with a roughed-in powder room.

It wasn't much compared to what I owned with Jamie or even Tori's place. You could probably fit five of these houses in the one I was moving out of, but it had a porch, a fenced-in yard for Sir that was decent sized, enough bedrooms for expanding, and it was close to both of our jobs.

I could live here and be really fucking happy with Syd. I could live in a gutter and be happy with her, but if she didn't like it, I'd find someplace else.

Whatever she wanted.

The slider was open when I walked around the corner and entered the kitchen. I stepped outside onto the small deck and saw Syd standing at the railing, looking out at the yard.

She turned when she heard my footsteps, leaned back against the railing with her hands stretched out and gripping onto it behind her, bent her knee, and planted her foot on a spindle all while staring at me, eyes hard and mouth pulled into a frown.

Fuck.

I halted a few feet away and scrubbed at my face with both hands.

"Fuck. You don't like it," I guessed, letting my arms drop and clenching my jaw through a tight inhale.

I thought this was it. I thought for sure I knew what she'd want.

"What don't you like?" I asked, stepping closer. "Is it shit I can fix? Or is it everything? The layout? Location? Would you rather have..."

My voice trailed off when Syd blinded me with a smile, pushed off from the railing, and charged at me like she was always doing lately, leaping into the air when she was close enough and I could catch her, hands on her hips then sliding to her ass, pulling her higher and nearer as she wrapped her arms around my neck and her legs around my waist.

"I love it!" she squealed, pressing kisses all over my face.

"Yeah?" I asked in a tight voice.

I needed to be sure.

"Yes! Everything about it. God...*everything*, Brian! Especially the bedrooms and the yard and the porch. *And* the kitchen and the cute little living room. Oh, and the basement. I don't even care that it's not finished. It has so much potential, Trouble. We could turn it into a big game room or another TV area. My creative juices are flowing like crazy. I can't wait to decorate! And did you see the size of the master bath? It's *huge*!"

It wasn't. It was a standard-size master bath, but Syd was excited.

I breathed a sigh of relief and kissed the corner of her mouth.

"Glad to know you approve. And thanks a fucking lot for making me worry." I nipped at her bottom lip. "Think I need my dick sucked for that."

She perked up, straightened her spine, and lifted an intrigued brow.

"Feel like christening the place? I could blow you in every room for good juju and then let you fuck me in our giant bathroom so you can watch my tits in the mirror."

My groin tightened.

Christ, her fucking mouth.

Syd must've felt my reaction 'cause she rotated her hips and bared down on me.

"That feels like a yes," she teased, her voice dripping sex. "Wanna get started?"

"In a minute."

"*In a minute?*" She felt my forehead and examined me closely. "Are you feeling okay? Do we need to go back to the hospital?"

I shook her hand off.

She moved it back to my neck and squeezed me there.

"Brian Savage doesn't want sex, I'm shocked."

"Want it," I said, pulling her hips closer until she felt my proof pressing hard between her legs.

She moaned and tried coming in for a kiss.

I had shit to clarify first and she was feeling greedy so I didn't stall.

"Know where this is going, don't you?" I asked, dipping to avoid her mouth and pressing my lips to her jaw so she could speak.

"Where what's going?" she questioned back.

"Wouldn't be buying us a house if I didn't plan on giving you my last name, babe."

I felt her pulse jump against my lips as I moved down her neck and sucked there.

"I..." She swallowed thickly and started breathing heavier. "We have to wait a year," she said, sounding quiet and sad, tilting her head back and offering me her throat. "I won't be legally divorced until it's been a year."

"Know that, and straight up, Wild, I fuckin' hate it," I growled. "Takes everything in me not to find that motherfucker and beat the shit outta him just for doing you like he did, add to that the fact he gets to have ties to you that I don't get to have until some fuckin' judge says I can..."

I felt my muscles lock in anger.

Wild moved her hands to the back of my head, pressed her lips to my ear, and softly admitted, "I know, honey. I hate it, too."

I kissed the spot just above her collarbone, then leaned back to look into her eyes.

"Shit keeps me up at night. Never wanted something this much before and I'm gonna be a miserable fuckin' prick waiting for it."

She touched my cheek. Her eyes were calming.

"We can be miserable fucking pricks together," she said on a smile, then let it soften, moved her other hand to my opposite cheek, dipped closer, looking serious now, and added, "I was married for six years and it never felt like this. Not even when it was good. Not even when it was great and I wanted it more than anything, because it wasn't right. It wasn't *us*. You and me. I've never wanted something this much before either and I never will, which is why I'm saying yes to this now, yes to this in a year, because I know my answer won't change no matter when you ask me."

My breath caught.

Fuck.

I slid my hand up her back to her neck and curled my fingers there.

"Syd," I murmured.

"And I promise you, Brian Savage, the day I'm legally divorced is the day we're getting hitched. I will not wait any longer than that," she stated firmly. "I'll sign those papers, free myself completely of Marcus, and then I'm signing my life over to you."

My muscles locked again but not in anger this time.

Fuck that year. Wild was mine. Now and always.

On a growl that shook the earth, I pulled Syd down and took her mouth, her tongue, and her breath, my hand on her neck moving up, twisting in her hair and gripping while my other hand stayed on her ass and held her weight.

Her hands were all over me, working down my neck to my shoulders to between us, where she tugged at my shirt.

"Please," she whispered. "Brian . . . take me."

I spun us and moved my girl inside, shutting the door and rushing through the kitchen in the direction of the master bedroom.

"You gonna give me that greedy pussy?" I asked, digging my fingers into her ass and kneading her flesh.

She moaned inside our kiss, sucked in a breath like she was startled, then murmured, "The dog."

Fuck that. I was taking her. He'd be fine.

I turned my head, allowing her lips to move to my cheek, and called out, "Sir!" as we stepped into the living room.

Seconds later he came galloping down the hallway, leash in his mouth and dragging it behind him.

Syd leaned away and turned to look at him.

Sir whipped the leash around playfully while growling like it was putting up a fight, released it out of his mouth, stepped back, dropped down on his front legs, and wagged his tail excitedly. Then he waited a few seconds and pounced on it again.

"Sir Duke, that is not a chew toy," Syd reprimanded him in a stern voice, calling him by his full name. She glanced around the empty room, then sighed, looking back at him to add, "But I guess it's all you have to keep you occupied for the next fifteen minutes."

I glared at her profile.

"Double that, babe."

She turned to look at me, flushed cheeks and eyes burning as she pulled that fat bottom lip into her mouth and started sucking on it.

Christ. She wanted it. So fucking greedy.

"You keep looking at me like that and I'm not making it to the bathroom," I warned her.

She released her lip and shrugged innocently.

"I can't help it. I'm so wet, I can feel it dripping down to my... you know." Her eyes widened and she shifted in my arms. "You could probably fuck me there without lube if you wanted."

I groaned. "Jesus Christ. Don't say shit like that to me."

"Why not?" She giggled.

I started moving us through the living room again, passing Sir, who was hanging by the front door, and headed down the hallway.

"Because I'll fucking do it."

"And that's a problem?"

"It is if I wanna make good on lasting thirty minutes."

Syd gave me a look of understanding, nodded once, then watched over my shoulder.

"Is he okay playing while we go do you know what?" she asked, tilting her head to the side so I could kiss her neck.

"Nothing for him to get into and he can't get out. He'll be fine," I told her, crossing into the bedroom and making for the master bath.

"You sure? What about the basement steps? Those are pretty steep."

"He's a dog, babe. Not a baby. He can handle steps."

I stepped inside the bathroom, flicked the light on, closed the door behind us so Sir wouldn't see that as an open invitation to cock-block me, and let Syd slide down my body.

She stood between me and the vanity, looking up nervously.

"You sure?" she asked again.

I cocked my head.

"Would you rather he join us in here so you can keep an eye on him while I'm buried inside you?"

She jerked back.

"Uh... no, that would be weird," she replied quickly. "Not to mention traumatizing for him, I'd imagine. You fuck dirty."

I smirked, reached back over my shoulder, fisted my shirt, and tugged it off.

"Fuck you sweet, too," I told her, dropping my shirt and reaching for hers.

"Sometimes," she murmured through a smile. She lifted her arms over her head so I could get her top off.

I tossed it next to mine then tugged the drawstring on her pants loose, causing them to drop and bunch at her ankles as she made quick work of her bra.

I stared at her tits when she freed them.

Full and sitting high on her chest, her rose-colored nipples the perfect size for my mouth.

"Fuck." I squeezed my cock through my shorts, then explained further, "Think you get a bit of both every time, Wild. Hard for me not to give you sweet when you're giving it and even harder not to dirty you up when you're begging for it." I lifted my eyes to hers. "Know you're getting both now."

Syd kicked off her shoes and stepped out of her pants. Panties came next, then with a coy smile, she stepped closer, reached for my shorts, and popped the button, asking, "Why am I getting both now?"

She lowered the zipper.

I moaned when her fingers brushed my cock.

"Mentioned letting me take your ass. Means you're already feeling dirty tonight so that's what you'll be getting." My shorts slid down my legs. I dropped my head back, eyes closing when she wrapped her hand around me and started stroking. "*Syd.*"

"And the sweet?" she asked, sounding playful.

I tipped my head down and held her eyes.

"Said you'd marry me," I reminded her. "Can't imagine not making love to you right now after hearing that."

Her hand stilled.

I moved in, forcing my girl to lose her hold on me.

"Gonna do that now. You good with that?" I asked, gripping the backs of her legs and lifting.

"Yes," she answered, nodding quickly while squeezing my neck. "I'm good with that."

I sat her on the edge of the vanity, spread her legs wide, and stared between her face and her cunt.

"Still dripping?" I slid my finger through her pussy to test. Moisture trickled onto my palm. *"Fuck."*

She grabbed my face and kissed me, slow and deep, shaking when I added a second.

"God," she moaned.

I bent down and gave her a long lick, tasting her in my throat.

She cried out and reached for me but I was already standing, fisting the base of my cock and stepping into her, then her head fell back and her eyes rolled closed as I pushed in that first inch.

Crazy.

Beautiful.

Mine.

"Brian." Syd's voice vibrated up my spine.

I slid in farther, slowly stretching her, her pussy drawing me in with tight little pulses until I was fully seated and my balls ached with the need to pound us both toward madness.

I fought it and gripped her hips.

This was our sweet. Paced and rhythmed. I wouldn't be desperate yet.

"Eyes, babe."

Immediately, Syd tilted her head down and blinked at me.

When I had her, I started thrusting slowly. Deliberately. Her desire dripped to my balls. She'd never been this wet.

I'd never felt this lost.

"Fuck, Wild...keep watching me," I told her. My voice was strained. "Keep looking at me like that. Always like that."

"Always."

She gasped when I started circling her clit with my thumb.

I pulled her hips so she was hanging over the edge of the vanity, slid my hands to the backs of her knees, and opened her up, spreading her legs wider and pressing them closer to her chest.

She whimpered and bit her lip as I drove in deeper, bottoming out each time.

"You like that," I stated, knowing she did as I watched my cock move inside the tightest pussy I'd ever fucked. "God...*tell me.* Tell me you like it."

"I like it," she breathed.

"Is this what your greedy little cunt wants? My cock filling it? Fucking it?"

"Brian," she gasped.

Her pussy clenched.

I sucked in a breath. *"Damn,"* I groaned, gripped her hips again, and lifted my eyes, catching hers still on me, glowing like she was lit from within and burning with that fire she had behind her love.

Love for me she was promising forever.

Forever.

Fuck.

I was the luckiest motherfucker alive.

I kept our pace, building it slow while I toyed with her clit until she moved her legs higher up my back and pushed her chest out, begging for my mouth.

"Suck them. Brian...*please*, suck them."

Gripping the edge of the vanity, I leaned in and circled her tight nipple with my tongue. I couldn't stop my hips from thrusting faster as I sucked hard, drawing the peak into my mouth.

She cried out, legs shaking against my sides and tensing against my back.

She was close, her orgasm right there. I could feel it humming beneath her skin.

I moved my thumb furiously over her clit to get her there as my other hand kept her anchored down, then on a gasp, she came and fell back against the mirror, taking me with her, squeezing my dick so goddamned hard I felt it in my spine.

"Wild," I whispered between her tits.

Her back arched and her voice caught.

I leaned away, fucking her through it, and watched those fat lips part and her features go slack.

She came down as beautifully as she'd climbed, head rolling to the side and eyes fluttering, those hot little moans rolling off her tongue.

I pulled out and tugged on her hips.

Syd slid off the vanity with a gasp, startled by the movement.

"Turn around and lean forward," I growled, stroking my wet dick.

She looked from my hand to my face with heavy eyes, filled with heat. She nodded quickly, then did as I directed and spun around, braced her hands on either side of the sink, and bent forward, jutting her ass out and spreading her legs.

"You came all over me," I said, my lips against her ear as I stepped up behind her.

She met my gaze in the mirror, swallowed, then nodded.

"You're gonna do it again," I promised, gliding my hands up her stomach to her tits, squeezing them and tugging on her nipples. "Aren't you?"

Her head rolled back and hit my shoulder.

"Yes," she whispered.

Fisting her ponytail with one hand, I slid my other up her back and tilted her forward at the angle I needed, lined up at her heat, and drove in, hitting bottom in one hard thrust.

"Oh, God!" she cried, her head snapping back when I pulled.

Then I started really moving, pleasure gripping me between my hips as I beat into her from behind.

I wasn't going to last. I was already close to coming when Syd went tight around me and now she was swollen and shaking and so fucking wet I could hear it.

Wild heard it, too. Her cheeks pinked and she bit her lip in shame.

I slid my hand around her waist and between her legs as I kept pounding hard. I pressed my lips to her cheek.

"Don't," I said, watching her eyes lift in the mirror. "Nothing sexier than hearing you, Wild. Nothing, you got me? Give me this." I rubbed her clit with the palm of my hand.

She gasped, closed her eyes, and pressed back, taking it deeper.

Our noises filled the bathroom, hers and mine. The squelching of our bodies and the slapping of skin, moans and incoherent words that broke apart before they left our tongues.

I fucked her until my legs burned. I became sloppy and clumsy with my thrusts, rutting at a maddening pace.

Syd loved it. She begged for more. For harder. For dirty, and I gave it.

I squeezed her tits harshly and slapped them.

I slid my cock between her lips and asked if she liked the taste of her pussy.

I told her I'd take her ass and I did, sliding two fingers inside while I bucked into her from behind.

Syd took it all. No hesitation. No shame.

She held my eyes in the mirror and got off on everything I was giving.

"Brian...oh, fuck, Brian," she groaned, and trembled in my arms.

My orgasm chased hers and seconds later I dropped my head to her back, cursed, and shot off deep.

I kept my arms around her. I never wanted to let go.

"One year," I said hoarsely when I had breath in my lungs again. My lips moved over her skin. "One fucking year."

Syd reached back and held me. She knew I needed it.

"It'll be here before we know it," she soothed.

I closed my eyes.

We didn't move until Sir started clawing and whining at the door. After we cleaned up and dressed, Syd scooped him up and we both went looking for his leash.

We found it in the kitchen. The little bastard had chewed it in half.

I smiled and pulled my girl close as she quietly scolded the clueless puppy for his wrongdoing.

He could've chewed a hole in the wall and I wouldn't have cared. Not that day.

Syd loved the house and was taking my name in a year.

Let the countdown begin.

Chapter Eighteen

SYDNEY

It was moving day and everyone was lending a hand.

Jamie and Cole were helping Brian with the heavy stuff and unloading the moving truck. Tori and I emptied out the back of my car and transported boxes and décor I didn't bother packing, including lamps and cute accent pillows I'd picked up at Target. When Shay arrived after her shift ended, she started unpacking and putting stuff away in the kitchen for me, and Kali, bless her heart, was doing what she could, which consisted of being amazing company and chatting us up while we worked since she was busy balancing a squirming Cameron on her hip.

I called for a break after setting the box labeled *Games and Shit* in the living room, not knowing what all *shit* meant and leaving that for Brian to relocate if needed since he was the one writing vague descriptive terms on stuff he packed up.

One of his boxes he'd labeled with a question mark. I stuck that one in the basement.

It seemed appropriate. I didn't know what we were putting down there.

The girls, plus Cameron and Sir, were hanging out in the kitchen, talking and digging into the pizzas I ordered as a thank-you to everyone for helping out. We were all standing around the small island, except for Kali, since the table and chairs hadn't been brought inside yet.

Kali was crouched down by the slider and watching over Cameron, who was on the floor, squealing and waving his arms excitedly as Sir sniffed and licked his toes.

"*Ga-ga-ya*," Cameron yelled, bopping Sir on the head in a happy baby way and not at all trying to be cruel.

Sir thought it was playful and kept on sniffing and licking.

"I think it's nice Jamie and that other guy offered to help out today," Kali said, looking over at us.

"What's nice about it?" Tori shot back, studying her chipped polish. "*We're* helping. It's the right thing to do. You shouldn't be rewarded for being a decent human being."

Kali slowly looked away, looking uncomfortable.

Shay muffled a giggle and resumed eating her slice.

I shook my head, shooting a disapproving glare at Tori.

She'd never give Jamie an inch.

While avoiding him wasn't an option today, Tori still managed to ignore Jamie every chance she got, paying him no mind when he was speaking either to her or in general.

She was still holding tight to that grudge developed on the night of the party but, if asked, would never admit to Jamie's actions affecting her.

Not ever.

She'd die first. I was convinced.

"I agree. I think it's nice," I added, standing a little taller.

Tori slowly slid her eyes to mine and narrowed them.

I ignored that, turning my head when Brian came around the corner. He was walking backward while carrying one side of the rectangular dining room table.

Jamie had the other end and entered the kitchen next, followed by Cole, who was walking behind and somehow managing to carry four chairs at once, making it look effortless.

"Coming that way," Brian warned over his shoulder. "Might wanna get the little guy up."

"Oh, right." Kali snatched Cameron up off the floor and carried him over to the island.

Sir automatically moved out of the way, rope in his mouth, and dashed over to his water bowl by the pantry. He dropped the toy beside the dish and went in for a drink.

"In front of the slider," Brian directed.

The guys lowered the table to the floor in the small dining room area we had. Once it was in the spot I okayed with a thumbs-up, Cole walked around the table and scooted a chair in on each side.

Some of our furniture was coming from Brian's old place with Jamie, including his bed, an extra couch they had stored in the basement, and the dining room table.

Jamie never used it so he didn't care if Brian took it with him when he moved out.

Now it was ours and I planned on cooking a lot of new recipes and getting plenty of use out of it.

I was extremely excited over a piece of furniture.

"Go grab the screwdriver. One of the legs is loose," Brian said to Jamie, then squatted down and examined underneath the table.

Jamie left the room.

"*Da-ba-da!*" Cameron craned his neck around, trying to see where Sir went. "*Da!*"

Kali rubbed his back.

"He's thirsty, baby. Let him get a drink."

Cam grabbed a fistful of Kali's hair and tried eating it.

"No, no, no. Not Mommy's hair." Kali pulled his hand down. "Come on," she said, bouncing him. "Let's go get some Cheerios."

Kali carried Cam out of the kitchen in search of her diaper bag, I guessed.

"*Da!*" Cam yelled out after they left the room.

Cole came up to the island, flipped a pizza box open, grabbed a paper plate, and took out a slice. "Appreciate the food," he said, giving me a smile.

I gave him one back. "No problem." Then I turned my head as Jamie entered the room again.

"Flat head or Phillips?" he called out, moving toward the table.

"Phillips," Brian answered.

I watched Jamie tuck one tool into his back pocket and hold on to another one.

What happened next was choreographed and well planned. I'd die convinced of this.

Just as Jamie was moving behind her, Tori stretched out across the island with her arms in front of her like a cat bathing in the sunlight, popped her jean short covered butt out, dropped her cheek on her shoulder, closed her eyes, and *moaned*, low and long and deep in her throat, doing this while giving her hips a little sway.

My mouth dropped open.

Something hit the tile floor with a sharp clink, followed by Jamie's voice groaning an ache-filled, *"Motherfucker."*

He was standing directly behind Tori and staring hungrily at her ass, looking ready to step up and take her in front of everyone right here.

"What the...you expecting me to reach that, dickhead?" Brian hissed from underneath the table. "Pick it up. I'm not crawling over there."

Tori straightened up a little and opened her eyes, slowly looking over her shoulder and doing so while keeping her bent-over position. She breathed a short, unimpressed laugh, then turned back around, keeping her weight on her elbows now and resumed facing forward, all while smiling proudly at herself.

"Hello?" Brian nearly shouted.

Jamie pulled out of his trance with a shake of his head and pushed the screwdriver to Brian with his foot, mumbling something about a cock tease under his breath.

"Jesus," Cole mumbled, looking at Tori like he was feeling that moan deep in his *own* throat. He blinked like he was trying to clear his mind, then stepped away from the island and stood by the table with the guys.

While they conversed among themselves, I took a step sideways and got closer to Tori.

"What was that?" I whispered, leaning down.

"What?" she asked, playing innocent and keeping her own voice lowered. She shrugged. "I had to stretch."

"You had to stretch," I repeated, disbelieving every word she was uttering.

That was no stretch.

"My back felt tight," she elaborated, picking at her cuticle. "We lifted a lot today."

We did no such thing.

I put my lips next to her ear.

"You totally did that to get a reaction out of Jamie. No other reason."

Tori turned her head and brought us nose to nose.

"You have never been more wrong in your life," she whispered with a straight face.

"Really?"

"Really."

"You weren't trying to get his attention at all?"

"He doesn't even exist to me."

"Mm. Okay." I stood tall and lifted my head. "So, Jamie, that big competition you're going out to Cali for in a few weeks, do you think you're gonna win?"

Tori glared at me.

I didn't see it, considering my eyes were on Jamie's head as it swiveled in my direction. No, I *felt* that glare. And it was filled with irritation and steel-like fortitude, I just knew it, because I was boldly calling my best friend's bluff.

This wasn't random conversation. Not at all. Jamie could run this topic in his sleep, brag about himself and do it without rebuttals because he was the best, indisputably. Everyone knew that, including Tori, and there was something undeniably sexy about a man who couldn't be topped.

And no matter if they were loved or hated, those men existed to *everyone*.

Stubborn women included.

"Do I think I'm gonna win?" Jamie echoed condescendingly with his arms crossed over his chest. "Ain't no thinking about it, Sunshine. Know I'm gonna win." He smiled, jerked his head to get the curling hair out of his eyes, and lightly shrugged. "No competition."

"Only 'cause I'm not entering," Brian announced from underneath the table.

My eyes were now taking up the majority of my face. I probably looked ridiculous but I couldn't help it.

I couldn't believe what I'd just heard.

Hope bloomed in my chest as I stood on my toes to look at my boy, saw he was on his back, knees bent and arms raised, working on tightening the table leg that was loose.

We'd talked about surfing only a couple of times since I knew Brian's reason for giving it up.

Guilt. It was still holding tight to pieces of him, causing Brian to deny himself something he loved doing, something he shared with his closest friends and the one thing he'd built his entire career around.

I was working on healing that piece of him and didn't think I was hitting deep enough yet, but maybe I was close. He never willingly talked about surfing. Never brought it up. Never joked about it.

He was joking about it now. I heard it in his voice.

"Still time to enter, brother," Jamie encouraged him, keeping the smile he'd given me and directing it toward the table. "You can take second just like the old days. Knock Cole down a seat."

"I'm standing right here, you know," Cole threw out.

"Right," Brian chuckled. "Wouldn't want to embarrass either one of you. I'll pass."

"Suit yourself," Jamie replied, then looked at Cole and nodded. "You can relax. Second's all yours."

Cole flipped him off.

Jamie threw his head back with a laugh.

I fought off tears, not wanting to draw attention to this maybe I was hearing and the feelings it was giving me for fear I'd ruin the moment and cause regression, kept myself composed, and decided to continue on with the mission to prove my point.

"Is this a big deal? Are you gonna get a new title or something?" I asked Jamie, assuming he'd win.

He looked to me, his chest puffing out in arrogance.

"World Pro Am Champion. Never won it before."

Tori turned her head hearing this and questioned with a tone, "Someone actually *beat* you? I thought you said that doesn't happen."

Jamie slid his deep blues to Tori, stared at her long enough without saying anything that she grew irritated, which only took three seconds, after which she pushed to a standing position, stuck her hand on her hip, and jutted it out impatiently while drumming her nails on the counter.

I gave myself a mental pat on the back. My plan was working like a charm.

"Did you hear what I said?" Tori asked when the silent staring continued.

Jamie's smile broadened.

"I heard you, Legs. Just processing the fact that you actually pay attention when I'm speaking. Didn't think that was the case, so if you don't mind, I'm gonna let this soak in a little before I give you an answer." He breathed deep and released it slowly. "Feels good."

"Don't read into it," she suggested. "Your ego is so loud, the people in the next state can hear you."

"Yeah, but I don't give a fuck about them," he replied bluntly, his face growing serious. "If I enter, I don't lose. First time entering this one, and you knowing that fact about me is something I give a fuck about."

"Well, you shouldn't."

"I do."

"I'm telling you not to."

"Doesn't work like that."

"*This*," Tori hissed with exasperation, tipped forward, and gestured with a quick hand between her and Jamie, "will never happen, so you giving a fuck is a waste of your time."

"*This*"—Jamie mimicked her gesture but kept his voice smooth and even—"has been happening for a while, Legs, and no part of it is a waste of my time. Not even this back and forth shit where you pretend you're not hard up for me."

Tori rolled her eyes, then she slid her gaze to Cole, who was standing there watching the drama but not looking as invested in it as Shay and myself, gave him the charming the pants off smile she'd perfected and informed *the room*, not just Cole, "I hope you take first."

Cole's eyebrows shot up.

"Uh, thanks," he replied, sounding unsure. "Appreciate it."

"What are you doing?" Jamie asked Tori, his eyes hot as they fell back on her.

I knew what she was doing. I was pretty sure everyone in the room knew what she was doing.

And I was *shocked* she was going there, mainly because unless I'd dreamed my last conversation with Tori, I was certain she was holding firm to the notion of Jamie not existing to her, yet here she was, admitting he existed by trying to make the man jealous.

This was good.

And I was totally right.

I shelved my excitement and decided on bringing that to her attention another time. She was getting ready to throw back some sass by the way her head was tilting, and I didn't want to miss it.

"What does it look like I'm doing?" Tori returned with the sass I'd predicted.

"Don't play with me, Legs."

"I'm not playing."

"And *I don't lose*," Jamie bit out, bringing back his words from earlier only this time saying them a little louder, a little firmer, and implying an entirely different meaning than before when he was speaking of surfing competitions.

I was picking up on that. Loud and clear.

So was Tori.

She sucked in a sharp breath. Her sass evaporated.

Jamie slowly grinned, flashing straight teeth and billboard-worthy dimples Tori was missing since she was refusing to look his way any longer.

Then everyone's attention turned to Brian when he stood and spun the screwdriver on his palm.

"Think that's it. Truck's unloaded." He met my eyes. "You get everything out of your car?"

"Yep. Just need to unpack."

I scrunched up my nose in disgust.

I hated unpacking. I would rather pack than unpack any day.

I was terrible at assigning things places and organizing.

"You want some help with that?" Tori asked. "I can hang around a little longer."

"Yeah, me, too," Shay offered.

I gave them both a smile.

I did want help, absolutely, but I also wanted some alone time with Brian in our new home. We hadn't had any yet and I was starting to get the shakes.

"That's okay," I told them. "It's not that much. I'll get to it later." I looked between Cole and Jamie and gestured at the pizza boxes. "You guys want any more? We have plenty."

They both declined, shaking their heads.

"I'm gonna get going," Cole announced, stepping forward and setting his plate on the counter. "Wanna beat the rain and get out on the water a bit."

"Same." Jamie turned his head. "You want a hand mounting the TV before I head out?" He directed this at Brian.

"I got it," Brian replied, setting the screwdriver on the table behind him, then moving in my direction. "Appreciate the help today."

"Yep," Jamie said.

"Anytime," Cole assured.

I grabbed the last slice of supreme, slid it onto a paper plate, and held it out as Brian came to stand beside me.

He smirked, threw his arm over my shoulder, and tugged me close like he was always doing, kissed the top of my head, then used his other hand to take the plate I was offering and placed it on the counter in front of him. He picked up the slice and lifted it to his mouth.

Kali entered the kitchen just as I was getting ready to combine the remaining slices into one box.

"I don't know where my head is today but I didn't bring it with me," she announced, bouncing Cameron on her hip and looking frazzled. "I forgot the Cheerios *and* the wipes, and this one is both starving and in need of a change. I'm gonna need to get going." She turned her eyes on me. "I'm sorry, Syd. I thought for sure I had extras in my car but I just spent the last ten minutes searching and the only thing I found was a bag of Goldfish that were so stale I wouldn't even risk feeding them to Sir."

Responding to his name being said, Sir barked at my feet.

"*Da-de-da!*" Cameron squealed, waving his arms excitedly and whipping his head around looking all over for the puppy.

"Don't worry about it. Everyone's heading out now anyway," I told her, watching the regret keeping weight. She wasn't letting go of it.

Kali shook her head and slid her hand up higher on Cameron's back, keeping him steady.

"No, I told you I'd help today and I didn't even get to really do that. I'm so irritated with myself right now."

"Taking care of your kid takes precedence over carrying boxes," Cole put in, trying to make her feel better and, in doing so, earning high merits from me. "Just saying. And it's not like we didn't manage. Everything's done."

"What he said," Brian mumbled around his bite of pizza.

"Plus, you kept Sir occupied for me while we were in and out of the house," I added, bending down and picking him up when he started pawing at my leg. "You *and* Cam were a help today. Big ones."

Kali gave me a soft smile, finally accepting my appreciation.

"Okay," she said, turning Cam and allowing his roaming eyes to spot the puppy in my arms now.

He reached out with both hands.

"*Da!*"

I carried Sir over to Kali and let the two new friends say their good-byes, which consisted of Sir licking all over Cameron's face and Cam giggling sweetly and bopping Sir on the head a couple times, caught up in the excitement of puppy kisses and unable to contain it.

I fully understood the struggle. I got caught up myself at least once a day.

Everyone left at the same time after that, giving farewells to one another. All except for Tori and Jamie.

Jamie gave his. Tori ignored it and made a point to single out the rest of us.

I rolled my eyes at my best friend and waved when she got to her car, then after making sure Sir was on the correct side of it, closed the front door and collapsed backward into Brian's waiting arms.

He kissed the top of my head.

It was four in the afternoon, and the only thing I wanted to do was curl up on our mattress surrounded by my boy's limbs and scent and the dirty words he'd whisper to me when I was nearly asleep. Nothing else would do.

"Wanna unpack now or wait a bit?" he asked, tightening his hold.

On the list of things that wouldn't do, unpacking was at the very top.

"Is never an option? 'Cause if I'm being honest, that seems the most appealing."

I felt Brian's warm breath tickle the top of my skull.

"Not an option if you want to live here with me," he murmured. "You still feeling that?"

Underneath his palms, my stomach muscles tensed.

I spun around, wrapped my hands around his neck, gave him a calming smile, and whispered, "I'm still feeling that."

"Good." He tugged me closer, moved his hands down to my ass, and squeezed. "You wanna feel me now?"

My belly dipped.

That calming smile I was wearing turned into something that could light up a large city. I was sure of it.

"Absolutely." I went up on my toes for a kiss. "That's my favorite option."

* * *

I came hard on a cry, losing suction on Brian's cock when my back arched and I pushed up, hands splaying across his lower stomach, elbows locked, and weight on my knees with Brian's face between them sucking perfectly on my clit.

"OhGodOhGodOhGod," I chanted as my hips jerked, smearing my desire over his lips and chin.

I was making such a mess. I could feel it, *hear* it, and Brian, God, he loved when I was like this. He wanted me dripping.

It turned him on like nothing else.

He moaned greedily and lapped at my slit. He wrapped his arms around me and pinned me down or pressed up with his face when I squirmed and held back.

He fucked me with his tongue and sucked me with his lips until I was panting and dizzy and building fast to another slow burn.

"Brian," I gasped with shaking legs. "*Please.* If you don't get inside me soon, I might die. This is not an exaggeration."

Warm breath burst against my flesh as he laughed. Then his tongue gave me a long, slow lick.

I gasped, shuddered, then glanced over my shoulder to peek at the top of his head.

"Are you *hearing me?*" I hissed.

I yelped when he bit my inner thigh.

He was hearing me.

"*Please*," I urged. "I'm being seriohh!"

He slid his hands to my hips and quickly shifted me off and onto the mattress beside him, sending me falling over on a yelp, then he was up on his knees and dragging me down to my back, spreading me wide with his big hands hooking behind my legs as he settled and stared between them.

"Play with yourself, babe. Want you coming again on my cock," he ordered, stroking himself slowly.

I could've told him there was no need, that I'd be coming again with or without assisting, I always did, but I wanted to do it.

Anything he asked of me, I wanted just as badly.

I slid my hand down my body and between my legs.

I was swollen and sensitive from Brian's mouth, but I still pressed with two fingers and rubbed, teasing that tiny bundle of nerves.

It hurt to touch. It hurt worse not to.

Then he surged forward and filled me, hitting deep.

"*Fuck*," he growled, thrusting slow. "Goddamn, I want you, Syd. Never wanted anything like I want you."

Oh, God. He just said that.

"Me either," I breathed, running my hand over the tight muscles of his stomach up to his chest and pressing there.

His heart raced under my palm.

"Wanna give you everything." He licked his lips and stared at my mouth. "Everyfuckingthing, Wild."

"I just want you." I cupped his cheek while my other hand worked between us. "I only want you."

"No."

I blinked, saying nothing.

No?

He read my confusion, smirked, and with hips dragging slow told me, "Not good enough. Not with what you've given me."

I didn't understand.

But before I could question any of it, Brian bent lower, dropped his forehead until we were touching, and said words I will never forget no matter how many years I walk on this earth.

"Wanna set your whole fucking world on fire, babe, 'cause that's what you've done to mine."

I stared up at him, unable to breathe. My one hand stilling between us. My other pressing firmer to his chest with fingers tensing and curling under, reaching for his perfect heart.

Tears filled my eyes.

"You're killing me," I whispered.

He was. Saying words like that to me, I'd never heard anything more beautiful before in my entire life.

And like everything else with this man, I wanted it. I wanted it all.

Kill me, I thought.

Let me die for this love.

"Know the feeling," he murmured, still moving inside me.

I couldn't take it.

I grabbed the back of Brian's neck and pulled him down at the same time as pushing up, going for his mouth and getting it as he continued driving into me, over and over, his one hand covering my breast and his other pinning my hips to the bed.

I went a little mad after that, holding him tighter and begging him louder and kissing him harder than I'd ever kissed him.

Brian drove deeper, staring into my eyes, his gaze intense as he took me.

And took me.

And took me.

"Fuck, you're so fuckin' tight, Wild," he rasped, fingers digging into my flesh. "Squeezing me like that...*Jesus.*"

"I told you I was little down there," I said, smiling against his mouth and risking ruining the moment we were sharing but deep down knowing I could never truly ruin it.

Not with him inside me.

And this was only confirmed when Brian kept on fucking.

"Weren't lying, babe. Shit is like a vise around my cock. Christ, I'm fucking close already."

"You're welcome," I whispered, giggling when he leaned back and shot me a glare.

Again, a risk, but I really couldn't help it.

"Don't be cute while I'm fucking you, Syd," Brian grated.

"I can't control my cuteness, Brian. It just flows naturally."

He glared harder. His hips stilled.

"You're being cute again."

"Completely accidental," I explained, wiggling underneath him and smiling big. "Come on, big boy. I've heard I'm wild when I come. You don't want me cute, better do something about it."

His eyes flashed, then he started pumping, hard and heavy, swiveling his hips and grinding low.

I dug my fingernails into his back and shuddered with need.

Oh, God, yes.

Yes. Yes. Yes. Yes. YES.

"Trouble," I panted.

He growled, twisted my nipple, and hit that spot inside that made my body tremble and tighten.

"Wait," he grunted, thrusting harder. Deeper.

I shook my head, warning, "I can't."

"*Wait*, Syd."

"Oh, God," I moaned, squeezing my eyes shut and taking my hand out from between us, putting it on his hip and holding on.

Brian dipped his head and sucked on the skin of my neck, murmuring *so good* and *so fucking good* and *fuck, Wild, FUCK.* He kept thrusting and working my nipple, and I felt his breath catch just below my ear before his lips touched my cheek and he groaned, "Now, baby."

Baby.

Oh, I liked that. I liked that a lot.

I liked it so much, I came harder than the first time, my head slamming back, hitting half pillow/half mattress, my nails cutting and dragging across skin and my hips pressing down, forcing Brian deeper.

He leaned back to look at me, meeting my eyes, and I saw his were nearly black and mad with want. He looked possessed. He looked *beautiful*.

Always. He was the most beautiful man I'd ever seen, inside and out.

Then on a moan, he buried deep, cursed, and gave it to me, spilling his pleasure inside and sliding out at the last second to watch the last shot bathe my pussy.

"Shit, Wild," he panted, then took his thumb and smeared it over my clit.

I gasped, reached down, and caught his wrist.

"Sensitive," I breathed, still working for air. "It aches a little."

He bent and kissed the top of my hand before I released him, then eased his thumb away, sat back on his heels, and continued staring between my legs while he rubbed my thighs restlessly.

His chest heaved. He looked like he wanted to eat me alive.

"Know I usually clean you up, but gotta say, babe, I like seeing you like this. I like it a lot," he admitted, lifting his eyes. "You want a towel or are you good?"

The way Brian was looking at me right now, I'd be good for a while.

I hooked my feet behind his waist, bent my knees to draw him in, and reached for him.

"I'm good. Come here."

He crawled over me, covering my body with his, and gave me a slow, wet kiss I felt all the way in my toes, then he rolled onto his back and took me with him, tucking me against his side so I was lying partially on his chest and partially on the mattress, my arm slung over his waist and my knee bent, resting across his hip. He slid his hand down my spine and cupped my ass, giving it a squeeze, then bent his other arm and tucked it behind his head.

I pressed a kiss to his chest and felt his fingers tense on my rear.

"That was amazing," I told him.

"Always is," he admitted.

"I know. I'm so good at it."

He tickled my side until I squirmed and cried out.

"I'm agreeing!"

"You're being cute," he argued, keeping me in his hold when my body bucked uncontrollably. "What'd I say about that?"

"You're not fucking me! And I told you, I can't help it!"

I wiggled and tried moving away, but Brian held on tighter and kept pressing his fingers into the skin above my hip.

My eyes watered. Laughter caught in my throat and tangled with my breath.

I could've fought harder but I didn't. I hated being tickled, but if he was doing it, I loved it.

I adored playful Brian.

I imagined a younger version of him in moments like this, youthful and spirited, a beautiful boy who didn't have worries or regrets or burdens, who always smelled like salt water and sunscreen and the hot July sun.

"Brian!" I giggled louder when he went for the sensitive spot above my collarbone.

Sir barked at the door. His nails scratched the wood.

Brian stopped tickling me but kept his hold just as firm.

"Fuck," he mumbled.

I twisted, pushed hard against his chest, and forced a stern look, hiding my happiness.

"You roused the boy. Now we can't have alone cuddles," I hissed, shook off his arms, and slid out of bed.

Brian fell back onto his pillow.

"Alone cuddles?" he repeated, fighting a smile while tucking his hands underneath his head and stretching his body out.

His cock was still half hard and lay heavy on his thigh.

I *really* wanted alone cuddles with that.

I snatched my panties off the floor, explaining, "Yes. I wanted time with you before Sir got done licking the peanut butter out of his Kong toy and came looking for us. Now because of your antics, we won't have that. I can't just ignore him."

"Sure you're heartbroken over it," Brian joked. "Think you like time with Sir over time with me."

I stopped halfway to the bathroom, panties in hand, shot him a look over my shoulder with eyes hard and narrowing, and firmly disagreed.

"That's absurd."

"Yeah?"

"Absolutely."

"See you're not arguing it, though."

"It's absurd and doesn't even warrant the time to argue."

"Using time to tell me it's absurd, Wild. Could be using that time to tell me I'm wrong, but you're not."

My eyes narrowed farther.

"Now *you're* the one being cute," I told him because he was.

He grinned then, full lips stretching wide, and it was so beautiful I couldn't keep my eyes narrowed for fear I'd miss the full impact of a grin like that.

My face relaxed, my breath left me in a whoosh, and the flip and twist happened, right on cue.

"What?" Brian asked after I kept staring silently.

I swallowed.

"I just love you," I said with a quiet voice, shrugging. "That's all. Nothing new, it's just, I'm feeling it on a deeper level right now. You're hitting my soul. No one's ever hit that."

His grin wavered, softening to something equally beautiful.

"Come here," he murmured.

I bit my lip.

"Um . . ." I looked down at my thighs pressing together then back up at him. "I'd love to, so much, but I need to get cleaned up. And I need to get Sir before he destroys something."

He sat up and swung his legs over the edge of the bed, keeping his eyes on me.

"Handle what you need to handle in there, then I want you back in this bed and in my arms. I got Sir."

He stood, grabbed his boxers off the floor, and started pulling them on.

I stared at Brian while he did this, running my gaze over his hard body and appreciating the view.

His muscled back, leaned out hips, and fantastic ass, sculpted to perfection.

Damn.

I was totally an ass girl now. Not that I'd ever heard women declaring something like that before, that was typically a guy thing, but if the trend ever picked up for the female population, I knew where I stood.

Sir barked again at the door and scratched once more on the wood. He was growing impatient.

Instinctively, I turned to let him in.

"Go," Brian said with a firm tone, halting me and reminding me of my instructions. He snapped the band of his boxers against his stomach and moved around the bed.

I stepped inside the bathroom and quickly cleaned myself up before pulling on my panties. After a quick check on my reflection in the mirror, finger-combing my roughed-up locks and wiping underneath my bottom lip, where my rose-tinted ChapStick had smudged, I cut the light and went back out into the bedroom.

Both of my boys were on the bed, as expected.

Brian was on his side with his arm out, pushing Sir back when he got too close but doing it gently and in a way Sir found playful.

He was growling back at Brian, bouncing swiftly right and then left, trying to pounce on him from every angle and getting denied, his little stubbed tail wagging back and forth at a rapid pace.

I smiled at the two of them as I came to my side of the bed.

Bending, I grabbed the top I'd been wearing all day and slipped it on, planted my knee on the edge of the bed, put my weight on it, and was pulling up my other knee to climb on when my cell rang.

"Shoot."

I rocked back, getting to my feet again, walked over to where my phone was charging on the dresser, saw the caller's name flashing on the screen, and left it to ring, returning to the bed.

"Who is it?" Brian asked, pushing Sir away again.

I shook my head. "No one I want to talk to right now."

Brian kept looking at me after I sat on the bed and started playing with Sir. I could feel his attention, then our eyes locked and he asked, "Who?" in a way I knew he was thinking it was Marcus calling. His tone was flat and uninterested but had an edge to it.

He hated Marcus, for reasons justified and ones he couldn't explain.

I understood it.

When you loved someone, they became your only and you wanted to be theirs, but the reality was sometimes you could only be their now and possibly their forever if you were lucky enough, but you could never be their only.

Never. These were the facts and they sucked.

However, reality or not, this was something I chose not to believe.

I was Wild. I could do that.

I could never be anyone's but Brian's. Not in my heart. Not ever. That was my choice and I was choosing it.

Screw the facts. And screw Marcus. I wouldn't have answered if it was him calling, now or any other time, but it wasn't and I didn't want Brian thinking it was for another second.

"It's my mom," I told him, pulling Sir into my lap and kissing the top of his head.

"You're not gonna answer it?" Brian asked, staying propped up on his elbow. "Thought you said you wanted her to know about us and what we're doing."

He was right. I had said that and it was definitely something I wanted.

I sighed, met his eyes again, and went on to explain, "I do, but it's our first night in our new house and I don't want her tainting any of it, and I'm afraid if I talk to her, that's exactly what she's going to do."

Brian reached out, tucked some red behind my ear, dropped his hand to my leg, and gave it a squeeze.

"Been a while since you last spoke to her. She might surprise you."

"She might not," I countered.

"You won't know unless you talk to her, babe," he argued gently, rubbing his thumb over my skin in a soothing way. "I get why you're avoiding her, but I know this is important to you. You want her to see what we got and support the life you're living now. Only way that's gonna happen is if you share it with her. She's reaching out. She might stop reaching out at some point. Think about that."

I thought about it while I scratched the underside of Sir's neck the way he liked.

Brian was right. Again. If I kept avoiding my mom, she might stop calling altogether, putting even more strain on our relationship and making it harder to build it back up, then I'd be the one struggling to get her on the line.

What if she never answered me?

I huffed out a breath. "Fine. Okay. I'll talk to her." Then I scooted Sir off my lap, leaned down until my forehead was flush with Brian's, and glared at him. "You being right all the time is getting a little old," I shared.

He smirked. "Can't help it, babe. Just flows naturally."

I rolled my eyes, laughing a little because he was using my words against me and in turn, being cute again, slid off the bed, and grabbed my phone off the dresser.

I swiped my thumb across the screen, went to my missed calls, and dialed her back.

She answered when my butt hit the bed.

"Well, didn't think I existed to you anymore. Surprised you're even bothering with this phone call," she snapped, sounding angry and maybe a little hurt. I couldn't tell. "A daughter ignoring her own mother. Really, Sydney, you should be ashamed of yourself."

I looked at Brian, conveying with my eyes that this call was already starting off on a high note.

"You know why I wasn't answering you, Mom," I replied.

"I'm not sure what's gotten into you lately, but I feel as if I don't even know you anymore," she argued.

"Why's that? I'm the same as I've always been. Actually...I'm better. I'm *me*."

"You most certainly are not *you*. The daughter I raised wouldn't leave her husband, choosing a life of sin over what God had planned for her. No...that is not my daughter. I brought you up better than that, Sydney Grace."

I pinched my eyes shut, breathed deep, then opened them to tell her, "I want to talk to you, Mom, okay? That's why I'm calling. I love you and I miss you and I want to talk to you, but for the last time, I did not leave Marcus. He ended it. He found another girl he wanted to be with and decided what we had wasn't worth holding on to anymore. He chose it first, okay? Then I chose it when I came to Dogwood to start my life over because I didn't have one with him anymore, and I chose it again when I met the man I'm living with now."

She pulled in a breath.

I shocked her. I realized this. My mother didn't know anything about Brian, and I'd just thrown it all on her instead of giving it to her a little at a time.

Maybe not the best tactic but I had committed to it. Saw it through and put it out there. No way could I take it back now.

I looked to Brian. He appeared a little shocked by my forwardness as well.

I ignored his raised brow and widened stare because I knew he'd recover quickly—we were in this together. I watched Sir roll onto his back and stretch his paws, smiled at his cuteness, then looked at my lap and continued speaking.

"You see, Mom? Marcus chose a life without me. He wanted me gone so I went and in doing so found someone who has made me happier than I ever thought possible, happier than I ever came close to being with Marcus, and if that wasn't part of God's plan for me, then he needs to take a step back and reevaluate some things because there is no way what I'm feeling right now is wrong. It can't be. I've never felt like this."

Brian grabbed the hand I had resting on my knee and held it with his.

We looked into each other's eyes, and I wanted so badly to kiss him, but I knew if I did that I wouldn't stop kissing him and I was in the middle of an important conversation I needed to see through.

So I held him back instead, curling my fingers around the back of his hand and hoping to convey the feelings I was fighting against.

"You're living with another man?" Mom spoke after several tense seconds, her voice eerily quiet. "You aren't even divorced yet, Sydney, and you're already moved in with someone else? I…I can't believe what I'm hearing. No. Absolutely not. This is wrong and I will not support this. I will not support any of this. I knew you moving to Dogwood would be trouble and *look* at what you're doing."

"What am I doing, Mom? I'm in love and I'm happy."

"You're practically having an affair," she hissed.

My spine straightened. I felt my pulse spike and the hand holding Brian's tense and grip tighter.

Then I let her have it.

"I am *not* having an affair. I would never do that, no matter if Marcus cheated on me or not, which he did, Mom. In case you're interested in knowing. *That's* what happened. He did this to *me*. Now I'll admit, what we had wasn't working anymore, our marriage was struggling and had been struggling for months, but I stuck it out. I never even considered any other options and that's all he was doing, considering other options. He gave me up for someone else, asked me to leave, and I did, and you know what? It was the best decision of my life 'cause it led me to Brian. That's who I'm living with. That's the man who healed my heart and that's the man I love with *every piece of it*. Marcus and I are legally separated now and have been since before Brian and I got together. We were no longer committed to each other when Brian and I started talking, meaning when I fell in love with him, I did so with a heart I could give away. Marcus wasn't holding it anymore. That was his doing. His choice. I will not say that again."

My chest was heaving and my eyes were pricking with tears. I was on the verge of crying or screaming, I wasn't sure which, but I did know I was fully regretting this phone call. That was for certain.

"Don't you take that tone with me, young lady. I will not be disrespected by my own daughter," she spat, her voice rising. "And if you think I'm going to support you in any of this, you can think again. Living with a man under *any* circumstance without being married to him is a sin in the eyes of God. It is shameful and *wrong*. You signing separation papers doesn't change that."

"Plenty of people live together before they get married, Mom. This isn't the fifties."

"You can make that argument to God when you stand before him at the end of your time. See what he has to say about that."

I closed my eyes and lowered my head.

"As for the matter of Marcus stepping out on you, he'll have to answer for his own sins," she continued. "And like I've told you several times already, you should've stuck it out and allowed him to repent. Fought for your marriage. Worked through it together as a unit. Instead you walked away. You left your family and now look at you. What a mess you've made of yourself."

My mouth dropped open in shock, air moving in and out of my lungs rapidly and erratically.

I didn't scream. God...I wanted to. I wanted my anger to rule my reaction, but it didn't.

Disappointment overwhelmed me. I chose to cry instead.

With tears wetting my cheeks and lips trembling, I kept my head lowered, my shoulders hunched forward, and Brian's hand in mine.

"I left the man who stopped loving me," I replied, voice shaking while I stared at my lap. "I didn't leave my family. You did."

"Excuse me?"

"You left me," I whispered. "Barrett died and you left me like I died right along with him, and even at twelve years old, I understood your reason. I knew you were in pain and you needed help, Mom, so even though I was sad, too, and I missed you so, so much, I didn't hate you for leaving me behind to find your peace. I didn't even hate you when you found it and forgot to come back for me. I couldn't.

I was happy for you and I was happy for myself because I got Tori and I got her parents. They became my family when you'd stay late at church or go to another prayer meeting. They supported me, and I know in my heart they'd support me still. They wouldn't judge me like this. They'd care about my happiness because that's what family does. *They* are my family. And the friends I have now, the ones I've met since moving to Dogwood, they are also my family. And Brian. He is my family. Not Marcus. Never Marcus. Family doesn't turn their back on you and treat you like you're nothing. Like you never mattered. They don't forget about you after getting themselves to a better place. I left Marcus but I never left my family, and I never will. It's too bad you can't say the same."

"Those people are *not* your family," she snapped. "I am your mother. I am your family, and when you took a husband, that man became your family. Marcus is your family."

"I'm not talking about this anymore." I wiped at my face. "It's useless. You're not hearing me."

"Oh, I'm hearing you. I'm hearing you say a bunch of people you don't share blood or bond with are the people who matter most to you. That's what I'm hearing."

"Good, 'cause that's *exactly* what I'm saying," I hissed through tears, coming up on my knees and blocking Sir when he jumped up excitedly, ready to play.

Brian sat up and got him settled, pulling him to his side.

I continued on from my defensive stance, feeling the weight of Brian's touch on my back.

"Sometimes family isn't made up of who you're born to or who you share a name with. Sometimes it's made up of a strange man you accidentally dial up and cuss out, or waitresses at a seaside restaurant, or seven-year-old twins who tell you you're awesome and super pretty. Family are the people who support you and love you no matter what. Who care about your happiness and who don't pass judgment. Who heal you. Who *accept* you and the life you're living. That's what family is, Mom."

"Well, then I guess it's a good thing Barrett died and you gave up on your marriage so you could find that family, sweetheart. Otherwise you'd just be stuck with me, right? And Lord knows you don't want that."

I flinched. Breath caught in my throat.

"Mom," I whispered, voice quivering and anxious to explain. "That's not what I meant at all. I want more than anything for you to be in my life. I wouldn't have called back if I didn't. I'm just saying—"

"I'm honestly not sure why you called back," she replied, cutting me off. "Unless you're moving back to Raleigh and fixing what you left behind, we don't have anything to talk about."

I rocked back onto my heels.

I was no longer defensive. My body slouched brokenly as the tears kept falling, as my lungs worked exhaustively through my sobs.

"I love him," I cried. "I love Brian, Mom. I'm not going back to Raleigh."

She breathed in my ear, slow and patiently, and for a moment I thought maybe she didn't hear what I'd said, that maybe this wasn't the end of whatever relationship we had left because I knew in my heart if she'd heard me, it was over.

And still, knowing that risk, I'd never take back those words or say them so she couldn't hear. I would never be quiet with my love for Brian. Not ever. Not even if it meant the end.

And it did.

She'd heard me. The call disconnected, then the dial tone sounded. That's how I knew.

It was over.

I let the phone drop and took my face in my hands, sobbing hard and ugly and alone but only for a breath before Brian's arms were wrapping around me and pulling me onto my side and against his chest, where he held me close. Dipping his head next to mine, he whispered, "Shh, baby," against my ear while his hand stroked my hair, then he moved his lips to my cheek and kissed my tears as they fell.

I cried. That was all I could do.

And Brian held me through it all.

"I'm sorry. Wild, I'm so sorry," he told me over and over, soothing me with his voice and with his arms holding tight.

Sir tried digging between us at one point but we were one, fused together. Nothing was penetrating.

Our love grew stronger in those minutes.

I felt movement at the foot of the bed as Sir settled there. He gave up. He was smart doing that.

I burrowed deeper into my boy's heartbeat.

"I meant everything I said," I sobbed into his chest. "Everything. You and Tori, everyone I've met here, you are the most important people to me."

He rubbed my back.

"Even Jamie. I'm *really* rooting for him."

"He knows, babe. He appreciates it."

I quickly composed myself and leaned away.

"I want to start having family dinners on Sundays," I informed Brian, watching his eyes flick wider. "I'll cook. Everyone can bring a side dish or beverages if they'd like, but it's not required. We have a large table and I'd like to utilize that, although we'll need more chairs. What's your sister's work schedule like?"

He stared at me for a moment before responding.

"Babe."

"Mm?"

"You sure you wanna be talking about this right now?"

I sniffed and wiped away a lonely tear.

"Yes. I'd very much like to talk about this right now," I replied a little curtly. "Why wouldn't I?"

"Considering you've just had a conversation that didn't end so well and you've been crying in my arms for a solid thirty, I'm thinking this might not be the best time to lock down weekly plans that involve a solid commitment from you in terms of cooking."

I tipped my chin up.

"I'm not sure what you mean exactly, but if you're trying to say I'm not in a right frame of mind to guarantee delicious meals for the people I love, I suggest you carve some time out of your schedule and get to know me a little better. Even in times of distress, I know what's most important, Trouble."

His lip twitched.

"Sounds good," he mumbled, giving me a squeeze. "Feel like I know you, but I'm all for carving out more time and digging a little deeper, Wild." He kissed my forehead.

I moaned and melted closer.

He was right. That did sound good.

"Jenna's off on weekends," he said.

"That's good," I replied, turning my head and resting my cheek against his chest. "I really want her and the twins there whenever they can make it."

"I'll make sure to tell her."

"Tomorrow. Give her enough notice. And the guys. I'll handle getting the word out to the girls."

A laugh rumbled behind his ribs.

"Whatever you want, babe," he said, so much meaning behind those words, they fought off my sadness.

Brian settled, sat his chin on top of my head, draped his leg over both of mine, and locked me against him like he always did when we lay facing each other.

I yawned, sleepy sighed, and wrapped my hand around his back.

"You okay?" he asked, moving his fingers through my hair.

I closed my eyes.

I wasn't sure if I had a mom anymore, but I had Brian. I had family. I had love.

If I wasn't okay, I knew I would be.

Tipping my head back, I kissed the underside of his jaw, flattened my cheek to his chest, closed my eyes again, and within seconds fell fast asleep, clinging to love and the assurance everything would be okay.

Chapter Nineteen

BRIAN

I thought I was protecting her.

I thought if I kept Syd ignorant to the dirty deeds of my past, we'd be untouchable, growing in love and building on the future I wanted us to have, the one I wanted to give her.

I was a fucking moron.

I thought I was protecting her.

But in the end I destroyed everything we'd ever have.

Chapter Twenty

SYDNEY

One Month Later

I was standing at the kitchen island crushing up Doritos in a Ziploc bag while humming along to "Suspicious Minds" as it played through my one earbud, my other ear going without the soothing voice of the King since I didn't want to risk missing the timer on the oven and burning my Mexican Chicken Bake, another new recipe I was trying out for Sunday family dinner.

This would be our fourth one. Meaning this was the fourth new recipe I was experimenting with and testing out on our friends.

It was a risk not sticking to the familiar since I was feeding such a large group, but it was paying off. The past three recipes had all been highly praised and devoured by everyone, meaning the number of recipes I was now comfortable making had doubled since moving to Dogwood.

I had high hopes for the Mexican Chicken Bake.

Not only because of my track record but also because of the delicious aroma coming from the oven as the chicken was baking, and according to reviews, it was an excellent meal to cook ahead of time and warm in the oven when you were ready to consume it.

That was why I chose it for today and why I was cooking it four hours before everyone was due to come over.

Brian and I had plans this afternoon. Important plans. Plans I wouldn't miss for the world or take any time away from because I had to get home and make a meal.

For the first time in five months, my boy was getting back out on the water.

This was huge.

Huge.

And I was overwhelmed with joy because of it, so much so I'd cried last night when he announced what we were doing today and I'd cried twice already this morning just thinking about our plans.

Last night was unexpected. He'd caught me completely off guard.

We were lying in bed with Sir between us, talking about nothing and everything like we always did, when Brian blindsided me.

He'd been thinking about surfing a lot, mainly because I kept bringing it up hoping it would spark discussion, which never seemed to happen. He'd change the subject or distract me with his mouth pressing to my skin and I'd forget all about it. But it got him to thinking he might be ready to give it a go again, but under one condition.

He needed me there. Me. No one else.

Today was going to be one of those days I'd never forget as long as I lived.

I *could not wait*.

Setting the one Ziploc bag aside after getting all the chips crushed to the consistency I needed them in, I filled another Ziploc bag with Doritos, sealed it good, flattened it on the counter in front of me, and took my rolling pin over it, breaking apart all the chips.

The song in my ear ended and "Can't Help Falling in Love" started playing.

I smiled. I loved this song.

Like *loved* this song, so much so I wanted it to be what Marcus and I shared our first dance to at our wedding.

It wasn't. We danced to some overplayed top forty hit instead.

Once Marcus shot down my choice saying he wouldn't dance with me to some old-ass shit his mother probably got down to back in her day, I didn't really care what we danced to. I just picked something slow I'd heard a hundred different times on the radio, figuring his mother probably didn't listen to that station and I'd be in the clear of her ever getting down to it.

Looking back, I should've told him to shove it and danced by myself to the song I wanted. I never should've compromised on that.

Marcus wasn't worth it.

Getting lost in the lyrics like I always did, swaying my hips slowly and closing my eyes through the chorus, I didn't see or hear Brian move into the kitchen or step up behind me, only becoming aware of his presence when he snaked his arm around my waist and kissed my neck.

I sucked in as my eyes flashed open, let go of the rolling pin, and squeezed his arm that was holding me.

"You scared me," I said, sounding a little breathless, then tipped my head to the side and dropped it back, leaning into him.

He brushed my hair behind my shoulder and took the earbud out of my ear.

"What are you listening to?"

I spun around and watched him bring the earbud up to his ear, hold it there, and listen for few seconds while keeping his eyes on me. His mouth tipped up in the corner.

"Should've guessed." He handed the earbud back, doing so while looking amused.

This wasn't the first time Brian had caught me getting lost in the King. Wouldn't be the last either.

I pulled my cell out of my pocket, stopped the song, unplugged my headphones, and set everything on the island behind me.

"Smells good in here, babe," Brian said, turning his head as if he was sniffing the air.

"Thanks."

He stepped forward and reached around me. I heard chips crunching.

"What's with the Doritos?"

"Ah." I slid over so I wasn't standing between him and the island anymore, picked up the other bag of Doritos I'd pulverized, and held it up, looking at it and explaining, "It's the topping for the Mexican Chicken Bake. When the timer goes off, I'll sprinkle these on top then bake it for another ten. It adds a tasty crunch. Plus, it's totally kid friendly." I moved my eyes to Brian. "The twins like Doritos, right?"

He shrugged. "They're kids. Pretty sure they like all chips."

I nodded, replying, "That's what I was thinking."

We both dropped our bags of Doritos onto the island.

"Is your sister still bringing dessert?"

"Last I heard."

"Good. Only thing we have is popsicles and that's *our* thing."

It totally was.

Brian had gotten us a house with a porch for the sole purpose of eating popsicles together on it. No other reason. It was totally our thing now.

"In terms of Jamie bringing something, I was thinking," I began, watching Brian's eyebrows lift in curiosity. "Maybe you could see if he wants to wear his shiny new medal to dinner. I'm sure everyone would love to see it. I know I would. I've never seen a World Pro Am Champion medal before."

Brian stared at me.

"Babe."

"Mm?"

"Love you."

I smiled big.

"Love you, too."

He didn't smile back. He stood taller, stuck his hands in his pockets of his shorts, and looked at me carefully when he went on to say, "But maybe you need to ease off your girl a little."

I stuck my hand on my hip and cocked it out.

"What's that supposed to mean?" I asked.

"It means I think you're trying to force something that's not happening. She's not feeling Jamie," he replied.

"She's feeling him," I shot back. "She just doesn't want to admit it yet. I'm only helping it along."

"No, you're not."

I cocked my hip out farther.

"Excuse me?"

Brian looked at my cocked hip, then back into my eyes to say, "You're not helping, Wild. Your girl is a push away from losing her shit during dinner. Look at what happened two weeks ago."

I thought back to two weeks ago. That was the last meal we shared with both Tori and Jamie since Jamie was in Cali last weekend and didn't get back until Tuesday. Nothing unusual was standing out about that dinner, and I told Brian that.

"It was a delightful evening. Everyone loved my beef stroganoff."

He tilted his head.

"You assigned seats with place cards."

"So?"

"Think you went a little too far with that one."

"They sat next to each other, didn't they?" I reminded him. "And it forced conversation. They talked a lot."

"They argued a lot," he corrected.

I leaned forward.

"That's still conversation, Brian."

He breathed a laugh, shaking his head at me just as my cell started ringing on the island.

It was Tori. Taylor Swift was singing to me.

I made a face at him before spinning around and snatching up my phone. "Hey, what's up?" I answered.

"Syd, you need to come over here right now, okay? Right now. Don't say anything to Brian, just get in your car and get over here. Tell me you're gonna do what I'm asking."

Tori was panicked, her words were running together she was speaking so fast, and her breathing was tense, quickened as if she was pacing the floor.

"Okay, um," I stammered, looking up at Brian, who was watching me. I started twirling a lock of my hair. "Can you tell me what's going on first?"

"No!" she shrieked. "I need you to get over here like I asked!"

"Tori..."

"Please, Syd, okay? Please! Get over here now! This is urgent!"

Wes. His name flashed in my mind.

"Okay, okay, I'm coming," I told her. "I'll be right there."

"Alone! Come alone!"

"All right!" I hollered.

She disconnected the call.

I stopped twirling my hair and stuck my phone into my back pocket.

"What's up?" Brian asked.

"No idea, but I gotta go over to Tori's. She's flipping out about something."

His brow furrowed.

"She didn't say what?" he questioned.

I shook my head. Then I pointed behind him at the stove.

"When the timer goes off, can you put the Doritos on top and then bake it for another ten? I'll be back as soon as I get her settled. Hopefully it won't be too long. I don't want to be cutting into what we have planned this afternoon."

"Do what you gotta do," he said, stepping closer, grabbing my face and kissing me. "We got time."

"Okay." I kissed him back.

Then I grabbed my keys, met Sir at the front door and told him he was staying home, stepped out onto the porch, and jogged to my car.

* * *

Tori had the front door swinging open before I even reached it, waving at me to hurry up.

"What's going on?" I asked when I got inside. "You are officially freaking me out."

She shut the door, grabbed my hand, and tugged me through the house.

"To preface what I'm about to show you, I need you to know why I was browsing a site like this. You keep forcing me to participate in family dinners and if I have to be around Jamie and his stupidly hot face, I can't be doing it all worked up. It makes ignoring him a challenge," she said, pulling me up the stairs.

I stared at the back of her head as we climbed higher.

"What in the world are you talking about?" I questioned, officially confused.

We reached the top of the stairs and Tori directed me down the hall to her bedroom, pushed the door open, released my hand, and moved to stand beside the bed.

Her sheets were messy and she had her laptop opened on it, facing the pillows so I couldn't see the screen.

"Syd," she began gently, reaching across her body to grip her elbow. "How well do you know Brian?"

I frowned at her question. This wasn't about Wes?

"Pretty well, I think," I replied. "Tori, what's going on?"

She sat on the edge of the bed and spun the laptop around so it was facing me.

"Did you know he did this?" she asked, hitting a key and waking it up.

I moved closer so I could see what she was trying to show me.

A video was playing with the volume turned down so I couldn't hear, but I didn't need sound. I could tell exactly what type of video this was.

A man was thrusting into the woman lying beneath him on a bed, really going at her with vigor by the looks of it. The camera was angled behind them so I could only see his naked back and her limbs and her dark hair fanning out on the white sheet over his shoulder.

I gasped, looking to Tori. "Why are you showing me this?"

"Keep watching," she said, her expression one of concern and worry.

I did as I was told because of that expression and looked back at the screen.

The man kept thrusting. The woman moved her hands to his shoulders and hitched her legs up higher on his back, her knee-high socks appearing to be the only clothing she'd left on.

Then the camera panned to the side to catch their profiles.

"Oh, my God!" I slapped my hand over my mouth and watched my boy move in and out of the girl he was fucking. Drawn to it because I couldn't believe what I was seeing, I climbed on the bed and hovered over the laptop. "Oh, my God! What is this? Why is Brian on the Internet?" I shrieked, looking to Tori and gripping the sides of the screen.

"It's a porn site. He's all over it," she answered.

Air raced in and out of my lungs. My nose started stinging.

"What do you mean, he's all over it?" I asked weakly.

"He's on the home page. Look."

She reached around the screen, forcing me to let go of one side, and hit the Back button. The video vanished and a website appeared in its place. Xstasy.com scrawled in scripted red font across the top against a black background, and in the center of the screen, there was a still image of Brian taking some girl from behind.

Get Done by Dash flashed below the image.

"Oh, my God," I whispered, covering my mouth again.

"Dash. That's what Jamie calls him, isn't it?" Tori questioned, pulling my eyes up to hers.

I nodded on the verge of tears while I stared at his hands on her hips and his mouth, opened on her neck and sucking.

My stomach rolled and twisted into a knot.

"He's got his own channel, Syd. I looked. It's him and the same three girls, it looks like, plus some of just him, you know, going solo. They're dated. They're all from this year. Some of them are from just a couple of months ago. Did he say anything to you about this?"

I cut my eyes to her.

She quickly shook her head through a frown.

"I'm sorry. Stupid question. I just . . ." She swallowed. "I can't believe he'd keep this from you. He must've known you'd eventually find out."

I looked back at the screen.

I was trembling. My entire body shuddered as I stared at that image.

"Why," I whispered, my voice shaking. Tears fell to my cheeks. "Why was he doing this? Why? This isn't who he is. He's not a porn star. He's not. He would never do something like this." I lifted my eyes again. "It wasn't him. It's not him."

"Hon." Tori reached for my hand. There were tears in her eyes, too.

My best friend *never* cried.

"It's not him!" I shrieked, pulling away from her. "It's not! I'll show you. Watch." I started moving my finger over the mouse pad to open up a video when Tori grabbed my hand. "Stop!" I pulled away again. "I wanna see them!"

"You don't, Syd."

"Yes I do!" I cried, fighting against her arms, which were reaching for me. "Yes I do! I wanna see them. Let me see them! LET ME SEE WHAT HE'S DONE!" I was screaming. I couldn't control it.

She slammed the laptop closed, slid it over, and grabbed my shoulders so hard I flinched.

"It's him. Trust me, it's him, and you do not want to see that, hon. You don't." She shook her head and let her own tears fall. "You don't wanna see it," she whispered, her bottom lip quivering. "Honey, please. Please don't watch."

I dropped my head and sobbed as my best friend's arms wrapped around me.

I knew it was Brian. Tori wouldn't lie and I knew I shouldn't look.

But I did.

I had to.

"He's mine. Let me see him," I whispered brokenly against her hair. I lifted my head, shrugging off Tori easily this time, and reached for the laptop.

She cried with her hand over her mouth as I flipped the screen up and navigated the mouse with my finger.

I wiped at my face.

I was determined to watch every video no matter how many there were or how long it would take me.

I got through three before I ran to the bathroom and vomited into the toilet.

Tori held my hair for me and rubbed my back.

A true best friend did more than sympathize with your pain. They allowed themselves to feel it, too.

My tears were her tears. We shared them. We cried together.

I emptied my stomach, slumped over the bowl, and wept while dirty images polluted my mind and the mantra my mother used to soothe herself with rang out in my ears.

Don't get comfortable being happy. It'll only hurt worse when it's gone.

I didn't think her words could touch me. Nothing could touch me.

I had been floating, high above order and reality. Blessedly and blissfully in love.

I thought my mother was spouting bullshit. Her words didn't have meaning. They would never be true for me.

I was comfortable in my happy. And love? It was beautiful.

Perfect.

Crazy.

Wildly beautiful.

I had thought about calling my mother, if we were speaking, which we weren't, and telling her she was wrong, that you could be happy without fear of losing it, because I was. I wasn't scared.

I should've been.

God...I should've been terrified.

I floated on my cloud of perfect love, delirious and oblivious to the dirty beneath me.

And when I came down, I didn't float.

I fell. I crashed. And it hurt.

Worse than any pain I'd ever felt.

It was unbearable.

"Where are you going?" Tori asked as I left her in the bathroom after rinsing out my mouth in the sink.

"I need to talk to Brian. I need to hear it from him," I called out on my way down the stairs.

Her quick footsteps followed behind.

"I'll drive you. You can't drive right now."

"Fine."

I didn't have it in me to argue, and I knew I'd be coming back here with Tori anyway so what was the difference?

I saved my energy for the conversation I was about to have.

When we stepped outside, I tossed Tori my keys and slid into the passenger seat. My phone started ringing from my pocket as we pulled away from the house.

I ignored it.

Only one person was most likely calling me right now. I'd been gone awhile and Brian would want to know why.

He could wait to find out. I didn't owe him a damn thing.

Images of the man I thought I knew filled my head as we drove, ones of him touching and kissing and fucking girls who weren't me. I put words into his mouth and heard him calling them *Wild* and *Babe* and moaning *Baby Baby Baby* when he was coming. It was torture.

I cried with my head against the window and Tori's hand in mine.

"Wait here," I told her after she pulled into the driveway and shifted into Park.

She unbuckled her seat belt, regarding me sadly and uncertainly. "You sure?"

I nodded, gave her hand one last squeeze, and exited the car.

I'm not sure why I did the next thing I did. Maybe it was because I didn't feel as if I belonged here anymore. Maybe it was because it was all a dream and I was finally awake. I never really lived here.

I climbed the porch and knocked instead of entering.

Sir barked a few times, then Brian opened the door and flinched at the sight of me.

"Babe, what are you doing?" He reached for me.

I took a step back.

"Can I please come inside?" I asked, wiping a tear away.

He stared at me, taking in my sadness and behavior.

"Wild, what the fuck?"

He made a move to step outside and I halted him with my hand raised.

"Brian," I began in a warning tone, freezing him in the doorway. "I am asking you if I can come inside. I don't want to do this out here."

Something flashed in his eyes then, recollection of what he did or realization of what I knew, I wasn't sure which, but he suddenly looked as empty as I felt and it took everything in me not to reach out and hold him.

Love is stupid like that.

He silently stepped aside and held the door open for me to enter.

I closed the door, ignoring Sir, who was jumping up at my feet for attention. He gave up after he wasn't getting it and moved on, leaving me to watch Brian as he padded across the room, rubbing harshly at his face with both hands. He stopped behind the couch and gripped the back of it, keeping his head down and his eyes fixated on the cushions.

"You need to know why I did it," he said quietly.

"I do, but it won't change anything."

His head snapped up at my words.

"Wild," he whispered.

"Don't call me that," I said, fresh tears brimming my eyes as I took a step forward. "You don't get to call me that. My boy calls me that and you are *not* him."

His spine straightened.

"The fuck I'm not," he growled.

I ignored his defiance and probed for the answers I needed.

"Why, Brian? Why were you doing that and why didn't you tell me? How could you keep that from me?"

"I was trying to protect you," he countered, his tone gentler now as he tried to explain. "I didn't want you ever seeing that. I didn't want you knowing about it. I knew it would hurt you." He looked back to the cushions and murmured, "I didn't think you would ever see it."

"Well, I did," I spat, gaining his attention again. "I did see it. I watched you with them. I watched the man I care about more than anything making love to those women."

"That is not what I was doing."

"Fine. *Fucking*," I hissed. "I watched you fuck those fake, nasty porn stars. I watched it! Do you have any idea what that was like for me? Having my best friend show me something like that? Sitting there not knowing *anything* about the man I love because he was doing this behind my back for *months*! I saw you get off on them! I saw enough to make me *sick*!"

"You think I wasn't sick going through with it?" he shouted, turning to face me now. "You think that's the kind of man I am? Fucking for money because I *wanted* it?" He jammed a finger at his chest. "You think that's me?"

"I know what I saw," I replied curtly. "Your dick was hard, so explain to me how you didn't want it."

"I had to take a fuckin' pill to go through with it, Syd," he spat. "None of that was real. None of what you saw meant *anything*. I fuckin' hated it. All of it. I was just doin' what I had to do."

"Why?" I asked. "Why were you doing it? I don't understand...why would you need to do something like that?"

"Because I needed the money."

"For what?" I yelled, moving even closer as I cried openly for him to see. "Why would you need money?"

"BECAUSE OF THAT FUCKING KID!" he bellowed, his face as red as the center of a flame.

I jerked back. My hand covered my mouth.

Oh, God.

Oh, my God.

No...

"Brian," I whispered.

He lowered his head. Fists clenched at his sides, he heaved deep breaths in and out of his nose. He looked as sick as I'd felt watching those videos.

I stood there, crying silently, and waited. I needed to hear it.

He lifted his head.

"There were bills, all right? Thousands of dollars' worth of hospital bills and that shit was gonna keep piling up for them and I couldn't just let that happen! I couldn't do nothing!" he roared. His voice was thunderous. "Not after what I did. I fucked up their lives. I put them there. Me! No one else. Fucking *me*, Syd! And I was gonna do anything I could to ease some of that burden. Anything. I WOULD'VE DONE ANYTHING!"

I was sobbing, hand to my mouth, while Brian's entire body shook with the bad he was finally letting go of.

The cords in his neck were bulging. His chest was heaving. Knuckles white.

He closed his eyes, made a choking sound in the back of his throat, then slowed his breath enough to continue on.

"And I did," he said, jaw tight but appearing slightly calmer. "I did anything. Found an ad in the paper when I was doing a crossword. Gig was paying eight hundred a scene. I saw the opportunity and to me it was the only option. You gotta know...Syd, I wasn't in a good place. In my head, all that fucking guilt, I wasn't thinking about how fucked up this was. I wouldn't let anyone help me. Jamie and Cole offered to give me cash but it wasn't their fuckup. I couldn't take it. I couldn't drag people into this shit with me. I couldn't fuckin' do that! This was mine! *I* had to fix this, but I swear to you...I swear to fuckin' God I hated it. Zoned out, got paid, then delivered the money. I didn't keep a fuckin' dime. I wouldn't do that."

"I believe you," I told him, because I did. I believed every word.

He made a move to come toward me, but I kept him back with a shake of my head.

"They knew you were giving them money?" I asked.

That didn't make sense to me. I still remembered the look on the father's face that night at Friendly's when he recognized Brian. That wasn't how you looked at someone you were seeing frequently because they were handing over cash.

Brian shook his head.

"No. I either stuck it in their mailbox or I gave it to this woman who runs a horse-riding place where the kid is doing therapy. It was supposed to help him so I was making sure he was getting to do that, too. I didn't want them knowing it was coming from me. I didn't want to risk them not taking it."

"So you kept this from everyone except Jamie and Cole," I offered, feeling my lip start quivering again. "Nice of them not to share it with me."

"They knew I didn't want anyone knowing," he murmured.

I looked away.

That hurt. They were my friends. Friends look out for each other. They should've told me.

Brian should've told me.

I felt my shoulders drop. Air rushed out of my lungs.

"Oh, my God," I whispered as more tears fell, looking back to Brian. "This was why, wasn't it? This was why you didn't want to know me. You were afraid I'd recognize you from that site." My eyes widened. "You asked me. You asked me if I recognized you the night of the party. This was what you meant."

"Knew you'd end it if you knew who I was," he admitted. "I couldn't lose you. I couldn't risk you finding out. Figured if I gave you my last name or any other shit, you'd search for me and something might come up."

"You were selfish," I put out.

He nodded. He wasn't disagreeing.

"You lied to me," I added a beat later.

His eyes got hard.

"I never lied to you," he returned quickly and with a rough voice. "Not once. I would never fuckin' lie to you."

"You didn't tell me the truth. That's the same thing as lying," I shot back, watching his mouth open to speak and cutting him off before that happened. "How long? The whole time? Were you doing this behind my back the whole time you were talking to me? In the beginning when we were just friends and then when we became more, were you with those girls? Did you ever stop? Oh, my God." I held my face with my hands and cried out, "*Are you still doing it?*"

"No," Brian answered with panic in his eyes, crossing the room to get to me and doing so without me stopping him. He grabbed my wrists and pulled my hands away. "Fuck, no, Jesus, I would never do that to you. Look at me," he ordered, lifting my quivering chin. "I would never fuckin' do that to you. I stopped after that night you attacked the car. Switched to solos after that. There was no one else." He held my face. "Once I had you, there was no one else. I swear on my fuckin' life, Syd."

Brian wiped my tears away, then his face tensed again through a breath and he did something that completely shocked me.

He stepped back.

I gaped at him.

"Before I tell you this, know I realize how different things could've been if I would've thought of this option five months ago," he said. His voice was shaking.

I braced myself, pressing the pads of my fingers to my mouth.

I could barely breathe.

"After that night of the party when I finally got you, when I finally got my girl, I knew I couldn't keep going to that warehouse and filming, solos or not. I wanted out. I needed another way. I had you and I wouldn't jeopardize it, so I convinced Jamie to buy me out of Wax."

My lips parted.

"What?" I asked, blinking up at him.

Brian nodded as if to confirm I wasn't hearing things.

"Sold my share and gave all the money to that family, and it was a lot of fuckin' money, Syd. More than I had given them up to that point. I didn't even think about it. Months ago, selling out didn't cross my mind. I was so fucked up over this shit, I wasn't thinkin' straight. I wasn't seeing other outs. If I had, I swear to you that's what I would've done. You gotta believe me."

"I do. I believe you," I told him, watching his face soften and then eliminating that soft when I bit out, "What I *can't* believe is you letting me think, for *months*, that you still owned Wax. You kept the truth from me, Brian. Again! I was getting everyone to go to the shop my boy owned because I was proud, and that whole time you let me think something that wasn't true."

"What could I have said?" he asked tensely, his voice growing louder. "Tell me. What the fuck could I have said to you? Why would I sell out?"

"You could've told me the truth!" I screamed. "But you didn't! You didn't tell me anything! You kept *everything* from me!"

"I was trying to protect you!"

"Well, you didn't, did you? You didn't protect me! You hurt me worse than anyone ever has!"

He sucked in a breath, then stepped closer, reaching out.

I stepped back.

"No," I said, my hand raised between us. "You kept everything from me, Brian. You had plenty of time to tell me the truth but you didn't."

"I was planning on telling you. I was just waiting for the right time. I needed you to understand..."

"Stop," I interrupted. "I don't wanna hear your excuses. They don't matter."

He looked away briefly, then met my eyes again. "I'll fix it," he rasped. He sounded desperate. "Let me fix it. You know everything now, Wild. Everything."

"Don't call me that," I whispered through my tears, then somehow with a softer voice added, "You lied to me."

His chin jerked back, then his jaw got hard.

"Never lied to you," he repeated gently but with eyes that were burning right through me. "Never touched another girl after you gave me that night on the phone. Kept things from you and did that because I thought that was the right move. Didn't want you getting hurt and would've done anything, know this, Syd, would've done fuckin' *anything* to keep that from happening. Can't stand the thought of you hurting. From the beginning, couldn't stand it. Thought about finding that ex of yours and killing that motherfucker more times than I could count. You did me in that night you called me. Lit my fucking world up. Had shit in my life, nothing but shit, then I got you, and *fuck*, baby, you gave me so much good." He smiled a little, then lost it to continue on, "So much good, and I didn't deserve any of it but you gave it. Got dick back but that didn't stop you. Gave me that good and I took it. I was selfish, I know I was. I couldn't risk losing you. And I'd apologize if I was sorry for getting your heart but I can't be sorry for that." He shook his head as tears filled his eyes again. "I'm trying. Right now, looking at you, I'm trying, Syd. I can be sorry for a lot of things and I am, I regret a lot of shit, but getting you? Fuck that. I'm not sorry. I'm in love with you. I'll die being in love with you."

Oh, God.

I cried with my hand to my mouth. My body was throbbing and my eyes were burning.

I wanted so badly to hold him. There was something wrong with me.

And Brian wasn't finished.

"I fucked up," he whispered, tears falling down his face. "I fucked up by not telling you that first night I had you in my arms. That I am sorry for. Not giving you what you deserved knowing, keeping shit from you, you finding out the way you did, for the rest of my life I'll feel this. I deserve to feel it." He wiped at his face. "Just tell me, Syd, tell me I'm gonna feel it with you next to me because I can't—"

"Brian," I cut him off, shaking my head.

He was asking something of me I couldn't guarantee. Even after listening to his explanation and hearing all he'd just said, even with my heart still reaching for him, I couldn't guarantee something I wasn't sure of.

Brian closed his eyes, opened them, and then begged, "Please, Wild. Don't leave me. It's over. All of that shit is over—"

"It's not over," I interrupted him. "It's not. Those videos are still out there. Anyone can see them. My mom. Your family. Years from now..." I paused through a sob, the reason behind my pain coming to light and Brian getting it.

He knew what I meant. I saw in the way the saddest boy on earth grew sadder, his body going still and pain sinking in his features.

I didn't have to say it but I did. I needed him to hear this from me.

"Years from now," I continued, still crying, "kids will search for anything on the Internet. Being curious, they could search for you, and that website will take them right to those videos, and what would you say? What *could* you say? They'd see their daddy with somebody else. How could you fix that?" He opened his mouth to speak but I kept going. "Or me?" I asked, breaking into tears again. "I watched three of those videos before I got sick. I saw everything you did with those women. How are you gonna fix that?"

"I will," he promised, stepping closer.

"You can't," I returned, and he froze. "You can't fix this, Brian."

"Wild—"

"You remember what you said to me the first time you called? You said if I didn't want to speak to you anymore, you'd disappear. You'd leave me alone."

Brian shook his head.

"Don't," he urged.

"I'm asking that of you right now," I told him, trying to sound firm and resolute in my request but finding that to be a difficult task with a voice that wouldn't stop quaking and a heart that didn't want me to speak. I powered through the best I could. "I'm packing my stuff and I'm going to Tori's, and I am asking you to leave me be. Don't call me. Don't text me. Don't follow me. Don't come there. Leave me alone."

"I can't do that."

"You'll do it, or you'll never see me again," I promised.

Brian flinched.

He killed me. Now I was killing him.

"I need time to think," I said, sniffing and looking around the room. "I might need a lot of time, and I need to do that without looking at you. If I want to talk to you, I'll reach out. If I don't..." My voice trailed off.

Sir entered the room from the kitchen carrying his rope toy in his mouth.

God...I was gonna have to leave him, too.

"I'm gonna fix this," Brian assured me once more, turning my head. "*I will fix this.*"

I could've said something back. So many words danced on my tongue as I stood there staring at the boy who built my heart up just to break it.

You won't.

You can't.

I hope you do.

God, please fix this.

Instead, I left him standing there and went to the bedroom, packed all the things I could fit into one duffle bag, slung it over my shoulder, and walked to the front door.

Sir met me there.

Brian hadn't moved from his spot.

I bent down and loved on my puppy for a minute, whispering to him and scratching underneath his neck the way he liked.

When I was finished, I turned and looked right into Brian's eyes. Then I said good-bye.

If it was our last good-bye, I wanted it to be one worth remembering. I wanted to see him.

He didn't say it back.

I opened the door, stepped outside onto the porch, fought back tears, and didn't let them fall until I got back to Tori's, back into my old bed, and wrapped in the same sheets that held me while I was falling in love with a boy.

Chapter Twenty-one

BRIAN

The front door shut behind Syd.

I heard a car starting in the driveway, another door shutting, and then the sound of my girl leaving me.

Fucking leaving me.

It was all I could do not to follow her.

I looked at the floor and scrubbed my face with my hands, my muscles burning as they locked up while I fought against the urge to punch holes in every goddamn wall in this house.

Watching your reason for living falling apart after shit you did, ain't nothing more devastating than that.

Except maybe hearing that reason tell you to stay away.

And that's what she did.

I couldn't go to Syd. Couldn't call or text. Couldn't hold her while she cried or wipe away the tears she was shedding because of what I'd done.

Hell. I was in it.

Thought I'd been here before but I was wrong. This was it.

And it was my fault. All of it. I put myself here. I deserved to feel this pain.

But Wild, she didn't deserve any of it.

I'd kill a motherfucker for putting this type of hurt on my girl, yet I was the one dragging Syd through hell with me.

She got here, looking broken already, and I knew why—she didn't need to say. Then I laid it out, all of that ugly, meant every word I said about regrets and the ones I don't have, gave Syd the truth she was justified all along in getting, not knowing what was gonna come out of it, if she would understand, forgive and stay mine, or if she would do the right thing, give me what I deserved back and end it, leave, take herself away from me because after everything I did, no fucking way did I earn the right to be with her.

I didn't deserve her good.

After hearing me out, my girl chose right. She chose what should've happened. I understood that. Even in hell, I understood it.

Didn't mean it was what I wanted.

Never could want that. I wanted her with me. I would always want her with me.

I got her choice.

Didn't mean I wouldn't beg to keep her.

I would beg for the rest of my miserable fucking life, miserable without her in it.

I warranted her leaving me.

Didn't mean I wouldn't do everything to get her back.

I would. I'd fix this. Promised her and I would. I'd be the man she deserved. I'd protect Syd like I should've done months ago.

I would never hurt her again. I'd die first.

I knew what I had to do.

Grabbing my keys, I crated Sir so he wouldn't roam and get into shit, stepped out of the house, locked up, and brought my phone to my ear as I was striding toward my Jeep.

"Yeah?" Jamie answered on the second ring.

"Meet me at the warehouse. Got shit I need to handle there and I might need backup." I swung the driver's side door open and climbed inside.

"Backup? For what?" he asked. "Thought you were done with that place."

I gritted my teeth and started the engine.

"I fuckin' am! Jesus, do I ask you for shit? Ever? Can you just fuckin' meet me there without giving me the third degree?"

"All right, I was just askin'. Christ," Jamie returned. "Give me twenty."

"Give you ten. Leave now," I shot back, shifting into Reverse. "Got a feeling I'm gonna need you to pull me off Mike before I fuckin' kill him."

"*Fuck*," he muttered.

Jamie knew about Mike. Knew enough to know I hated the bastard and wouldn't mind laying him out if I had the chance.

I didn't need to explain further.

"Right. Leavin' now," Jamie threw out.

I hung up, tossed my phone on the seat, backed out of the driveway, and rode to Xstasy.

There weren't a ton of cars in the lot, but there were enough to know people were shooting, which meant Mike was there.

He didn't trust anyone shooting and using his equipment without keeping an eye on things.

I parked by the door, cut the engine, and got out. I scanned the lot for Jamie.

He wasn't here yet.

Fuck.

Cracking my knuckles, I debated waiting until he showed before I handled this. Then I pictured Syd.

Standing on the porch looking like she didn't belong in that house with me.

Crying and giving me her pain.

Telling me she was leaving, and if I followed, it would be over…

I stalked to the door, threw it open, and went inside.

There was music playing off to the left. Heavy bass vibrated off the walls. I glanced at the gathering of people standing over by the scene they were shooting, scanned for Mike, and when I didn't see him, slid my eyes to the office door at the other end of the room and made for that.

I didn't knock.

Fuck courtesies.

Turning the knob, I went right in.

Mike looked up from his desk. He jerked straight in his chair, hit me with hate-filled eyes, and told the person he was listening to on the phone, "Gotta go. I'll call you back," then he disconnected the call, slammed the phone down on his desk, stood with hands bracing on the papers in front of him so he was leaning forward, heaved through his breaths, and bared his fucking teeth.

"You got balls stepping in here," he growled, trying to sound threatening. "Get the fuck outta my building, you piece of shit."

I stalked forward.

I wasn't afraid of Mike, but he was damn sure afraid of me, which was good. I needed that fear. It was the only way I'd get cooperation from him.

I was six-two. He was barely taller than my girl.

I had muscle and could throw a punch and have that shit hurt. He had a gut that hung over his belt and got winded from standing.

I wasn't here to negotiate. He was about to find that out.

Mike's spineless body shot ramrod straight when I got opposite him with only the desk separating us, slammed my own hands down on top of the cluster of shit he had covering it, and leaned forward.

"Want you to take down all those videos you got of me," I growled. "All of them. Want off that site and I want it happening today, right the fuck now, cocksucker." I pointed at his chair, which had slid out when he stood. "So sit your fat ass down and get to fuckin' work. I'm not leaving until it's done."

Mike stared at me like he wasn't expecting those words to come out of my mouth.

Then he grabbed his stomach, threw his head back, and laughed like he'd just heard the funniest fucking thing ever.

"You fucking asshole." He shook his head with a smile. "I *own* your shit, Dash! Own it all, motherfucker! I'm not taking down *jack*." He leaned forward on jack and pointed at my face. "You're outta luck, dickhead. I'm gonna make money off you until the day I fucking die."

My pulse jumped.

Something coiled tight in my stomach.

"I didn't sign anything saying what I shot belonged to you," I grated out, reminding him of the contract we never had, feeling my hands curl into fists on top of the papers I was crushing. "I never signed a damn thing, meaning you own *nothin'*."

"Not how it works," he shot back, lowering his arm. "Whatever you did when you stepped inside this building belongs to *me*. We had a verbal agreement and I will hold you to that, motherfucker. Shot you fucking and jerking your load on *my* cameras, uploaded that shit to *my* site, and that's where they're fucking staying. And just so we're clear"—he cocked his head—"you didn't have me signing shit either, meaning you got nothing to force my hand."

"I got plenty to force your hand," I snarled, leaning closer and watching Mike move back. "Take that shit down."

"Not fucking happening," he replied coldly, then slumped back into his chair and held his arms out like he was waiting for me to crucify him. "What are you gonna do, Dash? Kill me? Huh? Let me ask you this." He gripped the arms of his chair and slid up to the desk. "Why now? Why come here now asking me to remove your shit? You up and bailed weeks ago. Didn't say nothing in that bullshit text you sent me about taking anything down, now all of a sudden..." He paused, his eyes flashed, and I watched a smirk twist across his mouth. "Oh, fuck me." He leaned back and started rocking. "Fuck me. You gotta bitch, don't you? That's what this is about. Tell me I'm right, Dash. You got some hot pussy at home who doesn't like that you stuck your dick in a bunch of whores."

My nostrils flared.

"Shut your fuckin' mouth," I hissed, itching to hit him.

"Did you confess to it?" he asked, grinning. "Or did she see it? I bet she liked that one where you fucked Jayden in every hole she has. Fuck it." He waved his hand. "Get your bitch in here. Maybe she wants to make a little cash on the side too. I like uptight pussy."

Fuck waiting for Jamie.

Growling like a caged animal, I reached across the desk and grabbed Mike by his shirt, yanked his fat ass out of his chair, and dragged him over to where I was standing, throwing his body down onto the hard concrete floor next to the desk.

"*Fuck!*" he groaned, arching his back.

I heard the computer monitor take a crash landing and bust to pieces as I straddled his waist, bent low, and started pounding my fist into the side of his face.

"You fuckin' piece of shit motherfucker!" I snarled through my hits, bone cracking against bone and blood splattering. "You ever talk about my girl again and I will *fuckin'* kill you! You hear me! I WILL FUCKIN' KILL YOU!"

I hit his jaw, his cheek, I felt his nose break under my knuckle.

Mike whined and moaned and whimpered beneath me. His legs thrashed out and his arms tried to block or push me away, but I just kept coming.

And coming.

And coming.

I was going to kill him.

"Dash!"

I heard Jamie yell at my back, then he hooked my arm when it cocked for another hit, trapping it, wrapped his other arm around my chest, and pulled me off.

"Jesus Christ!" Jamie got me to my feet, then he shoved against my chest. "Fuck, you said ten minutes! You couldn't wait for me?"

"You're late," I bit out, shaking my hand and trying to flex it.

Mike made a gurgling noise, then he turned his head and started spitting blood out of his mouth.

"Fuck this," Jamie murmured. "We gotta go."

He grabbed my bicep and pushed me in the direction of the door. We ran through the warehouse, gaining some attention but not giving any back.

Once we got outside, Jamie turned to me. He pushed his hand through his hair.

"What the fuck are you doing?" he asked. "If I'd been any later, you would've killed him."

I shrugged. "Good thing you weren't any later, then."

His eyes widened.

"Are you fuckin' nuts? What's gotten into you? He's gonna call the cops and your ass is gonna get arrested."

I dug my keys out of my pocket with my left hand.

"He's not gonna do shit," I replied, spinning around and walking to my Jeep.

Jamie stayed with me. "Care to explain that?"

I turned my head when I reached the door.

"Mike isn't exactly running a legit business here, Jamie. No fucking way would he get cops here when he hasn't been paying taxes on any of that money he's been pulling in. It's all under the table. And with his fucking ego being the way it is, ain't no way he'd point a finger and admit it was me who bested him."

Mike hated me just as much as I hated him. He'd never admit to this. He couldn't lose to me.

Jamie's eyes widened again, this time in realization.

"Still, we better go," he suggested, looking around the lot and then back at me. "What the fuck brought this on anyway?"

I clenched my jaw, answering through my teeth, "I fucked up."

* * *

Icing my hand, I sat at the dining room table trying to come up with another plan for getting those videos taken down.

I sat there for hours.

Nothing.

Fucking *nothing* came to me.

There was nothing else I could do.

Besides getting on my knees and groveling to Mike, which, considering I beat the shit out of him, I was doubting he'd do me any favors. Not that I'd fucking grovel to that worthless motherfucker but I'd at least keep my hands off him when I made my second request.

I was officially out of options.

Mike ran the site. He controlled what went on there.

I was fucked.

My phone sat on the table in front of me. Taunting me. My girl was a call away and I couldn't do shit about it.

I needed something. I needed to find some way to get those videos down. I needed . . .

A knock sounded on the front door.

Wild.

I jumped out of my chair, letting the bag of peas I was icing my hand with fall to the floor, ran to the door, told Sir to get back, and swung it open, ready to greet my girl with a fuckton of begging.

"Uncle Brian!" Olivia shrieked, bouncing up and down on the porch.

"Hey, Uncle Brian," Oliver greeted me. He held up his DS. "Brought this so we can play after dinner."

Dinner.

Family dinner.

"Fuck," I muttered, pinching my eyes shut and then looking between the two of them.

Olivia gasped, covered her mouth, then giggled. Oliver smiled big.

"Brian, really?" my sister scolded, standing behind them carrying a large casserole dish. She looked down at the twins. "Nobody is allowed to repeat what Uncle Brian just said. Am I clear?"

Olivia mouthed the word over and over as she stayed facing away from Jenna, smiling as she did it.

Oliver grinned at his sister, slid his glasses higher on his nose, then turned facing forward, replying for the both of them, "We won't."

"Good." Jenna lifted her eyes to me. "I know we're a little early but the kids wanted to play with Sir." She studied me intently. "You look awful. Are you feeling okay?"

"No," I replied honestly.

My entire fucking world was gone.

"Hi, Sir!" Olivia bent down when Sir pushed through my legs and stuck his head out the door. "I brought you treats. They're in my pocket," she whispered.

"Sorry," I apologized, rubbing at my face and looking to Jenna. "For cussing and because I meant to call. Dinner's canceled."

Her brow furrowed.

"What? Really?" she asked, sounding disappointed. "Because you're not feeling well?"

"Aw, man." Oliver made a fist and punched the front of his thigh. "This is the worst day of my *life*!"

"Oliver, please, you said that yesterday when you couldn't find your *Star Wars* shirt," Jenna said.

"That was a really bad day, Mom," Oliver argued. "So is this. I wanted to hang out."

"We're not staying?" Olivia asked, blinking up at me but staying crouched down. "But Syd promised she'd braid my hair all twisty again."

"Syd's not here," I told her.

My chest grew tight.

"She's not?" Jenna asked. "Where is she? Did she get called into work?"

I breathed deep.

What the fuck was I supposed to say?

"She's..." My voice trailed off when Jamie's car pulled into the driveway and parked behind Jenna's.

"Uncle Jamie!" Oliver spun around, leaned around his mother, and waved, holding up his DS with his other hand. "Brought my DS!"

"Cool!" Jamie shouted, then shut his car door and jogged to the porch. He tipped his chin at Jenna. "Hey, Jenna."

"Hey," she returned pleasantly.

"What are you doing here?" I asked when he climbed the porch.

He gave me a peculiar look.

"Dinner," he stated matter-of-factly.

"Are you *shittin'* me?" I grated.

"Brian!" Jenna warned.

Oliver and Olivia both started giggling.

"Sorry," I told her, then looked at Jamie again. "What makes you think we're still having dinner after the shi...stuff that went down today?"

"That's another reason why I'm here," he replied. "We gotta figure this out. There's gotta be somethin' else you can do."

I stared at Jamie. Something tightened in my chest.

He wanted to help. He was always wanting to help and I never took it. I never took it from anyone.

And look where that fucking got me.

The only person I ever let in was Syd. She was it. I didn't fight her when she wanted to heal me. I didn't tell her I had to do it myself.

I let her in. And it felt fucking *good*.

It was time I let the rest of them in. I had to. I couldn't do this alone. I never could.

I needed help.

"Wait, what went down?" Jenna asked, looking between myself and Jamie, who was standing behind her.

"Dash screwed up. Syd's gone," he informed her, knowing the details because I gave them to him before we both hauled ass away from the warehouse and went our separate ways.

"Thanks, man. Appreciate it," I said sarcastically, getting a shrug in return.

"What? Syd's *gone*?" Jenna whipped her head around and glared at me. "What did you do?"

I stepped back and held the door open.

"Come inside. I'll explain everything," I told Jenna.

The kids barreled in first and went straight for the couch with Sir on their tails. Jenna stepped in next, keeping the glare and giving it to me before she carried her dish to the kitchen.

I reached out and stopped Jamie from following behind with a hand to his chest.

He turned his head and looked at me.

"What's up?"

"Need your help with this," I confessed, letting my hand drop since he wasn't resisting.

His eyes flickered wider.

He wasn't expecting to hear this from me.

Jamie came here offering help knowing I'd resist, and still, he was here, offering it.

Jamie McCade was one of the best fucking men I'd ever met.

"I can't do this alone," I continued. "I've got nothing. I'm out of ways to make this shit right."

He grinned slowly, no doubt savoring this moment, and I let him 'cause I was done fighting this, then he slapped my shoulder, declaring, "That's why I'm here, man. I got your back. We'll figure something out." He urged me to walk toward the kitchen. "Come on. I'm starving. I need to eat before we hash out a plan."

I still had skepticism about hashing out anything, but I kept that to myself and moved to the kitchen.

Jenna was standing at the island with her arms crossed under her chest. Her dish was on the counter in front of her.

"What happened?" she started the second I entered the room. "I told you not to screw it up with her, Brian. She was the best thing that's ever happened to you."

"Jen," I began, tipping my head at the table. "You're gonna want to sit down."

She stuck out her chest.

"I'm fine where I am."

"Go sit, Jenna," Jamie encouraged, giving her shoulder a squeeze when he moved behind her to get to the fridge. "Brian has a lot to say and you're gonna want to be sittin'. Trust me."

She gave me a worried look, then dropped her arms, rounded the island, and put herself in a chair.

I joined her, taking the seat beside her at the head of the table, propped my elbows up, and careful of my hand, linked my fingers.

Then I proceeded to tell her everything.

Jenna sat silent, no doubt stunned by what she was hearing.

I wouldn't look at her. I kept my eyes on the table as I spoke, not even looking up at Jamie when he joined us and started eating.

It made me sick talking about it. It made me sicker when I got to the parts that involved Syd, her reaction, and the reason she wasn't here anymore.

I saw her face covered in tears. I thought about what she was doing now, if she was still crying and if she needed me.

If she knew I'd be there if I could.

When I was done confessing everything, I slouched back in my chair, kicked my legs out, and rubbed my good hand over my face.

A chair slid against the floor, then I felt Jenna's arm come around my back as she gave me a hug, leaning her head on my shoulder.

"Oh, Brian," she said softly, sounding on the verge of tears. "That accident was not your fault, sweetie."

"I know," I told her, keeping my head down. "Syd got me there."

She had. I no longer thought about that accident the same way I did before I met her. I knew now it was all by chance. Nothing more.

"I can't believe you gave that family all of that money," she said, leaning away and letting her hand slide to the back of my neck and squeeze there. When I turned my head and looked over at her, she added, "That's unbelievable. I bet they are incredibly grateful for that."

I dragged in a breath and shook my head.

"Doesn't matter. None of it matters. I lost Syd, and unless by some miracle those videos disappear on their own, I'm fucked."

"Let's brainstorm, brother," Jamie said, dropping his fork on his empty plate and sitting tall, flattening his hands on the table. "There's gotta be somethin'. Some other way."

"Like what?" I asked, my voice picking up edge. "There's nothing else I can do."

"Actually," Jenna started, tapping her finger on her lip as her eyes lost focus on the table. "You didn't sign anything, ever, when you were working for them?" she asked, looking at me.

"No."

"Hm."

"Hm?" I sat forward, curious. "What's that mean?"

She bit her lip with her eyes lowered, then stood and announced, "I'm gonna make a quick call. Be right back."

"To who?" I asked.

"A partner at my firm. There might be another way," she informed. "I need to grab my phone. It's in the car." She turned to walk away, stopped herself, then turned back and asked me, "How did you get the Viagra? You weren't, like, going to a drug dealer, were you?"

Jamie laughed.

When I told Jenna everything, I didn't leave shit out.

"Got it from my PCP," I returned. "Said I was feeling depressed after the accident and couldn't get it up. He prescribed it."

"Oh." She nodded, lost in thought. "That makes sense. Okay, good, that's good. I'll be back."

She left the room and said something to the kids, then I heard the front door opening and closing.

"See?"

I turned to Jamie after he spoke.

He was smiling.

"Told you there had to be somethin'," he said, leaning back and tucking his hands behind his head.

Hope bloomed in my chest. It felt strange.

It felt fucking *good*.

I let my eyes fall to my phone and thought about Syd.

I'm fixing this, Wild.

"Uncle Brian, Mommy said we can get something to eat if we want," Olivia said, moving into the kitchen.

Oliver followed behind her. He had his head down and his eyes focused on his DS screen.

"Yeah, sure." I stood up from the chair and went to the stove, where Syd's Mexican Chicken thing had cooled down, then I grabbed two plates out of the cabinet and a couple of forks from the drawer.

"Oh, cool! Are those Doritos?" Olivia asked, coming up to stand beside me as I was scooping some out onto a plate.

I smiled.

"Yeah. You like Doritos?" I asked her.

"I love them! They're the best chip *ever*, and they go so good with whatever that is, Uncle Brian. I can tell."

"What about you, Oliver? You like Doritos?" I turned my head to where he was standing at the corner of the island.

"Cool Ranch or Regular?" he asked, eyes still focused on the screen.

"Regular," Olivia answered.

"Yep," he replied. "Can I get extra on mine?"

"Me, too!" Olivia jumped up and down, pointing at the dish.

"You bet," I replied. "Get yourselves something to drink and sit down. I gotta heat this up."

Olivia moved behind me to get to the fridge while I scooped out more of the Mexican Chicken and dumped it onto the other plate, then I got one heating in the microwave and grabbed some napkins for both of them.

"When will Syd be back?" Olivia asked as I was sliding napkins in front of her and Oliver, who was showing Jamie something on his DS screen.

I straightened and gripped the back of a chair.

"Don't know, Liv," I answered honestly, watching her mouth pull down as she sank on her knees in her seat.

"Is she sad at you? Mommy gets sad sometimes and she says it's because of a boy."

My teeth clenched.

That fucking dickhead. I should fly out to Denver when my hand heals up and knock his fucking teeth out.

Forcing my jaw to relax, I gave her my reply.

"Yeah, Liv, she is. I made her sad."

Olivia lifted her one shoulder and spoke casually when she said, "Then you should fix it."

Just like that. As if it were that simple.

"Trying." I nodded, giving her a small smile in hopes that would reassure her.

She smiled back bigger, as if she knew everything was gonna work out.

The microwave beeped.

I switched out the plates and heated the second one, carrying both over to the table at the same time so they could start eating together, stood across from them gripping the back of a chair, and glared over my shoulder in the direction of the living room.

What the fuck was Jenna doing?

Finally, the front door opened, shut, then quick footsteps padded on the floor and Jenna came darting into the kitchen.

"You get your phone?" I asked, straightening and turning toward her.

"Nope." She smiled. "Already made the call."

I leaned closer. My heart crawled up into my throat.

"And?"

She smiled bigger.

"There's another way."

* * *

Three days later I was standing in Mike's office with a crowd surrounding him.

Crystal, Holly, and Jayden were there, the girls I'd shot with who were agreeing to say the videos of us were personal property, something they could say since nobody signed shit before filming, meaning Mike didn't own them and didn't have rights to share. We'd all met up last night and Jenna explained the plan, asking the girls if they'd be willing to threaten a lawsuit against Mike if he didn't take down the videos and images. Not only were they willing, but they were also sick of Mike's shit, and on top of backing me, they were there to tell Mike they were done.

He was pretty pissed about that. Oh fucking well.

Jamie stood off to the side, positioned there in case I felt the urge to break the other side of Mike's face, and Calvin, the partner at Jenna's firm who was doing me a solid by standing in and being a presence, making the threat of suing carry a little more weight, was standing beside me.

"You gotta be fucking shitting me," Mike spat after hearing everyone's piece, finding my eyes in the crowd the best he could with the one eye he had open.

The other was still swollen shut.

"Mr. Galloway," Calvin stated, gaining Mike's attention. "I suggest you take action immediately, sir, or I will. All the videos and still images containing Brian Savage are to be removed from your site. If anything is left up by accident or deliberately, my clients will be taking legal action against you. This is very serious."

"No, you wanna know what's serious?" Mike snarled, leaning forward in his seat and stubbing out his cigarette. He pointed directly at me. "What I'm gonna do to that motherfucker right there. *That's* what's serious. I'm gonna tear—"

"I suggest you stop right there, Mr. Galloway," Calvin interrupted. "Unless you'd like me to call the authorities for threats of violence."

Mike lowered his hand and slid his eye to me.

I smiled right at him, letting him eat it.

"Get the fuck out." He pushed his hand through the air. "All of you! Get out!"

Slowly, everyone filed out of the office. I hung back and watched Calvin approach the desk.

Mike looked up at him.

"If you'd like to go ahead and get started on removing my client from your site." Calvin pointed at the brand-new monitor gracing Mike's desk. "We'll leave when you're finished," he added before stepping back and taking a seat.

Mike glared at me with his one eye.

"I'll stand. I'm good," I told him.

Then I watched as Mike removed all traces of me from Xstasy, and I did it grinning.

Fucking grinning.

It was over.

I shook Calvin's hand when we got outside to the parking lot. "Thanks a lot. Really appreciate you coming down here and helping me out."

"No problem. Happy to help." He released my hand, produced a business card out of his suit pocket, and handed it to me. "Take care of yourself. You need anything, give me a call."

"Thanks."

I slid the card away.

Calvin got in his black Lexus and I crossed the lot, reaching Jamie, who was waiting for me by my Jeep.

"See?" He held his hands out, looking arrogant. "Told you somethin' would work out. Now you can go get your girl." He slapped my shoulder.

"Yeah." I nodded, scrubbing at my face with my hands. "Fuck," I muttered.

I couldn't believe I was about to get her.

"You got the store, right?" I asked him, tugging out my keys.

He backed away toward his motorcycle.

Fucking idiot actually bought the thing.

"We're good, man. Go. Do what you gotta do."

"Appreciate it."

He jerked his chin, spun around, and got to his ride.

I climbed in the Jeep and started it up. I made it to the end of the lot when my phone started ringing in my back pocket.

Leaning over, I yanked my cell out and checked the screen. I didn't recognize the number.

"This is Brian," I answered, pulling out onto the road and heading in the direction of Tori's house.

I wasn't sure if Syd was working today or not so I was starting there.

"Brian, it's Mona."

"Oh, hey. How's it going?" I asked.

It was weird she was calling me, but I was too focused on Syd to think anything of it.

"I...I didn't know if I should call you or not, but I figured you'd want to know if something happens. You were so involved with helping him."

A strange pressure built in my chest.

I stopped at a red light and pressed my foot down hard on the brake.

"Mona, what's going on?"

"It's Owen. He's sick, Brian. He's really sick, and they don't know if he's gonna make it. I just got a call from his mom. It doesn't look good."

"What?"

I sat forward in my seat. My heart dropped to my stomach.

"He's at NHC. He's been intubated."

I floored it, ignoring the light, cutting the wheel, and turning around in the middle of the intersection. I nearly sideswiped a van and gave a half-assed apologetic wave as I sped down the road in the opposite direction I was heading, passing the warehouse.

"Brian? Did you hear me?"

"Yeah." I gripped the wheel tight. I felt sick. "Yeah, I heard you."

"I'm sorry," Mona cried softly.

Chapter Twenty-two

SYDNEY

I kept replaying my last conversation with Brian over and over again in my head.

I relived it. I allowed myself to feel that agony all over again, seeing the pain in his eyes and hearing the hurt and hatred in his voice as he admitted what he'd been doing and why he'd been doing it.

The why was getting to me. And the disgust for his own actions, I felt that right along with him.

It was what had me telling Tori under no circumstance was she allowed to let me leave the house the past two days. I handed over my keys and my cell. I wasn't on schedule to work, and I knew if I had my phone, I'd call, or if I left, I'd go to Brian and give him the comfort I was dying to give him, to tell him I understood why he did it and to ignore my own broken heart to make sure his was still beating.

Only my boy would let guilt swallow him up like that.

And I felt sorry for him. I did.

I cried and I cried, thinking about what had to have been going through his mind five months ago. How shattered he must've felt. The internal struggle he was battling and how it probably tore him apart.

He didn't want to shoot those videos. He didn't want any part of it. I believed that in my gut.

I wondered how different it would've been if Marcus had tossed me aside before that accident and if I would've met Brian under different circumstances. In my soul I knew I would've, Brian and I would've found each other somehow, and maybe I could've gotten him to a place where he never got to feel that blame the way he did, meaning he never would've sold himself to pay back that debt.

I could've stopped this entire nightmare from happening.

I could've kept Brian from that dirty.

I could've given him Wild like I'd promised so it was the only thing he was feeling.

My heart was crazy.

Officially.

Love made you stupid and I was now the reigning mayor of Idiot Town.

I was hurting, unbearably so, but I cared more about how Brian was doing through all of this. I wondered if he was crying or ripping shit apart. I wondered if it was killing him not reaching out or coming over. I wondered if he was staring up at his bedroom ceiling thinking about me like I was thinking about him.

See? Crazy.

It took everything in me not to go to him.

Time ticked away my misery while I lay in my bed wrapped up in Tori's Christmas quilt. I thought about the past two months with Brian, the strange way we came together and the unbelievable weeks that followed. I smiled at the memories we'd made already, and I cried at the ones I didn't know if we'd ever have. I thought about everything, from start to finish and in between, and I asked myself the same questions over and over again.

Would I have left Brian if he'd given me the truth months ago when I deserved to hear it? Would I have walked away from everything, including the best thing I ever felt?

I couldn't answer those questions.

I tried. God, I tried. It should've been easy. Yes or no.

He broke my heart—yes, I would've left him.

I understood why he did it and I felt his guilt-driven reason as if it were my own—no. I loved him. I would never leave. Not even if he could never get those videos taken down, which I was convinced of. I didn't see how that was possible.

Still, I would've stayed by his side because of what I knew.

Brian said he was trying to protect me. I believed that.

That heart was mine.

But he still hurt me. Worse than Marcus.

I couldn't give an answer.

What was I supposed to do?

I was grateful for work on Tuesday. It was supposed to be a distraction, one I desperately needed. NHC was a demanding hospital, and normally, even on days when I didn't want to keep my mind off Brian, I was too busy to think about him.

Of course, that wasn't the case today.

We were so slow, my supervisor had sent one of my co-workers home.

When I got word of this happening, I hid in the bathroom for fifteen minutes so I wouldn't get the ax, too.

I couldn't go home, because I wouldn't go home.

I'd go to Brian.

There was no doubt in my mind.

Taking my chances and returning to the department after an amount of time I felt was appropriate, I relaxed, realizing with three of us left and two OR cases going on at the same time, the other two techs handling those upon my return, I was safe from being told to leave.

I sat by the printer waiting for a requisition to print out, and when it did, I'd go handle house patients or x-rays that needed to be done in the emergency room.

Even handling all of that by myself, I still wasn't busy.

But at least I was here and not in my car on my way to Brian's.

Things were looking up.

Sort of.

I say this because I was currently filling out a crossword puzzle from the Sunday paper we had lying around the department, waiting for another requisition to print out, thinking about Brian because I was filling out a crossword puzzle.

I wasn't even reading the clues. I was just filling out four letter word blocks with whatever came to mind.

Love.

Wild.

Hate.

Risk.

Liar.

Fuck.

Fuck.

FUCK.

If someone were to find this paper when I was finished with it, there was a chance they could use it as evidence when I went on trial for my sanity.

I'd be sent to the psych ward for sure.

Yet knowing that, I still filled in my own answers.

When the department phone started ringing on the desk in front of me, I dropped my pen and reached for the receiver just as a requisition started printing out.

"X-ray, this is Syd," I answered.

"Hey, it's Melissa up in ICU. I just put in an order for a stat portable chest to check a line placement. Can you come do it right away? The doctor is waiting."

I stood and grabbed the requisition off the printer.

"Yep. It just printed out. I'll be right up."

"Thanks."

I hung up the phone and studied the order.

It was for an eight-year-old boy with pneumonia. I immediately thought about Oliver.

My nose starting stinging.

Shaking those thoughts away, I snatched the key off the desk, took the requisition, and left the department, stepping out into the hallway where we kept our portable machines plugged in and charging.

When I reached the fifth floor, I pushed the machine off the elevator and started down the hallway, looking up at the room numbers because I always forgot where they began.

I was at Room 17 and the patient was in Room 4. That was on the opposite side of the department.

"X-ray," one of the nurses called out to me when I was passing by the reception desk.

I looked to her and stopped pushing the machine.

She was carrying an IV bag when she came closer, stopped at the tall counter that circled the desk, and said to me, "Just hang around up here for a minute. The doctors are in there working on him. They might still need it."

The way she was speaking, I knew what that meant.

I nodded and gave her a sullen smile.

"Okay, thanks."

Then I pushed the machine past the desk, cut down the small corridor connecting the two sides of the department to get to the even-numbered rooms, turned the corner, and froze.

I couldn't believe what I was seeing.

"Brian?"

My boy was standing in the hallway outside Room 4, staring through the glass and watching the doctors work on the patient I was supposed to be x-raying, but when I said his name, Brian turned his head.

My heart seized in my chest.

He looked devastated. His skin was pale and his eyes were lifeless as they locked on to mine.

It was like I was staring at a ghost.

I parked the portable machine against the wall and ran to him.

I had to.

"What are you doing here?" I asked when I reached his side, but before he could give me an answer, I got it for myself.

I turned my head and looked through the glass at the boy in the bed, who was currently getting CPR administered on him. A doctor was hovering over and compressing down on his chest while a nurse was squeezing the bag attached to this breathing tube, giving him air.

There was a crash cart next to the bed and several other nurses circling and doing their jobs, plus other workers standing around watching. Then my eyes cut through the crowd and fell on the parents, who were huddled together at the back of the room, holding each other and crying.

I recognized the father first. He was facing the door. Then I recognized the kid when I looked back at the bed.

His wheelchair was in the corner next to the bathroom.

"Oh, God," I whispered, bringing my hand up to my mouth. "Oh, my God."

Brian didn't say anything, but I heard him make a noise deep in his throat like he was choking, and I reached down and grabbed his hand, slid my fingers between his, and held on tight.

He held me back.

We stood outside that room together, watching as the doctors and nurses did everything they could to keep that boy alive. They worked tirelessly, switching off with compressions after several minutes, and at one point a doctor looked up and motioned for me to come in and shoot the x-ray, but then the heart monitor started alarming again and they had to go back to doing CPR.

Brian and I didn't speak. We didn't look at each other. I didn't let go and neither did he.

Pneumonia can be a complication of spinal cord injuries.

People died from pneumonia. I wished that little boy could've been the exception that day.

But he wasn't.

After eleven minutes, the doctors and nurses stopped working. There was nothing more they could do. His body gave up.

The parents ran to his side and held him as the team cleared the room to give them their privacy.

I was already crying but started crying harder.

I was devastated for them.

Brian dropped his head into the hand I wasn't holding and fell apart next to me. His big, strong body nearly buckled in half.

"Honey," I soothed, my voice trembling. I turned into him and wrapped my arms around his shoulders, holding the back of his head as he buried his face in my neck and pressed closer, his tears absorbing into my skin, his arms holding so tight around my back it hurt, but I let it.

I had to comfort him.

"It wasn't your fault," I whispered as we cried together, because I didn't know if Brian was allowing himself to think that again and I couldn't let him do that. I couldn't. "Don't go to that place, Brian. You didn't do this, okay? This is not on you."

He didn't say anything back, but his arms squeezed tighter.

I winced and came up on my toes.

I didn't tell him to stop. I kept comforting him.

And he kept holding tight.

I have no idea how long we stood there, but I did know I would stand there for as long as he needed.

"What...what are you doing here?"

Brian and I pulled away from each other at the sound of a woman's voice at my back.

I turned my head and saw the parents of the boy standing just outside the room now. They were both staring at Brian, tears still filling the eyes of the father and the mother with fresh ones on her cheeks.

Brian didn't respond. I looked to him and he was staring back, his body rigid and yet shaking somehow.

I grabbed his hand again and did the only thing I could think of.

"He's the one who's been giving you all that money," I told the parents, feeling Brian's hand tense in mine. "For your son. It's all been from him."

The father's shoulders dropped. He stared in disbelief at Brian.

The mother sucked in a breath, her eyes widening as they slid from my face and looked to the man standing next to me. Then her lip started quivering, new tears built behind her lashes, her head started shaking, and she came forward, crying again as she threw her arms around Brian and gave him a hug.

I felt Brian stop shaking and his body go perfectly still. He didn't reciprocate the affection and he never let go of my hand.

The hug lasted only a couple of seconds and she never said a word to him, then the mother stepped back, covered her mouth, and moved back into the room.

The father came in front of Brian then and placed his hand on

Brian's shoulder. He looked him in the eyes and I knew the man was expressing his gratitude even though he didn't speak the words.

Maybe he couldn't.

But Brian heard them. I could feel the tension leaving his body.

When the father stepped away, I looked up at Brian. His eyes had lost their focus and his breathing was shallow.

He was processing what he'd just been given.

It was a lot. I could tell.

I was sure he never expected it.

Brian gave that money knowing he'd never take credit for it.

I stood there silent and allowed him to process, wiping tears away and slowly composing myself.

Then Brian blinked several times through a deep breath, brought our hands that were still together in front of him, and wrapped his other hand around the back of mine.

He stared at our joining.

Someone paged X-ray on the intercom overhead. I told myself I'd respond to that in a minute.

I just needed another minute.

Just one.

"I'm so sorry, Brian," I told him, finally speaking again, not remembering if I had said that already when I was comforting him minutes ago.

I whispered a lot. I know I whispered I loved him. I couldn't help it.

His eyes lifted to my face, and I saw how bright they appeared now, still shadowed with sadness but not as much as they were when I first rounded the corner and saw him standing here. He looked different, relieved maybe, but it was almost as if he was hiding that behind a different shade of pain now.

Pain for the parents who had just lost their child. The kind of pain anyone would feel and sympathize with. And pain because he was looking at me and he didn't know what that meant, where we stood, or how I was feeling, and he worried the worst while thinking it was useless to hope for the best.

"I—"

"I fixed it," Brian interrupted my sad attempt at small talk, because I honestly didn't know what to say to him and knew if I didn't say something and kept watching him hold me and look at me like that, I'd end up kissing him.

I blinked up at Brian, absorbing his words.

"What?" I asked, stepping closer.

He sniffed, and the corner of his mouth tilted up the tiniest bit.

"Those videos are gone, Wild," he shared. His voice was confident. "All of them. Got everything taken down from that site. There's nothing left of me on there, and there's no trace of it anywhere else. It's gone."

I heard what he was saying. I understood what he was saying.

I just didn't believe it.

"How? How did you do that?"

He shook his head and held my hand tighter with both of his, telling me, "Doesn't matter. It's done."

"But what about if someone saved those videos on their own computer or something? They could share them all over the Internet."

That had become a worry of mine that I'd discovered while lying in bed that first night without Brian.

It stressed me out so badly, I didn't fall asleep until the sun came up.

"Not an option," he answered firmly. "That dickhead running the site wouldn't allow anyone seeing his shit and not paying for it. You couldn't save images or videos on your own devices. He made sure of that."

"Oh," I replied, pulling my lips between my teeth and looking away.

My heart started beating faster.

He fixed it, just like he said he would.

"Wild."

My eyes slid back to Brian's.

He opened his mouth, and I knew what he was going to ask me, and for some reason I couldn't explain, I panicked.

I covered his mouth with my other hand and prevented him from speaking.

"I can't, Brian," I blurted out, suddenly feeling overwhelmed, watching his brows pull together, his eyes go sad, and feeling his breath burst against my palm. "I can't. I'm...I just need to think a little more, okay? This has been really hard and I just, I don't know if I'm ready." I slid my hand away and stepped back, pulling my other out of his hold. "I'm sorry."

Then, so I wouldn't see that look on his face any longer, that look that was killing me and making it hard to breathe, I turned and ran out of the ICU, leaving the portable machine behind.

Brian called out for me but I kept running.

I rode the elevators to the bottom floor and hurried back to my department, shutting myself in the room I was slowly going crazy in and busying myself with the work waiting for me.

Work I was grateful for. I needed that distraction now more than ever.

Hours ticked by, and even though my focus was on my job because it had to be, my mind still wandered. And the more it wandered, the more I thought about Brian, and the more I thought about Brian, the more I thought about everything, him fixing us and the reaction I had to it, bringing me to the conclusion I didn't want to make while being stuck at work.

I'd made a mistake.

What I'd said to Brian wasn't entirely true.

Yes, it *was* really hard finding out what Brian had been doing and learning what all he'd kept from me.

It broke my heart.

Yes, I *didn't know* if I was ready to go back to the life I was sharing with Brian, if I could allow myself to feel that kind of love again when I knew what losing it felt like.

Love was a risk. It was wild and unpredictable. You could either hold on for the ride, not knowing how it would end, or you could let go and never know the amazing you could've had.

And yes, I *was* sorry. I was sorry for what happened to us. I was sorry for everything Brian had to face without me.

But what wasn't true was that I didn't need to think. I didn't need to convince myself who I wanted to hand my heart over to so they could heal it. I didn't need to weigh the pros and cons of sharing my life with someone who had it in him to make me happy again, the happiest, and I didn't need to wonder if choosing Brian was the right choice, because I knew the answer.

He was never a choice. He was my fate. My boy. Everything he ever promised me he made sure to see through.

He fixed it, just like he said he would.

And running from him was a mistake I needed to make right on.

I was holding on for this ride. I'd never let go of it.

I loved him. I'd die loving him.

Heart racing and ready, I counted down the remaining seconds of my shift while staring at the time clock, on the verge of screaming, it was taking so long. After punching out and grabbing my things, I ran through the hospital and out to my car, tossed my book bag on the passenger seat, started it up, and peeled out.

I drove moderately fast to get to the house, figuring if I was to get pulled over, I'd just explain my situation to the police, hoping they were understanding of a woman needing to right her wrongs and get the love of her life back.

If they weren't and issued me a ticket, so be it. I wasn't slowing down.

Throwing the car into Park and cutting the engine, I ran up the driveway, jumped up onto the porch, stood in front of the door while taking in several calming breaths, getting my nerves in check, and then knocked.

I felt it was the appropriate thing to do, all things considered.

The door swung open before I had time to lower my hand, and before Brian could question what I was doing there or ask why I was knocking again, since he looked geared up to do just that, I opened my mouth and beat him to speaking.

"Hey, Trouble."

He blinked, looking shocked at my greeting, which I understood.

I was falling back into old habits. It was as if nothing had changed between us.

"Hey, Wild," he replied, falling with me.

The flip and twist happened.

God, that felt good.

I cleared my throat, tipped my chin up, and requested, "Can I come in?"

Brian's mouth twitched. Fighting a smile, he stepped back and held the door open.

"Thank you," I said, moving inside. I looked around, noticing the TV was on and expecting more noise.

"He's outside," Brian said behind me, reading my mind. He shut the door and crossed the room, grabbing the remote off the couch and turning down the volume.

"How is he?" I asked.

"Good. Misses you." Brian dropped the remote and took a step closer. "I miss you."

I watched him keep coming, slowly eliminating the distance between us.

Holding up my hand, I told him, "I've been doing some thinking, and before you come any closer or say anything else that'll make me want to kiss you instead of saying what I need to say, I'd like to share my thoughts while keeping some space."

Brian stopped moving toward me.

"You wanna kiss me?" he asked.

"Yes, but I know once we start kissing, I won't wanna stop."

He didn't fight that smile anymore. He gave it to me, big and bright.

And it was beautiful.

"That's not a bad thing, babe," he said, tucking his hands inside his pockets. "Feel the same way, and now that I know you want that kiss as bad as I do, I suggest you get to talking. It's been too long since I had your mouth and I'm feeling pretty impatient right now."

I sucked in a breath. He was feeling impatient.

As instructed, I didn't waste any time.

"I made a mistake," I whispered.

Brian lost the smile. His eyes softened.

"I don't need time to think," I continued with tears building behind my lashes. "I don't. I don't know why I said that. I think I was just overwhelmed by everything, and hearing you tell me you fixed it . . . I wanted that so bad, Brian. I did, but I didn't think it was possible. You promised me you would and I was so scared you'd fail. I was scared we'd never have us again. I didn't want that. I would never want that. I love you. I love you so much."

"Wild," he said quietly.

"And I've been in agony being apart. The worst pain I've ever felt. I reached for my phone so many times to call you," I continued, wiping a tear from my cheek.

"Babe," he prompted.

"Mm?"

"Fuckin' *dying here*."

I knew what he meant. Brian wanted to get to me. I'd asked him to give me space and he was at the end of his patience.

So I told him it was okay and I did this by moving first and not doing it slowly.

I rushed at him and not a second later he rushed at me. We collided together somewhere in the middle, Brian wrapping his arms around me and squeezing tight while I wrapped my arms around him and squeezed tighter. My head was pressed to his chest, turned so I could listen to his heartbeat while his face was lowered and buried in my hair.

"I love you," he whispered over and over while I cried tears of joy and ones I knew were for everything we'd been through.

And like he always did, Brian held me through it.

When I composed myself enough to speak, I leaned back, tipped my head up, met his eyes, and said, "You're still my boy. I didn't really mean it when I said you weren't. I was just—"

He shook his head, halting my explanation.

"You fixed it," I blurted out, worrying he'd halt those words, too, and needing them to be heard.

His chest moved with a breath, then he bent and pressed his lips to my forehead.

"Yeah, baby."

Baby.

I closed my eyes, moaned, and melted closer.

"Babe."

"Mm?"

"Look at me."

I opened my eyes.

Brian was staring down at me, looking like the saddest boy on earth again.

"I am so fucking sorry," he said, his voice sounding thick as he slid his hands to my hips. "I fucked up. I don't deserve you. I don't deserve to be holding you right now. Doubt I ever will again. I just—"

"Trouble," I interrupted him.

"Yeah?"

"I get to decide who holds me and I'm choosing you."

He swallowed and kept looking into my eyes.

"I know you're sorry," I continued. "I know even though I'm telling you I forgive you, you'll keep giving me your sorry. Just know you don't have to. I feel it. You never meant to hurt me, and I know you really thought you were protecting me. I get that now." I placed my hand on his cheek. He leaned into it. "I get why you did it, too," I added a little quieter.

Brian closed his eyes, inhaled and exhaled slowly, then resumed looking at me.

"You told them about the money," he rasped.

"They needed to know."

He bent closer. "Thank you."

My eyes flickered wider, and my breathing paused. Brian straightened again and kept his eyes on my face.

I knew what he was meaning. He wasn't thanking me for giving him recognition. He was thanking me for healing that last final piece of his soul.

Those people didn't blame Brian. They were grateful for his gift.

He was finally free of that guilt.

I closed my eyes, nuzzled his chest, and announced, figuring he needed to know my plans, "Moving back in."

Brian's arm tensed around me.

"Good. Missed you," he replied with a smile in his voice.

"Missed you, too," I said. "And I wanna meet your parents."

"Think they'd like that."

"I don't care anymore if you meet my mom. I have everything I need with the family we got here."

I felt Brian's face graze the top of my head again. His breath warmed my hair.

"You change your mind, you tell me. I'll make that happen," he vowed.

I didn't think I'd ever change my mind, but it felt good knowing Brian was with me if I did.

Opening my eyes, I looked up to ask, "Can we dance to 'Can't Help Falling in Love' at our wedding?"

I had to know.

If Brian wanted to compromise on this, I would. I loved that song but I loved Brian more.

But I had a feeling . . .

His eyes went soft as he stared back at me. I knew he was picturing that day.

I was picturing it, too.

Then his arm tugged me closer as his other hand came underneath my chin and tilted it back at the same time as he bent down, bringing our mouths together where he pledged, "Whatever you want, babe."

Whatever I want.

He was promising. That meant it was going to happen, just like everything else he ever promised me.

My feeling was right.

I smiled against his lips, then I kissed him.

And just like every other kiss Brian gave me, it was the best.

Epilogue

SYDNEY

One Week Later

"Wild, you ready?" Brian called out from somewhere in the house, most likely near the front door since he'd been waiting on me for the past twenty minutes to get changed, a task which always took me less than five, just like today, except Brian didn't know that.

I was making him think the task was taking longer than usual.

"Almost!" I hollered back, then looked away from the window I was peering out of and glanced at the clock on the wall.

It was almost six. The mail typically ran between two and two thirty.

This was unacceptable.

"Come on," I whispered to the empty room, shifting on my feet, then turned my head and resumed looking out for the mail truck through the shutter blinds I was holding apart.

"Just going to the beach. You know this, right?" Brian yelled. "Not sure what all you're putting on back there but you only need your suit."

"I'm accessorizing!"

Lie.

Although I was finally wearing the turquoise hair wrap I'd purchased months ago, using it like a headband so it kept the hair out of my face. It was tied off at the base of my skull and then interwoven

with my ponytail so it concealed the boring elastic band holding everything together.

And like predicted, it looked amazing against my red.

"You're *what*?" Brian called back, sounding confused.

I turned to the door.

"Just give me another minute! I'm finishing up!" Then I turned
back to the window and muttered, "Someone is *not* getting a Christmas card this year."

I was referring to our mailman.

Today was an important day, for two reasons.

First, Brian and I were finally going to the beach so he could get
back out on the water.

This was huge.

I was beyond excited to leave and get him out there, but we
couldn't leave yet, hence the reason I was stalling and saying I wasn't
ready when I'd been ready for the past fifteen minutes.

This was because of reason number two.

Something was set to arrive in the mail today, and because of the
importance of it, I didn't want us to be gone when it arrived.

However, I wasn't sure how much longer I'd be able to stall. Eventually Brian would come back to the bedroom and find me ready to
go, and I had a feeling my time was running out along with his patience.

I narrowed my eyes and stared at the street.

I liked our mailman. He was a nice guy, but he was seriously
messing up my plans here.

Life was perfect, but I knew it had the potential of becoming even
more perfect for Brian, and I wanted that.

Two days after I moved back in, Brian and I were sitting on the
couch watching TV when the local news came on. The man running
the adult film company Brian had been shooting for was arrested on
charges of tax evasion, shutting down the operation and destroying
any remaining ties Brian had to them.

We were both happy hearing this, although I was more relieved
than anything. I hated knowing that place was around, and after
hearing Brian tell me everything that happened during our three

days apart, what all he went through to get the videos taken down and learning about that scumbag owner, I wanted to punch him in the face myself.

Now he was in jail, and he would be for a very long time.

Brian was completely free of that monster, and knowing there was no risk of us ever running into Mike, he was loving life.

And he was about to love it even more if the damn mail would ever come.

Footsteps turned my head as they grew louder in the hallway.

Shit!

"Babe, seriously, whatever you're wearing, I'm sure is fine." Brian's voice carried with his steps.

I sucked in a breath, looked back at the street, and saw the white and blue mail truck making its way toward our house.

"Coming!" I yelled, crossing the room and yanking the door open. "The mail is here. Let's grab it before we head out," I suggested casually, darting past him where he stood in the hallway and briefly catching his eyes.

"What the hell were you doing in there?" he asked at my back.

"I told you. Accessorizing." I glanced over my shoulder and saw he was moving this way now, eyeing me suspiciously. "The wrap was complicated," I threw out.

Lie.

I spun around and walked backward.

His eyes went to my hair. "I like it. Looks good on you," he said, moving in my direction.

My cheeks warmed.

"Thanks," I replied, giving him a wink, then I spun around when I reached the foyer. "Sir, get back." I eased my puppy out of the way and wrenched the front door open, darted outside, jogged across the lawn, and waved at the mailman as he pulled up in front of our house.

"You're late," I scoffed as I took the mail he was holding out, then I didn't linger and spun back around, jogged across the lawn again, jumped up onto the porch, and rushed inside.

"Come on. Let's look through this real quick and then we'll head out," I proposed, my breaths coming hurriedly and rushing the words out of my mouth.

I crossed the room and moved into the kitchen, stepped up to the island, dropped the mail on the counter, and then whirled around, waiting for Brian to join me.

He followed but he did it leisurely. My foot was tapping when he finally entered the room.

"You're acting weird," he pointed out, coming to stand beside me.

"No, I'm not," I argued, even though I knew he was right.

I was never this eager about checking the mail. It only ever contained bills.

I fished through the envelopes and sale flyers.

"I'm hoping my new Target Red Card is in here. I want to start earning my five percent off."

Lie.

"That couldn't wait until after we got back from the beach?" Brian asked.

I turned my head and looked at him, my hands stilling their search.

"I might want to stop on our way home and pick something up," I explained, committing to my story. "And I'll be upset if we do that and then get home and my card was here waiting for me. Five percent is five percent."

His mouth twitched.

"You're a cute liar, Wild."

I narrowed my eyes.

"Thank you, but I'm not lying," I lied. "Now, if you don't mind..." I turned my head back to the counter and resumed fishing through the mail, ignoring Brian's deep, muted chuckle, then spotted the envelope I was looking for. "Here!" I picked it up, swiveled, and held it out for Brian to take.

"That's not from Target," he stated, taking the envelope and studying it.

It was addressed to him and had a P.O. box for the return. No name for the sender.

I tilted my head with a smile.

"I'm a cute liar. What can I say?" I shrugged, watching the slow shake of his head. "Open it."

"You know what this is?"

I nodded and grabbed a stray lock of hair and started twirling it while Brian ripped open the envelope and pulled out the contents—a folded piece of paper and a check.

"Holy fuck," he muttered, looking at the check first. His eyes lifted to mine.

"Read the letter." I tapped the folded paper in his hand.

Brian sat the check down on the counter and unfolded the letter, then he proceeded to read it, breathing slowly and evenly then quicker and a little stressed, not anxious, more like when you're excited about something.

When he reached the end of the letter, all of the air left his lungs in a pant.

He lifted his eyes to me again. They were round now, the whites swallowing up his green. He looked shocked.

"Wild, you knew?" he asked, stepping closer.

I took the letter from him.

"I did," I said, placing the letter on the counter next to the check, then looking up at Brian. "They wanted to make sure we'd be home when they mailed this."

Brian stared at me. His lips were slightly parted and he was back to breathing slow.

I stepped closer until our fronts were touching and placed my hands on his chest.

"That money you gave when you sold to Jamie, Owen's parents barely tapped into it, and because of you and everything you'd already given them, they don't have use for this money. It's yours, Brian. They wanted you to have it back."

"But..." His eyes slid to the check, then back to my face, as his hands held my hips. "They're caught up? They're good? You're sure?"

"I'm sure," I replied, tipping my chin up. "You did an amazing thing, helping them. They appreciated it so much."

I watched his neck work with a swallow.

"What do you want to do with the money?" I asked.

"I don't know. I don't need it."

"Can I make a suggestion?"

He looked at my mouth, nodding.

"You could be part owner of Wax again."

He contemplated this for all of two seconds, then argued, "I'm fine with just working there."

"But you said it was your dream growing up."

His hands slid around to my back and he jerked me closer.

"I'm holding my fuckin' dream," he muttered, tilting his head down and smiling lazily.

My heart fluttered. And wouldn't you know it, the flip and twist happened.

"You give me butterflies," I shared, sounding breathless, watching his lazy smile grow so it lifted both sides of his mouth now. "And I love being your dream, but I want you to have all of your dreams, Brian, just like you've given me all of mine."

His eyes went soft and absorbing. Then he pulled in a slow breath, let it out while looking over at the check again, thought for a beat, and optioned, "What about something in memory of Owen? Like a fund or something?" He looked at me. "Might be able to put something together with Mona, the woman who runs the riding place. Have a thing set up so families who can't afford it can get the therapy. I don't know. Is that dumb?"

I sucked on my lip to keep it from trembling.

My boy had the most selfless heart in the world. I was sure of it.

"No," I said quickly, fighting against my emotions, sliding my hands around his neck and squeezing there. "No, that's not dumb at all. That's sweet, Trouble."

His lip twitched.

"But it's a lot of money," I reminded him, feeling strongly about my suggestion. "You could set up that fund and still keep some for yourself."

"And buy back part of Wax?" His eyebrow lifted.

"Why not? Do you think Jamie will let you?"

Brian breathed a laugh, replying, "Yeah, I do. He fucking hated me selling out."

"Is he coming to the beach? You could ask him about it tonight."

"Not sure," he replied. "Said he was getting dinner first at White-caps, and depending on if your girl was working, he might hang out there for a while and nag her."

I smiled big.

"She's working."

Brian shook his head.

I ignored that because he knew where I stood on the situation and I knew where he stood. And we had more important things to talk about right now.

"So." I stood on my toes and moved in to give him my mouth. "You decided then?"

I loved Brian's idea for the money but I was hoping he would do something for himself with it, too.

If anyone deserved all of their dreams, it was him.

"Yeah," he whispered, sliding his lips along mine and kissing me slow and sweet. "I'll contact Mona and talk to Jamie."

I closed my eyes and took that kiss, going harder and deeper when I couldn't help it anymore.

I was the happiest girl in the world.

Brian was getting all of his dreams, just like I had all of mine.

My heart couldn't wait.

They hate each other. They want each other.
And now they need each other.

Don't miss J. Daniels's stunning next installment of
the Dirty Deeds series featuring Tori and Jamie!

HIT THE SPOT

Available Winter 2016